Praise for the novels of *New York Times*
and *USA TODAY* bestselling author

CANDACE CAMP

"Camp's newest Matchmaker novel features her usual vivid
characterization, touches of subtle humor and plenty of
misunderstandings, guilt and passion. You won't want to
miss this poignant and charming tale."
—*RT Book Reviews* on *The Courtship Dance*

"Delightful...Camp is firmly at home here, enlivening
the romantic quest between her engaging lovers
with a set of believable and colorful secondaries."
—*Publishers Weekly* on *The Wedding Challenge*

"A beautifully crafted, poignant love story."
—*RT Book Reviews* on *The Wedding Challenge*

"Lively and energetic secondaries round out
the formidable leads...assuring readers a surprise ending
well worth waiting for."
—*Publishers Weekly* on *The Bridal Quest*

"A clever mystery adds intrigue to this lively
and gently humorous tale, which simmers with
well-handled sexual tension."
—*Library Journal* on *A Dangerous Man*

"The talented Camp has deftly mixed romance and
intrigue to create another highly enjoyable Regency
romance."
—*Booklist* on *An Independent Woman*

"A smart, fun-filled romp."
—*Publishers Weekly* on *Impetuous*

CANDACE CAMP

Suddenly

HQN™

Recycling programs
for this product may
not exist in your area.

ISBN-13: 978-0-373-77445-6

SUDDENLY

www.HQNBooks.com

Printed in U.S.A.

Suddenly

PROLOGUE

London
1871

CHARITY HAD HER escape all planned.

The important thing was that no one should know that she had left the house, not even the servants or her sister Serena, for any of them might tell her parents. They would think it was for her own good, of course; a well-bred young lady could not be seen walking through the streets of London unaccompanied without severe damage being done to her reputation. No one, not even her affable, loving father, would excuse such behavior. They would not accept her reasoning that, since she would make sure no one in society saw her, it could hardly damage her reputation. Worse, they would try to worm out of her why she had left Aunt Ermintrude's house this morning without even a maid to accompany her.

And *that* she simply could not reveal, for, if being alone walking down the quiet, elegant streets of Mayfair was reprehensible, it was nothing compared to the social horror of what she proposed to do.

After a great deal of thinking, Charity had decided that the best time to leave would be immediately after she ate breakfast. Her mother and sisters would still be asleep, for with the constant round of parties they had attended since they'd come to London for Serena's and Elspeth's debuts, they had adopted town hours, staying up until the wee hours of the morning and often sleeping until noon. So they would not know she was gone—she hoped not until after she came back. And her father, an early riser like herself, would leave for his daily walk as soon as he ate breakfast. The servants, busy with their tasks, would not wonder where she was as long as they did not see her slip out the door alone.

So, as soon as she had eaten and her father had left, she crept cautiously downstairs, bonnet in hand, and with a final glance around to make sure there were no servants about, she slid out the front door. Thrusting her bonnet on her head, she ran lightly down the steps and along the street, glancing back once to make sure there was no one pursuing her. She hailed a hansom cab, and within minutes she was pulling up in front of Dure House, a tall, imposing white Georgian-style edifice.

Charity paid the cabdriver and marched up the steps of Dure House as if it were something she did every day, knowing that the best thing when one was uncertain was to act as if one knew precisely what one was doing. She raised the bright brass ring in the mouth of the lion's-head door knocker and brought it down with a sharp crack.

A tall, cadaverously thin manservant opened the door. His expression was so haughty that Charity was sure he must be the butler of the house. His supercilious look deepened when he took in Charity, standing alone on the doorstep in her country-sewn dress.

"Yes?" he inquired, his eyebrows rising in a way that

spoke volumes about his opinion of her breeding and her purpose on the earl of Dure's doorstep.

Charity's chin came up, and she returned an equally cool gaze. Not for nothing were there centuries of dukes and earls in her family's background; she was not about to let a butler stare her down.

"I am the Honorable Miss Charity Emerson," she said in her best imitation of her mother's aristocratic tone. "I am here to see Lord Dure, if you will be so good as to inform him."

She saw the man hesitate, and she knew he was struggling with an urge to toss her out forthwith. But Charity was certain that he recognized the name Emerson, and he wasn't likely to take it upon himself to turn her away.

Finally he stepped back grudgingly, allowing her to enter, and said, "If you will kindly remain here, I will see if His Lordship is at home."

This, Charity knew, was a euphemism for asking Lord Dure if he was willing to see this insolent chit who had arrived unheralded and unaccompanied on his doorstep. Charity occupied herself with looking around at the wide, formal entry, tiled in white marble. A wide staircase swept upward elegantly, parting halfway to curve in two matching wings the rest of the way to the next floor.

It was up these stairs that the butler went and down them that, after a few minutes, he returned in the same measured tread. He gave a slight bow in Charity's direction and said, "If you will follow me, miss…"

Charity's knees went weak. She had not realized until this moment how tensely she had been waiting, afraid that the earl would turn her down and her whole adventure would have been in vain. She drew a breath and followed him up the stairs and into a comfortable study.

"The Honorable Miss Charity Emerson," the butler intoned, then withdrew, leaving Charity alone facing Simon Westport, the Earl of Dure.

He had been seated behind his desk, and he rose at her entrance. This, she thought, was a dangerous man.

Everyone had said he was; they called him Devil Dure. Now, seeing him, she could understand the rumors. He was big and cold and hard, an imposing and intimidating figure from the top of his leonine black mane of hair down through the swelling muscles of his arms and chest and thighs, which not even the excellent cut of his clothes could conceal. His clean-shaven face gave nothing away; his features were as regular and hard as if they had been carved from granite. His eyes were an odd, dark color somewhere between the green of a deep, mossy pool and the gray of slate. They pierced her now, icy and sharp, like a pin through a butterfly, leaving her wriggling helplessly.

Charity's mouth went dry. *Perhaps she had been foolhardy to come here.*

"Yes, Miss Emerson?" the Earl asked, his eyes surveying her coolly. "How can I be of service to you?"

Charity squared her shoulders. She had never run from anything in her life, and she was not about to start now. Besides, her sister's entire future was at stake.

"I came," she told him clearly, "to ask you to marry me."

CHAPTER ONE

THERE WAS A MOMENT of stunned silence. The Earl of Dure stared at Charity, baffled.

He had been amazed when his butler, Chaney, announced that Charity Emerson was at the door. He knew that Charity was Serena's sister, though he had never met the girl. He had been intrigued, as well, for he could not imagine what bizarre circumstance could have brought her to his doorstep. Even though rumors had been flying for the past two or three weeks that he was on the verge of offering for Serena, he was not yet in any way related to the Emersons, and it was social disaster for a young woman to visit the house of a man who was not kin to her.

When Charity stepped into his study, he had been surprised again, for he had expected Serena's younger sister to be a schoolroom miss, not the obviously grown, youthfully blooming young woman who stood before him. It was, however, quite easy to see why Charity had been left with the younger daughters in the schoolroom, instead of being brought out with her sisters, Serena and Elspeth. Her excellent figure and glowing blond beauty would have cast both of the others into the shade. He had felt an immediate and definite tightening of his loins as he looked at her.

Her question left him speechless. Finally he cleared his throat and said, "I beg your pardon?"

Charity blushed, realizing how baldly her words had come out. "That is, I mean, well, you are in the market for a wife, are you not?"

The Earl's eyebrows rose lazily. Whatever surprise he felt did not show on his cool, composed face. "I doubt that the matter is any of your concern, Miss Emerson, but, yes, I do intend to marry soon. Since my grandfather died, I have a duty to the estate to produce an heir."

"Well, that is why I am here."

"You are saying you intend to, ah, put yourself upon the market?"

Charity's flush deepened to a bright red. She had not said at all what she intended to. Her plan had been to state her case coolly and logically, but somehow, as so often happened to her, the words had just seemed to come tumbling out of her mouth.

"I am not—" She had started to retort hotly, then stopped. "Well, yes in a way—but not as you're implying."

"Indeed." His dark eyes were tinged with amusement. "Pray, may I ask, in what way *are* you offering yourself?"

There was a dark, subtle undertone in his voice that sent a shiver up Charity's spine. She knew that she should be insulted at his words, that he was implying that she was not a lady, but the timbre of his voice made her feel more weak in the knees than indignant.

She stiffened her spine, reminding herself of what was at stake here, and said, "Everyone says that you are planning to ask my sister to marry you. Even Papa told Mama last night that he thought you would come up to scratch soon."

"Indeed?" The Earl's mouth twitched.

"Yes. When I heard that, I knew I had to do something desperate."

"Did you, now? And what might that be?"

"To ask you to marry me, instead of Serena."

"You're trying to steal a march on your sister?"

Charity looked horrified. "No! It's not like that, my lord. You mustn't think that I would ever do anything to hurt Serena. It's just the opposite. I am rescuing her."

"Rescuing her? From marriage to me?" His brows vaulted upward. "I had not realized that it was so horrible a fate. Indeed, I thought Miss Serena seemed perfectly, ah…resigned to it."

"Oh, she is," Charity assured him gravely. "She knows that it is her duty to marry you, and, you see, Serena is the kind of woman who always does her duty to her family. She will most certainly marry you if someone doesn't do anything to stop it, and then she will be thoroughly miserable the rest of her life!"

There was a moment of silence, then Dure mused, "I was unaware what a poor husband I would be."

Charity blushed, realizing how tactless her statement had been. "I—I'm sorry. I didn't mean to say that marriage to you would make a person miserable, ordinarily—for if that were so, I don't think I would have offered to marry you in her place. Truly, I'm afraid I'm not that unselfish a person." Her brows knit a little as she regarded this failing in herself. "No doubt Serena would have done so for me, but she is a vastly superior person."

"I find her quite above the ordinary," Simon admitted, and his dark eyes danced with amusement, changing his hard face in a startling way. "That is why I was intending to offer for her."

"But you are not in love with her, are you?" Charity asked anxiously. "Serena did not think you were. She and Papa both said that you were not interested in love with a wife. That is true, isn't it?"

"It is true that I am looking for a more reasonable arrangement," he admitted. "I tried love once, and I have little intention of falling into that pit again. But I am afraid I still don't understand why—"

"Well, it isn't that Serena's afraid of you. She isn't— or, at least, only a little bit."

"I am vastly relieved."

Charity glanced at him, and, catching the glimmer in his eyes, she relaxed and grinned. "I'm sorry. I'm making a proper mess of it, aren't I? The problem is this—Serena is in love with another man. You can understand, can't you, how she would not want to marry you, when her heart has been given to another?"

Dure frowned thoughtfully. "Your sister never mentioned this to me. She seemed quite agreeable to my advances. If she did not wish to marry me, why didn't she say so?"

"That is not her way. She is a dutiful daughter, and Papa and Mama very much want her to make this marriage. You see, with five daughters, it is very difficult. For even one of them to make a splendid marriage would be so advantageous. Once Serena is married to you, then she can bring out all her younger sisters."

Simon let out a faint groan at the thought of bringing out a succession of girls in his house, and Charity nodded commiseratingly. "You're right. You would not enjoy it at all. Especially Belinda, for she is a spoiled brat. But Serena feels that she has to marry you for the sake of our family, even though it breaks her heart. You see, she is in love with the parson back home, at Siddley-on-the-Marsh. Reverend Anthony Woodson. He's a very good man, but, of course, he has no fortune. Serena doesn't mind. She just wants to marry him and be happy and do good works. She would be a wonderful parson's wife, for she's very good and kind, you know, and she wants to help people. She truly doesn't mind wearing old clothes and not going to balls and such."

Charity's nose wrinkled as she considered this oddity in her sister.

"I had no idea," Dure said gravely. "I assure you, I do not wish to marry your sister if she is in love with another man. It was never my intention to force her into marriage."

"Of course not. I was sure it was that you did not know— After all, how could you? Serena would never tell you herself, and Papa and Mama don't even know that she is in love with Reverend Woodson. They would not approve, you see, since he has no money."

"I give you my word that I will relieve your sister's mind on that score." He hesitated, curiously reluctant to send his visitor away. "Now, Miss Emerson, having accomplished your mission, you must return home. I am afraid it would do considerable damage to your reputation if it ever got out that you were in a gentleman's quarters. Especially mine," he added truthfully.

"I know. Aunt Ermintrude would say I was brassy. She often says so, anyway. And Mama did say that you had something of a reputation. At first she was somewhat concerned, you see, about whether your intentions toward Serena were honorable, but Papa assured her that you never took up with young females of virtue."

Simon let out a bark of laughter. Charity looked somewhat abashed. "I'm sorry. I've done it again, haven't I? Even Serena says that I let my tongue run away with me. I hope I haven't offended you."

"Not at all. In fact, you've added a considerable amount of amusement—not to mention enlightenment—to my morning. But you must go now. I will have Chaney get you a hack. I am afraid my own carriage would arouse too much notice."

"Wait!" Charity jumped to her feet. "You haven't said— I mean, you can't just not marry Serena! Mama will murder me if she finds out I talked you out of offering for Serena and then someone else, like that odious Lady Amanda, gets you instead."

"I can assure you that I have no plans to offer for Lady Amanda Tilford's hand," Simon retorted flatly.

"Of course not. You would not be so foolish, I am sure. But, don't you see, it must be one of *us*— Oh, I wouldn't have come here if I hadn't thought you would be willing to take me instead! Papa says it's absolutely vital that Serena marry you, so we won't wind up in the poorhouse." She paused, then added judiciously, "I don't believe he meant that quite literally, but it's true that we are in a real case. I've had to turn these gloves, and this bonnet is Serena's old one that I retrimmed. And Papa told us that no one else could have new dresses this year so that he could pay for Serena's and Elspeth's coming out. Mama and Papa married for love, you see, and neither of them had a feather to fly with. Fortunately Aunt Grimmedge left Mama a competence, or I don't know what we would have done these past years. But Mama would never consider any of us marrying someone in trade, even if we were starving.

She's proud, you see, what with her cousin being a duke and all. But your family is impeccable enough even for her—except for that scandal back in the time of King Charles II, but Mama excuses that because, after all, she says, everyone was quite scandalous then."

"I'm sure that the Dowager Countess will be elated to hear that your mother finds the earldom of Dure acceptable."

"Oh, dear. Have I offended you?"

"No. However, I don't think this marriage swap is quite as easy a matter as trading one horse for another."

"But it is!" Charity assured him earnestly. "I mean, what you want is an heir, is it not? And I am quite as capable of producing one as Serena. I am fully grown and perfectly healthy." She held her hands a little out to the sides, inviting him to look at her.

"Yes," he agreed, his dark eyes lighting for an instant. "You are perfectly healthy."

"There! I am as likely as anyone to bear healthy heirs. And my bloodlines are exactly the same as Serena's. So I'm just as respectable."

"Not if you often frequent bachelors' quarters this way," he pointed out.

"I am not in the habit of it," Charity rejoined indignantly, her blue eyes flashing. "I came here only in desperation, I told you that. I had to save my sister."

"And you are willing to, uh…be the sacrificial lamb?"

Her brief moment of indignation passed, and Charity had to giggle at his description. "Well, I was the only one. Elspeth would not have done it. She's scared witless of you. You wouldn't want her, anyway. She whines all the time, and is a perfect bore. Belinda and Horatia are both too

young. So that leaves me. Besides, I would not call it a sac-
rifice, exactly. You are, after all, an earl, and a wealthy man,
and—" she tilted her head judiciously and studied him "—a
rather attractive one, at that, if you like the dark, brooding
sort."

"And do you like that sort?"

The low tone of his voice set up an odd, unsettling
stirring in Charity's abdomen. "I do not dislike it," she
replied demurely, casting her eyes down, as a modest
maiden should, but with such an air of mischief that Simon
found it hard not to chuckle.

"You do not fear me?"

"No. Actually, I'm not afraid of much of anything.
Mama has frequently said that I am sadly lacking in sensi-
tivity."

Simon did laugh aloud this time. "You are a minx, I fear,
and a man would doubtless do well to stay away from
you."

Charity shrugged. "That is what my father has told me."
She pursed her lips in a way that was unconsciously
alluring, and Simon felt his loins tighten again in response.

"This is absurd," he said roughly. "You haven't any
idea what you are doing."

"No, I nearly always know exactly what I'm about.
That is why I do it." She gazed at him with her clear,
candid blue eyes. "And I have to tell you that I usually end
up getting what I set out to."

Dure turned and walked away, shaking his head, though
there was indecision in the lines of his body.

"I understand that you have doubts, since you do not
know me," Charity went on cheerfully. "But the truth is, I
would be a far better wife for you than Serena. You see,

you spend a good deal of your time in London, but Serena would be miserable here all the time. Worse than that, for you, she would probably try to reform your ways."

"That *would* have been awkward," Simon murmured, fighting a smile as he looked out the window.

"On the other hand, I enjoy the city," Charity continued. "I would love to go to parties and dinners and the opera and all those things. Truthfully," she admitted, "I'm nearly eaten up with envy watching Elspeth and Serena get to do such things, when they don't even really enjoy them."

She paused and frowned. "Of course, I would have to bring out Belinda and Horatia and try to find Elspeth a husband, as well. It would be my duty. But—" she brightened "—it will be much easier with me doing it. I will be better able to make them fashionable, and I will rid us of them much sooner."

Simon made a strangled noise, and she peered across the room at him. "What's wrong? Is something the matter?"

"No." He turned back, his lips pressed together. He stood regarding her for a moment, then shook his head. "My dear girl, you tempt me, but I'm afraid it would not suit."

Charity's face fell ludicrously, and she looked so woebegone that for a moment Simon thought she was about to cry.

"Oh, no!" she wailed. "Now I've gone and ruined it! Mama will be furious with me for interfering. Truly, I wouldn't have come here if I hadn't thought you would be as willing to marry me as Serena." She looked at him plaintively. "Why do you not want me for a bride, my lord? Is it because I'm too bold? I am direct, I know. Mama is forever telling me that I must put a rein on my tongue. And sometimes I am a little lively, even impulsive, but I'm sure that I will grow more sedate as I get older. Don't you think so? And I would never do anything to bring dishonor or embarrassment on your name."

A smile curled Simon's lips. "I am not inclined to see you less lively or direct, my dear Miss Emerson. You are…quite diverting."

"Oh." She looked perplexed. "Then is it my features? You prefer Serena's coloring? Or her slenderness? I am too rounded." She sat down with a thump on the nearest chair, her face glum.

Heat flooded Simon's loins. "You are 'rounded' perfectly. I cannot imagine any man who would find you less than lovely. Surely you must know that."

"I've been told so once or twice," Charity admitted. "That is one reason why I thought you would not be averse to the switch. I thought you would hold me as attractive as Serena."

"You are." He thought of this sunny, beautiful girl in his bed, instead of the composed Serena, and the heat in his abdomen grew alarmingly. "It is no fault in you," he said shortly, and turned away, fighting the urge to go to her and reassure her of her desirability. "It is simply unsuitable. You are far too young."

Charity came back up on her feet, once more hopeful. "But no—I am eighteen, only three years younger than Serena. I would have come out this year, except that the expense for three of us would have been far too great."

Simon turned and looked at her. He did not think she was aware of the other factor that must have weighed with her parents—how much she would have outshone her older sisters.

"Still, it is twelve years between us," Simon reminded her. "I am too old and…jaded, I think, for one such as you."

A dimple sprang into Charity's cheek as she smiled teasingly at him. "Nevertheless, I do not think you are entirely decrepit yet. I may be young, but I know what I want to do. Anyone who knows me can tell you—I am not indecisive or fickle. There are many who marry with much more difference between them than that."

"Perhaps twelve years is not such a problem, but your youth is," he replied brusquely, ignoring the small voice inside him that kept pointing out how entertaining this girl would be to live with, how desirable she would be in his bed. "I am not looking for some romantic young miss, I require a sensible, mature wife, one who can accept a loveless marriage and will not expect me to be constantly dancing attendance upon her or flattering her or cajoling her into a pleasant mood with words of undying love or expensive gifts."

"But I do not expect that!" Charity protested. "I am fully aware what sort of marriage you contemplate, and I assure you that I am quite prepared for it. I would be much better than Serena, for despite her calm exterior, she is very much a romantic at heart. A homebody. She would want a husband's love and attention, and would wither without it. But I, on the other hand, am quite capable of taking care of myself. I will be happy following my own pursuits. I will have my own friends—I make friends easily, you see—and I shall do things with them. Go to balls and dances and the opera and—oh, all the exciting things there are to do here in London. I promise I will not be begging you to accompany me everywhere. And I will not expect romance from you."

"Don't be a fool," he said, scowling darkly. "You will fall in love someday, and then what will you do? You will be stuck in a loveless marriage."

"Oh, no!" Charity looked shocked, and once more indignant. "I would never betray my husband!"

"I did not say you would. But you would not be able to stop your unhappiness, and I do not wish an unhappy wife, either."

"But I will not be unhappy, I assure you," Charity responded blithely. "I am the most unromantic of women. I have never lost my heart to anyone. I have never swooned and sighed over any young man, as so many other girls I know do. I do not think I am suited for love."

"At eighteen, you have hardly had the opportunity."

"Oh, but I have," she assured him naively, and Simon was aware of a sudden, strange spurt of anger inside him. "I've been to assemblies back home, and my dance card is always full. I am much admired," she said loftily, lifting her nose in the air, but then she spoiled the pose by giggling. "I have even had two proposals of marriage—though I must confess one of them doesn't count, because I think he was only trying to lure me out into the garden."

"Someone dared to try to accost you?" Simon scowled fiercely.

"No, of course not. I was not such a fool as to go into the garden with him. I told you, I am well able to take care of myself. And my heart has never been in danger. Believe me, I have no wish to be in love. I have seen what happens when a couple marries for love. I have seen what my parents did, and then, after a few years, they fell out of love. Honestly, now I think they hardly even like each other. Mama blames Papa, saying she could have married higher than the younger son of the younger son of an earl, and sometimes Papa gets exasperated and says he wished that she would have. It is very sad, and not at all something I wish to happen to me. I decided long ago that I would not marry in the heat of love—and more recently I think I've discovered that it is not in me to feel that heat. It's no doubt very ungenteel and unfeminine of me, but—" Charity shrugged "—there it is. I am perfectly suited to a marriage such as you propose, and I would be quite happy in it. For I would like to have children, and I would be very happy spending time with them. And that, after all, is why you want to marry, is it not? For children?"

"Yes." A flame sparked in his eyes. "I want children."

"Then you see? We are not at all unsuitable. We want the same things."

"You are so innocent. You haven't the faintest idea what marriage is about." Simon's voice was rough. He strode over to her, his expression dark and forbidding. "Marriage is not some pretty little watercolor scene of parties and fashionable clothes and children all dressed up in neat little clothes." He grasped her arms, startling her, and said, "This is what marriage to me would involve."

He pulled her up hard against him, and his mouth came down to cover hers.

CHAPTER TWO

CHARITY FROZE IN SURPRISE. At first she was aware, in some amazement, only of how very hard and muscled Dure's body was against hers, and then of how incredibly soft his lips were in contrast. His mouth moved on hers, hot and seeking, his lips pressing hers apart. His tongue flicked along the seam of her lips, and she gasped a little. He seized the opportunity to slip his tongue into her mouth, shocking her even more.

Charity had been kissed once or twice, but those had been chaste and naive things, nothing like this, so curiously hard and soft, so heated and demanding. She pressed against Simon in return, her own lips responding, and her arms stole up to clasp his neck, holding on to him as wild sensations rocked her body. She had never felt anything so wonderful, so exciting, as the way his hot tongue explored her mouth and his lips rocked against hers. His arms were like iron around her, enfolding her in his heat, and even that was exciting. Her body trembled in his arms.

Simon made a harsh noise deep in his throat and released her abruptly, stepping back. Charity staggered back a little, and her hand went out to grasp the back of the chair. She wasn't sure that she could stand upright without its support. She gazed at him for a moment in astonishment, her eyes wide with wonder, her face flushed, and her mouth soft and glistening.

Desire thrummed through Simon's veins, and his chest rose and fell with his harsh panting. He had intended to kiss the girl just to prove his point, to frighten her off and show her how little she knew about the marital state she so blithely wanted to enter. But when his lips touched hers, fire had ignited him. He wanted to keep on kissing her, and to do much more than kiss her. Her mouth had been sweet, her breasts soft and yielding against his chest…. Even now, just looking at her, her lips soft and damp from his mouth, her eyes lambent, he wanted to pull her back into his arms and kiss her again. More than that, he wanted her in his bed. Yet he knew that he could not, must not—she was too innocent, too young, for him. And she was certain to be repelled by what he had just done; she would do exactly as he had intended, and flee the room. It was what he wanted; it was for the best. Yet he could not quiet the passion that boiled in him, telling him to chase after her if she did run from him.

"Is that—is that what a man's kiss is like?" Charity asked wonderingly. Her tongue tentatively touched her lip, tasting him there.

A shudder ran through Simon at the gesture, so unconsciously seductive. "Yes." He ground out the single word, his fists clenching in an effort to hold back from her.

"And is that what you do when you marry—to make children?"

"Yes, and more. Much more."

Her eyes widened, and he was sure that she would cry out in horror and leave. But instead she said, "Then I—I think that I should like marriage very much."

Dure stifled a groan as he struggled to hold on to his composure. He whipped around and strode away from her to the window. For a long moment, he gazed out, his back to her, his body rigid. Then he turned and, giving her a short bow, said, "All right, Miss Emerson, you have persuaded me. I shall call on your father this afternoon to ask for your hand in marriage."

Charity leaned back against the seat of the hack, staring sightlessly across its gloomy interior. Her entire body felt as if it were glowing. *He had kissed her!* And such a kiss— Charity had never imagined that anything could feel the way his kiss had. She could still feel his body, hard and masculine, against hers, his arms wrapped tightly around her so that she seemed almost surrounded by him. It should have been frightening, she thought, to be held that way by such a large, strong man, a veritable stranger to her. Instead, it had been exhilarating.

She smiled a little to herself, and her gloved fingertips went unconsciously to her mouth. His lips had claimed hers, taken her as his own. To think that this was what happened between a husband and wife! She had never been entirely sure, being a genteel young lady brought up in the most sheltered way, but she had assumed that whatever the married state entailed, it was something rather boring. Few husbands and wives of her acquaintance looked as if they had ever shared anything exciting. Yet they must have done what Lord Dure had just done with her, if that was the way one set about making children. She found the idea hard to reconcile with what she had seen of marriage.

It occurred to her that perhaps what she had felt was not

commonly experienced by married couples. Perhaps Lord Dure was special…different…. Perhaps the delicious feelings that had run through her when she was in his embrace were something that only he was capable of arousing. She thought about the things that were whispered of him, the way her mother had protested that he was given to lewd company, and she wondered if he had acquired the hot, wonderful way he kissed in that company. Was it perhaps an unseemly thing that loose women had taught him?

Then thank God for their training, she thought, and a delightful shiver ran through her. It was probably quite base of her to think so, Charity knew, but then, she had long ago become accustomed to not thinking or feeling the way she was supposed to. Her spirit had never been the delicate, shy, sweet one of a true lady, and her mother had often despaired of her. Charity had never understood why she was the way she was—different from her sisters and, indeed, from all the young ladies she knew—any more than she had understood why the things she said so often shocked those around her.

But Lord Dure had not seemed to be shocked by what she said—surprised, true, but not horrified or disgusted. He had seemed more amused than anything. She had not missed his hidden smiles or his choked laughs, and they had given her hope that he would accept her plan. He was not stodgy, as were most of the men she knew. She had sensed that he was different the first time she saw him, peering down through the banisters with her younger sisters. Belinda, the silly chit, had said that he looked dangerous, but Charity had not thought so. There was a hardness to his features, true, and his coloring was dark, giving him a mysterious, almost foreign aspect. But there had been something about him, Charity was not sure what, that intrigued her. He had looked like someone grimly doing his duty, coming to call on Serena, and it had confirmed Charity's opinion that he had no interest in Serena, only in marrying a suitable young woman. Charity had also thought that it would not be so bad to be married to him, that he didn't look frightening to her, only bored and a little impatient, and she wondered what he looked like when he smiled. It was then that the first spark of her idea had come to life in her brain.

And now—she hugged the knowledge to herself—her scheme had come to fruition. He had accepted her idea; he had not sent her away in indignant outrage, or treated her like a foolish child. Instead, he had agreed. He had kissed her.

The hack stopped a block from her aunt's house, and Charity walked the rest of the way. She slipped in the side door and made her way up to her room, thankful to meet neither of her parents on the way.

Serena was in the bedroom they shared, seated by the window reading a book, and she looked up, relief flooding her face, when Charity entered. "There you are! Wherever have you been all morning? I was worried sick. I made excuses to Mama, of course, but I had no idea if I was doing right."

"You did wonderfully well," Charity returned gaily. "I've been out walking. What else?"

"This long? You woke me up slipping out of the room this morning. Why were you so furtive, if you were just going for a walk? And where could you have gone?"

"Why, I went to Hyde Park, of course, and I'm afraid I did spend rather too much time there. I miss the country, and—" She broke off at her sister's skeptical stare. "Oh, all right. You know me too well. I did go somewhere else, but I'm not going to tell you, not yet. First I want to make sure that it works out. I don't want to get your hopes up."

"My hopes?" Serena questioned warily. She was a pretty young woman, with a pleasant expression and a sweet smile, but at the moment, her looks were marred by knit brows and a mouth thinned by suspicion. "Charity, exactly what were you doing? You had better tell me, you know. Have you gotten yourself into another scrape?"

"Of course not!" Charity retorted indignantly. "I haven't gotten into a scrape in…oh, ages." She waved her hand airily.

"Then what were you doing?" Serena persisted.

Charity grimaced. She didn't want to tell Serena what she had done. Serena would be thoroughly shocked. Charity knew that it would never occur to her sister to do something so scandalous as visit a bachelor in his home, nor would she have countenanced it in her sister, even if it would free her from a marriage she did not want. That was why Charity had been careful not to reveal her plan to Serena before she put it into action. Serena would have done everything she could to stop her from acting so impetuously—perhaps even reveal Charity's plan to their parents. And now, even though the thing was done and Serena could not undo it, she would still scold her for doing something so outrageous.

But Charity was not one to avoid trouble. So she sighed and straightened her shoulders and told Serena the truth. "I went to Lord Dure's house and asked him not to marry you. I suggested that he marry me, instead."

Serena stared, too shocked by what Charity had said to even scold. "What?"

Charity started to repeat what she had said, but Serena waved her hand. "No, no, I did not mean that. I heard you. I just could not believe you. Charity, did you actually go to that man's home?"

Charity nodded. "Yes."

Serena's cheeks flooded with color, and she put her hands up to them, as if to cool them. "Oh, no... What will he think of you? Of me? Oh, Charity, how could you have done such a thing?"

Charity gnawed uncertainly at her lower lip. "I thought it was for the best. Are you...terribly angry with me?"

"But what did he say? What did he do? Was he furious with you?"

"No. He was quite calm. Actually, I think he was rather entertained by me. He smiled and chuckled."

"Oh, no," Serena groaned, closing her eyes. "He was laughing at us? Is he going to tell everyone? Will we be the laughingstock of London?"

"No! Serena! Have you so little faith in me? He wouldn't spread such rumors about the future Lady Dure." She paused portentously. "He agreed to marry me instead of you."

Serena's eyes popped open. "What? He actually agreed to such a madcap scheme?"

"It wasn't madcap!" Charity protested. "It was very reasonable, and he saw that. He said he had no wish to marry someone who didn't want to marry him, and he agreed that he wanted to marry only for an heir, as you said, and that I would do as well as you."

"He said that?"

"Well, not in so many words," Charity admitted. "But he did agree to it. He told me that he would call on Papa this afternoon to ask for my hand."

"I cannot believe it."

Charity looked wounded. "You think no man would want to marry me, even one who was not marrying for love?"

"No, of course not. There will be many men who would give anything to marry you," Serena assured her warmly. "You are by far the prettiest of us, and you are so very kind and generous. But the earl of Dure! And after you had done something so improper, so scandalous! I cannot fathom it. Are you sure that he was not making a game of you? To repay you for your behavior?"

Cold fear knotted in Charity's stomach. *What if Serena was right? What if he had only been playing a joke with her?* Charity had painful visions of Dure's throwing Serena aside and laughing about Charity and her family through all the best salons of London. "No," she breathed, "he would not. He is not so cruel, nor so proud."

"He seems to me to be a very proud man," Serena retorted. "And I would think he could be quite cruel. He is a cold man."

The two sisters looked at each other. Charity lifted her chin. "No. I refuse to believe it. He was quite sincere. He had his doubts. He told me I was too young. But I convinced him in the end."

She thought of his kiss, seemingly his final test of her, and a blush tinged her cheeks. For the first time, she wondered if he had enjoyed it as much as she had, and if it had been that which had convinced him to marry her.

Serena did not notice her sister's embarrassment. She was staring blankly across the room, trying to absorb the news, fear and hope warring within her. "Can it really be?"

"Yes! I believe what he told me. He would not have lied

or played a game with me. I do not think he is that sort of man." She paused, anxiety tightening her stomach, and added, "But it is possible that he might change his mind, once he thinks it over. Perhaps he will decide that what I did was too scandalous for a future Lady Dure, that I would not be a fit wife for him."

"I did not mean that you would not be a fit wife for him—or any man!" Serena said, immediately contrite. She went to her sister and took her by the shoulders, saying earnestly, "You are the dearest and sweetest of women. And any man should be proud to have you for a wife. I should not have said what I did to you. I spoke hastily and out of fear. I was simply overset with worry about where you had been, and then, when you said that you'd been to see *him,* well…I snapped at you. What you did was improper, of course, and I do wish you would think before you jump in next time. But if the Earl decides that you are not a proper enough wife for him, then he does not deserve you. And if he is not what you think, and chooses to spread scandalous gossip of us around town, then he deserves neither of us."

Charity smiled at her gentle sister's pugnacious look, and gave her a quick hug. "I am afraid you look at me with a fond sister's eye, but thank you, anyway. Let us not think about the worst. Let us simply hope that he will be exactly as I think him." She hesitated, then went on tentatively, "Serena…have I done wrong? You are not upset with me, are you? You truly did not wish to marry the earl?"

Serena stared at her, too astonished to speak for a moment. "No! Charity, how can you even ask such a thing? You know of my feelings for Reverend Woodson. How could I want to marry any other? You know I would never agree to it if it were not my filial duty."

"I know." Charity frowned thoughtfully. "Serena, would you tell me the truth?"

"Of course." Serena looked affronted.

"Has the reverend ever kissed you?"

Serena's rosy blush was answer enough, but Serena also nodded, looking down. "It was bad of us, I know, for we knew that my parents would never approve of the match, but once, when we were walking down by Lichfield Wash…"

"And was it pleasurable?"

"Charity! Such questions!" But Serena had to smile. "Yes, you baggage. It was pleasurable. I felt…uplifted." Her eyes glowed, telling the truth of her words.

Charity relaxed. "And did His Lordship ever kiss you?"

"Lord Dure?" Serena looked amazed. "No, of course not. Why, we are barely acquaintances."

"But you were nigh on to betrothed to the man," Charity pointed out. "Didn't you wonder? Didn't he try?"

"Well, he kissed my hand several times, when he took his leave."

Charity rolled her eyes. "That is not when I mean."

"I know." Serena shrugged. "He was always a gentleman."

Charity suspected that the way he had acted with *her* would not be classified as gentlemanly, but it had felt wonderful.

The two sisters waited on pins and needles through the next few hours. Every time there was the sound of carriage wheels outside their window, they tensed, but none of the vehicles ever stopped for Lord Dure to disembark. Nor, hard as they strained their ears, could they hear the thud of the front door knocker up here on the third floor.

For a while, they passed their time by doing up Charity's hair. Over the years the girls had become adept at doing each other's hair, for they had not the money to spare for a personal maid. In a hurry this morning, Charity had taken the time only to catch her thick hair back in a soft roll. But now Serena pinned it up on her crown in a knot, letting a cluster of finger curls fall from it. It was a soft, bouncy style, well suited to her.

Then Charity changed into a pale pink afternoon dress, which actually belonged to Serena. Looking in the mirror, Charity was well pleased with her image. She appeared older and prettier, she thought, less of a country mouse.

After that, there was nothing to do but wait. Serena's doubts filled Charity's mind, and she fidgeted and paced and snapped irritably at Horatia and Belinda when they tumbled into the room in a boisterous game of tag. Belinda stuck out her tongue at Charity, and Charity retaliated by tossing a small pillow at her, and suddenly the four of them were romping about, like schoolgirls all, chasing and throwing pillows and tickling one another when caught. Finally Elspeth emerged from her small room. She, alone of the sisters, was given a room to herself, because her frequent insomnia was aggravated by having anyone sleeping in the room with her.

"You have awakened me," Elspeth told them in a whispery voice. "I had just gotten to sleep…I've been laid low by a headache today."

"Sorry, Ellie," Charity responded, but her blue eyes danced in a less-than-penitent manner.

It was then that one of their aunt's maids hurried up the stairs and came to a breathless halt in front of the sisters.

"Miss Charity, you're wanted in the front drawing room.

Right away, your father said." Her eyes were wide, and sparkling with interest.

Charity glanced at Serena, whose face had the same arrested expression that Charity was sure was on hers. Hope flooded her. *Dure had come!*

She whirled and hurried down the stairs, holding her dress up above her ankles. She would not let herself think about any other possibility, such as Dure's having sent word to their father of his daughter's highly improper behavior this morning. Lifting her head, she sailed across the hall and into the drawing room. The two men inside the room turned at her entrance.

Her face was flushed and her hair slightly mussed from the games she had been playing abovestairs with her younger siblings, and her eyes sparkled. Simon straightened unconsciously, his eyes sweeping over her, and he smiled. Lytton Emerson, on the other hand, simply gazed at her with the same slightly stunned expression that had been on his face for the past few minutes, ever since the earl of Dure had informed him that he wanted the hand of his third daughter in marriage, not that of his first.

"Ah, Charity, there you are." Lytton smiled, a little uneasily. Serena was a biddable girl, and would do as she was told. Charity he had some doubts about. It occurred to Mr. Emerson that she might refuse to marry a man she had never met, and then they would all be in severe trouble.

"Hello, Papa." Her eyes went inquiringly to Lord Dure, as she played the part of one who did not know the man.

"Charity, this is Lord Dure. I… He… The fact is, His Lordship has been gracious enough to ask for your hand in marriage."

"Indeed?" Charity opened her eyes wider, in a creditable look of surprise, and turned to Dure. "But, Your Lordship, you do not know me. How could you wish to marry me?"

Simon's lips thinned as he suppressed a smile. His dark eyes, lit with amusement, met hers. "Ah, but I have seen you from afar, Miss Emerson, and my affections were immediately engaged."

"You are a man who makes up his mind quickly." Charity dimpled, mischief lurking in her eyes.

"Yes, I am." Simon strode toward her. "I usually know what I want." He stopped in front of her, too close for politeness, looming over her, and his dark eyes glinted down at her. "What is your answer, Miss Emerson?"

Charity tilted back her head to look at him. "Why, yes, of course, my lord," she replied demurely. "What other answer could there be?"

"You have made me a very happy man," he replied formally, and raised her hands to his lips. A thrill darted through Charity at the touch of his mouth on her flesh. It was a common enough gesture, with little meaning, but still, the brush of his lips, warm and velvety against her skin, made her shiver.

She wondered how Serena could have experienced even this brief touch of his mouth on the back of her hand and not felt some excitement. Suddenly she was very glad that Serena had not, and even more glad that Dure had never kissed Serena on the mouth.

Charity was shocked to feel jealousy rear its ugly head within her. She had enjoyed her popularity at the assemblies she had attended, for she had pride aplenty. But never had she felt envy or jealousy when one of her squires danced or flirted with another young woman. But she realized that she had no desire to share anything of *this* man with anyone, including her favorite sister. She supposed it was because he would be her husband.

"I must take my leave now," Simon went on. "I shall see you again soon. Will you be attending Lady Rotterham's ball tomorrow night?"

"I don't know," Charity replied blankly.

"Of course," her father said genially, cutting in. "We shall be there."

"Good. Then I look forward to seeing you." Dure nodded to Charity, then her father, and strode from the room.

When they heard the front door close behind him, Lytton turned to his daughter, eyebrows shooting up. "Did you understand this?"

At that moment Charity's mother swept into the room, her face wreathed in smiles. Caroline Emerson's jaw dropped ludicrously when she saw Charity standing there with Lytton. "Charity! But where is Serena? What has happened? I know I heard Dure's voice in here."

"You did." Lytton turned his bewildered face toward his wife. "He was just here asking to marry Charity."

It took a moment for the words to sink in. Then Caroline gasped, "Charity! What do you mean?" She rounded on her daughter. "What have you done! How could you have done this to your own sister?"

"What are you talking about?" Lytton asked, confused.

"I have done nothing to her, except save her from a marriage she despised," Charity retorted hotly. She loved her mother, but Caroline was a proud woman of rigid beliefs, and they had quarreled often—and sometimes bitterly.

"Despised! How could Serena despise such a marriage?"

Caroline asked in honest astonishment. "Dure is an earl. She would be a countess!"

"Serena has no interest in being a countess."

"What nonsense! You are merely trying to excuse this trick you have played on her."

"I played no trick. Serena knows, and she approves of what I did."

"What did you do?" Lytton asked, still bewildered. "I don't understand. What is going on?"

"Oh, Lytton. It's obvious—Charity has somehow contrived to steal Lord Dure away from Serena."

"I did not steal him! I simply asked Lord Dure to marry me instead of Serena, because Serena did not want to marry him."

"But when— How—" Lytton sputtered. "You have never even met His Lordship."

"Lytton, do be quiet," Caroline snapped. "She has met him somehow. How else could she have managed to arrange this charade?" She swung back to her daughter. "But how can you say that Serena did not want to marry him? She said nothing of this to me."

"How could she? She knew how important it was to you and Papa, to the whole family, that she marry someone wealthy. She was going to do her duty, as she always does. But she dreaded it. You would know that, if you had heard her crying in her bed at night, as I have."

"But how could she be unhappy?" Lytton asked, puzzled and worried. "She would have been a countess. Dure is not old, or ugly, or mad. His family is excellent, and he has money and land. She could have had anything she wanted."

"Except the man she loves," Charity pointed out.

At that pronouncement her parents erupted into

bellows and squawks and torrent of questions. Caroline collapsed upon the nearest chair, fanning her face and threatening to swoon.

"What the devil is going on here?" an imperious old voice demanded, and Aunt Ermintrude hobbled into the room, leaning on her cane.

She was actually Charity's great-aunt, her father's aunt, and she had not aged gracefully. Rather, she had fought it tooth and nail. The necklines of her gowns were disgracefully low, revealing a great deal of wrinkled skin, and she dyed her hair an improbable shade of red. Charity's mother called her a relic from an age when people had few morals; Caroline deplored the bluntness of the woman's speech. For her part, Aunt Ermintrude disliked Caroline with equal vigor. However, she did take an interest in Charity and her sisters, and it was for their sake that she had invited the Emerson family to visit her for the season and bring out Serena and Elspeth.

She cast an irritated look around the room. "It sounds like a menagerie in here!"

"Lord Dure has offered for me," Charity told her succinctly.

"For you!" Aunt Ermintrude's eyes began to twinkle, and she banged her cane against the floor as she let out a cackle of laughter. "Why, you cunning little thing, you! Stole the march on your sister, eh?"

"I did not take him from Serena!" Charity protested. "Well, that is, I did, but not wickedly. She does not want to marry him."

"She says Serena loves another!" Caroline put in accusingly, glaring at Charity as if Serena's preference in suitors were her fault.

"Who?" Aunt Ermintrude asked, leaning forward with great interest.

"Reverend Woodson."

For once Charity's mother was speechless. Both she and Lytton simply stared at Charity, mouths agape in astonishment.

"Bah!" Aunt Ermintrude exclaimed in annoyance, and turned away. "Couldn't she find anyone more interesting than a pastor? I was hoping for a disinherited son, or a highwayman, something interesting."

"How would Serena know a highwayman?" Lytton asked his aunt, distracted by such a thought.

"For pity's sake, Lytton. Aunt Ermintrude is simply making one of her jests," his wife told him. "Serena cannot possibly think to marry that Woodson boy. Why, he hasn't a penny to his name."

"And he's a pastor," Lytton pointed out. "Dull sort of life, I should think."

Charity giggled. "I should think so, too, Papa, but that is what Serena wants. She doesn't want wealth or position. She wants to marry Reverend Woodson and do good works and lead an exemplary life."

"Well, she has to think of her family," Caroline declared. "She can't be selfish enough to marry into poverty."

"Why not?" Charity crossed to her mother to make her case. She knew where the real power in the family lay, and it was not in her vague, fox-hunting father. "I will be marrying well now. The Earl of Dure is still going to be your son-in-law."

"He offered a very generous settlement," Lytton put in. "Said he doesn't want us plaguing Charity for money."

"And, of course, I will be able to bring out the younger

girls, just as Serena would have." Charity went on, looking martyred, "Next year Elspeth can live with us for the season, if you can't find her a husband this year."

"A capital idea!" Lytton brightened even more. He far preferred living in the country with his hounds and horses. "We can stay in Siddley-on-the-Marsh and Charity can take care of all that. It sounds perfect, Caroline."

"So you see, Mama, we have lost nothing, and there is really no reason why Serena should not be allowed to marry as she wishes. She loves the reverend, and he loves her."

"They have been courting behind our backs?" Caroline's face darkened.

"No! You know Serena better than that. They have merely met and talked over all sorts of charitable works. She truly loves him, Mama, and you can't want her to pine away her whole life for him. She would not be happy marrying someone else, and now that the family no longer needs her to marry well, I am sure she will refuse any other suitors. She will wind up unhappy and unmarried."

"She should have told me," Caroline said stubbornly. "It was wicked of her to have hidden it from me."

"Ha!" Aunt Ermintrude put in bluntly. "As if you would have listened to anything the girl had to say. You didn't know it because you never asked or looked at the girl long enough to see that something was wrong. You were too busy pushing what you wanted on her."

Caroline started to bristle, and Charity intervened hastily. "Serena knew how much you and Papa wanted her to make an advantageous marriage, so she said nothing to you. But now, oh, please, Mama, say that she may have her pastor."

Caroline sighed. "I suppose so, if he comes to your father in a proper way once we get back—though why Serena should choose to live in that damp little manse, I don't know!"

"Thank you, Mama." Charity leaned forward and kissed her mother on the cheek.

"At least you had the good sense to take Dure," Caroline went on practically, brightening. "Let's see, what's to do first? An announcement to the newspapers, of course…"

Charity bounced up and went upstairs to tell Serena the good news, leaving her mother behind, absorbed in anticipating a grand wedding.

CHAPTER THREE

SIMON LEANED BACK against the seat of the hack as it made its way through the streets of London. He thought of Charity and how she had looked this afternoon when she came into the drawing room. All the way over to call on her father, he had wondered if he was committing a grave folly in agreeing to marry the girl. He thought of how young she was, of how little he knew her. His actions were too impulsive for a lifelong commitment such as marriage. Besides, the desire that stirred in him at the sight of Charity made him a trifle uneasy.

He was not about to enter upon another marriage in which his heart was engaged. He had learned that painful lesson the first time; giving one's heart into another's hand was the surest way to a living hell. He had been careful ever since then to avoid ladies, and the lures offered by their love. Instead, he had frequented the women of the demimonde; a paid mistress gave pleasure and did not put one's heart in danger. The sudden rush of passion that swept him when he kissed Charity had been so intense that it almost frightened him. *What if he came to care too much for her?*

But then Charity had waltzed into the room, her face aglow and smiling, and his doubts had vanished.

She was not precisely the woman he would have described as his ideal for a wife; she was far too lively and unpredictable. But now that he had met her, the prospect of marrying Serena or any of the other young women he had met in London seemed dull and flat. Life with Charity, he suspected, would never be dull. Surely it was better to marry a woman who amused and entertained him, who did not bore him with her company. It would be much easier to get an heir if making love with her was a pleasure, rather than a chore.

There was little risk that he would fall in love with her, he reassured himself. He had learned how to guard his heart, and lust, after all, was not the same as love. After a time it would fade, as it always did. Then he would be left with a pleasant relationship with his wife, a friendly sort of partnership in raising their children. He smiled, his thoughts turning toward blond-haired, blue-eyed children with dimpling mischievous grins. For the first time, it occurred to him that marriage could be an adventure.

The carriage pulled to a stop in front of a familiar house, and Simon climbed out. He never came here in his own carriage, his crest emblazoned on the side; he was too discreet for that. He crossed the street to a narrow but attractive house. This was a much less fashionable part of town than his own house in Arlington Street, but it was pleasant, nevertheless. He climbed the steps and knocked on the door, bracing himself for the scene that he was sure was about to follow.

He had known for some time that he had to break off this relationship. Indeed, he had tired of Theodora some weeks ago; her undeniable sensual lures had grown familiar, and her emotional excesses had become tiresome. He would have put an end to it sometime earlier, but he had put it off because he dreaded the kind of emotional scene that Theodora was likely to enact. It would not be because Theodora loved him, he knew. But she would very much dislike losing the money.

However, he could not continue with the relationship now that he was about to be married; it would clearly be an insult to his future wife to maintain such a liaison. He had to tell Theodora it was over.

Theodora's butler answered the door and permitted himself a wintry smile. Simon was their most welcome visitor. "My lord, how nice to see you."

"Sommers." Simon greeted the man as he stepped into the hall. "Is Mrs. Graves home?"

"Yes, my lord." Sommers led him to the drawing room and left him, saying he would tell Mrs. Graves that Simon was here.

Minutes later, there was the light sound of footsteps on the stairs, and a woman swept gracefully in. "Simon!" Her low, sultry voice vibrated with pleasure, and she walked over to him, hands extended.

"Theodora." He took her hands and raised one of them to his lips perfunctorily.

Theodora Graves was a beautiful woman. Thirty years old, she was one of those women who attained the height of her beauty with age. Her skin was milk-white, in vivid contrast to her black hair and large brown eyes. She was very proud of her skin, and loved to show it off in evening gowns with low necklines and short capped sleeves. She looked her best in the evenings, and she knew it, for the golden glow of lamplight gleamed on her pale skin, hiding all signs of the incipient wrinkles around her mouth and eyes. Her gowns were always of dark, warm colors, golds and greens and deep crimsons, and they took full advantage of her large, luscious breasts and small waist, cinched by corsets into nothingness. One of her admirers had once told her that she looked sinfully delicious, and she cherished the compliment.

She was not a member of the demimonde, as most of Dure's other mistresses in the past had been, but one of a dubious group who hovered on the fringes of society. Though she was only a tradesman's daughter, her beauty had won her a husband of good family, if straitened means; a cavalry officer, he had been killed in Ethiopia a few years ago. She moved among a circle of army officers and some flamboyant army wives and widows, considered a "loose" crowd by the more conservative matrons, but was now and then invited to very large crushes or taken there by one of her officer friends.

It was at such a function that she had met Simon a year earlier. He had been drawn to her sensual good looks and had easily recognized her as a woman who, while not a "lady of the night," was willing to give her favors outside the bounds of matrimony and expected to be supported in return. She had at that time been attached to a certain young gentleman, but she had been shrewd enough to realize that Simon was a far better catch, and within a few weeks' time she had rid herself of her gentleman and set her cap for Simon. He had maintained her household for several months now.

"How reserved you are," Theodora told him playfully now, retaining her grip on his hands when he would have released them. She leaned forward on tiptoe and kissed him on the lips.

Simon stood stiffly, not responding to her mouth, and

when she dropped back flat on her feet, a pout on her face, he glanced toward the door, saying mildly, "The servants."

"Oh, pooh." Theodora waved her hand. "Who cares what the servants think?" She dimpled up at him. "I did not know you were so stuffy, my love."

Simon, looking down at her, wondered why he had never noticed before how practiced her smile was. He thought of Charity's smile, which broke across her face like sunshine, dimples springing into her cheeks without artifice. He found himself looking at Theodora, comparing her voluptuous body to Charity's slender figure, with its firm, high breasts, and Theodora's lush beauty suddenly seemed excessive, like the heavy scent of patchouli that clung to her.

He stepped back from her. Theodora frowned faintly and went to close the door to the hallway. "I am so glad to see you," she went on, abandoning her pout. "It seems as if it's been ages since you've been here. A lonely heart makes the days seem longer, I suppose."

She stopped when she turned away from the doors and saw that Simon had seated himself in a chair, instead of the love seat or sofa, effectively isolating himself from her. She forced a smile and returned to stand in front of him. Once he would have reached up and pulled her down into his lap, but he did not this time, and after a moment she moved over to the sofa and perched on the edge of it.

"Shall I ring for tea?" she began brightly.

He shook his head. "No. I came to bring you this."

He reached into his jacket and withdrew a long, thin jewelry box. Theodora's eyes widened, and she quickly reached for the box, a smile curving her lips. She opened it, revealing a bracelet of sapphires and diamonds, and she drew in her breath sharply.

"Oh, Simon!" She stared at the bracelet with avid eyes. "It's lovely. Thank you, oh, thank you!" She took the bracelet out of its box and stretched out her arm toward him. "Here. Put it on me, will you?"

He did as she asked, and Theodora held her arm up, twisting it this way and that to admire the flash of the jewels. "You sly dog," she told him. "Here I was afraid that I had offended you somehow."

"No. You have not offended me. But I do have something to say. You know, perhaps, that I have decided to marry again."

Theodora's breath caught, and she gazed at him with glowing eyes. Simon, intent on what he had to say, did not notice her reaction.

"This afternoon I became engaged. For that reason, I am afraid that we must end our…arrangement."

He raised his head to look at her, and now he did notice that her face was white and her eyes were wide with shock.

"I'm sorry," he said quickly. "I have taken you off guard. I did not realize… I thought surely you would have been aware of the gossip. It seems half of London knows that I have been searching for a wife."

"A wife! Of course I know it!" Her eyes blazing, she jumped to her feet. "I had thought— But you love me!"

Simon stared at her. He rose, too, his face cool. This was the emotional scene he had dreaded. "No, madame," he said softly. "I have never given you cause to think that. I am certain of it. I never spoke words of love to you, never intimated that our relationship was anything more than what it was, a man and a woman who took pleasure in each other. You are a worldly woman. You were well aware of what we were to each other."

"You cannot do this to me!" Theodora cried passionately, tears welling in her eyes. "I love you! I have given myself to you, flung away my reputation, all for love of you."

Simon's mouth tightened. "I think, madame, that you forget William Pelling and the hussar captain who were both before me, and probably several others whom I do not know."

"You are insulting." Her great dark eyes flashed.

"I speak only the truth. We had a business arrangement, you and I, and we each received what we wanted from it. There was never any question of love or marriage, and you know that very well. If you have deceived yourself, I am very sorry."

Theodora let out an incoherent cry of rage and blindly picked up the closest thing at hand, a small crystal vase, and hurled it against the wall. "How dare you! How dare you! No man has ever cast me aside!" She collapsed into tears, flinging herself on the sofa.

Simon swallowed his distaste at her histrionics and went over to the couch to kneel on one knee beside her. He did, after all, owe Theodora something; he had partaken of her favors for several months, and even though he had kept her in good style in return, there had, at least at first, been some emotion between them. He disliked hurting her, and though he had little illusion that she loved him, he knew that he had dealt a blow to her feminine pride.

"Come, Thea, 'tis not so bad a thing. There are many other men in London who will be gleeful to find that I no longer visit your house. You can have your pick of any of them. No one will think that this is because of any lack on your part. They will know that I am to be married. It would be an insult to my bride to flaunt my mistress in her face."

"Your mistress!" Theodora sat up, her face blazing with color. "I would have been your wife!"

Simon gaped at her inelegantly, amazed by her words.

Theodora's eyes narrowed. "She stole you from me. Who is this chit that's taken your fancy?"

Simon's face tightened, and he rose to his feet. "No one stole me from you, Theodora. I was never your possession. I did not give you cause to think that our relationship was anything other than it was. And whatever it was, it is now over."

"Then go!" Theodora shrieked. "Get out of my house!"

Simon bowed and left the room. Theodora bounced to her feet, her fingers curling into claws, her chest heaving with fury. She grabbed a pillow from the sofa and hurled it after Simon. But it fell far shy of its mark, bouncing harmlessly, noiselessly, off the wall. Theodora let out an incoherent cry of rage and leaped for a small wooden box from the end table and sent it crashing into the hall. The noise was soothing to her, so she grabbed every object she could find and sent them after the box, until finally she had exhausted her supply. She collapsed to the floor then, panting and trembling.

So he thought that he could just put her away like that! The idea enraged Theodora, even more so because she had been sure that she had the Earl of Dure wrapped around her little finger, a slave to his passion for her. She was stunned that he had slipped those sexual bonds—and for some little milk-and-water miss! *As if one of those little bloodless debutantes could keep Simon satisfied!*

A smile curved her full lips as she recalled just how passionate and innovative Simon could be in bed. He had satisfied her far more than any of her other lovers had. It was one reason—besides the money and that title, of course— why she had hoped to bring him to marry her. *Well, he would find out what a bore his lady wife was, and then he would regret throwing away his chance with her!*

Theodora thought of this with great satisfaction. Hope began to rear its head inside her again. There was yet time; he would not marry the girl right away. *She could win him back!* No doubt Simon's family and friends had persuaded him to marry some maiden from the nobility, for the sake of his name. But he did not love her. He would soon grow tired of her, and he would begin to long for the hot passion he had had with Theodora.

Pleased with the idea, Theodora sat up straighter and began to wipe the tear streaks from her face, plans racing through her head. Tonight Lady Rotterham was having one of her vast crushes. Surely Simon would be at it, dancing attendance upon his new fiancée. And Theodora had an invitation. Since her name had been linked with Simon's, she had received more invitations to society functions. She would go, also, and she would see this chit for herself. She would dress beautifully, and take extra time with her toilette. *Let Simon see what he would be missing!*

"Breathe all the way out, Charity," Belinda said impatiently, holding the strings of Charity's corset. "It's still not enough."

Charity groaned and rolled her eyes. "How could it not be enough? I can scarcely breathe as it is!"

"It's not enough because Serena doesn't have a great thick waist like you!" Belinda retorted. "You can't get into her dress without the corset tight."

Charity whirled and glared at her younger sister. "I do not have a thick waist!"

"Of course you don't," Serena intervened soothingly, grimacing at Belinda. "Belinda, you apologize to your sister. She has a lovely figure, and you know it." 'Tis far better to have curves than to be straight as a board, as I am."

"I'm sorry," Belinda told Charity grudgingly, spoiling the apology by crossing her eyes at Charity.

"All right now, Charity," Serena went on, pressing her hands to the sides of the corset. "You take a deep breath, then exhale all the way out."

Charity did as she directed, and Serena clamped firmly down on the whalebones, drawing its sides together. Belinda pulled the strings tight and quickly tied them.

"There!" Belinda declared triumphantly. "Now Serena's dress will fit you."

"Yes, if I don't take a breath," Charity grumbled.

The whalebone stays of the corset pressed into her flesh, bruising it and squeezing the air from the bottom of her lungs. The only way she could breathe was shallowly. The corset also pushed her breasts upward uncomfortably. But there was nothing she could do about it. She was determined to go to Lady Rotterham's ball tonight, and she had to wear one of Serena's dresses.

Serena was a trifle shorter than Charity, and slenderer, too, but her mother had decreed that she would wear Serena's corset and flat-heeled slippers to make her suit the dress. It was, Charity thought, rather like Procrustes's bed, on which the travelers were stretched or chopped to fit the requirements of the bed instead of the bed's suiting them.

She tied on the little bustle in the rear. Then Serena and Belinda picked up the lacy white ball gown from the bed and lowered it over Charity's head. Serena shook the skirt out and settled it in place, while Belinda buttoned up the multitude of small round buttons in the back. Horatia, the youngest of the sisters, sat on the bed, legs crossed in an unladylike manner her mother would have decried had she been there, and watched the transformation with glowing eyes.

"Oh, my…" Charity breathed, looking at herself in the cheval glass. Perhaps the pain was worth it, after all.

The white satin gleamed in the lamplight, overlaid with lace. Charity's arms were bare, and the neckline was rounded and low-cut, trimmed in a cloud of tulle. Her creamy white breasts, pushed up by the tight corset and constrained by the too-tight dress, seemed ready to spill over the neckline at any unexpected movement, and her waist was reduced almost to nothingness. The skirt was pulled back to cascade down from the bustle into a train decorated with ruffles and bows.

Serena had already worked on Charity's hair, brushing the golden locks until they shone, then twisting them into a roll at the back of her head and securing it with pins. A spray of false gardenias decorated the line of the roll, and around her forehead, her face was softened by feathery little wisps of curls.

Charity's eyes gleamed as she gazed at her reflection. She looked older than she was, she thought, and much prettier. She gave most of the credit to Serena's artistry and the dress, instead of to her own bright eyes and prettily flushed cheeks. The dress was uncomfortable—the tulle scratched her, the waist pinched abominably, and the train was heavy to drag around—and she was faintly shocked by the wide expanse of white bosom and shoulders that it exposed. But she would bear such burdens gladly. *She was going to her first true fashionable ball, and she looked like a beautiful sophisticate!*

"You look like a fairy princess!" Horatia exclaimed, and Charity flashed her a dazzling smile.

Belinda frowned crossly and plopped down on the bed beside Horatia. "Oh, Horatia, you are so childish."

"She is not," Serena protested, smiling at first Horatia, then Charity. "She's right. Charity does look like a fairy princess."

Elspeth, reclining on the chaise, remarked lugubriously, "You will catch your death of cold in that thing, Charity, and then you'll never live to see your wedding day."

"Don't be such an old gloomy puss," Charity retorted. "You know I'm never ill."

Elspeth looked pained. "I know. You're as healthy as a milkmaid." She said it with no pleasure, being of the opinion that it was a mark of low birth or insensitivity—or both—to be so uninclined to illness.

"No one is as sick as you are," Belinda pointed out, indifferent as to which sister received her barbs.

Elspeth lifted her eyebrows at the girl and said pointedly, "Some of us are more delicate and refined than others."

"You two, hush," Serena ordered, always the elder sister.

"Their noses are out of joint because Charity's going to be a countess," Horatia explained.

"Ha!" Belinda retorted.

Elspeth shivered ostentatiously. "She's welcome to him. He frightened the life out of me."

Charity cast Elspeth an irritated glance. "There's nothing to be frightened of."

"No?" Belinda sat up straight, always eager to impart gossip. "I've heard that he's a terrible man."

"He has some considerable reputation for wild living," Serena admitted. "But then, many men do. It doesn't mean that they don't settle down and make exemplary husbands."

"Not that one!"

"I've heard his wife died at his hand."

"Yes, and his brother died mysteriously, too, making *him* the heir."

"Oh, pooh." Charity turned and flashed a scornful look over toward her sisters. "Papa talked to me about it. He said the earl's wife died in childbirth, and his brother was killed when his horse stumbled and went down when he was out riding. Hardly mysterious."

"Ah, but what made the horse stumble?" Belinda asked in a sepulchral voice.

Charity's eyes lit with a bright blue flame, and she set her hands on her hips pugnaciously. "A rabbit hole, no doubt. Or something equally innocuous. Honestly, Belinda, you are a gossipmonger. That's all it is—gossip. People have nothing better to do, so they malign someone. Just because Lord Dure doesn't stoop to answer their mean little whispers, that does not mean he is guilty!"

"His eyes are cold." Elspeth shuddered expressively. "I'm sure his heart is, as well."

Charity gaped at her sister, thinking of the fire that she had seen in His Lordship's dark green eyes. "What nonsense! You haven't any idea what you're talking about, either of you. You don't know the man."

"And you do?" Belinda shot back.

"Better than you. I, at least, have talked to him. It's no wonder that he looks at you coldly, Elspeth. No doubt you shrink into your chair and act as if he's about to strike you. It would be enough to irritate anyone."

"I don't know why you are defending the man," Elspeth retorted petulantly. "It isn't as if it's a love match."

"He is to be my husband!" Charity's temper flared. "And I won't allow him to be slandered, any more than I would let anyone slander one of you."

"Oh, dear," Belinda drawled. "Charity has found another cause to champion. Another stray."

"At least Charity is kind," Horatia pointed out.

"Girls, please!" Their mother stepped through the doorway, her gaze sweeping coolly over her daughters. "You sound like a gaggle of geese. I could hear you all the way down the hall. Please try to remember that you are young ladies, not magpies." She turned and surveyed Charity carefully, then gave a nod of approval. "You look quite charming, my dear. Now, pray, try to remember your station, and don't do anything untoward tonight."

"Yes, Mother." Charity gave her mother a saucy little curtsy and grinned.

Even Caroline's stiff demeanor had to soften under the warmth of Charity's smile, and she came forward and gave her daughter a peck on the cheek. "You do me proud, Charity. Imagine, you a countess!"

Her eyes glimmered with emotion for an instant. Then she moved away, saying briskly, "Come, girls, it's time to go. Your father is waiting for us downstairs."

Elspeth, Serena and Charity trailed out of the room after her, leaving Horatia and Belinda to wrangle with each other and their governess. Charity swept down the steps beside Serena, doing her best to keep her face tamed into a demure look.

"Oh, my!" Lytton Emerson gazed up at them with a beaming face. "What a bevy of beauties! I shall be the envy of all the men at the ball tonight, escorting such lovely women."

"Quite right," Aunt Ermintrude agreed loudly from the top of the stairs. She stalked down the stairs after them, a startling vision in her low-cut purple gown, with a fortune in diamonds around her throat and at her ears. "The Emersons were always a fine-looking lot. Except for Cousin Daphne, of course, but then, she got that horse face from her mother."

Charity's mother rolled her eyes but said nothing. Aunt Ermintrude stalked up to Charity and inspected her closely.

"Very nice, my girl, very nice. You look just as a future countess should. You'll have Lord Dure eating out of your hand in no time."

"Really, Aunt Ermintrude, must you use such vulgar expressions?" Caroline turned a more critical eye on Charity. "I am not quite sure about that neck. Doesn't it seem a trifle low for a young girl? It wouldn't do for Charity to be thought bold."

"Nonsense! A girl ought to show off her wares a little," Aunt Ermintrude argued, nodding with approval at Charity's attire. "Besides, she's already snagged her an earl, so she doesn't have to kowtow to those biddies."

The girls smothered their smiles at the old lady's words. Their mother glared at them.

"Serena's gown is a trifle small for me," Charity explained quickly, hoping to avert a battle between the two older women, and gave a vain tug to the front of her bodice.

Caroline reached out and fluffed up the tulle so that it covered more of Charity's breasts. "It will have to do until we get you some clothes made," she said with a sigh. "Just don't bend over, Charity."

"Yes, Mama."

"Humph! Not nearly as low as we used to wear them when I was a girl. Why, I remember once when Lady Derwentwater—Phoebe, that was, not that dreary creature that her son's married to—wore an evening gown cut so low, you could almost see her nip—"

"Aunt Ermintrude! Please! There are tender young ears present."

Aunt Ermintrude crackled with laughter. "As if they don't know what they've got on their own chests! Anyway, poor Phoebe made the mistake of bending over to pick up a fan she'd dropped, and demmed if one of her bosoms didn't pop right out, there in front of everyone."

The girls all stared at her with wide eyes. Caroline made a strangled noise and began shepherding them toward the front door. "I think that's enough, Aunt Ermintrude."

"What did she do?" Charity asked curiously.

"Why, Phoebe was always cool as a cucumber, no matter what. She just straightened up and popped it back in, as if nothing had happened, and everything went on. 'Twasn't nearly as embarrassing as the time that Mariana Vivier's drawers came untied on the dance floor and—"

Caroline interrupted hastily, shooing her daughters out of the house and down the steps into Aunt Ermintrude's waiting carriage, an old-fashioned landau. It was a tight squeeze, given the women's skirts.

"Why don't we just walk?" Charity asked innocently. "It's only two blocks."

Caroline and Aunt Ermintrude turned equally scandal-
ized eyes on her. "One must arrive in a carriage!" Aunt Ermintrude exclaimed.

"It simply isn't done," Caroline added with finality.

Charity shrugged and fell silent, watching out the
window with interest as their carriage moved along the
street and joined the line of carriages waiting outside Lady
Rotterham's house. They sat for twenty minutes before
their carriage reached the front of the line, but Charity
was well occupied watching the occupants of the other carriages emerge from their vehicles and walk up the steps to
the door. Jewelry glittered at necks and ears and wrists;
satins and velvets and lace gleamed in the lamplight.

After they were handed out of their carriage and walked
into the house, they had to wait again at the top of the
grandly curving stairway as the guests filed past the hostess
and her family. Then, at last, they were able to walk along
the gallery to the ballroom, passing a smaller drawing
room in which older ladies and a few gentlemen were
already engrossed in whist. The ballroom, a spacious,
ornate place with no fewer than three glittering glass
chandeliers, was filled with people. Many stood or sat
along the walls, and in the middle of the room, dancers
swirled in a waltz. Charity drew in a quick breath, dazzled
by the beauty of the scene. It was, she thought, exactly
what she had dreamed of.

She followed her mother and Aunt Ermintrude as they
made their way to empty seats, schooling her face into a
look as demure as Serena's. But her eyes roamed quickly
over the occupants of the room. She could not find Lord
Dure. Of course, there was the yellow anteroom, where
people could sit and converse in quiet surroundings, or the

refreshment room downstairs. He could be in either place, but she could not leave her mother's side and look for him.

Then something, she wasn't sure what—the swift susurration of noise that traveled from the crowd around the doorway, or merely the feeling of his eyes on her—made Charity turn her head toward the open doorway. Her breath caught in her throat, and her heart began to pound. Lord Dure had entered the room and was walking toward her.

CHAPTER FOUR

SIMON WAS DRESSED in the white shirt, black suit and white gloves that were de rigueur for such an occasion, and he looked inordinately handsome to Charity. There was something vital and strong about him, a physicality and depth that set him off apart the other men in the room. She smiled at him, her face suddenly luminous. She did not notice that now practically every eye in the place was turned toward them; even many of the dancers were sneaking peeks their way.

Simon's eyes flickered over Charity, and there was a gleam in their gray-green depths, but he spoke to her mother first, as was proper, bending over Mrs. Emerson's hand. Then, of course, he had to greet Aunt Ermintrude, Serena and Elspeth before at last he could turn to Charity.

"Miss Emerson."

"Lord Dure." Her voice was a trifle breathless as she looked up at him.

"You look lovely tonight." His eyes traveled down over her in a way that Charity suspected was improper, but warmed her in spite of that.

"Thank you, my lord." Her irrepressible dimple danced in her cheek, and she added, "So do you. Look handsome, I mean." She hesitated. "Or should I not say so?"

"I take no offense from it." He smiled. When he first saw her in the ballroom, it had taken him aback. She had no longer looked like the ingenuous girl he had met, but rather like a sophisticated and beautiful woman. Then she had smiled and somehow become both a mature beauty and the girl who had amused him.

His eyes drifted down to her breasts, straining against her gown, the white tops soft and quivering, and a heat most inappropriate to the time and place started in his loins. He wondered if Charity had any idea what a seductive picture she made, swathed in folds of virginal white, yet her full, soft mouth and sweetly rounded breasts offering untold physical delights. He wanted to stand and look at her, yet, curiously, he found himself wishing that she had worn something else that hid her looks more effectively from the other men in the room.

"Would you care to dance?" he asked formally. The waltz had ended while he was talking to her, and now couples were taking their places again on the floor.

"Indeed I would," Charity answered candidly. Instinctively she glanced at her mother for her permission, and Mrs. Emerson nodded. Charity took the arm Lord Dure proffered, and they made their way to an empty spot on the floor.

The music started. Dure bowed, and Charity curtsied; then he put his hand at her waist and took her other hand in his and swept her away into the waltz. Charity had waltzed before, at country assemblies or at private parties at estates near theirs. But this waltz was nothing like those other times. Simon was an expert dancer, unlike most of the boys with whom she had danced, and in his arms, looking up into his eyes, she felt as if she were flying. It was a wonderful, heady feeling, and everything, everyone, else in the room seemed to recede around her. There was nothing but Simon and the music and the gaily circling steps.

Charity was startled when the music ended and they stopped. Hurriedly she bobbed down into her curtsy, then took his arm. "That was marvelous!"

A smile touched his lips as he gazed down into her face; it was alight with pleasure, her eyes sparkling and her lips slightly parted. "Was it? I am glad."

"Oh, yes! It was everything I've ever dreamed of."

"Careful. You will puff me up with pride."

"As if you didn't know you are a wonderful dancer!" Charity laughed lightly.

"It is nice to hear you say so." Simon had an impulse to take her hand and bring it to his lips and kiss it lingeringly…and to kiss her lips, as well, if the truth be known. But, of course, neither would be acceptable in this public place. "It is easy to dance well with you."

Charity chuckled. "You know how to turn a compliment, too." She paused and glanced around her. "Why are we walking this way?"

"It is traditional to promenade at least a half turn around the room after a dance. To take a girl back immediately would be something of an insult, as if to say that she is not worthy of your attention."

"Oh," Charity responded, enlightened. "I have many things to learn, I'm sure. But you will teach me, won't you?" She looked up at him a little uncertainly. Lord Dure did not seem the sort of man to patiently tutor someone in anything, least of all the social arts.

But something sparked in his dark eyes at her words, and he said in a low voice, "Yes, I will be happy to teach you…many things."

Charity wasn't sure why, but his words, and the timbre of his voice, sent a shiver through her abdomen. "Thank you." She was suddenly a little breathless, and she wished again that she did not have to wear her corset so tight.

"Ah, there is someone I would like you to meet." Simon angled across to where a tall, lovely dark woman stood beside a man even taller than she, and as blond as she was dark. "Venetia…"

The couple turned at his voice and smiled at him. The woman he had called Venetia came toward Simon, holding her hands out and catching his. She went up on tiptoe and kissed his cheek. "How are you, dear?"

"Splendid," Simon responded. "No need to ask you the same question. You look radiant."

The blond man joined them, nodding to Simon, and Simon went on, "Venetia, Ashford, I would like you to meet my fiancée, Miss Charity Emerson. Charity, this is my sister Venetia, Lady Ashford, and her husband, Lord Ashford."

Venetia's eyes widened, and she looked from Simon to Charity, then back, as if she hardly knew which to stare at. "Are you jesting? Simon, you've never—" She smiled warmly at Charity then, and stepped forward to kiss her cheek. "My dear Miss Emerson, welcome to our family. Please forgive my shock. My brother had remained such an obdurate bachelor that I had given up all hope of his marrying again."

"Pleased to meet you," Lord Ashford said, smiling pleasantly. He was a nice-looking, placid man, one who looked as if worry or any other very strong emotion never ruffled his expression. He stepped forward to bow over Charity's hand. "Welcome to the family." He turned to Dure. "Congratulations, old fellow."

Charity smiled and made an appropriate response. She liked Lady Ashford's smile and warm eyes. She had worried that an earl's relatives might be stuffy and as apt to disapprove of her ways as her own mother—or even more so! But, looking at Venetia, Charity was sure that the woman would not scold or condemn her.

Venetia came over to Charity, suggesting a little shyly that they sit and talk. "I want to get to know you much better," she explained. "I'm sure you must be very special for Simon to have chosen to marry you."

"Thank you."

They walked over to an open window where there were, thankfully, two empty chairs. Venetia was a quiet woman, even a little timid, and when they first sat down, their conversation was a trifle awkward. But Charity rarely had trouble talking, and, once she got over her initial anxiety over making a good impression on a member of Lord Dure's family, she began to comment and question in her usual cheerful way. Before long, Venetia was relaxed, too, and the two of them were chatting like old friends. They discussed their sisters, then made plans to go shopping together one day the next week. Charity confessed that she had been forced to wear her sister's dress that evening, and Venetia chuckled over Charity's description of being tightened into her corset.

Venetia leaned closer and clasped Charity's hand warmly. "I'm glad that you are marrying Simon. He deserves to be happy, and I can tell that he will find that with you."

Charity wondered uneasily if Venetia thought that theirs was a love match. "I shall do my best to make him a good wife."

"I know you will. Simon is a good man, and he will be

a good husband. He's had…some sorrows, and I know that sometimes he may seem a bit distant. But, please, don't let that dismay you. He has a good heart."

Charity nodded. "I know."

Venetia smiled. "Good. I hoped you would."

The two women rose. They caught no sight of Simon, so they strolled toward Caroline Emerson, who sat across the ballroom, talking with another woman her age. As they walked, Charity had the distinct feeling that someone was watching her, not idly or in mild curiosity, but intently. She glanced around, and her gaze fell upon a woman who stood near the windows, chatting with a tall, brown-haired man who sported a neatly clipped brown beard. It was this woman who was staring at her, Charity realized. Even when Charity looked at her, the woman did not turn her eyes away, but continued to watch her.

Charity gazed back at her with equal curiosity. The woman was beautiful: dark and faintly mysterious, with a lushly rounded figure and creamy pale skin. Her hair was dark, almost black. She wore a deep maroon satin gown that set off her white skin and exposed an ample amount of bosom; there were jewels in her ears, and around her throat and wrist.

"Venetia, who is that woman?" Charity asked in an urgent undertone.

"Who? Where?" Venetia followed the direction of Charity's eyes. She stopped dead when she saw the woman, and a flush spread up her throat and across her face. "Uh…uh, it's no one. I mean, I don't know her."

Charity glanced at Lady Ashford in astonishment. It was obvious that Venetia had recognized the woman. *But why would Venetia disclaim all knowledge of her?* Charity took another look at the woman before Venetia firmly steered her over to Mrs. Emerson's chair.

Charity danced with several other young men after that, then once again with Simon. Afterward, he escorted her downstairs to partake of the light supper, as well. Charity barely ate, too excited—as well as too tightly cinched—to want food.

"You enjoy the ball," Dure said, faintly smiling as he watched her, his words more statement than question.

"Oh, yes! Don't you?"

He shrugged. "I am always welcome, for my name. But I have little liking for the whispers."

"Oh."

"You do not ask me, 'What whispers?'"

"No. I have heard them."

"And having heard them, you still wish to marry me?"

"I don't believe them," Charity replied simply.

"Indeed? So easily?"

Charity shrugged. "My father told me what really happened, and Papa would not lie to me."

"Your father might not know what really happened," he pointed out.

"That's true. But I wouldn't have believed them in any case, once I met you. You are not a murderer."

"Thank you, my dear."

"Why do you not simply tell them the truth, and shut their mouths?" Charity wondered.

A corner of Dure's mouth quirked up sardonically. "What am I to do? Walk into a party and say, 'I am not a murderer'? Cry out that when I lost my brother, it was like losing a part of myself?"

Charity's ready sympathy went out to him. "I'm sorry."

She laid her gloved hand on his wrist and looked up earnestly into his eyes. "I did not think. I'm afraid it is one of my besetting sins. Of course you cannot deny where no one directly accuses. Rumors are the hardest to fight. But why do they follow you so?"

Simon's expression hardened, and he looked away from her. "I have enemies. Besides, some of the rumors are true. I have gambled and drunk to excess."

"And taken mistresses," Charity added candidly.

His dark expression was surprised into a smile. "You should not know of such things," he scolded her teasingly.

"How could I not? I've heard it from all sides, ever since you started calling on Serena." She paused, frowning. "Are you really a libertine?"

Dure's eyes widened, and he let out a chuckle. "This is a highly improper conversation for us to be having, Miss Emerson."

"No doubt it is," she agreed, then prodded him further. "Well, are you?"

Simon gazed down at her. He wondered if she had any idea how his blood stirred at talking about such things with her. Though she had withdrawn her hand from his wrist, he could still feel it where she had touched him. He looked at her bare white arms above the long evening gloves and thought of sliding his hands up the smooth flesh until he touched the froth of tulle at the neckline. He could imagine the faint scratchiness of the net beneath his fingers, contrasting with the supreme softness of her skin.

"I…am fond of women," he said carefully.

Charity dimpled. "Thank heavens for that. I should hate to marry a man who was not."

"I have had mistresses, and I have eschewed the company of 'good' women."

Charity hazarded a guess. "Because they bored you?"

He chuckled. "Sometimes. Lord knows I cannot say that about the 'good' woman I am about to marry."

Charity smiled. "Good. I shall always endeavor to amuse you, my lord."

It surprised Simon how intensely he wanted this woman under his roof—to see that bright, sunny smile across the breakfast table from him, to hear her laughter rippling down the hallways of his home, to have her in his bed, white and sweet and welcoming his touch. He wondered if that spark of passion he had felt in her kiss would prove true—if she would not, as Sybilla had, remain cold and stiff in his arms, but would indeed awaken to him and take pleasure in their coupling. And not the jaded pretense of passion that he had sometimes seen in his mistresses, but a true, sweet hunger.

He turned his head away, shaken by the wave of desire that had surged through him. It was dangerous to spend much time with Charity; he was all too easily aroused by her. When he had thought of taking a wife, he had assumed that their engagement would last the customary year; he had felt no urgency about marrying. But now the idea chafed him; he realized that anything but a short engagement could prove to be torture for him.

"My lord?" Charity leaned forward and laid a hand on his arm in concern. "Have I spoken amiss? My mother says I have a lamentable tendency to frivolity. I should not have made light of—"

"No." He swung his head back to her, his eyes bright and intense. "Never lose your sense of frivolity. There is nothing amiss with you."

She chuckled. "There are those who would disagree with you."

"There may be. But, remember, you no longer need to please any of them."

"Only my husband."

"Yes." His eyes darkened. "Only me."

Charity stared at him, her eyes caught by his, her lips slightly apart. A strange warmth crept through her as he looked at her, and she felt breathless and tingling. She wished that he would kiss her again, as he had that day at his house. She knew that such a thought was probably scandalous and unladylike, but she could not help it. She wanted to taste his mouth again, to feel his hard body pressed against hers, all the way up and down. *Would he be shocked if he knew?* Charity supposed that he would.

Finally Simon tore his eyes away and said hoarsely, "I should take you back to your mother."

That was the last place Charity wanted to go. What she really would like would be to slip outside with this man, into some dark corner of Lady Rotterham's garden, and ask him to kiss her. However, she knew that would be unconscionably bold, and he would probably be repelled by her. So she said only, "All right, my lord," and rose with him to go back upstairs to the ballroom.

She reached down to pick up her fan from the table where she had laid it, and as she did so, a small square of paper toppled off. Surprised, she picked up the little square and unfolded it. Written on it were the words *Do not marry Dure, or you will regret it.*

She froze, staring at the words. For a moment, the words made no sense, and then, with a wave of hot anger, she understood them. Someone was warning her away from

Lord Dure, implying, no doubt, that he would cause her death, too. She went pale, then flushed, and was swept with a fury so intense it startled her.

"Charity? What's the matter? What is that?"

"What? Oh." Charity looked up at Dure, recalled to where she was. Quickly she crumpled the paper in her palm and dropped it into the glass she had used, where it soaked up the remaining punch. She wasn't about to burden her fiancé with the malicious contents of this note, not after the conversation they'd just had about the rumors that plagued him. "It was nothing, just a scrap of paper."

"But you looked—"

"I stood up too fast," she lied glibly, "and it made me feel a trifle dizzy. Or perhaps there was something too strong for me in the punch." She smiled brightly and took his arm.

When Simon left her with her mother, Charity sat down and lapsed into an unaccustomed silence. Two young men asked her to dance, and she politely did so, but she found that her mind was distracted. She could not stop thinking about that note and wondering who had written it. Many people had strolled past where she and Dure were sitting in the refreshment room; anyone could have dropped the little piece of paper onto her fan, where she would be sure to notice it later. But who had thought it necessary to warn her against her future husband?

She supposed it could be someone who believed the rumors and was genuinely concerned about a young woman marrying a "murderer." But Charity did not think so. She detected the hand of malice here, and she was sure it was directed against Dure. After all, she did not know anyone here—how could anyone wish her harm? No, someone wanted to throw a spoke in Dure's wheels. It made Charity furious; she wished the attack had come openly, so that she could answer it.

"Charity…Charity!"

Charity jumped a little, startled, and turned back to her mother.

"Goodness, child, where has your mind been?"

"Sorry, Mama." She wasn't about to reveal to her mother that she had been dwelling on Lord Dure. "Did you want something?"

"Only to introduce you to Mr. Faraday Reed." Mrs. Emerson waved her fan toward the tall, slimly elegant man standing before them. "Mr Reed, this is my daughter, Charity."

"Miss Emerson." The man bowed expertly over her hand. "It is indeed a pleasure to make your acquaintance."

Charity smiled politely up at him. Faraday Reed was slender and tall, with light brown hair, hazel eyes and a small, neatly trimmed beard and mustache. He was handsome—though of course, Charity thought, his rather monotone attractiveness could not begin to compare with Dure's powerful build and fiercely compelling face. Then she realized, with a start, that this was the man whom she had seen earlier in conversation with the stunning beauty who had stared at her.

Her curiosity was piqued. She wanted to know who that woman was; there was a certain mystery that hovered about her dark beauty. And Charity could not fathom why the woman would have been looking so intently at her. Venetia's odd reaction had aroused her curiosity even more.

However, she could think of no way to ask Mr. Reed

about the woman, not with her mother sitting right there listening to every word that was spoken. "Mr. Reed is married to Lady Frances Reed. I met her at the Athertons'," Caroline was saying. "You remember Lady Atherton, my dear. She is my second cousin."

"Yes, Mama," Charity murmured, her brain furiously working on a way to work the dark woman into the conversation.

"I was hoping that you would allow me the honor of dancing with you, Miss Emerson," the man ventured. "I have already asked your mother's permission."

"Certainly, Mr. Reed." Charity seized on the excuse to get away from her mother, where she could question Mr. Reed about the mystery woman. She put her hand on his arm and let him lead her onto the floor.

Faraday Reed, she found, was almost as a good a dancer as Lord Dure, though she felt nothing of the excitement with him that had bubbled up when she was in Dure's arms.

"I have not had the pleasure of seeing you before tonight," Reed said, smiling down at her, his eyes warm. "I cannot believe that I could have missed such a glowing beauty as yours."

Charity arched a brow at his effusive compliment. She could not think of any way to answer it. *Hadn't her mother just said that Reed was a married man?* It seemed strange to her that a married man would flirt like that, but she didn't know how people acted in London. Perhaps it was commonplace here.

"Tonight is my first party," she admitted, deciding to ignore the compliment altogether.

"And are the rumors which I have been hearing true?

Has Dure stolen a march on all the rest of London and already seized you for himself?"

"I would hardly say he *seized* me," Charity replied thoughtfully. "However, he did offer for me, and I accepted. If that is what the rumors say, then they are true."

Reed assumed a sad expression. "There will be many a heartbroken man in the company tonight, then."

Charity smiled thinly. "But not you, surely, Mr. Reed. After all, you are already taken."

"Ah, but, Miss Emerson, a man cannot keep from looking when a woman is as lovely as you." He smiled down at her, his brown eyes glowing.

Charity giggled. She was sure that he charmed many women, but his exaggerated comments, and the soulful looks that accompanied them, seemed comical to her. She left the topic of conversation, which did not interest her, and plunged into the subject uppermost in her mind. "I saw you with a very beautiful woman earlier. She had black hair and fair skin."

When Charity did not respond to his flirtatious bantering, irritation had flitted across Reed's features, but at her question, his eyes began to twinkle. "Ah," he said with a secret smile, "that must have been Mrs. Graves."

"I had the oddest sensation that she was staring at me."

"But you must have felt that many times tonight. You are lovely and young and new to everyone here. Why should people not stare at you?"

Charity drew breath to reply, but she looked past Reed and saw, to her astonishment, that Lord Dure was stalking through the whirling dancers, straight toward her, his face dark and set in grim lines. She stared, faltering in her steps, and Reed's arms tightened to steady her.

Then Dure was beside them, and his hand lashed out, taking Charity's arm in an iron grip and pulling her from Reed's grasp. They stumbled to a halt, and Charity gaped at her fiancé in amazement. His face was furious, his eyes dark and glittering.

"What the devil do you think you're doing?" he barked at Charity. He fixed the other man with a deadly gaze. "Leave Miss Emerson alone."

Dure turned and left the dance floor, dragging Charity along with him. Charity went with him, too astounded to do anything else, but by the time they reached the edge of the dance floor, she had recovered enough to stop and jerk her arm away.

"What do *you* think *you* are doing?" she gasped, a flush spreading up her face. Everyone in the ballroom was looking at them, either openly or covertly.

Dure turned and faced her. "You will not dance with that man again. Nor speak to him, either. From now on, avoid him."

Charity's jaw dropped. "What? *Why?*"

"He is not someone you should know," Dure replied shortly, and he reached out to take her arm again. "Come, I will take you to your mother."

Charity's chin jutted out ominously, and she dug in her heels. "I think not. Let go of me this instant. I may be betrothed to you, but that does not make me one of your servants. You cannot order me about."

She whirled and strode off through the interested crowd of people. Behind her, Dure flushed darkly and started after her. At the doorway of the ballroom, he caught up with her. Wrapping his hand around her in a grip she could not break, he pulled her down the gallery, away from the other guests. Charity went with him, unwilling to make a further scene by trying to break away from his iron grip, but her indignation built.

Finally he turned the corner and found the library, quiet and unoccupied, dimly lit by the fire in the fireplace. He pulled her inside and closed the door after them, reaching over to turn up the low-burning light in the wall sconce. Charity jerked away from him, and he let her go easily now. She strode to the center of the room and whirled to face him.

"How dare you!" she said, seething.

"I dare a great deal more than that. I am your husband."

"Not yet!" she snapped. "And not likely to be, if this is any indication of the way you act. You neglected to inform me that you are a madman."

He looked at her, his face set like stone. "Hardly that. I have good and ample reason for warning you away from Faraday Reed."

"And for humiliating me in front of that entire group of people?" Charity retorted, her hands on her hips.

"You humiliated yourself, letting him hold you so tightly, laughing and gazing up into his face like a moon-struck calf!"

"What?" Charity's voice rose in a shriek.

"You heard me. And hear this, too—you will not see Faraday Reed in the future."

Charity's jaw set mutinously. "I will if I choose to."

"No." His voice was implacable, his face hard. "I will brook no disobedience in my wife."

"It is no surprise to me that you are not married, then!" Charity whirled and began to pace furiously about the room, her hands balled up into fists, making her wide skirts swing wildly. She wanted to scream, to hit him, all the liking that had built up in her toward Dure turning into indignation and painful disillusionment. "I am not your slave, nor will I be, *if* I marry you."

If... The word pierced him like an arrow, cutting hotly through the jealousy and rage that had sprung up the instant Simon saw Charity in Reed's arms. At that moment, he had wanted to knock the blackguard to the floor, and it had taken all his self-control to do no more than pull Charity away from him. Her defiance had fed the hot anger within him. But now her beauty stirred him in a different way. His emotions churned, confusing him.

"There is no *if* about it," he growled. "You pledged yourself to me."

"Engagements can be broken." Charity whirled and walked rapidly back toward him. Her cheeks were flushed with anger, her eyes bright and glittering, and she spoke in a fast, high voice, fairly quavering with emotion. "I'll not be treated like your dog, ordered to go here, stay there. No, not your dog, for doubtless you would treat a dumb animal better than you would your wife."

"I would treat my wife with every courtesy." His words were ground out between his teeth.

Charity, almost breathless from her angry spate of words, stopped. There was something odd in his face, a look no longer just of anger, but of something heavier, hotter. His mouth softened, and his eyes slid down from her face to the tops of her breasts, which were quivering and threatening to escape their confines at every heavy step she took. Charity felt suddenly, strangely dizzy.

Simon crossed the last few strides to her and pulled her against him. His arms wrapped around her like iron, and he bent his head and kissed her.

His kiss was hard and demanding, his lips plundering her mouth. Charity made a noise—whether of protest or pleasure, she wasn't sure. His arms tightened around her, pressing her into his hard chest, as his mouth devoured hers. Desire surged through Charity; she felt dizzy and weak. She tried to draw in a breath, but she was hampered by Simon's arms around her and his mouth on hers.

Panicked, she tried to twist and pull away, but he only tightened his hold on her. She began to struggle in earnest, but just as her struggles pierced the haze of his desire and Simon slackened his grip, lifting his head from hers, blackness washed over Charity.

With a little sigh, she fainted in his arms.

CHAPTER FIVE

FOR A MOMENT, Simon simply stared down at Charity in shock, his arms tightening automatically to hold up her suddenly limp weight. Fear, like an icy knife, pierced his bowels.

"Oh, God," he breathed. "Charity… Sweet Lord, what have I done?"

He lifted her up and laid her on the sofa, carefully propping up her head with one of the small sofa pillows. He knelt beside her, chafing her wrists gently, his eyes fixed on her pale face.

"Charity, please…" He kissed the back of her hand, then continued to rub her wrist. Guilt burned in him. "Wake up. I'm sorry. I didn't mean to hurt you. Please, believe me, I would never try to harm you. You were so beautiful, standing there spitting out fire at me—but I was a blackguard to force myself on you. I didn't think."

Charity's eyelids fluttered open, and she gazed at him blankly. Simon let out a sigh of relief. "Thank God. I was furious when I saw you dancing with him. You are so young and innocent—you have no idea what someone like that can do to you. But I should not have dragged you from the dance floor. I apologize. Then, to attack you myself—"

His jaw tightened, and he turned his head away. Through clenched teeth, he muttered, "Usually I have better control of myself. I promise you, it will not happen again.

Charity let out a chuckle. "Not ever, my lord?" she asked teasingly.

His head snapped back, and he stared at her smiling face. "You—you aren't angry at me?"

"Of course I am," Charity replied, but the smile didn't leave her eyes. "You were impossible—rude and over-bearing, a thorough tyrant. I don't think I should like that in a husband."

He looked at her uncertainly. "I don't think I should like to be that sort of husband, either. I acted hastily, without thinking."

He smoothed a hand across her forehead. Charity's skin was as soft as rose petals beneath his fingers, and it made him tremble. "I am sorry for hurting you. I was rough and clumsy. Normally I am not such an inept lover."

Charity grinned impishly, her dimple lurking in her cheek. "I should probably hold it over your head," she said consideringly, then shrugged and sighed. "But I don't have it in me, I'm afraid. I didn't faint because you were too rough. I mean, well, not exactly."

He frowned. "What do you mean?"

"I fainted because I couldn't breathe. Partly it was because you were holding me so tightly, but it was also because I'd been dancing and was out of breath. Then I was mad, and scolding you so hard that I couldn't catch my breath. So I fainted."

Simon cocked a disbelieving eyebrow. "You fainted because you were angry and talking too fast?"

"Not exactly." Charity sighed. "Mama would murder me for saying it, for it's most indelicate, but the truth is, I couldn't breathe because my stays are too tight."

He stared at her blankly. "What?"

"This corset—it's cinched too tightly. You see, I didn't have a gown good enough for a ball, so I had to wear one of Serena's. But Serena is slimmer than I, so I had to tighten my corset to fit into her dress."

Simon's eyes drifted down over the bodice of her dress, lingering on her breasts, which were pushing against the material and swelling out over the top. "I see."

His mouth was suddenly dry as dust. His gaze went to her waist, infinitesimally small, and he spread his hand over her stomach. He could feel the stiff corset beneath the satin.

"I do not like to think of your flesh so cruelly pinched," he told her in a low voice. He raised his eyes to her, and the dark fire in them sent a quiver through Charity. "You are beautiful enough, without squeezing the breath out of you in order to reduce your waist to that of a child. Do not wear a corset again."

He smoothed his hand gently over her stomach; the satin was cool and slick beneath his skin. Charity let out an odd, breathless chuckle. His touch sent strange sensations shooting through her. She knew that Simon should not be touching her like this, but it felt far too wonderful for her to make him stop. She scarcely even noticed that he had issued another command.

She said only, her voice a trifle unsteady, "'Tis easy enough for you to say, but I would split the dress wide open if I did not wear stays."

Simon's hand strayed upward, grazing the underside of

her breast. "It would seem to me," he said meditatively, "that you are already in some danger of bursting out of this dress."

The prospect did not appear to displease him. Simon's voice was like brandy, warming and seductive, and Charity closed her eyes against a wave of hot pleasure.

"My lord," she breathed.

Simon looked at her. Her eyes were closed, her face was faintly flushed, her mouth was soft and moist. He recognized the stirrings of passion in her expression, and it heated his own blood. Experimentally he curved his hand around her breast, and he was rewarded by the way desire rippled over Charity's features and her mouth opened in a soft *O* of surprised arousal.

"I think," he said softly, "that we are close enough that you could call me by my name, rather than 'my lord.'"

"Simon."

The soft flutter of sound made his abdomen tighten and prickle. Simon could not keep from bending over her and placing his mouth upon hers. Charity did not resist or pull away; instead, she wrapped her arms around his neck and held on, her lips pressing back against his. Simon groaned and sank his mouth hungrily into hers. His tongue filled her mouth, greedy and demanding. She tasted as sweet as honey to him, and desire spiraled through Simon. He waited, dread warring with passion, for Charity to tighten and pull away in disgust at his hot, earthy kiss. When she did not, instead curling her own tongue tentatively around his, he shuddered with delight. His hand caressed her breast. Her nipple tightened and strained against the dress.

Charity's untutored response shattered Simon's uncertain control. He kissed her again and again, changing the slant of his mouth on hers or pulling back slightly, only to have the pleasure of meeting her lips once more. Charity clung to him, emitting little whimpers of desire every time his mouth and hands sent a new wave of pleasure through her. She had never imagined anything like the sensations he was arousing in her, and the pleasure was almost overwhelming. She squeezed her legs together, aware of a growing, insistent ache there. She stirred on the couch, moving her hips unconsciously. She wanted to feel his hand there, where the yearning blossomed between her legs, and the thought was so licentious that it shocked her even as it sent a fresh wave of heat through her. She wondered if Simon would think her lewd and shocking if he knew what she wanted. Then all thought flew out of her head as his lips left hers and trailed a burning path down her neck, to her chest.

"Simon…" Charity twined her fingers into his thick hair. Her breath was fast, hard panting, and she moved her legs restlessly. She was aching and raw with passion, yet it was all so new to her that she could not even identify what she felt.

Simon, more experienced, blazed at her innocent desire. His body was suddenly a furnace, and he trembled under the force of his need. He mumbled her name against her skin, his lips trailing down onto the soft, quivering tops of her breasts. That exquisite softness was almost too much for him, and he buried his face between her breasts, breathing in her scent.

"Charity, oh Charity…" he groaned, and abruptly pulled away from her.

Charity reached out for him instinctively, appalled at the loss. "No, wait! Simon!" She opened her eyes and looked up at him, her eyes dark blue in the dim light, startled, regretful, and glowing with unspent passion.

Simon groaned and clenched his hands in his hair, using the pain to pull his hungry senses back from the precipice of desire. He knew he was about to slide down into that dark, hot spiral of hunger and need from which there was no returning.

"Oh, God—" he grated the words out "—what am I doing?"

He surged to his feet and began to pace the room, struggling to contain the primitive hungers raging within him. Charity swung her feet off the couch and sat up. Her heart was pounding in her chest, and confused emotions churned within her. She had been wrong to act this way, she knew, yet she could not say that she regretted it. Every part of her had thrilled to Simon's kiss, to the sweet caress of his hand.

But he had turned away from her—no, more than that, flung himself away. *Had he, perhaps, been displeased by her boldness? Had she acted like a loose woman?* Her mother had always told her that a man wanted a proper lady for a wife. *And he had already been upset with her for acting in a way he didn't think was proper.* Charity smoothed her hands down her dress and cast a troubled glance over at Simon's ungiving back.

He turned back to face her, his face a cold, blank mask. "I beg your pardon," he said stiffly, his hands clasped behind his back. "That never should have happened."

Charity's heart sank. He looked like a stranger—a disapproving stranger. "I—I am sorry, my lord." Her gaze dropped; she could not bear to look at his cold face. "Did I displease you? If I was overbold, I—"

Simon's nostrils flared, and a light sprang into his eyes. "No," he said huskily.

He sat down beside her on the sofa and took her hand. Charity could feel the heat radiating from his body. She looked up into his face and saw in his eyes the same heat that had been in them earlier. Relief flooded her; she had not repelled him. She smiled, and his eyes dropped to her mouth. The flame in his eyes burned even more brightly.

"You have done nothing wrong. I promise, nothing you did here displeases me. It is I who was wrong. I have acted like a cad. I took advantage of your innocence. I should never have brought you to this private room, and once here, I should not have given way to…" His eyes fell to her breasts, and his voice faltered. He jumped to his feet and cleared his throat. "Ah, that is, I, uh, should not have given way to my desires."

"But you are to be my husband," Charity said reasonably.

"Even that does not give me allowance to— My God, Charity, a few more minutes and I would not have been able to stop!" he exploded. "I must have taken leave of my senses. That door was unlocked. Anyone could have come in here at any moment. Your reputation would have been ruined."

"Oh. And then you would have been unable to marry me."

He stared at her, shocked. "Good Lord, no! How could you think that? I am not such a blackguard."

"But if my reputation was ruined, I would not be suitable for the Countess of Dure." She gazed back at him blandly.

"Of course I would have married you!" he said through clenched teeth. "But it would not have been pleasant for you to have such a thing hanging over your head—the gossip and the whispers."

Charity immediately softened. "I know. You have had to endure that already. You are right. It was wrong of us." Then she beamed at him, her smile breaking across her face like sunshine. "But there was no harm done. No one came in, so we are safe. In the future, we shall simply have to be more careful."

"There will be no future," he replied grimly. "I mean, there will be no repetition of this. I lost control of myself. It shall not happen again."

"Yes, my lord." Charity sighed. She had rather liked Dure's losing his control. She had especially liked the idea that she had the ability to make him "take leave of his senses."

"So, we are back to 'my lord'?" he asked. Charity glanced up to see a faint smile on his lips. His eyes were warm and caressing. "We had progressed to 'Simon.'"

"I thought perhaps it would sound too intimate."

"I like the sound of it." He crossed the few steps to her and reached down, pulling her to her feet. He cupped her face with his hand and gazed down at her intently. "I look forward, my dear, to being intimate with you. When you are my wife, I plan to repeat what happened tonight—and much more."

Charity's eyes darkened sensually. "I am glad."

Simon drew in a sharp breath. "Sweet Jesus, but you tempt me." His hand slid caressingly down her throat, then fell to his side. "But I have promised I will not. Go back to the ballroom. I am leaving."

He turned and strode to the door. He opened it and paused, looking back at Charity. "But when our wedding night comes, sweet Charity, I promise you it will be long and full."

He walked out the door. Charity sank back down onto the couch, suddenly weak in the knees.

Simon had intended to have a brief and forceful conversation with Faraday Reed before he left the ball. The passion seething inside him yearned for an outlet in fury. But as he started down the gallery, he saw Reed standing outside the door to the ballroom, chatting with Theodora Graves. Theodora was smiling up at Reed, her fan wafting languidly, while Reed was ogling the deep bosom of her dress. Simon had seen Theodora almost as soon as he arrived at the ball, and her presence had alarmed him. He had been afraid that she had come there to accost Charity. Theodora was a great lover of scenes, and he had had little hope that she would hold back from one tonight, just because it was so public. Simon did not particularly care whether Theodora managed to blacken his name further; he had long ago given up caring what others thought of him. However, he was filled with a quiet, icy rage at the idea that she might subject Charity to public humiliation, and he had waited tensely, ready to stride over and sweep Theodora away if she approached Charity.

But she had not, and Simon had finally decided, watching Theodora preen herself and flirt and laugh, that she had come there this evening merely with the hope of making him jealous. Since there was little possibility of that, he had relaxed. Now, seeing her flirt with Reed, he thought that she had met her match. Reed was probably figuring up the cost of her diamond necklace while he leered down her neckline.

Simon turned and went down the staircase instead of approaching Reed. He had no desire to speak to Theodora, and he did not want her to think that when he laced into Reed for dancing with Charity, he was doing it out of jealousy because he'd seen Theodora flirting with Faraday Reed.

Simon did not glance back around, and so he did not see Faraday Reed watching him as he disappeared down the elegant staircase. Reed's face settled for a moment into bitter, resentful lines. Then he turned his eyes to the woman in front of him again, schooling his face into its usual expression of patrician charm. Personally, he found Theodora's charms too lush for his liking, although, of course, he was sure that he would before long sample those charms much more intimately. He liked the thought of taking one of Simon's women. He had done it several times before, and it always gave him a piquant satisfaction. Not as much, of course, as he would have when he took Dure's bride before the man tasted her himself.

He was sure that it would happen. He had infinite confidence in his own skills with women. Besides, if by some odd chance Miss Emerson did not succumb to him willingly, he had no qualms about using force. But that, alas, must lie in the future. Right now, he wished for a more immediate revenge, to rid himself of the antsy feeling that seeing Simon Westport always left him with.

After a moment's thought, it came to him. It would be quite fun, and very useful, too. So, excusing himself to Theodora, he sauntered back into the ballroom and glanced around until finally his eyes alit on the person he sought. He waited for a few minutes, until she moved away from the knot of people with whom she had been conversing, and then he crossed the room, intersecting her path.

"Lady Ashford!" he said with pleased surprise, as if he had by chance come upon her.

Simon's sister stopped and looked at him warily. "Mr. Reed."

Venetia started to walk around him, but Reed shifted subtly, so that he was still in her path. "No, please, my lady, do not pass me by so easily." He paused and added, "Once you would not have."

"Once I was a green girl," Venetia snapped back. "I am not so foolish now."

"You wound me. Personally, I remember that time with great fondness. Indeed, I cherish my mementos of it."

Venetia went still, her face paling. "Mementos? What do you mean?"

"Not much, only a few letters…a ring. You remember them, do you not?"

Red flooded her cheeks now, replacing the paleness. "You kept them?"

"But of course." He smiled. "I am a man of sentiment. It warms my heart to look back upon them now and then."

Venetia glared, but there was fear lurking in her eyes. "What do you want?"

"I?" He assumed an air of injured innocence. "What could I want of you? You are, after all, a happily married woman. I do not know your husband, but perhaps I shall have the pleasure of making Lord Ashford's acquaintance in the future. We have so many things in common, I am sure that we would have much to talk about."

"Get out of my way." Venetia's voice was low, and shook with fury. "And stay away from me in the future."

"But of course, my lady." He stepped aside, sweeping her an exaggerated bow.

Venetia stalked past him, not once looking back at him, but her hands were clenched together tightly to hide their trembling. Faraday watched her go, a faint smile playing about his lips.

Faraday Reed came to call on the Emersons the next day. Caroline Emerson was charmed by the man. It was disappointing, of course, that he was already married, but such issues were no longer all-important, now that she had one daughter successfully engaged. And she found him so skilled in all the social graces, so handsome, so blandly charming, that soon he was always welcome in her drawing room.

Charity did not tell her mother of Dure's reaction to the man, which Caroline seemed to have been one of the few people not to witness. Her mother, had she known that Lord Dure disliked the man, would have refused him admittance immediately, for no man, no matter how socially pleasant, was worth offending as wealthy a son-in-law as the Earl of Dure. But Charity did not want her mother to refuse admittance to Faraday Reed.

It was not that she was particularly interested in Mr. Reed. He was light and amusing, and he was always full of compliments—though sometimes they were so flowery that Charity had to hide a smile. But he could not compare to Simon, who was far more handsome and exciting, and whose very presence sent a sort of electricity through her. Next to him, Faraday Reed seemed distinctly boring. However, Charity was determined to allow Mr. Reed to call on her, because she was still nettled by her fiancé's peremptory and domineering manner. She was not about to let any man, even Lord Dure, tell her with whom she could associate. Besides, though he had apologized for being a trifle rough with her and for causing a scene at the dance, he had not really taken back his commands or told her that he was sorry for ignoring her wishes and opinions in the matter. She saw no reason to give in to him. It would only set a bad precedent. So she did not avoid Mr. Reed when he came to call on them, and she did not tell her mother about Lord Dure's edict concerning the man.

A few days after the Rotterham ball, Mr. Reed invited Charity to go for a ride with him in Hyde Park. Charity's mother decided that it would be proper, since it was an open-air vehicle—as long as one of her sisters accompanied them. Charity grimaced when Mrs. Emerson assigned Elspeth the task of chaperoning, for she had long ago found that Elspeth usually put a damper on any activity. However, she had not been driving in the park yet, and she had heard several times that it was the fashionable thing to do. Also, she looked forward to getting a breath of fresh air. She had been used to tramping along the lanes and paths back in Siddley-on-the-Marsh, and life in London, where a girl could not go out in the street unless a maid accompanied her, had made her hungry for a bit of exercise and the outdoors. Besides, having Elspeth as a chaperone might blunt Dure's displeasure if he learned of her outing with Faraday Reed.

So she put on a smile, despite Elspeth's presence, and tied one of her prettiest bonnets on her head. Elspeth took quite a bit longer to bundle up against the imagined chill that might creep up on her outside, even though it was May, but at last she was ready, and Mr. Reed escorted the two of them outside and up into his victoria, an open, low-built carriage suitable for driving on a nice spring day. It was also the best sort of vehicle in which to see and be seen as one tooled around the park.

Faraday Reed was a charming companion, full of compliments and light tidbits of gossip. Charity never took his flowery compliments seriously, but it was fun to flirt a little with him, the way she had flirted with her father's friends back home. He was not as old as they were, but he was several years older than she, and he was married, and that put him the same category, Charity thought.

They drove along slowly, nodding and waving now and then to acquaintances. There were delays when the occupants of one vehicle stopped to talk to those in another, but they were in no hurry to get anywhere. The purpose, after all, was in the going.

As they drove along, two women and a man on horseback came trotting toward them. Charity straightened a little and looked with interest at them when she recognized one of the women as the lady who had been staring at her at Lady Rotterham's ball. The woman was dressed quite differently from the way she had been that night, for today she wore a smartly tailored riding habit in a military style, and her luxuriant dark hair was covered by a rakishly upturned hat with a plume. She looked, Charity thought with a touch of awe, the very picture of sophistication, and she wished for a moment that she had some of the woman's lush, sensual beauty.

"Faraday!" the woman exclaimed in surprise, and urged her horse forward to come up beside the carriage. "How nice to see you."

Reed swept his hat from his head and bowed to her. "My dear Theodora."

She smiled and glanced at Charity and Elspeth, sitting in the carriage with him. Charity smiled back in a friendly way.

"Oh, excuse me," Mr. Reed said politely. "Miss Emerson, this is Mrs. Graves. Mrs. Graves, the Misses Emerson."

"It's so nice to meet you," Mrs. Graves said, leaning down a little from her horse and shaking Charity's hand. She nodded at Elspeth. "I noticed you, you know, at Lady Rotterham's party. I said to Faraday, who is that attractive young woman, didn't I, Faraday? But at that time he didn't know you." Dimples deepened in her cheeks, and she cast a roguish glance at Mr. Reed. "But I can see you didn't waste any time making her acquaintance, did you, my dear?"

"I'm afraid you know me all to well, Thea."

They talked for a little while, saying the sort of small, social things one said at such a time. When another carriage pulled up behind them and waited impatiently, Reed pulled his carriage off to the side of the road, and Mrs. Graves followed, waving at her companions and telling them that she would catch up with them later.

Mrs. Graves dismounted, and Charity and Faraday got out of the carriage. Elspeth, languidly waving her fan, elected to stay in the victoria.

"Don't go too far," Elspeth called after Charity. "You mustn't get out of my sight."

"Is your sister feeling ill?" Reed asked in a concerned voice. "Perhaps I should take her home."

"Oh, no, Elspeth's always like that," Charity responded cheerfully. "She'd be sitting at home doing the same thing."

"Well, anyone can see that *you* are full of spirit," Theodora said, linking her arm with Charity's and propelling her forward. "I knew I would like you. Tell me, do you ride? Perhaps we could ride together one morning."

"No," Charity answered regretfully. She had sorely

missed riding since they had been in London. "I'm afraid I don't. Our horses are at home."

"What? And Dure has not given you the use of one of his animals?" Theodora's large dark eyes widened expressively. "'Tis well known he has an excellent stable."

"No." Charity wondered if she had committed some social gaffe by admitting this. *Was it wrong of Dure not to have set her up on a horse? Did it mean that he did not value her as he should?* "I'm sure His Lordship's horses would all be too high-spirited for me."

"Oh, well, then of course he would not. Dure is very particular about his horseflesh."

"Do you know Lord Dure?"

Mrs. Graves smiled faintly. "We have met. But I doubt His Lordship would remember my name."

"I cannot imagine any man forgetting a woman as lovely as you," Charity replied honestly.

Mrs. Graves looked startled, then chuckled and gave Charity's arm a squeeze. "What a dear child you are! Something tells me that you and I shall be good friends. Perhaps you would like to come to one of my little parties. They're nothing grand, of course, but I hope I am not being overly immodest when I say that everyone enjoys themselves."

"Your parties are delightful," Reed assured her.

"We're not stuffy," Mrs. Graves told her, her dark eyes glowing with good humor. "Just young people, you know, games, and sometimes a little impromptu dancing." She leaned closer confidentially and said, "No line of gray chaperones to look down their noses at one."

"It sounds delightful," Charity agreed honestly. She found the rules and conventions of society dreadfully constricting, and she often felt as if all the older ladies who sat and watched the dancing were like vultures, waiting to pounce on some social faux pas or the other. "However, I doubt that Mama would go to a party where there are just young people."

Theodora gazed at her blankly. "But, no, I meant you, not your mama."

Charity looked back at her just as blankly. "But how could I go without Mama and Serena and Elspeth?" She was new to London, but even she knew that a young unmarried girl never attended parties alone.

"But you are engaged now—why, almost a married woman."

"Oh." Charity's sunny smile crossed her face. "You mean that I shall be able to come when I am married to Dure. Of course. That sounds delightful."

Theodora's smile looked strained, but she said only, "Why, before that, I should hope. An engaged woman, if she has the proper escort, may go about more as she pleases."

"Do you honestly think so?" Charity asked, feeling rather doubtful on the point herself. "Well, I guess if Lord Dure took me, it would be all right."

"Yes, although we are probably not fine enough for His Lordship. But Faraday, of course, could escort you."

"My pleasure," Reed agreed.

Charity smiled politely and made a noncommittal reply, thinking to herself that the last thing that would make the party acceptable to the Earl of Dure was for Faraday Reed to act as her escort.

"There, I've overstepped myself," Theodora said quickly, looking crestfallen. She released Charity's arm.

"I'm sorry, I was pressing you, and I should not have. They are only simple little parties, and I'm sure not what you are used to. No doubt you would consider us poor creatures, to find amusement in them."

"Oh, no," Charity hastened to assure her, horrified that she had hurt the other woman's feelings by her reluctance. "Indeed, I would like to come. I am sure that I would enjoy myself very much."

"It is just that you seem like such a sweet young woman, and I would like to be your friend. I am sorry if I have been importunate."

"No. Truly, I would be happy to be your friend. It is only that my mama is quite strict, you see. And my fiancé would not—" She paused, searching to find some way to state the earl's objections without offending Faraday Reed.

"Dure?" Theodora's brows shot up, and she smiled faintly. "Do not tell me Dure has become such a puritan. Why, everyone knows—" She stopped abruptly, then went on, "Well, never mind."

"Knows what?" Charity asked mildly, preparing herself for another warning about Dure's reputation. She had endured at least ten such from family and friends so far.

"What? Oh, nothing. But I always say, what's sauce for the goose is sauce for the gander. Don't you think so? I find it sad that a man may go to parties wherever and whenever he likes, but a woman may only go where a man considers 'suitable.'"

Charity wondered if Theodora was speaking specifically about Lord Dure or about men in general. Was Dure going out to other parties when he was not with her? And what sort of parties were they? However, she couldn't bring herself to ask Theodora; it would be too embarrassing to admit that she did not know what her fiancé did.

Theodora smiled brightly and said, "Ah, well…I must try to catch my friends. I'm afraid I've spent too long here talking. It is just that you are so charming to talk to."

"Thank you. I enjoyed it, too. I hope we see each other again."

"But of course we will. You must promise that you will come to one of my parties."

She looked so entreating that Charity could not bear to tell her that she would not. "I would be happy to—if Mama allows it."

"Sometimes mamas are too strict," Theodora said in an indulgent voice. "My own mama was much the same. Perhaps it would be best simply not to tell her."

"You mean sneak out of the house?" Charity goggled at her, wondering if somehow Theodora could possibly know that Charity had done that very thing when she went to Dure's house to suggest their marriage scheme. But, no, there was no way she could, Charity reminded herself.

"Oh, dear," Theodora went on, touching Charity's arm, "now I have shocked you. I am sorry. I forgot how young you are. You are doubtless still quite terrified of disobeying your mama."

"It isn't that," Charity retorted, stung a little by Theodora's words. "It's just that—"

She stopped, unable to explain that she was willing to disobey her mother and even flout the conventions of society, but only for something terribly important, as she had done in going to see Simon that day. Something as frivolous as a party was different; she could not risk embarrassing her family or Simon over nothing more than that.

"I'm sorry," she said finally. "I just can't."

"Of course. I understand." Theodora flashed her a brilliant smile, although it seemed to Charity that sadness and hurt lurked in her eyes. "Good day, Miss Emerson. Mr. Reed." She turned and walked slowly back to her horse.

Charity felt guilty as she watched her. She could see that Theodora's hands were curled into fists, and Charity suspected that she was struggling to keep her emotions in check. Charity was tempted to run after Theodora and tell her that she would come to her party after all.

"I hurt her," she murmured. "I'm sorry. I didn't mean to."

"Don't worry. Theodora is accustomed to the small snubs of society."

"What?" Charity's eyes widened with horror. "Oh, no, did you think I was snubbing her? I wasn't, truly. It is only that Mama is so strict, and I couldn't do anything to embarrass her or Papa. Truly, I know they would not like it if I went to a party without a chaperone."

"I didn't mean that *you* had snubbed her, my dear Miss Emerson," Reed hastened to assure Charity. "I meant only that, well, many ladies don't attend her parties. Especially the older ones. So she is sure that your mother will not bring you. You see, she is not truly one of 'us.' Her family is respectable, of course, but only minor country gentry. Not the sort into which a baron's son usually marries. But Thea's beauty made Douglas Graves fall in love with her. He was a lieutenant in the dragoons. They never had much money, of course. He was only a younger son, you see. But while he was alive, they were accepted everywhere. Then, after he died, well, many people snubbed Theodora."

"Because her husband was dead?"

"It was his place in society that got her in. Without him, she was once again just a country nobody."

"But that's horrible!" Charity's ever-ready sympathy was easily engaged.

"No doubt. But that is the way London is, in general. There are some who remained her friend."

"Like you." Charity looked up at him. It occurred to her that there must be more to Faraday Reed than there seemed, some hidden depth of feeling.

He made a dismissive gesture. "She and Douglas had been my friends. I could hardly drop his widow, now, could I?"

"I can see that you would not." Charity smiled at Reed. She could not understand why Dure so disliked this man. "Anyone would be honored to have you for a friend."

She put her hand on Reed's arm, and they started toward the carriage.

CHAPTER SIX

As Charity and Mr. Reed strolled toward his carriage, they saw a young urchin come trotting up to the side of the victoria. The boy stopped and spoke to Elspeth. She shrank back from the dirty creature, shaking her head. The coachman turned and spoke to the boy, gesturing to him to be off, but he stood his ground. Finally the driver nodded toward Charity and Reed, and the boy turned and ran to them.

"Miss Emerson?" he asked in a thick cockney accent, coming to a halt in front of them. "Miss Charity Emerson?"

"Why, yes," Charity replied, surprised. "That is I."

"'ere." He thrust out a white envelope toward her.

Charity hesitated, then took the missive. "What in the world?"

Reed reached in his pocket and pulled out a coin, which he threw to the boy, and the urchin scampered off. Charity looked at the writing on the front: only her name, in blunt printing.

"How odd," she said, as she tore open the envelope. "Why would anyone—" She stopped as she opened the folded sheet of paper inside.

"What is it? You've gone pale as a sheet." Reed plucked the piece of paper from her nerveless fingers and read it aloud. "'Ask him what happened to his wife and his brother'? I say. What does this mean?"

Charity pressed her hand against her stomach. She felt ill. "I don't know. I wish you hadn't read that." She snatched the note back and looked at it again.

"Who sent it?" Reed went on. "Are they talking about Dure?"

"Yes. I'm sure so." Charity crumpled the note in her hand. "Oh! This makes me so angry! It's low and sneaky. Wait! Where's that boy?"

She looked around, but the urchin was already gone from sight. She let out a groan of frustration. "I should have stopped that boy and asked who gave this envelope to him. But I was so stunned, I didn't even think. Now I still don't know…."

"Have you gotten others like this?" Faraday asked.

"Yes," Charity admitted. "I found one at Lady Rotterham's ball. Someone dropped it on my table. I didn't see who. At first I didn't even notice it. Then, as we were leaving, I saw it and picked it up. It said, 'Don't marry Dure or you will regret it.'"

"Did you tell Dure?"

"No!" Charity turned horrified eyes on Reed. "I wasn't going to show him something like that!"

"But he would surely want to know if someone was bothering his fiancée."

"It would be awful for him to know that someone held such spite for him. Hated him that much—to try to stop his marriage."

"Well, then, your father. Did you tell him?"

"No. It would only upset him and Mother. I wouldn't want them to worry. And what if they began to doubt Lord

Dure? Besides, there was nothing anyone could do. I didn't see who dropped the note. And look at how this one is printed—they've disguised their handwriting. If only I had thought to ask that street urchin," she said mournfully.

"You were startled. It's quite understandable. I was, too."

"How would they have known to send it to me here?" Charity mused. "Who could have known that I would be here in the park at this moment? How did he know to come to me?"

"I see what you mean. That is a trifle odd. Hmm…I guess that anyone who'd been here in the park and seen you would know. Someone in another carriage, perhaps. It would have been easy enough to dash the note off and find an urchin outside to carry it. All they would have had to do was describe my victoria and tell him your name."

"Why would anyone want to frighten me?" Charity asked. "Do they hate me? Or is it Dure they hate that much?"

"No one could hate you," Reed replied, smiling. "I'm sure you have no enemies."

"But Dure does."

Reed shrugged. "Every man has enemies." He paused. "I think you should tell your father or Lord Dure."

"No. They won't be able to do anything, either, and it would just upset them. I—I don't want Dure to see how much someone hates him."

Reed sighed. "I think you're wrong. You should seek their help." He took her hands and gazed earnestly down into her eyes. "But if you will not, then I ask that you let me help you. I will stand as your friend."

Charity smiled at him and squeezed his hand. "Thank you, Mr. Reed. I need a friend, I think."

He raised her hand and kissed it gently. "You may rely on me."

Charity told herself that the notes she had received were merely some person's odd notion of a practical joke, or the work of some spiteful enemy of Lord Dure's. Except for the outrage they called up in her, and the distinctly uncomfortable feeling she had at social gatherings when she looked around and wondered what person among them might have sent the wicked things, they had done no actual harm. It seemed to her that all the sender could hope to accomplish was to frighten her so that she would cry off her engagement to Simon, thus causing him social embarrassment. And she wasn't about to do that.

Though the notes frightened her a little, what she felt was primarily uneasiness about the sender, because of the venom and secrecy of the act. About Simon, she never really held any doubts. She did not stop to wonder why she should so trust a man who was literally little more than a stranger to her. She simply knew that Simon could not have killed his wife and brother.

However, she was not so sure that the rest of her family would react with the same aplomb regarding the notes. Despite the advantages of her marrying Lord Dure, her mother would decide against the engagement if she began to suspect there was any truth to the vague rumors about Dure's past. And, somehow, these notes made the possibility seem more real than society's typically exaggerated rumors. She did not want to give Caroline even an opportunity to have any second thoughts.

Therefore, she did not mention her notes to anyone, even her sisters. Serena would worry, and Elspeth would doubtless have hysterics, and Belinda would remind her of the times she had said that Dure was reputed to be a dangerous man.

Charity was tempted many times to confide in Dure, for she knew that it would make her feel easier. But she refused to allow his unknown enemy to use her in that way to hurt him. If it shook her to read the notes, how much more must it bother Simon, toward whom the hate was directed? Why, it might even make him begin to wonder if she believed the notes. She wasn't about to put that sort of gnawing worm right at the core of their marriage.

Besides, she was finding, to her disappointment, that she did not see very much of Simon—at least, not alone. Her days and nights were filled with a whirl of social events, from morning and afternoon calls to soirees and dinners and balls, until it seemed she never had a minute to rest. In the evenings Simon often joined them at one party or another, but they were always surrounded by a crush of people at such events and could do little more than chat or perhaps dance. While Charity found dancing with Simon divine, their rather formal public conversations left her dissatisfied. Even when he came to call on her in the afternoons, there were always other visitors, or at least her mother or sisters, as chaperones, and her mother managed to keep the conversations on the safest, dullest topics.

She wished that she could be alone with him, that their conversation could flow freely, as it had that time in his office. Simon looked as bored as she was with the sort of light social inanities that callers engaged in. And though she often found him looking at her with a spark in his eyes that made her pulse begin to race, there was never any opportunity to find out to what interesting place that look might lead. The traditional yearlong engagement began to seem interminable to her.

There were other amusements, of course. Venetia, true to her word, took Charity out on a shopping expedition. Venetia was a quiet person, but she warmed up quickly around Charity's effervescence, and the two of them enjoyed the afternoon tremendously. Though Charity's budget was limited, she had never before been given such license from her mother to buy as she pleased, and to her the amount seemed tremendous. Charity firmly turned down Venetia's suggestion that Lord Dure pay for her clothes, and barely noticed when Venetia took the modiste of the very elegant establishment aside and whispered a few words to her. Charity was pleasantly surprised to find that the prices of these elegant London gowns were little more than what she would pay in the country, and she was able to buy several gowns and day dresses.

The evening dresses, of course, were the virginal white required of young unmarried girls, but she was able to persuade both the modiste and Venetia that an ice-blue dress would be suitable for afternoons, as would a soft pink one. She had enough left over to purchase a new pair of gloves, as well as pieces of ribbons and lace with which to update several of her old dresses to make them suitable for London wear. Venetia, who had never had to economize in her life, found it delightful fun to rummage through goods, laughing and discussing materials and styles. Later, she realized, it had not been the task so much as Charity's lively stories about life with her sisters in their country manor that had made the afternoon enjoyable.

They sent their purchases home in Venetia's carriage, and the two women strolled back to Aunt Ermintrude's house in Mayfair, chatting contentedly about their afternoon. Venetia, inspired by Charity's economical approach to shopping, had also bought several new items that were, she said, simply too great a bargain to pass up.

Charity listened to her reasoning with a smile and agreed that Venetia had, indeed, purchased wisely. "Why, you must have saved at least fifty pounds," she said, looking at Venetia with big, grave eyes.

"Oh, yes," Venetia agreed. Her eye caught Charity's and she began to grin. "And at a cost of only several hundred pounds more!"

The two young women began to laugh, and Venetia linked arms with Charity as they continued down the street. "I must have a dinner party," Venetia went on, "to introduce you to the family, you know. Our uncle, Ambrose, and his son, Evelyn. Uncle Ambrose is Dure's heir—for the present, that is. He is rather stuffy, but you'll like Evelyn. He practically grew up with us. Of course, we will have to invite Aunt Genevieve, too, and my sister, Elizabeth. At least Cousin Louisa is out of town, so you will be spared her chatter about her children."

"I would like to meet your family," Charity told her. "I know so little about Simon."

"He isn't one to talk about himself. And though we are very fond of each other, he is six years older than I. Elizabeth was between us. He has never confided in me." She paused, frowning. "But I do know that he has not been a happy man these past few years."

"Since his first wife died?" Charity ventured.

Venetia nodded. "Yes. She and their baby. They died

together, you see, at its birth. After that, Simon came to London and spent most of his time here," Venetia continued. She turned and looked at Charity earnestly. "If you hear tales of his wildness, please do not take them too much to heart."

Charity murmured a polite denial. She could not tell her that such rumors were not the ones that occupied her mind.

"He did, perhaps, turn to some wicked ways and bad companions, but I think he was almost mad with grief. He did not continue them long, and he was never evil in it. And he was still young, only twenty-three when Sybilla died. He is not an unkind man. He has always been very good to me. Those who say he is hard or cruel don't know him as I do."

"He must have loved her very much," Charity mused softly. Obviously, the truth was the opposite of what the note had said. Simon had grieved greatly for his wife, had been driven to drink by her death. He had loved her, not murdered her. It gave her a strange, almost aching feeling in her chest to think of Sybilla, and of Simon's love for her. She thought of his insistence on a loveless marriage, and she wondered if he could not give his love to another woman because he was still in love with Sybilla.

"He did," Venetia agreed, her thoughts so focused on the past that she did not even glance at Charity and see the uncertainty in her face. "It was a love match. My father was opposed to it. He said that Simon and Sybilla were too young. And I suppose they were. Simon was only twenty, Sybilla just seventeen. But Simon was adamant. He and Father argued horribly about it. Father did not disown Simon, in the end, but they were stiff and formal with one another after that, barely speaking. Even after Sybilla died, they remained cool."

"What was she like?" Charity found herself suddenly consumed with curiosity about this woman of whom she had scarcely thought before. But now she wondered what sort of woman had taken her lord's heart and left him so wounded.

"Sybilla?" Venetia frowned. "I'm not sure. I was still in the schoolroom then. She was three years older than I, and already out. I didn't really know her. After they were married, they did not visit much, because Father and Simon were so angry with each other. She was very lovely. She had blond hair, but not like yours, very pale. Gray eyes. And the most beautiful pale skin. She was like a cameo, I thought."

Charity thought about following such perfection, and even her sturdy spirit quailed a little. She did not expect Simon to love her; she had been quite honest in telling him that she would live contentedly in the sort of arrangement he envisioned. But she had thought that affection would grow between them, a sort of closeness and friendship. Now she wondered if perhaps his heart was too much locked away to permit even that. She did not like to think of living for the rest of her life with a man who compared her always to another, perfect image of a wife.

Venetia sighed and shrugged. "But Sybilla never warmed to me, nor I to her. No doubt I was too young for her to become friends with me, and, I confess, I was rather jealous of her, for she had taken away my beloved big brother." She smiled a little sheepishly. "I had always worshiped Simon, though I confess back then he hardly seemed to know I was alive. He was closest to Hal, our brother. Only a year separated them, and they had grown up almost as twins—a masculine fortress, you see, against us girls."

"And Hal died, too." Once again, Charity thought, the note-writer had written of hatred and murder, yet the truth was that Simon had loved his brother. What drove the writer to so turn the events around? What made him hate Dure so much? "It must have been horrible for Simon."

"Yes. We all missed him, but Simon most of all. It was only a year after Sybilla and the baby died. I think Simon almost felt as if he were cursed. And people were so cruel…. There were whispers that it was too much for mere bad luck, that Simon must have played a part in their deaths."

"Why? Who?" Charity looked at her. Perhaps she could find out the source of the notes through Venetia. Whoever who had spread the rumors might be the same one who had sent the notes.

"I do not know. They were so vague. No one spoke of it to me directly, of course. There were just allusions…and whispers that stopped when I came near. But I knew what they were saying. Even Ashford heard them." A faint smile curved her lips as she thought of her husband. "Poor George. The most phlegmatic of men—and he almost got into a fistfight at his club one night because of it. He's always been Simon's friend."

"Good for him. The man needed a thrashing, I'm sure, for spreading such rumors."

"I don't think there was any malice in him. He was only repeating what he had heard. It was not he who began the rumors."

"But who, then?"

"I don't know." Tears came suddenly into Venetia's

eyes, and she looked away. "It was awful for Simon. That's one reason why he is so often alone. So often grim. I am sure he was pierced by their unkind suspicions. But he just set his face and went about his life, ignoring them. Giving everyone that haughty stare." She sighed. "Even now, I still sometimes hear people talk about the scandal in his past."

Charity's eyes flashed, and her fists tightened. "They had better not say so to me, or I'll give them an answer that will make their ears ring!"

Venetia chuckled. "I believe you would."

"But why would someone dislike Simon enough to spread lies?"

Venetia smiled wryly. "Simon can be blunt, and he cares little what people think about him. He has offended more than one person."

"But to slander him like that!"

"Once said, words are not easily taken back. Over the years, in the retelling, doubtless the stories have grown and become blacker. And Simon, of course, is too proud to do or say anything to squelch them."

"Of course." Charity already knew him well enough to realize that.

They were almost to Charity's house, their steps desultory as they talked. A man rounded the corner, walking briskly, a gold-headed walking stick in his hand. He pulled up when he saw them, and a smile crossed his face.

"Ladies!" he cried, and came forward to bow to them, sweeping off his hat. "What a pleasant surprise to come upon you like this."

"Mr. Reed," Charity replied, smiling. Beside her,

Venetia stiffened, and, though she nodded to Reed, she said nothing in greeting.

"I have just come from your charming mother, Miss Emerson, and I was desolated to find you not at home. Little did I know how fortune would smile on me—that I would not only see you, but find you with Lady Ashford, as well…." He smiled pointedly at Venetia, who still said nothing, only looked away from him.

Faraday turned back to Charity, saying, "You have no need to introduce us, you see. Lady Ashford and I have known each other for years."

His eyes seemed lit with an inner amusement that Charity did not understand. He turned and escorted them to Charity's house. Charity noticed that Venetia shifted position so that Charity was walking between her and Faraday. Venetia's behavior seemed odd to her. Simon obviously did not like Reed, but Venetia seemed more uncomfortable than loyalty to one's brother required. Charity wondered once again what had happened to make Simon and his sister dislike Faraday Reed.

Reed escorted them to Charity's door. Charity started up the steps to her door, but Venetia stopped. "I—I must get home now," she said, turning toward her carriage, which had brought home their purchases and now stood waiting for her.

Charity glanced at Venetia curiously, but said only, "All right. Thank you for taking me shopping."

"I had a lovely time," Venetia assured her honestly.

She started toward her carriage, and Reed stepped forward quickly, politely taking her arm. "Let me help you into your carriage, Lady Ashford."

Charity continued up the steps as Reed escorted Venetia to the elegant barouche.

"Have you thought about what I said the other night?" Reed asked in a low voice.

Venetia looked up at him, her eyes wide. "No. Please, you aren't really going to say anything to George, are you?"

Reed smiled coldly as he reached out to open her carriage door, giving her a little bow as he did so. Venetia knew that to the world he looked like a gentleman being polite; to her, he looked terrifying.

"Of course I am. Unless, of course, you were to help me out a little. I think a hundred and fifty pounds should be enough."

"A hundred and fifty pounds!" Venetia gasped. "I couldn't possibly."

"It's amazing what one can do if one is pressed." Reed handed her up into her carriage, squeezing her fingers so tightly that Venetia had to press her lips together to keep from crying out. "I'll give you one week, my lady."

"No, please."

"Yes." His voice was firm, and his eyes were as hard as stones as he closed the door.

The carriage rumbled off, and Reed turned away. He smiled up at Charity, who waited on the upper step, watching him. He hurried up the steps to join her.

"I am sorry to have kept you waiting."

"It's perfectly all right," Charity assured him. She paused, then probed curiously. "Lady Ashford seemed a trifle…uncomfortable."

Reed sighed. "Yes. It's sad. We once were friends, but now… Well, she is a loyal sister."

"Why does Lord Dure dislike you?" Charity asked impulsively. "I don't understand. You've shown yourself to be a good friend. Even the other day, when I received that note, you didn't take the opportunity to malign him. Instead, you promised to help me find out who is saying such things about him."

Reed shrugged.

"No, please. There must be some reason. Please tell me. Dure refuses to say a word about it—as if I were a child who only needs to be told *what* to do, not why."

Reed looked at her consideringly for a moment, then took her arm. "Let us take a little stroll, and I will tell you."

They started down the street in the direction from which Charity had just come. Reed began, "We were never friends, Dure and I, only acquaintances. I knew Venetia—I mean, Lady Ashford—better. But after…our falling-out, I bore him no grudge. It was Dure who was unable to forgive me. 'Tis odd, since it was he who won. But, then, when it comes to an affair of the heart, it is not always easy to be rational."

Charity's head snapped toward him, and her heart began to pound furiously. She felt a sudden, inexplicable rage, and it was difficult for her to keep her voice steady as she said, "You and Dure fought over a lady?"

A smile curved Reed's lips. "Well, we did not actually come to fisticuffs or pistols at dawn or anything so dramatic. And the woman in question was not exactly a lady…." He let his voice trail off suggestively, then finished. "But we were competitors."

So the two of them had competed over the favors of a soiled dove! No wonder Dure had not wanted to explain the matter to her. Charity clenched her jaw and thought of a dozen cutting things she would like to say to the Earl of Dure the next time she saw him. She would not, of course. Ladies were not supposed to even know of the existence of the women of the night, let alone take their fiancés to task over a former relationship with one. Men were granted their little peccadilloes, as long as they were discreet. Besides, that was something that had happened before she even met Lord Dure; it was no concern of hers. It would be most unfair of her to be angry at him about it.

She was, in truth, a little astonished that she was as upset by the knowledge as she was. But reason had little to do with the red-hot lance of jealousy that stabbed through her. What really hurt, she realized suddenly, was not so much that Dure had sought out such women, but that he had cared so much about the woman in question that he still despised the other man. *Had he loved her deeply? Did he still love her?* It had been bad enough to learn from Venetia that Simon had loved his first wife very much. It was even worse to think that there might be a woman still around whom he loved. If that was the case, it would probably preclude his ever loving his new wife. It also made her wonder if, even now, while he was engaged to marry her, he might still be keeping a mistress.

Tears sprang into her eyes at the thought, startling her.

"Thank you for telling me, Mr. Reed," she said in a slightly choked voice. "I am pleased that you thought enough of me not to keep me in the dark. But I think I should like to go home now."

"Of course," Reed said smoothly, turning and starting back along the street. "I hope I have not upset you by telling you."

"Of course not." Charity put on a pleasant, if rather

forced, smile. It was foolish and unworthy of her to allow this jealous anger to overcome her. Theirs was not a marriage of love, after all, but an arrangement of mutual satisfaction. She did not love Dure, and she could not expect him to love her.

Still…it was one thing to have a husband who did not love you, but it was quite another thing altogether to have a husband who loved another! Who might, even at this moment, be spending a happy evening with his mistress.

CHAPTER SEVEN

CHARITY WAS AWAKENED a few mornings later by the screeches of her younger sisters. A quarrel had broken out between Horatia and Belinda. Cooped up as they were in the city, without their normal outlets for their energy and denied the entertainments that occupied their older sisters, the two girls had become restless and irritable. The slightest provocation was apt to start an argument between them. This one had begun over a hairbrush, belonging to Belinda, which Horatia had borrowed and not returned, and before long it had escalated into screeches and hair-pulling.

Elspeth then began to scold them for giving her a headache, and Serena and Charity ran into their room to pull them apart. It was no easy task, and Serena had to almost shout to be heard over the din the other three were creating.

"Hush!" Serena cried. "You stop that! You, too, Horatia. Whatever is the matter with you? You will wake Mama."

The others, acutely aware of their mother's formidable wrath if she was to be awakened and pulled into the scene, subsided into mutters and vengeful looks.

"It was *her* fault!" Belinda said, grimacing at her younger sister. "She never returns anything."

"At least I'm not a selfish crybaby like you!" Horatia retorted hotly.

"Girls!"

"They've been cooped up too much," Charity offered, yawning. "I have, too. We've hardly been out since we came to London—I mean, not parties and things, but just out for a walk or…or a romp on the lawn."

"At least you get to go to balls and soirees and the opera," Belinda put in sulkily. "I'm stuck here with this brat all day and all night."

"Don't call your sister a brat," Serena responded automatically. "Charity, you're right. I think what we all need is a breath of fresh air. Why don't we walk over to Hyde Park? The girls can run there, and it will do us good to get a little sunshine."

"It sounds heavenly," Charity agreed.

"It sounds tiring," Elspeth countered.

"Oh, Elspeth, it will be healthy for you." Serena smiled and went to take her by the arm, drawing her toward her room. "You'll see. The spring weather will take away your headache."

"Well, I suppose if I wore a shawl against the morning chill…"

"Just the thing," Serena agreed, and cast a dark look back at Charity, who had let out a groan at Elspeth's words.

Charity rolled her eyes, but she said nothing, just went to change into one of the older of the frocks that she had brought from home. She wasn't about to wear one of her better dresses for a romp in the park, and anyway, this early in the morning, there would be no one she knew around to be appalled at her attire.

Thirty minutes later, the five sisters set out for the park. Serena had thought that they should take one of Aunt Ermintrude's maids with them, but Charity at last convinced her that with five of them, they could hardly come to any harm, and that at this hour of the day no one would see them to comment on it.

At the park, Elspeth arranged herself on a bench, wrapped around with a heavy shawl, and Serena sat down beside her to pen a letter to the Reverend Woodson, but Charity entered into a lively game of tag with Horatia and Belinda. It wasn't long before they were romping freely about, even Belinda tossing aside her usual airs and gleefully chasing across the grass. Charity fell down once and smeared a long grass stain across her skirt, and her hair began to straggle loose from its pins, until several wisps had escaped and clung damply to her face.

A dog trotted out of the nearby trees and paused, watching them, his ears cocked up with interest. Then, with a gleeful bark, he bounded across the grass toward them. He joined in their game of tag, barking and leaping, then flinging himself into a stop, his hind end up and his tail wagging encouragingly. The girls laughed.

"What an ugly dog!" Elspeth exclaimed from her bench. "Send him away. He's filthy."

"Oh, Elspeth, don't be such a spoilsport. He's cute."

"Cute?" Elspeth looked affronted.

Charity turned back to look at the animal, and had to laugh. He was a large dog, with medium-length hair, absurdly long legs, and one ear that stood up proudly and another that flopped forward in a comical way. He was of some light color, indeterminate through the coat of dust and mud that covered most of his body. He seemed to grin at them, mouth parted and white teeth showing, his tongue lolling foolishly out of his mouth. He would have been an odd-looking dog under the best of circumstances, but liberally besplashed with mud, and with leaves and twigs clinging to his coat, he was undeniably ugly. Yet it was, somehow, an ugliness that was curiously endearing.

"Girls, be careful," Serena said, rising and looking doubtfully at the creature. "He doesn't look quite safe."

"He only wants to play," Charity assured her, chuckling. She looked around her on the ground and found a stick. Bending over, she picked it up, held it up for the dog to see, then hurled it away. The dog took after it delightedly.

He returned with it in his mouth and dropped it at Charity's feet, looking up at her with merry eyes, tail wagging. "What a clever dog," Charity told him, her heart already lost, and he reared up and planted his paws on her, mud and all. Charity patted him, heedless of the further ruin of her skirt, and threw the stick again.

She and Horatia amused themselves with playing fetch with their new canine friend, and soon Belinda joined in, not one to be left out. Charity threw herself on the grass beneath a tree, heedless of her skirt, and rested, watching the two younger girls play with the dog.

Time passed, moving toward noon, and the girls began to grow hungry. They decided that it was time to retire to their house.

"Besides," Serena added, glancing around at all of them in their old clothes, Charity and the younger girls all liberally bedaubed with mud from cavorting with the dog, "if we wait much longer, someone we know might see us, and that would be disastrous."

Charity chuckled, glancing down at her dress. "You don't think I look like a future countess?"

"More like a street urchin." Elspeth sniffed. "What's

worse, you encourage the younger girls. Horatia is becoming just like you."

"Oh, stuff and nonsense," Charity retorted with little rancor, too accustomed to wrangling with Elspeth to get angry. "Horatia is just like herself, and that's far better."

"I'd *like* to be like you," Horatia informed her loyally, sticking out her tongue at Elspeth.

Elspeth did not dignify Horatia's action with a reply, merely turned and started off down the path. The rest of the sisters followed her. Trotting right along with them came the dog.

"Oh, dear, look, he's following us," Serena said, frowning down at the creature. "What are we going to do? Charity, shoo him away."

"I like him," Charity protested. "Why don't we take him home? Once I get him cleaned up, he won't look so bad."

"We can't," Serena argued. "You know that Aunt Ermintrude doesn't like dogs."

"That's right." Charity looked downcast. "She won't let him in the house, will she?"

"I don't think so." Serena looked doubtfully down at the animal panting at Charity's side. "Not even if he were clean and pretty."

"Oh dear."

"You'd best leave him behind," Serena advised. She turned around and made shooing motions at the animal with her hands. He watched her interestedly, his tail wagging, but stuck close to Charity.

"Charity, do something," Elspeth told her.

"What? I refuse to kick him or throw something at him. And he doesn't look like he's leaving us otherwise."

That was certainly true. The dog was trotting along beside Charity as if he belonged to her.

"We'll have to think of someplace to put him," Charity said. "Maybe we know someone who would like to have him, or who would keep him until we go home. Papa would let us have him in the country."

"What about when you marry?" Elspeth pointed out. "Do you honestly think an earl is going to let his wife keep a dog that looks like that?"

"Dure!" Charity exclaimed happily. "Of course, why didn't I think of that? Come on, girls, let's look for something we can use as a leash for him. We can't take him out of the park without a lead. He might dash out into traffic and get hurt."

"Think of what?" Serena asked worriedly. "Charity… what are you thinking of? What does Lord Dure have to do with it?"

"Why, I shall simply ask him to take the dog in. He can take him to his country estate, and Lucky will be happy as can be there, with rabbits to chase."

"Lucky?"

"Yes, that's what I think I'll name him. Because it was so fortunate, you see, that he showed up there at the park at the very time we happened to be there."

"Ill fortune is more like it," Elspeth said darkly. "You can't seriously expect a man like lord Dure to take that cur into his house, can you?"

"First we will take him home and clean him up. Aunt Ermintrude will let me keep him long enough to bathe him, don't you think? Then I'll take him to Dure House."

"You can't take him to Dure House!" Elspeth gasped.

"Have you gone mad? It would be ruinous to your reputation—even if you are engaged to him."

"She's right, Charity," Serena said firmly, fixing her with a warning look.

"All right. Then I will send one of the footmen to take Lucky there, and I will write Lord Dure a note explaining everything."

"But Charity, I don't think that Lord Dure will want the animal," Serena pointed out reasonably.

"Don't be silly," Charity said calmly. "He will understand that we couldn't keep Lucky at Aunt Ermintrude's feeling the way she does about dogs, and he will see that this is the only reasonable course. I am certain he must like dogs. I can't imagine him not."

Serena cast another look at the dog and sighed. He was thoroughly unappealing, and she could not imagine an earl wanting to house him, even at his country estate. Nor could she imagine having the nerve to ask someone as forbidding as the dark, cold-faced Earl of Dure to take on the graceless animal.

Horatia found a piece of thick string on the ground and pounced on it gleefully. They doubled the long string and fastened it around Lucky's neck, and then they walked out of Hyde Park, with Lucky trotting happily at Charity's side, the makeshift leash in her hand.

Amazingly, the dog was well behaved as they walked along the streets, looking about with interest at the carriages and carts that rolled down the street and the people walking along. They would, perhaps, have done well enough, if they had not happened on the water cart.

It was stopped by the side of the street, and the horse pulling it had fallen to its knees. Beside the horse stood the carter, a man whipcord-thin and red in the face, raising his whip threateningly and shouting at the animal.

"Get up, you lazy good-for-nothing!" he cried, lifting his whip and bringing it down on the horse's back. "Get up, or it's off to the knacker's for you!"

The horse shuddered at the whip and struggled vainly to stand, but it could not. Charity and her sisters came to an abrupt halt at the scene, staring in shocked horror.

The man raised his whip again, and Charity cried out, "No! Stop that!"

The carter turned his head and gave the group of girls a cursory glance. "Go on," he said roughly. "It's no business of yours."

He turned back and lashed the horse again. Charity dropped Lucky's makeshift leash and darted out into the street. She grabbed the whip from the startled man's hand as he raised it again.

"Stop it, you brute!" Her eyes blazing with fury. "Leave that poor animal alone. Can't you see that there is something wrong with him? He's worked his heart out for you, and you repay him this way?"

"Charity!" Serena called worriedly, and Elspeth glanced around them, mortified to see that a crowd was quickly gathering around the scene.

"Now, see here, missy," the man spat out, stalking purposefully toward Charity. "This ain't no concern of yours. You get out of here, or I'll—"

Whatever he might have threatened was lost, for at that moment Lucky launched himself at the man with a growl, protecting his newfound mistress. The dog hit the carter full in the chest with all his weight, and the man staggered backward. He caught his heel on an uneven stone and fell heavily. A ripple of amusement ran through the crowd.

The carter's face turned bright red with anger, and he struggled to his feet, cursing. Lucky positioned himself between Charity and the man and growled, his head lowered and the fur on his neck standing up. The man bent to pick up a rock, his eyes remaining on Lucky. He pulled back his arm to throw it at the dog, and Charity lashed out with the whip, striking the carter on the arm with enough force to sting and make him drop the rock.

He gaped at Charity, clutching his hurt arm. Charity waited, the whip ready in her hand, Lucky still standing guard between them.

"You little bitch!" the carter raged, in frustration and pain. "You just wait till I get hold of you, and both you and that bloody hound of yours will be sorry you ever crossed Dan McConnigle." He launched into a series of invectives so harsh that many in the crowd around them gasped.

Fortunately, Charity and her sisters knew few of the words he hurled at her. They did, however, recognize the anger and threat in his voice, and her sisters moved protectively up beside her. All around them the crowd was growing and choosing up sides, calling out words of derision or encouragement.

Charity gripped the whip and faced the man down. She didn't know what she was going to do, but she wasn't about to back down before this bully.

It was with some relief that she saw out of the corner of her eye a man in a blue uniform shoving his way through the watchers until finally he burst through.

"Now, what's going on here?" the bobby demanded,

straightening his hat and glaring from the carter to Charity and her sisters and back.

"Constable!" Serena exclaimed with relief.

"This wench took my whip and hit me with it!" the carter cried, pointing at Charity.

Charity looked at him disdainfully. "Yes, I did," she said, dropping the whip on the ground. "This man is a brute. He was whipping his horse, and anyone can see that the poor animal could go no more."

The constable looked from Charity to the carter, and a faint smile twitched at his lips. "Did she now? Well, I can see how a lass like that could overpower you."

The carter flushed. "It wasn't only her. That brute attacked me, too." He pointed toward the dog.

"Lucky is not a brute!" Charity answered hotly. "He didn't even bite you. He merely came to my defense when you threatened me."

"I never touched her!" The carter swung back toward the constable, appealing to him. "The girl is mad. She attacked me with no reason. Interfering in my business— telling me what I should and should not do. Hasn't an honest businessman any rights anymore? This girl is running loose with a vicious dog, creating a disturbance. She's probably escaped from Bedlam."

"What?" Charity drew an indignant breath, her eyes flashing fire. "How dare you?"

"Here, now, miss." The constable ran a disapproving eye over Charity, and she realized suddenly at how much of a disadvantage she must appear. She and her sisters were dressed in old clothes, and after her romping about with the dog, her skirts were covered with mud and grass stains, and her hair was straggling out of its knot. She must indeed look like a wild woman.

"You can't be running about the streets, now, interfering with people's business," the constable went on. "I think you'd best go along home."

"You mean you aren't even going to do anything to him?" Charity gasped.

"To me? It's you he ought to be taking in." The carter, more confident now that the constable seemed to be leaning toward his side, turned toward the policeman and made his appeal. "Sir, she lost me time, and she took my whip from me. And that vicious animal of hers attacked me. Are you just going to let her go?"

"There's no harm in the lass," the constable said. "I don't see no need to be taking her in."

"I should say not!" Serena exclaimed, and all the sisters began to babble at once. Across from them, the carter argued that damage had been done to him, and various members of the crowd around them chimed in with their opinions.

The constable looked pained. He glanced around at the crowd. Already two men were arguing about which side of the argument was right. It wouldn't take much for a scene like this to develop into something more.

"All right, all right, miss." The constable reached out for Charity. "Why don't you just bring your dog, and let's sort this all out back at headquarters?"

Charity twitched her arm from him and drew herself up into the most commanding stance she could. She lifted her chin and looked down her nose at the man in the best imitation she could manage of her mother, and said, "Do you think to lay a hand on me? Do you intend to arrest the Countess of Dure?"

The constable froze, his mouth dropping open, and for a moment there was a great silence around them. Then someone in the crowd began to laugh.

"To be sure," the carter said bitingly. "Anyone can see that you are a countess. I told you, Constable—Bedlam." He tapped his forehead significantly.

"I am a countess!" Charity protested. "Or, at least, I will be soon. I am engaged to be married to the Earl of Dure."

The constable's eyes ran down her clothes and then to the muddied mongrel at her side. He sighed. "Miss… you're only making it worse for yourself by making such claims. I better take you back and send for your family to come get you."

Charity felt panicky. She could well imagine her mother's reaction to having to come down to Scotland Yard to fetch her daughters. And Dure—if word got out that she had been arrested, he would be a laughingstock.

She jutted her chin out and stepped forward. "I suggest that we go to Lord Dure's first. I doubt Lord Dure or my aunt, Lady Bankwell, will be particularly pleased at finding me incarcerated. If you value your job, I suggest you investigate my story before you lay hands on me."

The constable wavered. Her carriage and voice were those of a well-brought-up young lady, and there was a certain aristocratic set to her face when she looked at him the way she was now. Lord knew, the nobility had their eccentricities…. What if this *was* a future countess and only liked to amuse herself by running about the city all ragtag and muddy, with a great cur by her side?

He glanced around, frowning. "But we can't go disturbing His Lordship to ask him who you are."

"I should think it would be far preferable to his having

to come down to your headquarters to rescue me," Charity retorted.

Behind her, Elspeth groaned. Serena came up to stand beside her. Calmly, she said, "She truly is engaged to His Lordship."

"He dotes on her," Horatia piped up helpfully.

"Come, take me there. It isn't far from here. In Arlington Street."

Her insistence on going to see the Earl of Dure shook the constable's confidence. Finally he said, "All right, missy. But no tricks now."

He moved to take her arm, but Charity quelled him with a look and started to walk regally through the crowd. The constable marched along at her side, and the carter and Charity's sisters fell in behind them. Even several members of the crowd trailed after them, intrigued by the drama.

Charity strode confidently to Dure House, keeping her face set in a cool, disdainful mask, but inside, her heart quailed a little. *What would Dure say?*

It did not take long to reach the door of Dure House. Charity turned and looked at the constable with a great deal more assurance than she felt. "Here we are."

The constable hesitated, gazing up at the imposing edifice. All the way over, he had grown less and less sure that he was doing the right thing. Questioning an earl was not something that fell into his normal line of duties. He had a mortifying picture of the Earl throwing him out for bothering him with such idiocy. He glanced over at Charity nervously.

"Well? Aren't you going to knock?" she asked.

"Yes, miss." He straightened, tugging at his collar a little, and rapped the bronze knocker on the door.

A moment later the door opened soundlessly, and a grave butler appeared in the doorway. The butler looked at the constable blankly, then at the carter and the straggling procession behind him.

"Yes?" he inquired freezingly.

The constable cleared his throat. "I'm here on a matter, uh, er, concerning the earl of Dure. Ah, this is his residence, isn't it?"

"Of course." The butler looked at him as if he were half-witted.

"Well, the thing is, there's a girl here, who, uh…"

"Chaney—" Charity stepped forward beside the constable "—could you tell His Lordship that we are here to see him?"

For the first time, the butler's eyes went to Charity. He looked at her blankly for a moment. Then his mouth dropped open. He stared at her, then down at the dog, over at the constable and back to her again.

"Miss Emerson!"

"Yes, Chaney, it is I. There seems to be some problem as to my identity. My sisters and I required Lord Dure's help."

"Yes, miss." The butler pulled his face back into its customary haughty lines and stepped back from the door.

Charity swept into the entry hall, Lucky trotting happily at her side, and the constable stepped aside to let her sisters follow her. He motioned to the carter, who no longer looked so bellicose, to enter, also, then followed him inside. Chaney neatly closed the door on the stragglers.

He swept a look over the group, obviously trying to decide where he should put such a motley crew. The Misses Emerson, of course, belonged in the drawing room by rights, no matter how ragtag they looked, but the constable and the other, rough-looking individual most assuredly did not. He considered leaving the men in the entry and leading the sisters to the salon, but another look at Charity's stained dress and the muddy mongrel that stuck to her side decided him against that. With a bow, he went to find Lord Dure and put the matter squarely in his hands, where it belonged.

Charity could not resist shooting a triumphant look toward the constable and the carter, who both shifted uncomfortably and glanced around the spacious entry and the wide, graceful marble stairway up which the butler had disappeared.

A few moments later Simon came down the stairs. He wore a sumptuous dark brocade dressing gown over his trousers and spotless white shirt, and it was obvious that he had been disturbed while dressing or at his breakfast. He paused at the bottom of the stairs and coolly looked over each member of the group before him. The constable colored under his gaze and tugged at his collar.

Simon's eyes stopped at last on Charity.

CHAPTER EIGHT

"MY DEAR MISS EMERSON," Dure said finally, "how delightful to see you. You must forgive my surprise, but, as always, the sight of you—" his lips twitched, but he quickly controlled them "—uh, has quite taken my breath away. I see you have brought your sisters, as well. But who are these gentlemen? I don't believe I have had the pleasure of their acquaintance."

"Dure!" Charity let out a gusty sigh of relief and hurried toward him. "You must tell this constable who I am. They don't believe that I am your fiancée. He said I belonged in Bedlam—the carter, I mean—and the constable said he should take me in and find out who I belonged to. So I had to tell them that we were engaged."

"Of course," Simon replied imperturbably. His eyes fell to the animal at her side. "And who is your friend?"

"That's Lucky. We found him in the park, and we couldn't leave him."

"Of course not," Simon murmured, gazing at the dog with a fascinated eye. "He might have got dirty."

Charity giggled. "Oh, stop. This is serious."

"I can see that. Serious enough for a constable." His gaze rested ironically on that gentleman. The man glanced around, as if some means of escape might materialize.

"Now, suppose you tell me what this animal has to do with these two gentlemen."

Charity proceeded to lay out for him the pitiful plight of the horse and the wickedness of its owner. Dure listened, his gray-green eyes glinting with amusement, as Charity explained how she and her sisters had felt compelled to stop such cruelty, and how Lucky had bravely defended her.

"Then," she ended indignantly, "*he* was going to throw a rock at Lucky, so I had to hit his arm with the whip."

"You lashed him with the whip?" Dure asked, his eyebrows vaulting upward, and when Charity nodded yes, he let out a crack of laughter. "By God, I wish I had been there to see that!"

But the face he turned on the carter was anything but amused. "And you," he said with icy contempt, "having been bested by a slip of a girl and a mangy dog, had to call the constable to defend you."

The carter, who had been squirming throughout Charity's account, turned beet red at Dure's words. "They was interfering with me job! Poking their noses in where they didn't belong. What else was I supposed to do? Just let her ruin me business? I couldn't very well settle the matter with me fists, seeing as how she was a lady and all."

"A lady with a whip and a loyal dog," Dure amended. "I can understand your hesitation."

The carter thrust out a mutinous jaw but subsided into silence, crossing his arms over his chest and curling up into himself.

Serena spoke up firmly. "He would would have hit her. He was obviously threatening to. When Lucky stood him off, he called Charity terrible, vile names."

"Did he, now?" Dure's eyes flicked coldly over the

hapless carter. "Exactly what, sir, did you say about my fiancée?"

"Nothing," the man retorted in a surly manner, not looking at Dure.

"You are saying that my fiancée's sister is a liar?"

"No," the carter mumbled.

Dure turned his cold eyes on the constable. "And when you came upon this scene of a young lady threatened by a man, saved from him only by a brave dog, you decided to arrest the young lady."

"I didn't know who she was," the constable protested weakly.

"I see. So if she had not been the fiancée of an earl, merely a young woman of obvious integrity, breeding and courage, you would have hauled her down to Scotland Yard. What would have been her crime? Let me see… Compassion? Bravery?"

The constable was beginning to look very pale. "Well, uh, it *was* the man's horse. And she had taken away his whip and was acting, well, sort of wild, sir."

Dure glanced over at Charity, taking in her muddy, stained skirts and the disarray of her hair, her bonnet tipped back off her head and hanging down her back, bow still tied around her neck. A smile quirked up the corners of his mouth for a moment.

"Yes. So I see. However, I find, sir, that I am a peculiar enough man that I prefer a woman who would wade into a fight against a man twice her size in order to save a tormented animal to a cold woman who would avert her eyes and scurry away in ladylike horror."

Charity colored rosily and beamed at his compliment. "Thank you, Dure. I *knew* you would stand buff."

"Always, I hope. Though I trust that in the future, when we are married, I will protect you better than this." He turned, eyeing the constable and the carter with a chilling disfavor. "I do not like to think of you being subjected to such men as these."

He strode forward to the men, stopping only a foot from them and directing the full force of his stare at them. "Constable, I am sure that your superior would wish to be informed of the way in which you protect the citizens of London—keeping them safe from the depredations of such vicious criminals as an eighteen-year-old girl and a starved mutt of a dog."

"Dure...don't be too hard on him," Charity urged, pity rising in her at the constable's hangdog expression. "He did not know that I was unexceptionable. I don't look much the part of the lady." She glanced down ruefully at her dress. "I suppose he could not help thinking that I was a bit mad."

"Softhearted, as always." Dure looked at her and smiled faintly. "I suggest, Constable, that you think next time before you act."

The constable, taking his words as a dismissal, nodded emphatically, backing toward the front door. "Indeed I will, my lord. You can count on that."

Simon turned toward the carter. "As for you...I am not quite sure. I'm tempted to take you out and give you the thrashing you deserve."

"I don't have no quarrel with you," the carter protested sullenly.

"I'm sure you *don't* wish to quarrel with *me*. You are a bully and a coward, the sort who attacks women and animals."

"I didn't do her no harm."

"No. That is the only reason that I am going to let you go. Miss Emerson *is* all right. And I have no desire for this little episode to cause her any scandal or grief. Therefore, I am going to pay you what the knackers would for your horse. You are to bring it my stables, and the head groom will pay you. But if ever anyone, *anyone,* breathes a word of what happened today, I will come after you. And I can promise you, you will be a very sorry man."

"But what if someone else tells about it?" the man whined. "There was other people there—the constable, the ones who stopped to gawk."

"Then I presume you'd better pray that none of the others talk."

"But, my lord! That ain't fair."

Simon's brows rose in aristocratic disdain. "I hadn't realized that fairness was a concern of yours. But, of course, ill-treatment is different when it is you who receive it, not give it out. Get out of here."

The carter hesitated, and Simon added, "Now! Before I decide to change my mind."

At that, the man turned and hurried out the front door after the constable. Simon turned to the Emerson sisters, who were standing in a bedraggled group and gazing at him with awe. "And now, ladies, if you'd like to come into the drawing room, I think a little refreshment might be in order, don't you?"

"Oh, Si—I mean, Lord Dure! That was marvelous. I knew you would set everything straight." Charity beamed at Dure, going to him and linking her arm through his. Together they strolled to the drawing room, Charity's sisters following them.

"Lord Dure, I'm terribly sorry," Serena said stiffly as they walked up the stairs. "I am so mortified that all this should have been laid at your door."

"Don't be a prig, Serena," Charity told her blithely. "Who better to deal with it than Dure? I knew as soon as that constable started being obstinate that Dure was the one to handle it."

Serena shot her sister a look of reproach. "But it was so…so messy. His Lordship cannot have been pleased at the scene."

"On the contrary," Dure said, a faint smile playing about his lips, "I found it quite…entertaining."

"It was exciting!" Horatia spoke up, skipping to catch up with Dure and Charity. "I liked it best when you told that nasty man to get out."

Elspeth, too long left out of the conversation, raised a trembling hand to her forehead as they crossed the threshold into the drawing room. "My lord, I fear… I feel quite weak."

"Elspeth, do bear up," Serena pleaded, grasping her sister's arm. "We can't have another scene."

"My head is aching," Elspeth moaned. "All that noise and fighting…it is too much for my nerves."

"Honestly, Elspeth, as if you did anything," Horatia snapped, exasperated. "It was Charity who was in danger. You just stood there and groaned about how embarrassing it was."

Elspeth shot her youngest sister a dark look, then swayed dramatically and crumpled against Serena. Serena staggered back, struggling to hold her up. "Elspeth!"

"Of all things! Elspeth, you goose!" Charity exclaimed impatiently as Dure jumped forward to catch Elspeth and take the burden from Serena.

He lifted Elspeth up in his arms and carried her over to the couch. Serena hurried to put a pillow behind her head and to fan her.

"Belinda, get the smelling salts from my reticule," she commanded, and when Belinda handed them to her, she waved the bottle under Elspeth's nose.

Gradually, coughing gently, Elspeth began to revive. Dure cast a glance at her, then looked at Charity's disgusted face, and he had to clamp his lips firmly together to keep from chuckling.

"I'm sure a cup of tea would help revive Miss Emerson," Dure declared solemnly, and rang for Chaney.

Dure turned a pained gaze down at Lucky, who had left Charity's side finally and come to lean against Dure's leg and look hopefully up at him. "And what do you intend to do with this wretched animal?"

"Wretched animal!" Charity repeated indignantly. "Oh. You are teasing me, aren't you?" She beamed down at Lucky. "Of course, I would keep him if I could. He's a wonderful dog. Just think how he saved me when that dreadful man threatened me—I couldn't turn him loose to fend for himself after that. I'm sure he's probably quite handsome, once one gets all that mud off. The problem is, Aunt Ermintrude abhors dogs. She has two cats, big fat lazy Persian things that shed all over the furniture, and she won't let a dog near them. So I cannot take Lucky back to her house. We could keep him at our home back in Siddley-on-the-Marsh, but it may be ages before Papa goes back there. So…"

She paused, and Simon raised an eyebrow. "So?" Suddenly his eyebrows drew together suspiciously. "Just what *is* your scheme?"

"The answer is obvious. I shall give him to you. You have this big house, with plenty of room, and I am sure that you like dogs."

"Some dogs," Simon admitted, casting a jaundiced eye at Lucky, who was rubbing his head against Simon's knee, leaving a large streak of mud upon his trousers.

"Besides, I realized that you were probably lonely here and would welcome a companion."

"I am so gratified that you thought of me," Dure murmured sardonically.

Charity chuckled. "It won't be so bad. Lucky really is a good dog, and I can tell that he likes you already. See how he leans against your leg?"

Dure glanced down at his formerly spotless trousers and sighed. "Yes, I see."

"You can take him out to your country house when you go there next. Please, won't you say that you will keep him?"

Charity looked up at Simon with pleading eyes, and Dure could not help but smile. He wondered if she had any idea of the power of her great lambent blue eyes. A man, he thought, would do more than suffer a mangy hound for such a look.

"Yes, I will keep him."

At that moment, Chaney entered with their tea and cakes, and Simon turned to him with a smile. "Ah, Chaney, just the man I wanted to see."

"Yes, my lord?" Chaney asked, setting down the large silver tray on the table in front of the couch.

"The hero of this day must have a little refreshment, too. Take Lucky out to the kitchen and feed him. Then, I think, a bath would be in order."

"Lucky, my lord?"

"The dog. He will be staying with us for a while."

"Oh. Yes, of course, my lord." Chaney's carefully trained face did not give away his thoughts, but his voice faltered a little as he went on, "Give him a bath, my lord?"

"Yes. You have to admit that he's appallingly dirty. He can't stay in the house in that condition."

"Yes, my lord," Chaney replied feelingly. He looked at the dog askance, then bravely straightened his shoulders and started toward Lucky. "Here, dog. Nice dog."

The butler bent over, crooking his finger to the animal. Lucky watched him with interest, his tail wafting to and fro, but he made no move toward the man.

"I think, Chaney," Dure advised, "that you will have to touch the thing."

"Yes, my lord."

"Don't tease Chaney," Charity said reproachfully. "You know he can't want to get his white gloves dirty. Besides, I'm not sure that Lucky will go with him. He seems to have become attached to me. I'll take him down to the kitchen, Chaney," she told the butler cheerfully, picking up the makeshift lead. "Just show me the way."

"Oh, no, miss!" Chaney looked horrified. "I'll take him, miss." He set his jaw and moved forward to take the lead.

Lucky sat back on his haunches and emitted a low growl. Chaney pulled on the leash, but Lucky braced his legs, lowered his head and refused to budge. Chaney, gritting his teeth, reached out and wrapped his hands around the lead on the dog's neck and tugged. Slowly he pulled Lucky, still sitting, across the smooth marble floor and out the door.

Simon and Charity sat down with the others to partake

of the tea. Serena was stiff and uncomfortable, and Elspeth was too busy languishing in her chair and fanning herself to pay much attention to the food, but the other three sisters dug into the sweet cakes with youthful enthusiasm, chatting cheerfully with Simon as they ate. Horatia was in the middle of a more detailed description of the morning's events when a loud crash sounded somewhere in the house, followed by an angry bellow.

Simon and Charity looked at each other, the same thought forming in their minds. A moment later, there was a feminine shriek, then a loud male voice exclaiming, "Come back here, you hellhound!"

Another thud sounded, much closer now, and then the sound of a dog's claws scrabbling on the slick marble. An instant later, Lucky turned into the room at full speed, sliding sideways, claws clicking as he sought purchase on the ungiving floor. A footman, white wig knocked awry and face red, shirtfront splattered with mud, lunged after the dog, making a flying leap to grab him. But Lucky scooted away, and the footman hit the floor with an audible "Oof." Lucky tore across the room and flung all seventy pounds of himself into Charity's lap.

Serena and Elspeth shrieked. The footman came up cursing. Chaney rushed into the room, trying to straighten his clothes and hair and regain a look of dignity as he poured out apologies. Simon roared with laughter.

"Lucky! You poor thing!" Charity cried, wrapping her arms around the dog.

Lucky looked, if possible, worse. He was soaked, his fur clinging to his body, and the water had turned all the dirt and mud covering him into an extremely dirty mess.

"Charity!" Serena gasped. "He's getting you filthy!"

"I know, but he's scared." Charity petted him, crooning words of comfort into the big dog's ear, and Lucky's tail swung happily, knocking over a small vase on an end table. "Poor thing, he's in a strange place, with strange people shoving him into a tub. It's no wonder he panicked."

She looked crossly at Simon, who was still laughing help-lessly and wiping tears of mirth from his eyes. "Oh, stop."

"I can't help it," Simon gasped out, looking at the great dog, who was now snuggling up to Charity, getting her even dirtier and wetter.

Chaney hurried across the room and tried to pull Lucky off Charity's lap. Charity pushed the dog off onto the floor and stood up. "It's all right, Chaney. I'd better wash him myself."

"Oh, miss, no!" Chaney looked horrified at the thought.

"He won't stay still for anyone else," Charity pointed out reasonably, and started for the door, Lucky trotting along obediently by her side.

Chaney cast an anguished glance at Dure, who shrugged. "Best do as she says, Chaney. Obviously Miss Emerson has a way with the animal that the rest of us do not."

He stood up and joined Charity. "Come, my dear, let me escort you to the kitchen."

The two strolled through the door and along the hallway to the kitchen, Lucky trotting happily beside them. Chaney followed, looking stricken.

The kitchen looked as if it had been the scene of a minor war. A large tub, half full of soapy, dirty water, sat in the middle of the stone floor. The remainder of the water in the tub had obviously wound up on the floor around it. A small cabinet lay turned over, doors open and contents spilled out. Two straight-backed wooden chairs were turned over on their sides, and a clay pitcher lay in pieces on the floor. A wet, bedraggled maid was sweeping up the pieces, and another was trying to mop up the water, while a footman righted the cabinet. The cook had withdrawn to the huge stove and was standing with his arms crossed, gazing contemptuously at the scene before him.

When Charity and Lord Dure walked into the room, all the servants swung around to stare at them, gaping in amazement.

"My lord!" a plump older woman, identified by her dress and the keys on her belt as the housekeeper, exclaimed, and dropped a quick curtsy, which the maids hastened to copy.

They shot hasty, curious glances at Charity and the muddy dog by her side. Only the chef was not stricken into silence. He strode forward, gesturing and speaking volubly in French.

"Yes, I know, Jean-Louis, I know," Simon said soothingly. "I promise you, your kitchen will soon be back in its normal shape."

His words did little to calm the Frenchman, who grew redder and louder with each word. Charity smiled and stepped forward. "I am so sorry. Please forgive my dog." She laid a small, entreating hand on his arm and smiled up into his face. "I'm afraid it is my fault that your kitchen is in such a dreadful mess."

The man stopped talking, and the angry flush receded from his face. He gazed at Charity for a moment, then smiled at her, then began to speak in heavily accented English. "But, no, *mademoiselle,* it is nothing. I did not know the animal was yours."

Simon lifted an eyebrow at this exchange, and when the chef had retreated to his stove, he bent and whispered in her ear, "Had I known you could wrap my chef around your finger that way, I would have married you long ago."

He introduced Charity to the staff, who bowed or bobbed a curtsy, stealing curious glances at her from the corners of their eyes. Charity favored them all with one of her sunny smiles.

"It's very nice to meet all of you," she assured them. "Now I'll wash Lucky and get him out of your way."

The housekeeper gasped in horror. "Miss Emerson! No, you mustn't! We shall do it."

"It's all right," Charity assured the servants airily. "It's something I've done many times before. Besides, Dure will help me. Won't you, Dure?"

The servants turned even more astonished gazes on their employer. Dure merely smiled imperturbably. "Of course, my dear. I am sure my trousers and jacket are a small price to pay for Lucky's comfort." He turned to the servants and dismissed them with a nod. "Get on about your tasks. Miss Emerson and I will take care of the animal."

The servants all retreated to the far side of the kitchen, gaping, as the earl of Dure stripped off his jacket, then wrapped his arms around the large, filthy dog and put him into the tub. Later, one of the footmen was to tell the neighboring footman that he had never seen anything like the way His Lordship, usually so impeccably dressed and coolly visaged, waded into the task of cleaning the dog as if he'd been accustomed to it all his life. The Earl's valet, hearing all the commotion, had finally given way to curiosity and walked into the kitchen to see what was going on. When he saw His Lordship, half-drenched and laughing as he struggled with a mongrel in a tub, he was so appalled he had to leave the room.

Charity picked up the bar of soap in the tub and lathered Lucky up, while Simon fought to keep the animal still. Lucky, however, was not going down without a fight, even with his beloved new mistress giving him the bath, and he squirmed and twisted and tried to heave his bulk out of the tub, thoroughly splashing both Charity and Simon with water. Two maids timidly brought Charity pitchers full of clean water, which she sluiced over Lucky's head. The dog shook all over, sending water flying about the room, and Charity shrieked and laughed, holding up her hands to protect her face. Simon, watching her, laughed and lost his grip on Lucky, who promptly bounded out of the tub, shook himself again and rose up to put his paws on Charity's shoulders, trying to lick her face.

Charity wrestled the dog down, and Simon came to her aid, pulling Lucky back into the tub. He held him down more firmly while Charity poured another pitcher of clean water over him, then yet another, until at last the dog emerged, looking half-drowned but clean.

Though Simon held tightly to the dog, his eyes went nowhere except to Charity. Her struggles with the dog had soaked completely through her dress and underthings. They clung damply to her skin, outlining the curves of her full breasts and the small, tight buds of her nipples. Simon's throat was suddenly dry, and his amusement of the past few minutes vanished, replaced by a consuming heat. He wanted her, and each time she bent or turned as she worked, her breasts swaying gently, desire coiled even more tightly within him.

One of the footmen brought a large bath sheet, and Charity and Simon reached for it at the same time, their hands grazing. Simon felt the sizzling shock of the touch all through him. Together they wrapped the towel around Lucky and rubbed him dry. As they worked, Charity's breasts grazed Simon's arm. He kept his head down, hoping she would not read the desire in his face.

Finally they let Lucky go, and he tore about the kitchen and out into the hall, whirling and shaking himself off and sliding against the walls and over the floors in an attempt to rid himself of the dreadful dampness. Simon and Charity watched him, chuckling at his antics, but Simon could not keep his eyes from straying to Charity's bosom.

Simon took Charity's arm and steered her from the room, carefully keeping his own body between her and the servants. Lucky bounded after them, but, fortunately, one of the footmen was quick enough to grab him and hold him back, while one of the maids shut the door.

Simon and Charity started down the hall. Suddenly Simon pulled Charity down a side hall and into the small alcove beneath the back stairs. Charity glanced over at him in surprise and opened her mouth to ask what he was doing, but then his mouth covered hers, effectively stifling all questions.

CHAPTER NINE

FOR AN INSTANT CHARITY went still. Then she melted against Simon. She wrapped her arms around his neck and went up on tiptoe, her lips pressing eagerly into his. Simon made a noise deep in his throat, and his hands slid down her body, pressing her hips into his. His shirt was as wet as her bodice, and it was almost as if nothing lay between them. He could feel the lush swell of her breasts pressing into his hard chest, and the small, harder buttons of her nipples. Excitement poured through him. He plunged his fingers into Charity's hair, disturbing its few remaining pins, and it tumbled down over his hands like a silken waterfall.

A tremor ran through Simon, and he turned, moving Charity farther back into the alcove, until she was pressed into the wall. His mouth moved on hers, his tongue exploring the hot, wet cave of Charity's mouth. He could not get enough of kissing her; he felt as if he could sink into her soft warmth, to the very center of her being. He wanted to; he wanted to know her that intimately, to hold her that tightly.

Yet, even more than that, he yearned to touch her, so his body moved back from her a fraction, and his hand crept up from her waist and cupped her breast. Charity drew in a shaky breath at that touch, and Simon's desire rose even higher. His thumb dragged across the hard circle of her nipple. Charity shivered, and a shy noise of pleasure was torn from her mouth. Passion exploded within Simon, and it was all he could do not to pull her down to the floor and plunge into her right there.

"Oh, God," he muttered thickly, raining kisses over her face and down her throat. "You are so beautiful— I want you."

Charity sank her fingers into his hair, too stunned by the wonderful sensations assaulting her even to speak. She felt as if she were on fire inside, and her breath came hard and fast in her throat.

Simon took her nipple between his forefinger and thumb and gently rolled it between them. Charity jerked as if lightning had ripped through her and let out a little moan. Her hips moved unconsciously against him. She could feel a hard ridge of flesh pushing into her, and she sensed, even in her innocence, that it was evidence of Dure's desire for her.

Simon's fingers shook as they went to work on the buttons of her dress, moving with uncharacteristic clumsiness as he unbuttoned the fabric far enough to allow him to shove her dress back off her breasts and down her shoulders, pinioning her arms to her sides. He looked down at her breasts, covered now only in the thin lawn of her chemise. The wet material was almost transparent, clearly showing the rosy buds of her nipples. He gazed for a long moment; then his hands went to the chemise and worked it slowly down off her breasts, teasingly scraping it over her nipples. The little buttons tightened, thrusting toward him. He covered her breasts with his hands, and his thumbs caressed the engorged buds. Charity leaned back against the wall, her eyes closing in pleasure as his hands caressed her. She was the very picture of a woman in the throes of desire, and the sight of her stirred Simon even more.

He thought about shoving up her skirts and taking her, thrusting deep and hard into her. He clenched his teeth as a shudder of elemental desire rushed through him. Then, reluctantly, he pulled the chemise back up over her breasts and stepped away. He could not continue, or he would take Charity here and now, and he would be a cad to do so. She was a maiden, untouched and innocent, and she deserved to be taken gently, sweetly, in a soft bed, and with darkness to cover her embarrassment. She was to be his wife, and to take her in this way would be an insult to her.

Charity's eyelids fluttered open, and she gazed at him, bemused. "My lord? What— Why— Is something wrong?"

"Yes." He grated the word out, for her open face, full of yearning and puzzled loss at his pulling back, made the passion surge in him even harder. "I cannot— If I go any farther, I shall wind up taking you, and that would be the work of a blackguard."

"Oh." Charity straightened, blushing a little as she noticed her uncovered state and hastily pulled her dress back together. "I—I'm sorry." She averted her eyes as she began to rebutton her dress. "I didn't realize… I thought, since we were to be married, it was all right."

"It is all right. Do not look so. There was nothing wrong in what you did. But for me to take advantage of you for my own pleasure—to turn your first lovemaking into a hasty coupling beneath the stairs—would be abominable. I may not be a model of virtue, but I am gentleman enough to know that. We will wait until you are in my bed…when we have every right to do what we want, and all the time in the world to do it."

Charity's color rose even more at his frank statement, but she could not help but thrill to the eagerness and hunger implicit in his words. Dure wanted her—so much so that he had difficulty resisting, even though his sense of honor and morality told him he must.

"I understand," she said softly, finishing the last button and glancing up at him. Her blue eyes were soft and lambent, and Simon's breath caught in his throat at her gaze.

"I doubt that you truly do," he responded, a trifle shakily, then turned away with a curse. "I pray we are not to have a long engagement."

"The usual year, I would think," Charity replied honestly. "I am sure that is what my mother expects."

Simon grimaced. "Mothers be damned! She is not the one who has to keep his hands off you."

Charity giggled a little at his words. "I should think not, my lord!"

Her words wrung a reluctant smile from Dure. He bent and gave her a quick, hard kiss on the lips. "You are an imp," he murmured, "and I think I must have been mad to have offered for you."

"Do you regret it?" Charity looked up teasingly at him through her lashes, but her heart sped up a little with anxiety as she waited for his answer.

Simon's smile was slow and amused, yet also rife with sensuality. "No. No doubt I should, but I cannot bring myself to regret it."

Charity smiled. She wanted to lean into Simon and rest her head on his shoulder; she wanted him to kiss her again and move his hands in that unutterably delightful way over her breasts. But that, she knew, was impossible. With a faint sigh of regret, she moved away, stepping out of the alcove into the hallway.

"We should join the others, I imagine, my lord."

"Yes, no doubt." Simon joined her, offering her his arm in so formal a manner that Charity had to bite back a chuckle, remembering the situation they had been in only moments before. She took his arm and fixed a dignified expression on her face.

But as they walked back toward the drawing room and her sisters, Charity felt as if she were walking on air.

Venetia fastened her hat on her head securely, then pulled down the veil so that it covered her face. It was not her most attractive hat; Aunt Ursula had given it to her, and she had worn it only once before, to a funeral. But it had a heavier veil than any of her other headgear, and that was all she was interested in at the moment. She fervently hoped that no one she might see on the street would recognize her.

She slipped quietly out the front door, after glancing around once to make sure that none of the servants had come into sight. She had instructed her personal maid to tell all the others that she was taking a nap and should not be disturbed for any reason. George was at his club, and she was sure that he would not be home until this evening.

Letting out a sigh of relief as she pulled the door softly to behind her, Venetia skimmed down the steps and out to the sidewalk. There she turned and hurried up the street, head down to avoid having to greet anyone. She was afraid of someone recognizing her, but she was almost equally nervous about walking down the street without at least a maid for a companion. Whenever she went out by herself, she almost always took the Ashford carriage, but, of course, that was impossible in this instance.

She was too preoccupied with trying to be invisible to notice that, down the street, a man slipped out of a hack, paid the driver and started after her. A supremely ordinary-looking man, solidly middle-class in a brown suit and hat, he carried a rolled-up newspaper under his arm. He was the sort of man she had probably passed a hundred times in the street and not noticed.

Harding Crescent was not far away, only a few blocks, and Venetia soon reached the pretty little park that lay in its curve. Small trees and shrubs grew around its edges, affording some privacy to the green spot within, and there were benches scattered along its carefully tended walkways. Venetia glanced around the park assessingly as she made her way to the bench at the north end of the park, which was more secluded than any of the other benches. Fortunately there was no one in the place at the moment besides herself. She wished Reed had chosen some spot other than this park to meet; she knew Millicent Cardaway, who lived on Harding Crescent, fairly well, at least well enough to know that she was a terrible gossip and had eyes like a hawk. If Millicent saw Venetia here, especially with a man, her reputation would be destroyed. But Reed had been insistent; she thought he had derived considerable amusement from her pleas to change the meeting place.

She plopped down on the bench, turning so that her veiled face would not be seen by anyone in the rest of the park. *Where was Reed?* She would have thought that he would be on time to collect his money, at least.

"Hiding, my dear?" His smooth voice came from behind her, and Venetia jumped and whirled to face him. "My, my, you seem a little on edge. Must come from keeping all those guilty secrets."

Faraday looked as smooth and handsome as ever, not a wrinkle in his suit or a hair out of place. Venetia could hardly bear to look at him.

She dug into her reticule and pulled out an envelope. "Here." She shoved the envelope at him and started to leave, but he reached out and caught her arm.

"Not quite so fast, my dear Venetia. Let me count it first."

"I gave you what you asked for," Venetia replied stiffly. "*I* do not lie or cheat."

Faraday smiled mockingly. "How admirable. I'm sure you've told your good husband all about us by now."

Venetia caught her lip with her teeth, her face flushing.

"Ah, I see I have struck home." Faraday opened the envelope and ran through it, then stuck it inside his coat. "Some of us are rather selective in our lies. I find it much easier simply to be a cad, through and through. That way one is never confused."

"Very clever," Venetia said sourly. "I have lost my taste for your bons mots, however. I must go now."

She turned away, but his next words stopped her. "But, my dear girl, we haven't set a time and place for your next payment."

Blood drained from Venetia's face, and she turned back to him. "What?" She hastily rolled up her veil to the top of her hat in order to see him more clearly. "What did you say?"

"I was talking about your next…ah, 'gift.' I think a month would be ample time."

Venetia stared at him. "You can't be serious!"

"Oh, but I am. I am a man of many needs, and I am afraid my wife has grown somewhat less than generous."

"I would think she would pay you to leave the country!"

"Well, I haven't put that proposition to her yet. Perhaps she would. But, frankly, I prefer to stay in London. So many of my friends are here, you know."

"You have no friends!"

He raised a lazy eyebrow. "How unkind. And quite untrue, you know. For instance, the lovely young Miss Emerson—you know, the new bright shining star of London—regards herself as my friend."

"Leave Charity alone!" Venetia cried. "She is a sweet girl, and I won't have you ruining her!"

"That is something that is hardly in your hands. You can't keep a young girl from running headlong into destruction. You should know that."

"You pig!" Venetia spat.

Reed grinned evilly, then reached out and grabbed Venetia's arms and pulled her to him. He wrapped his arms around her, holding her still despite her struggles, and kissed her full on the mouth. He ground his lips hard against hers, so hard that one of her teeth cut her lip. When at last he released her, Venetia staggered back, her face filled with revulsion. Her gloved hand went to her mouth and came away with a spot of blood on it. She was filled with hatred and repulsion; the emotions rose in her like bile, flooding her throat with bitterness.

"Don't you ever touch me again!" she spat, her dark eyes for once so like her brother's that Reed took an unconscious step backward. "I'll kill you if you try to— God, I cannot fathom what ever attracted me to you! You are scum! You're evil."

"Careful what you say," Reed said lightly, recovering from his momentary surprise. "Remember, I am the one who sets your price."

"I will not continue to pay you!"

"Then you're prepared to have me tell Lord Ashford about you and me?"

"No!" Venetia's anger fled, replaced by fear and a sick hopelessness. "You can't. I paid you all you asked. You can't turn around now and ask for more."

"Oh? Are there rules for this sort of thing? I didn't know. To whom are you going to complain? A magistrate?"

"I can't get that kind of money again," Venetia protested. "You don't understand."

"Come now, do you expect me to believe that our dear George is not rolling in money? Everyone knows the Ashfords own half of Sussex."

"Yes, he has money, but much of it is tied up in the land, and the improvements he makes to it. He doesn't squeeze his people for every cent. I have no way of getting to his money, anyway."

"He gives you an allowance, doesn't he?"

"Yes, of course, but I've given you my clothes money for this quarter right there. I have nothing else."

"What about the household money? You could borrow from that, couldn't you?"

Venetia looked shocked. "No! George would notice if suddenly the quality of Cook's meals diminished or I stopped having parties or we let go some of the staff."

"Tell him some tale about an overdue bill or something. Say you made an unwise purchase. He'll give you extra money."

"I don't want to lie to him!"

"But you already have. I presume he doesn't know about our arrangement to meet here."

"Of course not!"

"Then what is one more lie? I'm certain that you will come up with some plausible excuse. And there are always your jewels. I'm sure they're worth a pretty penny. For instance, those earrings you have on right now should bring a fair price at the moneylender's."

Venetia clapped her hands to her ears, as if he might jerk the emeralds from her ears right there. "They were a gift from George. I could never—"

"Then perhaps you should borrow the money from your loving brother. He would be happy to help you out, as he did before."

"Why do you hate Simon? All he ever did was protect his sister. You act as if *he* had wronged *you.*"

"He spoiled my plans. I had to marry that loathsome slug. Pretend that I loved her and wanted her." His face twisted with disgust. "I have to dance to her tune if I want anything. Stay by her side, wait on her, beg her for every cent I get. It is her father who is wealthy. God knows he gives her ample money, but he gives it to *her.* She is free to do with it as she will. I have to live on her mercy. Even when he dies, it will be the same. She has told me that he has his entire fortune tied up in trusts, and the trustees will dole out money only on her say-so. If she dies, I have nothing."

"No doubt she and her father realized what kind of man you were. It sounds like a practical arrangement for someone married to a scoundrel."

Reed glared at her. "Your fee just went up. I want twenty pounds more next month."

"I can't give you even this much again!"

"You had best go home and figure out some way to do it. Because I will expect my money on the first of next month."

"How can you be so wicked? How could I ever have thought I was in love with you?"

Venetia whirled and hurried through the park toward the street, tears blurring her eyes. Behind her, Reed stood watching, his eyes narrowed and his mouth twisted. It had been sweet to take Venetia's money, sweeter still to hear her beg him not to make her pay any more, but it was not as pleasing as he had imagined it would be. It always turned out that way. Whatever kind of revenge he took against Dure, it was never as satisfying as he had dreamed it would be. Always, he wanted more.

Today was the same. He could look forward to squeezing more money out of Venetia. It would be fun to watch her squirm—and profitable to him, as well, which was always something to be considered. But he knew that it would not be enough to satisfy the need that burned in him, the need to humiliate Dure as he himself had been humiliated when Dure easily thrashed him and literally threw him out of the inn where Dure had caught him with Venetia. No, it was quite obvious, the only thing that would satisfy him, that would pay the high-and-mighty Earl of Dure back would be the publicly known seduction of his fiancée.

Just the thought of it made a chilly smile cross Reed's face. Thinking of his triumph—for he was already sure that the innocent little Miss Charity Emerson was becoming smitten with his charm—Reed strolled out of the park. So intent was he on his own thoughts that he did not notice, just as the distraught Venetia had not, that an ordinary-looking man in a brown suit stood at the opposite end of the park, half-hidden by a large bush. Nor did he see when the man slipped out of the park behind him and trailed him down the street.

"My lord?" The ever-correct Holloway stopped in front of Lord Ashford, who was in the elaborate process of readying a thick cigar for smoking—rolling it between his hands, sniffing it, cutting off the end with a small pair of gold-chased scissors.

Ashford looked up, suppressing his irritation. Holloway was never one to interrupt a man at leisure in his club unless it was something important. He raised his eyebrows questioningly. "Yes? What is it?"

"There is a…person outside who wishes to address you, my lord." Ashford knew from his tone, and the way he hesitated before he said "person," that whoever it was was not the sort who could be mistaken for a gentleman who would frequent a private club.

"A person?"

"Yes, my lord. A man in a brown suit. He said that you would most certainly wish to see him, and he asked that I present his card to you." The servant stretched forward his hand, in which lay a small silver platter.

Ashford took the card from the platter and read it. His face tightened. "Yes. Thank you, Holloway. I'm afraid he is right, and I must see him." He rose and followed Holloway through the smoking room and into the hall beyond. "I'll see him outside."

"Very well, my lord." Ashford knew Holloway would have been horrified if George asked him to bring the man inside—though, of course, such emotion would never have been allowed to touch his composed features.

Ashford opened the heavy wooden door at the front of the club and stepped outside. A man stood on the stoop, his back to the door, gazing idly across the street.

"Mr. Weaver?"

The man turned and smiled a little nervously at Ashford. It wasn't every day that he did business with a baron, and he felt a bit in awe of Ashford still, though the lord seemed a pleasant enough type. He was also very aware that the news he was bringing him was probably not what he wished to hear.

"I found out today, my lord," he said, stopping to clear his throat.

"Indeed?" Ashford felt his heart drop at the anxious expression on the other man's face. He gestured toward the street. "Why don't we take a little stroll?"

"Very well, sir." Weaver tugged a little at his collar and fell in with Ashford as he came down the steps.

They walked along the sidewalk, talking in quiet tones. There were few people around, and when someone did approach, they would fall silent, then resume their conversation when the others had passed.

"She left the house earlier than usual this morning, my lord, and she didn't take the carriage. Anyway, she went to Harding Crescent. There's a pretty little park there. It's a few blocks from your house."

"Yes, I know the location." Ashford paused, then went on, struggling to keep his voice even and unconcerned, "And what did she do there?"

"It was as you thought, my lord. She met a man. They talked for a while, animated like. She started away, and he took her arm and pulled her back, and they talked some more. He— They kissed."

"Damn!" George pressed his lips closed after the one brief, explosive curse.

"They kept on talking some more. Then she turned and walked out of the park. She looked angry, my lord. I didn't see much reason to follow her, so I stayed and went after the gentleman."

"Gentleman?" George repeated in ironic tones.

"Yessir," Weaver replied, unaware of the sarcasm of George's word. "He was dressed like a gentleman, right up to the mark, and he carried a gold-knobbed cane. Very smart, he was."

George made an impatient gesture. "Good God, man, I don't care what he wore. Who is he?"

The other man smiled smugly. "I followed him to his house, my lord. Nice place, it was, too, in Mayfair. I managed to make friends with a coachman what was sitting waiting for his master at a house across the street. He said the man was a Mr. Faraday Reed. A swell, just like I thought, looking at his house."

Faraday Reed! Ashford's hand clenched. *That snake!* George had not suspected him in his wildest imaginings. It was well known that Dure and Reed did not like one another. No one knew why; it was only whispers and speculation. It seemed bizarre that Venetia would take up with someone whom her brother despised. George had never even seen Faraday Reed come up and speak to his wife at a party—*except for that time the night Dure introduced Charity to them.*

Ashford recalled it now. At the time, he had made little of it. Venetia and Reed had spoken briefly, and though Venetia had looked a trifle pale afterward, George had put it down to her disliking Reed's impertinence. Now he saw that it must have had very different connotations.

Weaver glanced at his silent companion, then began tentatively, "Will you be wanting me to keep on, my lord? Following Her Ladyship, I mean?"

"What? Oh. No. I— That will be enough, Mr. Weaver. Quite enough."

Ashford paid the man, then turned and started back to his club. He felt strangely disconnected from himself. Normally, he knew, he would never even have thought of the possibility of his wife's being unfaithful. But he had begun to be suspicious, because Venetia seemed so unlike herself, often staring into space, jittery and jumpy all the time. A few days ago, he had found her crying in her dressing room. When he went to her, concerned, she had quickly brushed her tears away and told him that it was nothing. It had bothered him that she refused to tell him what was wrong, but what had really pierced him was that when she looked up at him, he saw a flash of fear in her eyes.

It was then that he had decided to hire Weaver. He had heard Winston Montague talking about him one day; Weaver had recovered some jewels for his wife, and Montague had sung his praises. Now Ashford realized that all along, even though he had told Weaver he wanted his wife followed to see if she was having an affair, what he had really wanted—what he had presumed, in fact—was that Weaver would tell him that his fears were unwarranted, that Venetia was not seeing another man. Now his half-hidden fears were realized; he could not hide from the truth. Venetia was in love with another man.

Hatred spurted within him as he thought of Faraday

Reed, and at the same time his heart burned with pain. *Venetia did not love him.* He wanted to strike out in rage, and he knew that if Reed had been there in front of him right then, he would have gone for his throat. That would have relieved some of his anger. But nothing could relieve the ache in his soul. He wished he had never hired Weaver.

Wearily Ashford climbed the steps to the front door of his club and went inside. He did not return to the smoking room. Instead he found a small, unoccupied room and sank down into one of its comfortable leather chairs. He leaned back, closing his eyes as if asleep, so that no one would disturb him, and let misery overtake him.

CHAPTER TEN

CHARITY STIFLED A YAWN as she brushed out her hair in front of the vanity mirror.

Serena, sitting on the bed behind her and doing the same thing to her own hair, smiled faintly. "Bored with this life already?"

"Tired, I think. The ball last night went on too long."

"I never thought I'd hear you say that," Serena teased.

"Me either." In truth, Charity was more bored and lonely than anything else. She had seen Simon only once since the day she had taken Lucky to him, almost a week ago. It had been at a dinner, and they had been seated far apart, without a chance to talk. The time had crept by. The social round was little fun without Simon. She worried that perhaps she had offended him by her behavior on the day they found Lucky. He had not seemed so, certainly, but perhaps, on reflection, he had decided she was too bold.

As though she had read her thoughts, Serena said, "I imagine that you will feel better this evening, when we go to the theater with Lady Ashford."

Charity smiled, her face lighting up. Simon would be in his sister's box, as well. "That's true." She turned back to the mirror, piling her hair up on her head in different ways and studying the effects. "I want to look especially pretty tonight. Do you think this style makes me look older?"

Serena chuckled. "Most women spend their time trying to look *younger,* not older."

"I know. But I don't want Si—Lord Dure to think I look babyish."

Serena studied her sister curiously. "You are fond of him, aren't you?"

"Of course." Charity looked at her with some surprise. "I am going to marry the man, after all."

"Marriage doesn't necessarily mean mutual regard," Serena reminded her softly.

Charity's eyes grew intent as she looked at her sister in the mirror. "Do you really think so—that the regard is mutual, I mean?"

Serena chuckled. "My dear, how can you doubt it, after the man took that wretched dog off your hands? He had to be smitten, not to show us all the door and cry off the engagement."

Charity smiled. "I know. But I haven't seen him since then. And whenever he calls, it's so horribly stiff!"

"It is difficult, with Mama and Elspeth and me there, too."

Charity grimaced. "It's *dreadful* with Mama and Elspeth there. If I say anything besides some insipid something or other, Elspeth jumps in, babbling about something else, and Mama looks daggers at me, then scolds me dreadfully after Dure leaves. And I have to stay in there with all those other dreadfully dull callers, as well. Sometimes I think it was more fun in the schoolroom."

"You were bored there, too," Serena reminded her.

"That's true," Charity agreed. "And it will be much

more fun when I'm married, for then Dure and I can talk anytime we want…about anything we want." She grinned. "Doesn't that sound wonderful? Can't you hardly wait for when you marry your pastor and can sit across from him at the breakfast table every morning? Or sit there in front of your vanity and talk while you're preparing your toilette?"

Serena blushed prettily. "Charity! What a shocking thing to be thinking of!"

Charity shrugged. "Well, it's true, isn't it? Don't you think you'll be together like this? I mean, you will be sharing a bed, how can you not be closer?"

Her older sister's cheeks turned beet red at Charity's last remark, and she shot her an agonized glance. "Charity, you must learn to hold your tongue! You simply cannot go around saying things alike that!"

"Why? I'm only talking to you. It isn't as if I blurted it out in front of a duchess."

"Thank heavens!" Serena replied with heartfelt gratitude, coming over behind Charity and taking the brush from her hands. She began to pin up her sister's hair, saying, "Sometimes, Charity, I cannot understand where you came by this want of propriety."

"I can't, either," Charity agreed, without rancor. "It must come from some bad apple in Papa's family. I can't imagine any of the Stanhopes being that way."

"I should hope not. Nor the Emersons, either."

"But, Serena," Charity went on, ignoring the issue of propriety, "don't you look forward to it?"

"Of course I do. I cannot help but be eager to be able to be with Mr. Woodson and…and commune with him in rightful solitude."

"Commune with him!" Charity gaped at her sister. She loved Serena dearly, but there were times when she was annoyingly priggish. Charity was not sure exactly what communing with a man in rightful solitude meant, but it sounded thoroughly boring. What she looked forward to was talking to Simon alone, saying whatever she wanted, her heart rising when she was able to draw laughter to his face or the light of passion to his eyes. She wanted to be with him in easy intimacy, no longer surrounded by other people, but free to kiss, to hold each other....

Charity pulled back her wayward thoughts, afraid that their nature might show on her expressive face. She had no doubt that Serena would be utterly shocked if she had any idea of what had passed between Charity and Simon.

"At least tonight at the theater I will be able to see him and talk to him. Even if there are lots of people there, it will be more fun than sitting in the drawing room with Mama watching us like a hawk."

Charity got up and walked over to the dresser, where a small vase of pink rosebuds stood. Simon had sent the flowers to her this morning; a maid had brought in the vase when she came into the room to wake them up. Charity bent to sniff their scent, and as she did so, she noticed a folded slip of white paper tucked deep amid the stems. She froze, staring at it. She had not noticed it before. *Had it been there when the maid brought in the flowers?*

She told herself that she simply had not seen it before because it was hidden deep amid the stems. She told herself that it was only a note from Simon accompanying the gift. But she remembered that the maid had handed her the small card with Simon's name on it when she brought

the vase. Charity's heart pounded, and her throat went dry.
She was certain it was another of *those* notes.

She glanced back at her sister and was glad to see that
Serena had not noticed her reaction. She had taken
Charity's place in front of the mirror and was absorbed in
brushing a long curl around her fingers. Charity reached
into the vase quickly and retrieved the piece of paper, then
unfolded it.

"You will be the monster's next victim."

Charity stared down at the note. Her fingers trembled
with rage, and she crushed the slip of paper in her hand.
She dropped it into the wastepaper basket, fury surging
through her. *How dare someone malign Simon this way?*
She wished that she could get her hands on the perpetra-
tor; her fingers itched to slap the coward who dared not
even make his accusations face-to-face.

Then, suddenly, she thought about where she had found
the note. It had not been delivered, nor had it been placed
in her possession at some large party, as the other notes
had. Instead, it had been here, in her own bedroom, tucked
into the very bouquet that Dure had sent her, like a poi-
sonous snake. Someone in this house had put it in there—
probably they had crept into her very bedroom to do it! She
and Serena had been in and out of the room since they had
arisen, going down to breakfast and across the hall to see
Horatia and Belinda. Serena had also left to borrow a
brooch from her mother, and Charity had spent some time
in Elspeth's room, retrieving a scarf Elspeth had borrowed.
It made Charity's skin crawl to think of someone slipping
into her room like that; she felt violated and uneasy.

Charity glanced around the room, almost as if she
would find someone still lurking in her bedroom. Serena

gave a final pat to her coiffure and rose from the vanity stool, smiling at Charity.

"Are you ready?" she asked.

Charity wanted to tell her sister about the note, to unburden herself of its evil, but she stopped herself. She could not show Serena that accusation about Simon; it seemed a betrayal of Simon to even admit that someone was accusing him of such a crime. So she fixed a smile on her face and answered her sister lightly, following her out the door and down the stairs to face the afternoon's callers.

They could hear by the sound of male voices that there were already visitors in the drawing room. Charity paused, tempted for a moment not even to go in. She didn't want to have to be polite to people she neither knew nor liked, when all she could think of was that note and the treacherous way it had turned up in her room.

Serena stopped at the door and turned toward her, her brows lifted enquiringly. Charity knew that if she didn't go in, she would have to explain her actions, at least to her sister, and then probably her mother or Aunt Ermintrude would come to see what was wrong. It was easier to put on a social mask and force herself through the call.

She joined Serena, and they entered the room. There were three men inside the room, as well as Aunt Ermintrude. Charity was relieved to see that her mother was not there. Aunt Ermintrude didn't have the eagle eye that Caroline did; she would not be likely to notice that there was anything wrong with Charity—especially since the old lady was having so much fun flirting. All the men stood up when the two women entered. One of the men was Faraday Reed. Charity's spirits brightened. Here, at least, was someone she could confide in. She exchanged polite greetings with everyone, and managed to maneuver herself into sitting in the chair beside Faraday.

"How lovely you look, Miss Emerson," he began, then stopped when he saw her expression.

"I must talk to you," Charity said in a low voice, looking at him intently.

"You've gotten another of them, haven't you?" he guessed.

"Yes. Just now, in my room."

His eyes widened. "In your very bedchamber? But that's—monstrous."

Charity nodded and began to tell him how she had found it. It was a relief to confide her fears and worries to him, instead of maintaining a polite social front. He had proven himself worthy of her confidence. Despite her fears to the contrary, there had been no mention of the notes from anyone since Reed had found out; obviously he had not seized on the opportunity to spread the juicy bit of gossip about Charity and Simon. Charity thought it was unfair of Simon to dislike the man so much. Even if they had loved the same woman, that didn't make Faraday a bad person. Faraday did not hold a grudge against Simon over it; it seemed to her that Simon should be able to unbend and get over the old rift, too. If only he knew how helpful Reed had been, how understanding and discreet...

"It was the same sort of thing—a warning that I would be in danger," Charity explained. "It called Dure a monster, and said that I would be his next victim." Charity's eyes flashed at the memory, though she kept her composure enough not to raise her voice. "How could they think I would believe such calumny about him?"

"No one who knew your loyal nature could," he replied soothingly.

"Why would they say such a thing? Why would anyone want to break off our engagement?"

"Perhaps a spurned suitor?" he suggested. "You are a beautiful girl—doubtless you've broken more than one heart by becoming engaged to Lord Dure."

Charity stared at him. "You can't be serious! Why, I never even attended a party here in London until Dure and I were engaged."

"But could there not be someone from your home in the country?"

Charity couldn't help but giggle, thinking about the country boys she had danced and flirted with, like the squire's son, Will, who was far more interested in his father's hunting pack than in any thoughts of marriage. "No. Really. It could not be that."

Reed sat silent for a moment, thinking. Finally he said, "Have you thought that perhaps it is someone who does not do it with malicious intent?"

"What do you mean? How could they not?"

"Perhaps it is a person who is merely concerned for you, though not close enough to you to express it. It could be that they really believe that you will be in danger if you marry Dure."

"What? That's preposterous! How can you even think that!"

"There have been rumors ever since his wife's death," he pointed out reasonably.

"Rumors do not make a thing true," Charity retorted heatedly. "Do not tell me that *you* think such a thing of Dure, too!"

"Of course not. Lord Dure and I have had our differences, as you know. But I have never believed that he murdered his wife. I was only pointing out that it might not necessarily be someone malicious or evil doing this, but someone who honestly believes that he is saving you."

"Well, whoever it is and whatever he thinks, I wish he would show his face, so that I could tell him what I think of him. It's a coward's way. If he had any honor or honesty, he would tell me directly."

"I have tried to find out," Reed told her. "Discreetly, of course. I could not ask outright questions."

"Oh, no. I don't want any of this getting out."

"But I could find no one who seemed to have a fierce enough grievance against Lord Dure to do this. There are those who have had disputes with him, of course, and some who believe the way he has lived indicates a weak moral tone. His manner is not always conducive to, uh, friendship. But no one seemed incensed or filled with hatred. Nor were there any rumors of such. That is why my mind turned toward your suitors, for I am sure there must be many men who, having met you, wished that they had had the chance to offer for your hand."

Charity smiled. "You are very flattering Mr. Reed, but I feel sure that—" She stopped abruptly, and her eyes brightened. "Why, that could be it!"

"You've thought of a suitor?"

"No. Not that. But what you said made me think— Perhaps it is someone in love with Simon—I mean, Lord Dure. No one was pursuing me before the engagement, but I am certain there were lots of women who were pursuing Dure. Hopeful debutantes, and their mothers. There are bound to have been, with a man like Dure."

Reed gazed at her blankly. "Uh, I don't really…"

"I know it isn't something I should be talking about. But

this is no time for polite convention. I must find out where those notes are coming from." She paused, chewing on her lower lip in thought. "You know, the more I think about it, the more inclined I am to think that it is a woman. Such dislike smacks of a lover scorned. I am so glad you suggested it."

"Actually, I didn't. You leaped to—"

"Yes, yes, I know, but it was you who gave me the idea." She smiled at him. "I feel much better now. If it is only another woman, hurt and grudging, that is something I can deal with. And I can investigate it myself."

"Miss Emerson!" Reed look alarmed. "No, you must not. You don't know what kind of danger you could be in."

"Nonsense. From a jealous woman?" Charity smiled benignly at him, thinking that men were foolishly protective. "I can hold my own with that sort. It will be easy for me to ask around. Everyone is always eager to carry tales to a future wife."

Reed still looked doubtful. "I do not believe that Lord Dure will be pleased at having his fiancée asking questions about his past—especially his romantic past."

"Don't be silly. For one thing, I doubt that he will know. I suspect that not too many people dare run to Lord Dure with tales of anything. Anyway, as His Lordship knows, I am my own woman and go my own way. It is the way we both prefer it."

"Indeed?" A speculative look entered his eyes. "You are an independent woman, then?"

"Certainly," Charity said briskly. The thought flickered through her mind that Lord Dure had not seemed to prefer her going her own way when it meant talking to Faraday Reed, but she shoved the idea away.

"There are other things I can do to find this note-sender," she went on. "Tomorrow I am going to talk to the maids. At first, when I found that note among my flowers, I assumed that the sender had actually crept into my bedroom and placed it among the blooms, but, of course, that would not have been the case. It would have been too easy for him to be caught. He—or she—must have bribed one of Aunt Ermintrude's servants. So I will question them."

"They aren't likely to admit to anything."

"Oh, I will worm it out of them somehow," Charity replied confidently. "'Tis quite possible that they did not even realize that there was any harm. They might have thought it was a missive from an admirer, or some such." She smiled warmly at Reed and reached out to squeeze his arm. "You have been so helpful. I feel much better. And I thank you for your discretion. You have been a gentleman and a good friend. I only wish Simon realized how wrong he is about you."

"I doubt that that will ever come about," Reed said dryly. "'Tis just as well that you don't try to convince him."

"But it's wrong," Charity protested, "when you have been doing all this to help me…and him."

"I have done it for you, Miss Emerson," Reed assured her, covering her hand with his and looking soulfully into her eyes.

Charity felt an inappropriate desire to giggle. He was looking at her in a moonstruck way that was, she thought, ridiculous. But she could not laugh, not after he had been so understanding and helpful about the wicked notes. She wondered if this sick-calf look was Reed's manner of flirting. It seemed strange to her for a married man to flirt in any way, especially with a woman who was about to be married herself. However, she had seen in the few weeks that she had been out that flirting was rampant throughout society, no matter what one's marital status, and her mother said that it was perfectly acceptable, that it didn't mean anything. Charity wondered why it was done, if it didn't mean anything. But she did not question her mother; she would only say that Charity was being frivolous or, worse, impertinent.

"Yes, I know," she replied matter-of-factly to Reed's emotion-tinged words, and discreetly tried to withdraw her hand from his. But his hand still clasped hers firmly. "And I appreciate it, I promise you."

It was at that moment that she became aware that all conversation around her had ceased. She raised her head curiously and saw that everyone else in the room was staring at the door. She turned and looked.

Simon was standing just inside the door, looking directly, chillingly, at her.

Her heart sank. It occurred to her then how her earnest discussion with Mr. Reed must look—the two of them, their voices soft, their heads close together, locked in a private conversation that excluded everyone else in the room. It was not the way a young woman of good breeding talked to a man who was not her fiancé. Her mother would have noticed and pulled her back into the general conversation, but Serena hadn't the skill to do it, and Aunt Ermintrude hadn't even noticed.

"Oh, dear," Charity murmured as Simon started across the floor toward her.

CHAPTER ELEVEN

SIMON NODDED POLITELY to Aunt Ermintrude and Serena and the two young men conversing with them. Then he turned toward Charity and Reed, and his eyes swept coldly over them.

"Good afternoon, Lord Dure," Charity began boldly, determined not to let him intimidate her. After all, she had been doing nothing wrong.

"My dear. I trust Mr. Reed has been keeping you entertained."

Reed shifted uneasily in his seat at Dure's icy tone, but Charity simply gazed back evenly and replied, "Yes, he has."

"Mr. Reed has always had a good deal of charm." He smiled in a chilling way as he looked at Reed. "Perhaps more than is wise for him."

Charity's eyebrows went up coolly at his words. She hoped that Dure wasn't about to cause a scene. She could see that Aunt Ermintrude and the others were watching them interestedly, their own conversations abandoned in favor of the more entertaining possibilities offered by Lord Dure's obvious antagonism.

"But now that I am here," Dure went on, speaking to Reed, "I can relieve you of the burden of entertaining my fiancée."

"It was no burden at all," Reed assured him blandly. "Miss Emerson is a sparkling conversationalist."

"Of course, but I am sure that you have other obligations you need to meet." Dure's eyes bored into him, and finally, flushing, Reed rose to his feet.

"It has been a pleasure, Miss Emerson," he said, turning to her and ignoring Dure.

"Thank you." Charity smiled at him warmly to counteract the sting of Dure's glowering disapproval.

Reed bowed to the others and made his departure. Dure stonily watched him go. He turned back to Charity and said stiffly, "Perhaps you would like to take a stroll around the garden, Miss Emerson."

Charity thought about telling Simon that she was fine where she was, just to thwart him, since he was acting so overbearing, but she had the suspicion that if she did not go outside with him, he would give her a lecture right here in front of the others. It would be better to receive a dressing-down in private, at least.

"Of course, my lord." She turned toward her great-aunt for permission.

Looking rather disappointed that she was going to miss the fireworks, Aunt Ermintrude nodded. "You young people run along."

Dure offered Charity his arm, and they walked silently out of the room and down the hall, then out the door to the formal garden behind Aunt Ermintrude's house. Charity cast a brief sideways glance at Simon's profile. His face might have been carved of stone. She suppressed a sigh. *Why was it that Dure had to be so obdurate on this issue?* It seemed rather unfair of him to order her not to talk to a man simply because he had once been a rival of his. Reed had proven himself her friend in this matter of the notes, which Charity found generous of him, considering the obvious dislike her fiancé held for him.

They walked in silence for a time. Charity could hear the audible grinding of the Earl's teeth, and she guessed that he was struggling to bring his anger under control. She remembered the other time, at Lady Rotterham's ball, when his anger had not been under control, and the way he had kissed her, his mouth so hot and hungry that she'd thought he might almost consume her. She flushed, thinking that she might prefer it if he lost his composure again.

But he did not. He seated her on the stone bench at the far end of the garden, then stood in front of her, his arms crossed over his chest like a stern schoolmaster. In an icy tone, he said, "Miss Emerson, do you seek out ways to defy me? Or are you merely foolish enough to think that I do not mean what I say?"

Charity gazed back at him, pride in every line of her face and body. "Defy you, my lord? Indeed, I have only gone about my own way, as you have gone about yours. It is, I believe, what we agreed our marriage would be like."

"We are not married yet."

"Then I would say that only makes it worse that you expect me to live under your thumb."

Dure's nostrils flared, and a fierce light flamed to life in his dark eyes. "I do *not* expect you to live under my thumb! I am not some brute who wants a cowed creature for his wife!"

"Indeed?" Charity returned coolly. "Then why do you seat me here and loom over me thus, as if I were some disobedient child and you my parent?"

"Damnation! I was attempting to be polite. Stand, then, if that's what you want!" He reached down and grasped her by the arms, jerking her to her feet. He stood for a moment only inches away from her, his fingers digging into her flesh and his eyes blazing down at her.

Then, with an oath, he dropped her arms and stepped back, half turning away from her. "God help me, I have never met a woman who could make me so—so damned uncivilized."

Charity let out a shaky little laugh. For a moment she had been uncertain whether he was going to shake her or kiss her breathless, as he had before. "Am I that annoying, my lord?"

"Yes, you are very much that annoying—and that enticing. You make me feel as if I were going to explode," he answered roughly, his gaze sweeping over her. "When I saw that cad Reed so close to you, and you smiling at him, touching his arm, it was all I could do not to floor him right there in your aunt's drawing room!"

"You were jealous?" Charity's brows vaulted upward. She had not considered this motive for Dure's forbidding her to see Reed; she had thought he simply disliked the man and expected his wife to form her friendships in accordance with his likes and dislikes. Given Dure's manner of marrying, she would not have thought that any emotions such as jealousy might stir him. She found the idea rather warming.

"You are to be my wife," he snapped, glaring at her. "I cannot allow any taint to attach itself to your name."

"Taint!" *So it was his pride and family name that he was jealously protective of, not her!* Charity drew herself up to her full height and glared right back at him.

"Yes, and worse than that, if you continue to associate with scum like Farady Reed."

"Mr. Reed is well accepted," Charity retorted.

"Society would accept a snake, if it spoke well enough and danced attendance upon all the old harridans who rule it."

"But you know better than they do?"

"Yes, I do. I know that Faraday Reed is a wicked man, and that he will ruin your virtue if given the slightest opportunity."

"You think that I have so little morals that I would permit any man who came along to seduce me?" Charity snapped, incensed.

"You do not have to be seduced to have your name ruined," Simon shot back. "Reed can make it appear that a woman's virtue has been compromised. Nor is he above forcing you, if that is the only way to do it."

Charity stared, shocked out of her anger for the moment. "Simon! No! You must be mistaken. He would not do such a thing. Why, he has been most kind to me. He even helped—" She broke off, remembering that she had not told Simon about the notes.

She was torn. If she told Simon how sympathetic and helpful Mr. Reed had been, despite the antipathy between him and Dure, then Simon would realize that he was being unfair to Reed. However, she wanted to protect Simon from the knowledge of those awful notes. It would be bound to bring back painful memories of his wife's death—and that of his child. It would be petty and unkind for her to expose him to those notes now, just so that she could make a point in an argument.

"He has helped what?" Simon asked, his brows drawing together suspiciously.

"He has helped me…fit in, you know, telling me who people are and how they are related. That sort of thing. He has helped me steer clear of some of the hidden rocks."

"You don't need his help. If you want to know something, ask your mother—or Venetia. But not Faraday Reed. I insist that you avoid him."

"My mother likes him and allows him to call. How can I avoid him?"

Simon grimaced. "Tell her what I told you, and I assure you that she will not permit him inside the house again. I expected you to do so when I first warned you about him. Obviously, you did not."

"You were being unreasonable. You still are. You make these vague accusations about Mr. Reed, but you won't tell me why you think he's wicked. What has he done to make you dislike him so? Why do you think he would try to ruin my reputation?"

"He would do so to get back at me. Believe me, he dislikes me as cordially as I dislike him. Perhaps even more so, as I won."

A bitter tongue of anger snaked through Charity. He was obviously referring to the woman of easy virtue that the two of them had pursued, and it bothered her that Simon would even think of her in Charity's presence.

In a tight voice, she asked, "Won what?"

Simon shook his head. "I cannot tell you."

"Of course. You issue orders and expect me to blindly obey you. And you say you don't want to force me to live under your thumb."

"The story is not mine to tell," Dure replied stiffly. "It involves a lady and her honor."

Charity was incensed. Reed had made it clear that the woman involved was a member of the demimonde, not a lady. How dare Dure pretend that the matter involved a lady's honor?

"Ha!" She let out a derisive laugh. "That's always the
last resort when a man doesn't want to tell you something.
It's too 'indelicate' for your poor female sensibilities, or
it involves a 'lady's honor,' or it's something you 'wouldn't
understand.'"

Dure's jaw jutted out. "It happens to be the truth. I don't
indulge in polite nonsense. It does involve a lady, and I
would be a poor excuse for a gentleman if I spread the story
around."

"I'm not asking you to 'spread it around.' I am asking
you to give me a reason why I should avoid Faraday Reed."

"Damnation, woman! Isn't the fact that I request it
reason enough?"

"You did not request it! You ordered it. There is a world
of difference. I am your fiancée, not your servant, and I will
not be ordered about. If what you want is someone you can
command, then I suggest that you find another woman to
be your wife!"

He gazed at her for a long moment, his head high and
proud, and Charity was afraid that he would tell her that
their engagement was at an end.

But then he gave her a stiff bow and said, "All right,
Miss Emerson. I am not ordering you. I am asking you, as
my future wife, to do this as a favor to me." His voice was
rigidly controlled, and he did not look at Charity until the
end. But then he looked straight into her eyes. "More than
that, I would like for you to believe me, to take my word
for it, even though I cannot tell you how I know, that Reed
is an evil man. I am asking that you trust me."

When he'd first begun to speak, Charity had felt a thrill
of triumph. She had, in a sense, tamed the wild, proud Lord
Dure, brought him to request it of her as an equal, not order

her as a child. But when he asked her to trust and believe him, his voice dark and laced with emotion, Charity had realized that he was asking far more of her than that she do as he requested. He wanted something deeper, a commitment of mind and belief. He was a man who had been hurt by rumors, a man about whom others whispered, a man known as "Devil Dure." Charity had had a glimpse of how much those rumors had pierced him, despite his cool exterior, and she knew that the trust of his wife was something he longed for, though his pride would not normally have let him ask for it. She knew, too, how much it had cost him to ask.

Charity reached out and took his hand in hers. "All right," she said quietly, gazing back into his eyes. "I believe you. And I will avoid Mr. Reed in the future."

Simon's hand tightened convulsively around hers. He raised her hand to his lips and kissed it. He turned her hand over and pressed a kiss into her palm, then cradled her hand against his cheek.

"Thank you." His voice was husky. "I should not have ordered you. I didn't think. When I saw him with you, I was so angry, so scared of what he might do to you, that I didn't think about how it would make you feel. Forgive me."

"Of course." Charity took a step closer to him, drawn by the emotion of his voice. She went up on tiptoe and brushed her lips against his cheek.

Instantly his arms were around her like iron bands, pressing her into him, and his mouth was seeking hers blindly. Charity melted against him, and her arms went around his neck, clinging to him. Simon kissed her deeply, thoroughly, and his hand slipped up and around to cup her breast. He groaned at the feel of the soft weight in his palm, and when her nipple tightened, pressing against his hand, a shudder ran through him.

Simon broke away and stepped back, sucking in great gulps of air. His face was flushed, his eyes were bright, and his mouth was wide and soft with passion. He curled his hands into fists, fighting to stay where he was.

"No," he said hoarsely. "We must not. Sweet Jesus, woman, I seem to have no control around you. You must think me a savage to leap on you like this at every opportunity."

"No," Charity replied softly, and her dimple flashed as she smiled happily up at him. "I like it when you kiss me."

Simon groaned. "Don't say that! You will completely break my will."

Charity stepped back, abashed. "I'm sorry." She twisted her hands together, gazing down at them, and said in a low voice, "Is what I said very wrong? Am I too bold?"

"No! Good God!" Simon whirled back around. "I…like very much for you to say that. To know that you take pleasure in my kiss. The fact is, I like it too much. I want to take you back in my arms and start kissing you again. And I am afraid I would not be able to stop. I must not dishonor you."

"Oh." Charity was flooded with heat at his words, and she felt breathless and a little giddy. She smiled at him, and an answering spark flared in his eyes.

He groaned deep in his throat and turned away, shoving his hands back through his hair. "I have to leave."

"What? So soon?"

"Yes, or I will forget myself entirely." Simon drew a long breath, staring out across the garden. Finally he turned back to Charity, and his face was set, his voice stiff. "The reason I came here this afternoon is to tell you that I plan to leave for the country tomorrow, so I shall miss tonight's theater party. I shall be at Deerfield Park for a few weeks."

Charity's heart sank. A few weeks! "But why?"

"Don't look at me like that. I have to go. If I stay, I—Damn it, it's torture being around you and not being able to have you!" He crossed the ground to her quickly and took her by the shoulders, gazing intently down into her face. "It's so hard to sit with you in your drawing room with your mother and sisters, making silly, polite chitchat, when all I want to do is to take you into my arms and never stop kissing you."

"Oh…" Charity breathed. Her knees felt dangerously weak, as if the fire that burned in Simon's eyes were melting her very bones.

"When I do get a chance to steal a kiss from you, it makes it even worse, for then I want to do so much more, and I know that I would be an absolute scoundrel if I did."

"But you will soon be my husband."

"Yes." His eyes flashed with a fierce possessiveness. "I shall, and then I shall take you to my bed and make you my wife with all the time and care that you deserve. Not hurriedly, behind some bushes in the garden, as if you were a common slut."

"If you leave town for a few weeks, then that won't happen?"

"It will help prevent it. Hopefully, alone in the solitude and peace of the country, I will be able to regain control of my wayward passions. I have spoken to your parents, and they have agreed to shorten the engagement to only six months. They felt anything less would appear to be unseemly haste. By going away, I can make the time of temptation even shorter."

"I shall miss you," Charity said simply.

"Will you? You have half of London dancing attendance upon you now. You have become quite the hit of the season."

Charity shrugged. "Only because I am engaged to be married to you. Otherwise, I would be a little nobody."

"I doubt that, my dear." Amusement laced his voice. "I do not think that you would ever go unnoticed in any situation."

Charity raised one eyebrow at him. "Is that a compliment, my lord?"

"Most definitely." He took her hand and raised it to his lips. "Now I must take my leave of you, else Aunt Ermintrude and her entourage will be out here hunting for us. Too long a walk in the garden, even with a scolding fiancé, would occasion comment."

"I know." Charity heaved a sigh. "There are so many more rules in London than in the country."

He grinned and held out his arm to her. "I trust you will be able to keep yourself out of trouble while I am gone?"

"Why, of course." Charity widened her eyes innocently. "Whatever do you mean?"

"Well, I shan't be there to save you from carters and bobbies."

Charity dimpled mischievously. "Or to advise me on whom I should speak to."

He cast her a darkling glance and added, "*Or* to house whatever poor unfortunate stray you should come upon."

"Come now, confess—you like Lucky, don't you?"

Simon rolled his eyes as they started along the path toward the house. "That hound has turned my entire household upside down. The footmen all hate to walk him, because he drags them down the street like a runaway train. The maids complain that he leaves hairs all over the furniture, and no one can keep him from sleeping on the beds."

Charity giggled.

"Ah, you think it's funny, do you? I doubt you would if it had been your newspaper he chewed to shreds, or your laundry he took exception to and attacked."

"Did he really?"

"Yes, really. He also seems to think that his rightful place to sleep at night is on the foot of *my* bed. Cook has threatened to leave if I don't get rid of him. By the way, that reminds me—this would be a perfect opportunity to take the mutt to the country."

"Oh, yes, he will love all that space to romp in."

"And London will be much safer without him."

"Come now, you cannot tell me that you don't really like him."

"Can I not?" He quirked an eyebrow at her. "He is a veritable hound from hell."

"*I* have heard that you are very fond of him."

"Who told you that? It's a dastardly lie."

"They say that he accompanies you whenever you ride in the park."

"He follows me and won't return home."

"And everyone says that you have quite started a new fashion in dogs."

"What? Ugly mutts?" Simon leaned his head back and laughed. "Now *that* I can believe. Everyone in London is so anxious not to be left out of the latest trend that they will follow any wild start."

He stopped outside the door to the house, pulling her to a halt, and he gazed down earnestly into her eyes. "Promise me that you will take care of yourself while I am gone?"

"I promise."

"Good. I want nothing to happen to you."

"What could happen?" Charity returned lightly.

He groaned. "I am sure I cannot even conceive of it yet." He bent and brushed his lips against her forehead. "I am beginning to see that life would be unbearably dull without you, Miss Emerson," he murmured.

Charity smiled. "I would find it the same without you."

His lips touched hers in a light, brief kiss. "I would like to take you in my arms and kiss you properly, but I'm afraid I would never leave if I did so."

He stepped back abruptly, and Charity let out a little sigh.

"Goodbye, my dear."

"Goodbye."

He opened the door and escorted her into the house. There he politely took his leave, and in a moment he was gone. Charity thought about the next few weeks and wanted to cry. How was she ever going to get through them without him?

CHAPTER TWELVE

SIMON WAS NOT in the best of moods as he stepped into his sister's house. He did not like the way he felt right now. *Damn it! He had meant for his marriage to be an easy, practical thing.* And it was turning out not to be so at all. He disliked the white-hot rage that had swept over him when he saw Charity in a tête-à-tête with Faraday Reed this afternoon. It had been, he was aware, not just anger that Charity had ignored what he told her, nor had it merely been concern that Charity would innocently bring scandal to his name. No, he had to admit that the single most compelling thing he had felt was jealousy—pure, acidic fear that Charity would turn from him to the smoother Reed. It had been all he could do not to jerk Reed out of that chair and pound him with his fists.

He had felt as close to losing his famed control as he had the other day, when he was kissing Charity under the back stairs. There, he knew, in another few minutes he would have been on the floor with her, frantically shoving up her skirts and taking her like an animal, heedless of who might walk past them.

Everything was different since he had met Charity. Sometimes he felt as if his world were upside down. Never before had he looked forward to a party with eagerness, as he did now, knowing that he would see her there. Never before had he had to hold back from calling on a woman every day, or force himself to leave after spending a polite time in her company. Whenever he saw her, all he wanted to do was to whisk Charity away from all the others and have her to himself.

He found himself daydreaming at his desk instead of doing his work, recalling the way Charity had smiled, or the flash of an ankle he had seen as he handed her up into her carriage, or the laughter that sparkled in her eyes. At night he often woke, sweating and hard, from a dream of making love to her.

The engagement period was torture. He wanted Charity right now, in every way. The only way he had been able to think of to endure it was to go away to the country, to spend time away from the constant lure of her. But, maddeningly, now that he was doing so, that prospect seemed unutterably dull and lifeless. Pain had squeezed his heart when he left her at her great-aunt's house. And *that* was the most infuriating thing of all. He did not want to miss her. He hated the fact that she had so quickly, so easily, become important to him. This was not the bloodless, painless marriage he had imagined—yet he knew he would not trade it for the world.

So it was that, after reflecting on such matters all the way over to Venetia's house, Simon was feeling thoroughly disgruntled with himself, Charity and the world in general. When one of the footmen answered the door and informed him that he would see if "my lady is at home," Simon firmly pushed the man aside, growling, "Of course she's at home. If she'd been out, you would have said so at once."

"But, Lord Dure..." the footman gasped, following on Simon's heels as he strode across the spacious tiled foyer toward the stairs.

"Where is she? Upstairs?" Simon snapped, ignoring the footman's anxious protestations. "In her sitting room?"

"I'm not sure, my lord. Pray, let me send one of the maids up to see."

"Don't bother," Simon told him, taking the stairs two at a time. "Venetia will see me."

He left the footman wringing his hands indecisively at the bottom of the stairs, and made his way to the small informal sitting room that lay next to Venetia's bedroom. It was empty, so he proceeded to the bedroom next door, rapping sharply on the door as he swung it open.

"Venetia?" He peered into the gloom.

The heavy drapes had been drawn, leaving the room in a twilight darkness, but he could make out his sister's form, curled up in the chair beside the bed. "What the devil are you doing there? Are you sick?"

"No, of course not," Venetia replied in a watery voice, and there was the distinct sound of a sniffle as she stood up. "What are you doing here, Simon? Why are you bursting into my chamber as if the devil were pursuing you?"

"I think he is," Simon replied. "Or at least the devil in the form of a blond young lady."

"Oh." Venetia dabbed at her face with a handkerchief. "It's Charity that's distressed you?"

"Yes. No. Oh, blast it, Venetia, I'm not even sure who's to blame. Me. No one. I don't know." He strode over to the window and yanked at the heavy draperies. "Why do you have it so damnably dark in here?"

"I, uh, had a headache." Venetia quickly moved away to a chair on the opposite side of the room and sat down. "Sit down and tell me what mischief Charity's gotten into now. Not another stray animal, I hope."

"No, thank God. She hasn't gotten into anything, exactly. It's that damn Reed. He's pursuing her. I told her to rebuff him, but she's as headstrong as…as…"

"As you?" Venetia suggested lightly.

Simon glowered at her for a moment. Then his sense of humor came to his rescue, and he had to chuckle. "Yes, as headstrong as I am. God help us." He sank down into the chair in which Venetia had been sitting earlier. "She lets him come calling on her. She didn't tell her mother what I said about him, and, of course, Mrs. Emerson thinks he's a wonderful gentleman, like all the other chuckleheaded ladies in town. Why don't any of them realize what a snake he is?"

"I am sure several of them do. But they probably found out about him through hard experience, and they are no more willing to tell everyone else why they refuse his calls than you or I were eight years ago."

"I know. But, bloody hell, Venetia, what am I going to do about Charity? She promised me today that she wouldn't see him again. But she only did it to please me. I can see that she doesn't believe it when I tell her he's a rogue."

"You should have told her why."

"And reveal what happened to you? Be sensible, Venetia. I couldn't betray you, even to Charity. I just wish she would *trust* me."

"I'm sure she will," Venetia replied soothingly. "Give her a little time. You've only just become engaged, you know. She really doesn't know you yet."

"This engagement ritual is a bunch of twaddle," Simon retorted. "Why do you have to wait so long? It isn't as if you get to know each other during that time. Why, you're never alone for more than a few moments. The only way you can even sit down and talk in private is to be married to a woman."

Venetia smiled. "Is that what all this storming around is all about? That you don't get to see enough of Charity?"

"Damn it, she's my fiancée. I'm not going to carry her off and ruin her, simply because they leave us alone for ten minutes. You'd think the chaperonage would loosen."

"Why, it does," Venetia responded teasingly. "Haven't you realized that you get to dance with her more than twice in an evening without causing a scandal? And you can sit beside her and glower at all the other young men who have the audacity to ask her to dance—which, I might add, I have seen you do on more than one occasion."

Her teasing remarks won a reluctant smile from Simon. "Oh, yes. That's a great advantage." He sighed. "I'm sorry, Venetia. I shouldn't have dropped all my grievances in your lap. Truly, that wasn't why I came."

"No? But that's what a sister is for, isn't it?"

"Is it?" Simon stood up and walked across the room to her. "That must be why you are such an admirable sister." He reached down and took her hands, pulling her up from the chair. "Come, say goodbye to me. I have to be on my way. That's why I came—to tell you that I'm leaving for the country for a few weeks."

"Ah," Venetia said knowingly. "I see."

"See what?"

"All this grumbling about your engagement. Your impending marriage has driven you to seek the solitude of Deerfield Park."

"The marriage that *isn't* impending soon enough is driving me," Simon told her.

"Well, the waiting will be over eventually," Venetia said, comfortingly.

"I've gotten Lytton to reduce the engagement to six months."

"That will be over in a flash!"

"Hardly."

"Yes, it will." Venetia linked her arm through her brother's, and they began to walk toward the door. "You'll see. Why, it's been nearly a month already, and by the time you get back from the country, the day will be practically upon you. And there will be the wedding preparations to pass the time."

"I'm afraid I have little to do with that."

"That's true. Well, the honeymoon to plan, then."

Simon smiled faintly, his mind turning to the prospect of a long journey alone with Charity. He would have to make sure that it was adequately long—perhaps a trip to Italy. He thought of the train ride across Europe, the two of them locked in their compartment, the wheels clicking rhythmically beneath them as they lay stretched out on their bed together.

As they stepped out into the better-lit hall, Simon glanced down at his sister and stopped abruptly. "You've been crying."

Venetia immediately put her hands up to her face. "Oh, dear. Are my eyes so red, then?"

"Enough to show that you've been crying. Besides, there are tearstains on your cheeks. And here I've been going on like a fool about my problems, none of which would merit crying over. What is it, Venny?"

Venetia tried to smile. "Nothing. You just caught me in one of those silly moods, I'm afraid. I'm just…a little blue. It's really nothing."

"Nothing? You closeted yourself in your room with all the curtains closed tight, and cried so hard I can still see it. I don't think it's 'nothing.'"

Simon turned and pulled her back into her bedroom, closing the door behind him. "All right. Now tell me what's wrong. You haven't been yourself for two weeks or more. Even I have noticed it. You look pale and distracted every time I see you, yet you always say there's nothing wrong with you. I'm sure George has noticed it, too. Have you at least confided in him?"

"George?" Venetia looked horrified, and shook her head quickly. "No! Goodness, no, I couldn't!"

"Couldn't tell your own husband? Nor your brother?"

"I can't tell anyone!" Venetia blurted out, and began to cry again.

"Here. I'm sorry. Venetia, please." Simon shifted nervously, appalled by the emotional storm he'd unleashed. "Don't cry. It can't be that bad."

Venetia's only answer was a wail as she cried even harder. Simon pulled out his pristine white handkerchief and handed it to her. She took it, gulping and sobbing, and pressed it to her eyes.

"Now calm down and tell me what's the matter."

"I—I can't," she said, her sobs subsiding as she wiped the tears away.

"Of course you can. You can tell me anything. Lord, Venetia, do you think I could condemn you? Have you— Well, that is, is there someone besides Ashford?"

Venetia gaped at him. "You mean, am I having an

affair?" Her voice vaulted upward, ending on a screech. "Simon! How could you think that of me?"

"You know I don't think anything badly of you. Have some sense, Venny. It's just that you're being so secretive…."

"It's Reed!" Venetia snapped, and began to cry again, burying her eyes in the handkerchief. "Oh, Simon, I don't know what I'm going to do!"

"Faraday Reed?" Simon's eyebrows drew together, and his face darkened. "What has he done? Has he been bothering you? Did he dare to make advances?"

"No! Not advances. I could deal with that. It's worse, much worse. He—he threatened to tell George! I had to pay him to keep him quiet. And now he wants more, and I don't know what to do! I gave him everything I had. I'd have to sell my jewels, and I can't do that. George gave me most of them, and the rest were Mother's. I can't give up any of them!"

"He's extorting money from you?" Simon looked thunderous. "That bloody bastard! I'll kill him!" He turned and started for the door.

"Simon! Wait!" Venetia shrieked, throwing herself after him and grabbing his arm. "Don't. You can't kill him."

"All right, I won't," Simon said impatiently. "He's not worth it. But I'll by God put a stop to his taking money from you."

"How? Simon, I don't want a scandal. George can't know about it! And I don't want you hurt."

"Don't worry about my getting hurt," Simon retorted scornfully. "That worm couldn't hurt me. He hasn't the nerve. He remembers what happened last time, and, believe me, he won't want that experience repeated."

"But he would tell George!"

"He is not going to reveal what happened between you. There is no benefit to him in that. You wouldn't pay him again, and odds are George would thrash him."

"But George would hate me!" Venetia wailed. "I can't risk it!"

"I doubt it. The man has been desperately in love with you for seven years."

"But he doesn't know the truth. If he did, he would hate me!"

"I'm telling you, George will not know. Reed would never risk telling him. He knows what I would do to him, and he's too much of a coward to face that. I don't think Reed would have followed through with telling George or anyone else. If everyone learned what he did to you, he would be just as ruined as you. No decent lady would let him in her house again. No, Reed has too much to lose. Once I've let him know I'm on to his game, he will stop threatening you. I promise. Just let me take care of it."

"Oh, Simon!" Venetia's face was suddenly radiant. She had felt as if her life were over, certain that she would be found out, that her husband would hate her, that she would be an outcast from the people she knew. Now Simon had cast her a lifeline. She had utter faith in him. He had saved her before from Reed; of course he would be able to do so again. "You're right. I should have told you earlier. I wasn't thinking. I was so scared…."

"Of course. But stop worrying now. I will take care of it—I'll do it this evening. He'll stay away from you. And if he doesn't, write to me at Deerfield. I will return."

Impulsively Venetia flung her arms around her brother's neck and hugged him. "You are the best brother. Absolutely."

Simon smiled and nipped her chin between his forefinger and thumb. "Then perhaps you can put in a good word for me with Charity. I fear she thinks I'm something of a tyrant."

"I'm sure not," Venetia protested, but Simon shook his head and bent to kiss her on the forehead.

"Don't worry," he assured her. "At least she promised to heed my advice—something she has not done in the past."

There was something in that fact that warmed him, though he wasn't sure what. It wasn't so much that Charity had bent to his wishes. Simon had no desire to see her turn into a milk-and-water miss who would not move a step without his permission; he enjoyed her spirit, and even found her defiance damnably arousing, somehow. No, what was important was that…that she had trusted him. Yes, that was it; she had not wanted to, but had agreed to because he had asked her to believe him, to trust that he had a good reason, even though he could not explain why.

The thought tempered his fury with Faraday Reed, and the act of searching for him gave Simon enough time to cool down, so that when he finally ran Faraday to ground at his club in Pall Mall, Simon did not commit the social solecism of pulling Reed out of his chair and pounding his fists into him, which was what he wanted to do. Instead, he strode purposefully through the mahogany-paneled rooms, looking grimly to left and right for his quarry, ignoring the curious glances thrown his way.

Finally he found him in one of the smoking rooms, standing and chatting with another man. Reed seemed to sense his presence, and turned. He stiffened when he saw Simon's set face, and glanced around a trifle nervously. But, reassured by the presence of other members not too far away, he faced Dure and stood waiting for him, arms folded negligently across his chest and a faint smile playing about his lips.

"My lord Dure." He greeted Simon with a sardonic bow. "How nice to see you again. We had so little chance to chat earlier this afternoon."

Simon, scowling, looked toward Reed's companion. "Herrington. Good to see you. I'm afraid you'll have to excuse Mr. Reed. He and I have a few things to discuss."

"Of course, of course," the other man said quickly, backing away. "Don't mind at all. Reed." He nodded his head toward Reed and was gone.

Reed looked after his retreating figure, then turned back to Simon, raising one eyebrow sardonically. "You certainly have a way with people. Are your manners as charming with your fiancée? No wonder the poor girl enjoys my company."

"My fiancée is none of your concern," Simon told him in a grating tone.

"Any beautiful, *bored* young lady is my concern." Faraday smiled suavely.

"Stay away from Charity."

Reed heaved a bored sigh. "Has no one ever told you how thoroughly tiresome you can be?"

Simon's smile was more a baring of teeth. "You will find me far worse than tiresome if you persist in dangling after my fiancée."

Reed's eyebrows rose to a peak of surprise. "My good fellow, *I* would not attempt to interfere with another man's marriage."

Simon grimaced. "I know you. I am well aware that you would welcome the chance to do me an ill turn. It doesn't matter. I am capable of taking care of myself. But I will not allow you to harm my wife in any way."

"I wouldn't dream of it." Faraday pressed his hand to his chest in an exaggerated way, opening his eyes wide, but his wolfish grin belied the innocent look. "How could I possibly hurt such a…delightful young woman?"

"I think there is very little of which you are not capable. However, I trust that your instincts for self-preservation will keep you from indulging in this particular bit of spite."

"Or what?" Reed asked languidly. "Will you challenge me to a duel over your fiancée?" Reed tsk-tsked mockingly. "Such a scandal would hardly do the girl any good."

"I wouldn't lower myself to duel with a worm like you," Simon returned contemptuously. "A whip on your backside would be more appropriate, I think."

A flush stained Reed's cheeks, and his hands clenched at the insult. Simon waited, ready, balanced lightly on his feet, his hands curving into fists. But Reed relaxed his stance into its former languid, rather insolent grace and forced a smile onto his face.

"No," he said swiftly. "Do not think that I will rise to your bait. There are always other means of dealing with you, Dure."

"Yes, I know your instincts run more to treachery and guile. That's what I came here to warn you about. My sister has told me about your extortion threats. You won't be receiving any more money that way."

"Indeed? You think she would rather face society's scorn?"

"She won't face anyone's scorn. I know you won't do it. You would be as ruined socially as she would. None of those silly matrons whom you've so charmed would let you near their houses again. Moreover, I'm sure you know that neither Lord Ashford nor I would take the slur to Venetia lightly. Lord Ashford may look placid, but I think you'd find him quite handy with his fists…or a gun. And if he did not finish you, you can be sure that I would be waiting. I think you've had enough of that experience."

Reed paled. His collar seemed suddenly far too tight for his neck; he wanted to run a nervous finger under it, but he managed to keep his hand by his side. He was aware that everyone in the room was staring at him and Dure; he could not let anyone see the fear that boiled inside him at Dure's words. Through lips that trembled slightly, he managed to say, "Neither of you would be willing to face the scandal."

"What scandal? If you had already ruined Venetia by spreading that rumor around, why would we hesitate? No, you will have hoisted yourself on your own petard if you reveal what happened eight years ago."

"You are being absurd." Reed strove for a lofty tone. "I never threatened Venetia. And I wouldn't stoop to taking money from her. She simply misunderstood a small jest I made."

"Oh. Of course." Simon's smile made it clear how little he believed Reed's face-saving statement. "Well, I suggest that you be a little less free with your jests." Simon turned and started to walk away, then swung back around. In a cold, crisp voice, he added, "Just keep in mind what I have told you…if you care for your skin."

Simon turned and left the room.

CHAPTER THIRTEEN

REMEMBERING HER PROMISE to Simon, Charity managed to avoid Faraday Reed the next day. It seemed cruel, when he had never done anything but be pleasant and helpful to her, and she felt very guilty about it. But she would not go back on a promise to Simon.

Two days later, Venetia arrived at Aunt Ermintrude's house at an unfashionably early hour and asked to see Charity.

Charity hurried downstairs and into the morning room, a more casual room where the ladies of the house often spent their time together when they did not have visitors. "Venetia! How pleasant to see you."

Venetia's smile was a trifle forced. "You are most kind to say so. I know it's horribly early in the day, and I apologize. But I had to make sure I saw you before you left to make calls or had visitors. It's important that I talk to you alone."

"Is something wrong?" Charity looked at the other woman closely. Venetia was pale, and there was an odd look in her dark green eyes, so like Simon's.

Venetia cast her an almost haunted look. "Yes, I— That is, no— Oh, I don't know where to begin. Charity, can we talk undisturbed here?"

Charity blinked, surprised. This sounded serious indeed.

Quickly she said, "I'm not sure. Mother or Aunt Ermintrude is apt to come in, particularly if they learn that you are here." She thought for a moment. "Let's go to the library. No one ever uses it, and it even has a lock on the door."

Venetia's grateful smile was more natural this time, though she continued to look pale and strained as Charity led her out of the morning room and down the hall to the library.

It was immediately apparent why no one made use of the room. The library was dark and gloomy, with meticulously arranged shelves of books and stiff, uncomfortable furniture. But Venetia seemed not to notice the surroundings. She sat down on the leather couch, then bounced back up and began to pace around the room, twisting her hands nervously. Charity, watching her, was more puzzled than ever by her behavior.

Charity turned the key in the lock with a decisive click and went to Venetia, saying, "What is it? You seem so… distracted."

"I— This is not easy for me. I would not have come here, except—well, you see, Simon has done so much for me. I had to at least do this much for him. But it's difficult. I knew the other day, when we saw him, that I should tell you, but it's difficult. I am afraid you will hate me for it."

Charity stared at her. "Venetia, what are you talking about? How could I hate you? You are a sweet, kind woman, and you've been a good friend to me."

"Not good enough. At first, you see, I didn't know that you knew Faraday Reed."

"Mr. Reed!" Charity's brows rose. This was the last

thing she would have expected Venetia to start talking about. "Well, yes, we met him at Lady Rotterham's ball." She hesitated. "Did Lord Dure ask you to discourage his calls?"

"No, Simon doesn't know I am here. He would never ask me to tell you this, any more than he would reveal it to you himself. As I said, at first I didn't realize that you even knew Mr. Reed, until that day I saw him here, when we had been shopping. I should have told you then, I know, but I hadn't the courage, and I hoped that Simon would discourage you from the association. Then Simon told me that Reed was still trying to fix his attention with you."

Charity chuckled. "Don't be silly, Venetia. Mr. Reed is a married man. He is not trying to win me. He has merely been a good friend to me. But I told Simon that I would not go riding with him again, or dance, or anything. He didn't need to tell you."

Charity could not suppress a sense of indignation that Simon had taken the problem to his sister. It was embarrassing to think that someone else knew all about their argument and that Simon had not trusted her to follow through on her promise.

One look at Charity's expressive face told Venetia what she was thinking, and she hastened to explain. "No, really, Simon did not ask me to come. He told me that you had said you would not see Reed again. But I knew I should have told the truth earlier. This situation has created a rift between you and Simon, and it is all my fault. You deserve to know the reason Simon insists on your not seeing Reed."

Venetia's face hardened, and she continued, "Faraday Reed is trying to win your affection. Believe me, his married state would not stop him from that. And he is doing it to revenge himself upon my brother."

"Surely you are mistaken," Charity said slowly. She found Venetia's words difficult to credit, and she could not understand how any of this could be Venetia's fault. "Lord Dure obviously detests Mr. Reed, but Mr. Reed has not said a word against him."

"That is because Faraday Reed has no honesty in him. He is playing a game with you, Charity. You are a pawn in some scheme of his, and I am certain that the object of that scheme is to hurt and disgrace Simon."

Venetia walked a few rapid paces away, then turned, her arms stiff, as if she were bracing herself. "Simon did not tell you why he hates Reed because it was not his story to tell. He would never betray me so, because he is a man of honor."

"Betray you!" Charity gasped. She felt suddenly weak in the knees, and the suspicion that she had been an awful fool began to creep through her.

"Yes, me. I was foolish when I was younger." Venetia's pale cheeks suddenly flamed with color, and she looked away. "Faraday Reed courted me. Simon did not like him, and he warned me not to trust the man. He sensed what a serpent Reed was. But I was too much in love to pay heed to him or to see the signs of wickedness that Simon saw in Reed. Reed wanted to marry me, but my grandfather would not consent. Reed had no money, you see, and Grandpapa and Simon were convinced he was a fortune hunter. They were right, but I wouldn't believe them. I was furious and heartbroken. I said terrible things to Grandpapa and Simon, things I still regret."

She pressed her hands to her flushed cheeks. Charity

went to her saying quickly, "You needn't tell me any more. This is too difficult for you. I believe you. I will no longer speak to Mr. Reed, and I will tell Mother that we must refuse to receive him."

"No." Venetia dropped her hands and looked straight at Charity, her gaze firm. "I have to tell you all. You must understand how wicked the man is, so that you will not be inclined to believe any lie he might tell you. So that you will understand exactly how deep his hatred of Simon is, how far he will go to revenge himself upon Simon."

She drew a shaky breath and continued. "Reed begged me to run away with him, to elope. He said my grandfather would have to accept our marriage. I was so angry with Grandpapa, so foolishly in love with Faraday, that I agreed. It was only after I had slipped out of the house and gotten in the carriage with him that I began to realize what an awful thing I had done. How I would bring disgrace upon my family. I began to regret my hasty decision. It had all seemed terribly romantic when I thought about doing it, but in reality it was rather—sordid." Venetia sighed. "Anyway, I told Faraday that I wanted to turn back, that I could not marry him this way. He tried to persuade me not to change my mind, but by that time I was insistent. He said that when we stopped at the next inn to change horses, we would turn around and go back. But when we stopped, he ordered a private room for us to eat a little dinner. And he…"

Venetia's voice dropped lower, and she turned her face aside. "He tried to seduce. When I would not do what he wanted, he—forced me."

Charity gasped, horror-stricken. "Oh, Venetia, no! I am so sorry! What a horrible thing!"

Impulsively she reached out and took Venetia's hand, squeezing it.

Venetia smiled weakly and pressed her hand. "Thank you. You are such a sweet girl. I imagine most people would have been shocked at my improper behavior and said that it was only what I deserved."

"No, surely not. Why, how could you have known?"

"Not everyone has your tender heart. I realized at last what my grandfather and Simon had tried to tell me from the start, that he had no interest in me, only in getting my money. He intended to take me to the town's border and marry me. He told me that I had no choice now that I…that he… Anyway, I don't know what I would have done. Then Simon came into the inn. He had followed us as soon as he found out what had happened, and he rescued me."

Charity clasped her hands together, her eyes shining. "Thank heaven Simon was able to find you."

"Yes. I felt as if God had answered my prayers. Simon was furious. He started hitting Reed, and I honestly don't know what he would have done if the innkeeper hadn't pulled him off. Simon broke Faraday's nose and injured him rather badly, I think. It was weeks before Faraday dared to show his face in town again because of the bruises. Simon didn't want to call Reed out, because everyone would have realized that there was some sort of scandal involving me, and it would have hurt my name. Besides, he told me, Reed was clearly not a gentleman. But Simon told Reed that if ever word got out of what had happened that night with me, Simon would personally see to it that Reed was ruined in society. Of course, Reed really could not tell, anyway, as it would have blackened his reputation, too, and ruined his chances of finding some other wealthy wife."

"No wonder Simon was furious with me when he saw me talking to Mr. Reed!" Blood rose in Charity's face as she thought of how wrong and naive she had been about Faraday Reed. "This is awful! Why didn't I believe Simon? I should have known he wouldn't be unreasonable. I've made a terrible mess of it. He must be furious with me for the way I've acted, the things I've said to him. I thought he was just being dogmatic and unreasonable, you see. Do you think Simon will ever forgive me?"

"Of course." Venetia smiled warmly. "I think my brother would forgive you many things, far worse than that. I have never seen him so smitten."

"Do you really think so?" Charity could not help but remember Dure's cold, calculating reasons for marrying, and his lack of concern over whether it was her or her sister. But, on the other hand, the kisses they shared had been anything but cold and indifferent; surely there was no calculation or reasonableness in his eager caresses. Could his sister be right? Was Simon coming to care for her as more than simply an "appropriate" wife?

"But of course, my dear! That is why I had to tell you, even though I have never told anyone else about what happened that night, not even George. I could not let Faraday Reed come between you and Simon. I could not let him worm his way into your confidence and use you to hurt Simon."

"It was terribly brave of you to tell me," Charity told her. "I'm sorry that you had to suffer through that ordeal again, even in recounting it."

"Well, 'tis over now and in the past." Venetia smiled brightly, though a shadow still lurked in her eyes. "No one ever learned of it. Once Reed was gone, I was able to see what a wonderful person Lord Ashford was, and now I have a husband whom I love very much."

Charity looked thoughtful. "I don't understand. Why does Reed hate Simon so much? I would think it is Simon who has far more reason to seek revenge than Mr. Reed."

"Because Faraday Reed is an unfeeling monster who thinks only of himself!" Venetia blurted out bitterly. "He never cared for me in the slightest. He pursued me only because my grandfather was wealthy, and he knew I would someday inherit money, which he would have control over. He is a vain man, and Simon humiliated him by beating him so soundly. He lost me, and he had to scramble to find some other heiress to marry. He has been bitter and angry with Simon ever since. All those rumors about Simon over the years—I'm certain that Reed is at the bottom of them. I have no way of proving it, but I'm positive that he spreads gossip about Simon and stirs up whatever there is already. He is a wicked man."

Charity gaped at her. "How can he be so evil?"

Venetia shook her head. "I don't know. He simply is. I don't know how I could ever have been so deceived by him. But I promise you that he has not changed. I am certain he has been hovering around you because he hopes to win you from Simon, to publicly humiliate Simon with his conquest of you. The fact that he is married will not stop him from trying to seduce you."

"But how could he think that I would turn from Simon to him?" Charity asked, in such genuine puzzlement that Venetia laughed.

"Because he does not know you or Simon, obviously. He thinks that he can win over any woman. His conceit is tremendous. Besides—" Venetia shrugged "—if he could not, he would not be above using force."

Charity gasped.

"He did with me," Venetia reminded her.

Charity shook her head. "He is so deceitful. I never dreamed… He always seemed such a good friend. He never said a word against Simon, yet he was able to make him appear in the wrong. Why, the very way he pretended to have nothing against Simon made Simon's stance seem unreasonable. He told me that they had quarreled over a woman. He made it seem as if it had been about a woman of the night, which put me out of sorts with Simon. And all the time the woman was you, and Mr. Reed had been completely in the wrong!"

Suddenly Charity straightened, knowledge dawning on her face. "Those notes!"

"What notes?" Venetia asked, perplexed.

"Why didn't I see it before? It never occurred to me. Those notes that I've been getting about Simon must have come from Mr. Reed!"

"What are you talking about? What notes about Simon?"

Quickly Charity filled Venetia in on the malicious letters. "And every time I got one, Faraday Reed was close by. The first was at the Rotterhams' ball. He was there—he could easily have done it. The next time, a boy ran up to me in the park and gave it to me. I was there with Mr. Reed. No wonder the lad was able to find me. No doubt Reed told him exactly where we would be. The last time, he called on me shortly after I found the note amongst a vase of flowers. I've asked all the servants, and none would admit putting it there or seeing anyone else do so. But if it was Reed who asked, of course they would think it was all right, especially if he slipped a few coins to them. They'd assume it was a love letter. Then, when I questioned them and they saw something *was* wrong, of course they would have denied doing it."

"Where are these notes? Did you show them to Simon?"

"Of course not. I didn't want him to read such hateful things about himself. There was no one I could tell, really. I didn't want my parents to read them, either, for fear they might begin to doubt Simon. My sisters would have been scared silly. They would have told my mother and father and who knows who else."

Venetia smiled. "It was very kind and loving of you to try to protect Simon. But you should have shown them to him. He would have been able to alleviate your doubt."

"I didn't *doubt* Simon. But I didn't want him even to wonder if I did. It seemed far better not to tell him. And Reed was always there to talk to." She jutted out her jaw. "I can see how it must have been now. He sent me the first note, hoping it would frighten me into calling off the engagement. Then, when I didn't scare so easily, he made sure he was with me when I got the next note, so that he could try to plant seeds of doubt in my mind. Once he even suggested that perhaps the sender thought the things he said were true. When I didn't respond the way he hoped, he used the notes as a way to worm his way into my confidence. He pretended to be my friend, to believe in Simon's innocence, so that I would like him and would rely on him. Oh, he must have laughed up his sleeve when I asked him to help me find who had sent the notes!"

Bright red spots of color flamed in Charity's cheeks. "Ooooh! I'd like to get hold of that man right now! I'd let him know what I think about him. I'd point out how very far he was from winning my affections. The next time I see him, I should go up to him and denounce him for what he's done. The world ought to know what a scoundrel he is!"

Venetia's eyes widened in alarm. "Charity, you can't! I mean, it would create a scandal. You have no real proof who sent the notes."

"No. You're right. And I couldn't reveal what he did to you, of course." Charity sighed. "I suppose that I shall have to keep my mouth shut. I will try to be content with giving him the cut direct. I'll tell Mother never to receive him again. Don't worry, I shan't reveal what you've told me. Simply saying that the Earl of Dure wishes it will be enough to convince her."

Venetia smiled and reached over to take her hand. "Thank you so much."

"For what? I am the one who should thank you. You came and revealed such a personal, painful thing, merely to help me. I'm very grateful."

"I am grateful to you for not turning away from me when I told you what I had done."

"Turn away from you?" Charity exclaimed. "No! How could you think that?"

"There are many who would. Who would refuse to receive a woman with a taint such as mine."

"You were never tainted. It was Faraday Reed who was at fault, not you! It's no sin to be too trusting, too loving." Charity's eyes flashed. "The world would be a far better place if more people were like you. It is Reed who should be shunned."

Tears formed in Venetia's eyes, and she blinked them away hastily. "Thank you. I am so glad that you are marrying Simon. I know you will make him happy." Impulsively, she leaned over and gave Charity a hug.

Charity squeezed her back. "I hope so. I want to."

"You will. I know it." Venetia smiled at her.

A few minutes later she took her leave. Charity sat back in her chair, trying to absorb all the things that Venetia had told her. Anger burned within her at what Reed had done to Venetia and what he had tried to do to her and Simon. She smiled grimly to herself. Faraday Reed might think she was a silly, naive country girl who could be easily twisted to his purpose. But he would soon find out that he had gotten hold of an entirely different sort of person.

Charity avoided Reed ostentatiously after that. She turned away whenever he approached her, and if he joined a group with whom she was in conversation, she would immediately leave the group. As soon as she told her mother that Lord Dure did not want her to associate with Reed, Caroline instructed the servants that the family was no longer "at home" to Reed.

Now, when she saw Reed across the room at a party, she could see that his smile was a little too smooth, that it touched his mouth but did not really reach his eyes. His courtesy appeared to her now to be blatant and false, not true coin. And when she compared his bland good looks and polished manner to Simon's rugged masculinity, it was laughable that Reed could ever have thought that he might be able to seduce her away from Simon.

Simon was what occupied her thoughts these days. Reed was a bit of a nuisance, trying to talk to her or dance with her at parties, "accidentally" running into her at a play, or calling on her, even though it was obvious that he was not being received in her home, but that was all he was. Simon, on the other hand, plagued her by his very absence.

All the parties—the dinners, the balls, the soirees—were deadly dull without him there. She received one rather stiff and impersonal letter from him. It was good that the missive was impersonal, she knew, since her mother insisted on reading her correspondence from him, but she couldn't help wishing that there had been more of his heart in the brief letter. She mailed a return to him, but it was equally stiff. She could not write about how much she missed him and wished him to return; she was afraid that would appear overbold from a woman he was marrying for purely "practical" reasons. She had, after all, told him that she would not cling or interfere with his activities, but would merrily go her own way. At the time, that promise had been easy. But the longer she knew Dure, the more she realized that she really did not want such a distant relationship with him. She wanted much more…but despite what Venetia had said, she was afraid that Dure did not feel the same way.

Two weeks after Dure left, Charity attended the opera with Aunt Ermintrude and one of her elderly swains. Her mother and sisters had gone to a ball, but she had chosen to go with Aunt Ermintrude instead. It depressed her spirits to stand and watch the dancing without being able to sweep out onto the floor in Simon's arms herself. Dancing with other gentlemen was little better. Charity was not particularly fond of the opera—in truth, she found it boring—but it seemed better than being bored and lonely at a glittering party. Besides, Aunt Ermintrude's beau, a retired military gentleman with a sweeping white mustache, occupied nearly all her great-aunt's time, leaving Charity free to pursue her own thoughts.

The opera had been going on for almost an hour when there was a soft tap at the door. Charity glanced at Aunt Ermintrude and General Popham, neither of whom had even heard it. Aunt Ermintrude was busy peering through her opera glasses at a box some distance from them, making whispered comments under her breath to her swain. He was leaning close to Aunt Ermintrude and whispering back, seizing the opportunity to nuzzle her ear. Aunt Ermintrude was giggling coquettishly and tapping him now and again on his arm with her fan. This sort of byplay had been going on between the two of them almost from the first notes of the opera, and Charity suspected that Aunt Ermintrude was surveying the crowd more for a reason to whisper back and forth with the general than out of any real curiosity.

Since neither of them even turned at the knock, Charity slipped quietly out of her chair and eased open the door. The Earl of Dure stood outside.

CHAPTER FOURTEEN

CHARITY STARTED TO SHRIEK, and had to clap a hand over her mouth to hold back the noise, Without thinking, she threw the door open and flung herself against Dure's chest. His arms closed automatically around her, and he lowered his face to her hair, breathing in her scent, luxuriating in her softness.

"Simon!" she whispered. "Oh, Simon, you're home! I'm so glad."

"Did you miss me?" he asked, in a less-than-steady voice.

"Yes, oh, yes, I did. It has been the most awful two weeks." She raised her glowing face to his, and Simon could not keep from kissing her.

It was glorious to feel Simon's warm lips on hers again, and Charity squeezed herself against him, delighting in his scent and touch and taste once more. He kissed her all over her face and neck—short, breathless kisses, as if he could not get enough of tasting her.

Finally common sense prevailed, and Simon realized what a spectacle they would present to anyone who happened along the corridor. Their embrace was decidedly improper, especially in a public place like an opera house, and kissing was absolutely out of the question. Reluctantly he loosed his hold and stepped back. Still, his hands remained clasped around hers; he could not completely break contact with her.

They stood for a moment, simply gazing at one another, smiling foolishly. Then Charity asked, "Why did you return early?"

"I found it made little difference whether I was there or here. I still kept thinking about you," he replied huskily. "I still wanted you all the time. Only there, I didn't have the pleasure of actually seeing you or hearing your voice. I decided it would be better to be tied up in knots, wanting you, here. At least I wouldn't be bored, as well."

His words were exactly what Charity had wished to hear. A smile blazed across her face. Simon brought her hand up to his mouth, laying a whisper of a kiss upon her skin.

He wanted to do much more. The past two weeks had been worse than his words had been able to express. He had found himself bored and lonely and missing Charity in a way he had never missed anyone. He realized how much she had brightened his life, how much each day had been laid around seeing her. Being away from her had only made him hunger more for her, not the opposite, as he had hoped.

It was not that he loved her, he told himself; it was just that he desired her, that he found her amusing, and that life with her promised to be entertaining and fun. She took the gloom away, her sunny spirit creeping into the shadows of death and pain and lost love that lay around him. He wanted to possess her, to make her his wife and take her to his bed. There were times when it seemed that his entire being ached to sink into her and find release. Waiting to marry her was torture, but not seeing her at all was even worse.

Charity pulled him into the opera box, and they sat down at the back of it. Aunt Ermintrude and Popham noticed their arrival no more than they had Charity's departure a few minutes earlier. Simon took Charity's hand, and they talked softly, their heads together.

"When did you get back?" Charity asked, more interested in the warmth of his hand around hers and in the closeness of his face than in his answer.

"Not long ago. I dressed and went to your house as soon as I arrived. The footman told me where you were, so I came straight here."

Charity smiled, pleased by the indication of his eagerness to see her. "And what of Lucky? Did he enjoy his new home?"

"Oh, yes. There was so much more sport for him there, you see—chasing the sheep and nipping at the cows' heels, jumping into the pond and coming back to shake off the muddy water on Mrs. Channing's waxed floors."

Charity chuckled. "I'm glad he's happy there."

Simon shifted in his seat, then cleared his throat, and said finally, "Well, actually…he isn't there. I brought him home with me."

"I knew you wouldn't have the heart to abandon him!" Charity exclaimed, squeezing his hand. The glow in the gaze she turned on him was enough to make his pulse speed up.

"Then you know more about me than I do," he said, forcing a casual tone. "I had every intention of leaving him…until today. He seemed to sense that I was going, and he was on my heels the whole time. When I got in the carriage and started down the drive, he ran after us the whole way, howling. I kept taking him back, but he kept following, until finally I let him up in the carriage with me." He sighed. "My town staff was quite downcast to see him with me when I returned. I could give no excuse except that I suffered from a temporary brain fever."

Charity giggled.

"And what have you done, Miss Emerson, while I have been tussling with the gravely misnamed Lucky?"

"Why, he's very well named," Charity retorted indignantly. "What could be luckier for a poor stray dog than to become the favored pet of a peer of the realm?"

"Perhaps I should have said it was the dog's keeper who was the victim of the misnomer."

"Well, you are luckier than I. I have been doing very little except attending the most boring of parties." She hesitated, then added softly, "I have not seen Mr. Reed since you left."

Simon gave her a searching look; then a faint smile touched his face, and he said, "Thank you."

"I was avoiding him, anyway, but then Venetia told me about…what happened to her."

His eyebrows vaulted upward. "She did?"

"Yes. She was worried that I might not do as you asked. She didn't want anything bad to happen between us because of her. It made me realize a lot of things. I—I have not been completely open with you about some things."

Dure's hand stiffened on hers, and his eyes narrowed. "What do you mean?" His voice was suddenly cool and remote.

"Please don't be angry." Quickly Charity told him about the notes she had received implicating him in murder and warning her against him. She explained how Reed had always been there and had offered his help. "I'm sorry," she finished. "I know I was awfully naive. It would probably have been obvious to you that it was Reed sending the notes."

"Yes. That swine." Simon's eyes glittered dangerously in the dim light of the opera box. "I should have done more than just threaten him the other day."

"You threatened him?"

"Yes. He's been trying to blackmail Venetia about what happened between them."

Charity gaped. "You mean, he would dare to extort money from her because of the way *he* wronged *her?* What unmitigated gall!"

"Faraday Reed is certainly not lacking in that. I'd like to draw and quarter the rogue. Perhaps I should pay him another visit. He seems to think that he can do whatever he likes to me and mine."

"No, please, Simon. It would only create a scandal. Everyone would wonder why you had done it. Venetia is very afraid of any word getting out."

"I know. That's why I haven't done anything to him before now. It would start tongues wagging. Besides, everything he does is so underhanded and secretive that it's difficult to catch him doing anything. Someday he'll go too far, though, and I will have to get rid of him." He paused, then asked quietly, "Why did you not tell me when you got those notes?"

"I did not want to hurt you."

Simon stared at her blankly. Finally he said, "You mean, *you* were trying to protect *me?*"

"Yes!" Charity snapped. "Why does everyone find that so strange? I didn't want to see you hurt by what the notes said. I thought it would make you feel bad to know that someone was spreading such lies about you."

"And you are so sure they are lies?"

Charity shot him a disgusted look. "Of course I am. You would not have killed someone, let alone three people. If you were the type to kill, you would, after all, have done in Faraday Reed long ago."

A faint smile quirked up the corner of his mouth. "You are a loyal person. Feisty. Brave." Simon smoothed the back of his hand down her soft cheek. "I am not sure anyone has ever tried to protect me before. Certainly not a female. I feel…honored."

"Honored?"

"Yes. That you have chosen me to marry. That you have given such courage and loyalty to me. I'm not sure I am worthy of it."

"I'll be the judge of that." Charity smiled at him, and Simon wished they were somewhere else, so that he could kiss her properly. But even such a lax chaperone as Aunt Ermintrude would be shocked if he pulled Charity into his arms here. So he had to content himself with pressing her hand to his lips again, letting his mouth linger on her skin. He wondered how he would be able to get through the four months until he and Charity could wed without comment.

Charity glanced around the ballroom. She still could not see Dure anywhere. He had planned to be at the Bannerfield ball tonight, or so he had told her, but so far he had not arrived. Charity knew that it was unlike Simon to arrive at any party this early, but her eagerness to see him kept playing her false, making her feel as if hours had passed. It seemed as if it had been days since she had been with him at the opera.

The ballroom was hot and airless, despite the opened doors leading to the terrace, and Charity's feet ached already from the new slippers she had worn. And as if that weren't bad enough, Faraday Reed was at the party, and had been pursuing her from the moment that she and her family walked through the door. She had managed to elude him every time he came close, but it was wearying. She also worried what would happen if he came face-to-face with Simon, given the way Simon felt about him.

Charity sighed and looked longingly toward the terrace doors. It would be so nice to step outside and feel the cool evening air on her face, to be away from the noise and the crowd.

She glanced at her mother beside her. Caroline was deep in conversation with Mrs. Greenbridge, on the other side. The Greenbridge girl had got married two months ago, and Caroline was finding her mother a fountain of information and advice.

Charity edged away from them. She looked back at Caroline; she was still thoroughly enthralled by the subject of wedding gowns. She scanned the floor; no one was watching her. Quickly she walked toward the outer doors, skirting clumps of conversationalists and smilingly turning down an offer of a dance from one of her admirers. With a final surreptitious glance around her, she slipped out the door and onto the flagstone terrace.

She sighed with relief at the touch of fresh air on her face, and walked quickly away from the door, putting the noise of the crowd behind her. There was a couple on the terrace, also, talking in quiet tones beside the balustrade. They did not even glance in her direction. Charity moved quietly away from them and down the shallow steps, onto the garden pathway. There was a full moon out, and the garden was bathed in its light. Charity had little trouble finding her way along the path that wound between the carefully tended flowers and plants. There was a small fountain in the midst of one square of flowers, and a low stone bench sat at the edge of the walkway beside the flowers. Charity sank down onto the bench and closed her eyes, listening to the soothing music of the cascading water. She gave herself up to thinking about Simon, recalling his voice, his eyes, the strength of his arms around her.

She was aroused by the scrape of a heel on the path, and she glanced up, startled. A man was coming down the path toward her. With dismay, she recognized him as Faraday Reed.

Charity jumped to her feet. She glanced in the opposite direction. That way only led deeper into the garden, and Reed would, without doubt, catch up with her. So she turned and walked toward him, her head aristocratically high, and when she neared him, she started to sweep around him without a word.

Reed, however, obviously had other plans in mind. He stepped quickly in front of her to block her path. "Charity! You must speak to me!"

Charity looked at him with an icy gaze. "Pray, step out of my way, Mr. Reed. I wish to return to the house."

"Not until you have talked to me. Tell me what is wrong. Why have you been avoiding me the past two weeks? I thought I was your friend. I thought you trusted me."

"Unfortunately, so did I," Charity replied crisply. "Obviously, I was naive. Now, please, let me pass."

"No!" Reed said explosively, reaching out and grasping Charity's upper arms. "Not until you tell me the reason why you won't see me anymore. Why you refuse me admittance when I come to call and avoid me at every social gathering. Is it because of Dure? Did he tell you something about me? Did he lie to you, try to blacken my character?"

"No, he did not!" Charity snapped back, wrenching herself out of his grasp. She knew that a proper lady would not even talk to him, but his slur upon Simon's character was too much for her loyalty. "Lord Dure would not lie. He is not a blackguard like you! He did not say anything about you except to warn me against you. He would not betray a woman's honor even that much. It was Venetia who told me the truth. She told me what you had done to her, how you had deceived and betrayed her."

"Venetia!" Reed's brows drew together ominously, and the smooth, pleasing expression he usually wore changed into something truer and far worse. His face became heavy, and his mouth twisted with bitterness. He looked somehow darker and older, and his eyes were pools of hate and evil. "Damn her to hell. She thinks she can play me thus!"

"I would say that Venetia was hardly playing. No doubt you cannot realize how much it costs a woman to reveal such a thing about herself. She was most noble and brave, to come to me and explain why I should not be in your presence anymore. She told me, too, about how much you hate her brother for foiling your wicked schemes. She told me about your campaign of malicious gossip against Dure all these years. How you have spread lies and insinuations about his wife's and brother's deaths. I realize now, sir, that it was probably *you* who sent those notes to me."

At Reed's startled look, Charity let out a brief, humorless laugh. "Yes, I saw through it all. It was easy, once I knew what a cad you were. You hoped to ruin my faith in

Lord Dure with those notes, and when that didn't work, you made sure you were always there to offer false words of friendship. You hoped to use them to win my trust, and then somehow turn that against Dure. Well, I can tell you this—it would not have worked, even if I had not found out about you. I would not have mistrusted Lord Dure. Nor would I have done anything to dishonor him."

Reed's mouth thinned, and his eyes glittered. "You think not, Miss Purity? You were ripe and ready. It would not have been long before you were swooning in my arms."

Charity's dumbstruck look, and the amazed laugh that escaped her, spoke more truly than words could have about the ludicrousness of his beliefs. "You think that I would have fallen in love with you? That I would have betrayed Simon? My heavens, even when I thought you were my friend, I never had even a *twinge* of romantic feeling for you. How could I possibly be interested in you, when I am already engaged to a man like Simon?"

Her spontaneous words, her laugh, the expression on her face, were like sparks to tinder, and Reed exploded into rage. His face was suffused with blood, and his eyes were suddenly lit with the fires of hell. With a low, enraged noise, he grabbed her and jerked her to him. With one arm tightly around Charity, he plunged his other hand beneath the low-cut neckline of her evening dress, clamping it around her breast.

"You wouldn't dishonor him, eh?" he panted, his breath hot on her face. "We'll see about that. We'll see how much His Lordship wants you when he finds you've been breached already. When he learns that it was my seed that first found a home in you."

Charity was so startled that for a moment she could not

even speak or move. He bent and kissed her, his lips bruising
hers. His tongue pushed against her, urgently seeking
entrance. Disgust poured through Charity. His clasp, his
kiss, his hand upon her, were nothing like the fiery, seductive things that Simon had done with her. She felt violated
and dirty, just from his touch. She knew that she would be
damned before she let him do anything worse to her.

She began to struggle violently, twisting her head aside
and pushing against his chest with both her arms. He was
too strong for her, and he chuckled at the futility of her
struggles. Holding her still with one arm, he reached out
with the other hand and seized her hair, pulling her head
back and holding it immobilized.

Reed expected her to swoon or give way to panic then.
Most other gently reared young ladies would have. After
all, he had experience in the matter. But Charity was, as
she had told Lord Dure once, not well acquainted with fear.
Moreover, she had grown up playing with the neighboring boys, both the squire's sons and the groundskeeper's
boy. She had learned quickly enough how to fight a larger
and stronger opponent, as well as where to hurt a male
most.

She did not scream. The last thing she wanted was for
everyone in the house to come flooding out and catch her
struggling in Faraday Reed's embrace. It would cause a
scandal, even though it would be obvious she was unwilling; everyone would say she should not have gone out to
the garden alone. And she did not want to be responsible
for any further scandal attached to Dure. So calling for help
was something she would do only as a last resort. Instead,
she went on the attack.

First Charity stamped down hard with her narrow heel

on Reed's instep. He let out a high-pitched noise of pain and loosened his hold on her. Charity took advantage of that to bring her knee up hard between his legs. Unfortunately, her skirts and petticoats hampered the blow, but it was still hard enough to make him yelp and bend over to grab at the pained area. Charity pulled back her arm, doubled her fist and hit him hard in the nose. There was a satisfying smack, and blood spurted from his nose. Reed let loose an animal howl, staggering back from her. Charity turned, lifted her voluminous skirts, and took off at a run for the house.

There were two men smoking cigars on the terrace who looked at her curiously as she flew up the steps, showing more ankle than was proper.

"I say," one of them said, "what was that noise?"

Charity shook her head and hurried past them, patting her hair and smoothing down her skirts. She didn't want to arouse comment and speculation with an untidy appearance, any more than she had wanted to scream and bring everyone onto the scene. She went through the doors at a quick pace, looking for her mother or sisters. Instead her eye fell on a dark man who was standing on the opposite side of the ballroom, scanning the crowd in much the same way she was.

"Simon!" Relief and happiness flashed through Charity, and she started toward him.

Dure's eyes fell on her as she hurried through the crowd toward him, unabashed happiness on her face, and the harsh lines of his own face softened. His chest seemed suddenly full and warm. He moved toward her, extending his hands to take hers. But instead, she threw herself against his chest and clung to him.

"Charity?" Simon asked, amazed, bending his head down to hers. "My love, are you all right? Is something wrong?"

There was a murmur around them, a swift susurration of sound, and Simon raised his head, expecting to find everyone staring at his embrace with Charity. Instead he saw that most eyes were turned toward the doors leading onto the terrace, and he, too, looked in that direction. Faraday Reed was coming through the door. His clothes were twisted and mussed, and his hair was disordered. He held a handkerchief to his face as he walked gingerly into the room.

In an instant, Simon realized what had happened. "Did he attack you?" he asked Charity, his words clipped and charged with fury. "Did he dare lay a hand on you?"

"What? How did you know?" Charity stepped back, gaping at him in astonishment. Then she followed the direction of his gaze and saw Reed.

"I will kill the son of a bitch," Simon growled and started toward Reed determinedly.

"No! Simon, wait!" Charity pleaded, grabbing his arm and holding on. "Please, don't do anything rash. Nothing happened. I'm all right, really. Please."

But Simon paid her no heed, simply shook off her restraining hand and strode through the crowd toward Reed. When he was a few feet away, Reed saw Simon approaching and his eyes widened in alarm. He whirled to run back out of the house, but Simon was too quick. Leaping forward, he grabbed Reed's arm and spun him back around, then punched him squarely in the jaw.

CHAPTER FIFTEEN

REED STUMBLED BACKWARD and crashed ignominiously on his derriere on the floor. Simon took a step forward and seized him by the lapels, jerking him up.

"God damn you!" he snarled, hauling his arm back for another blow.

"No!" Charity shrieked, and threw herself on Simon's arm, holding on tightly with both her arms wrapped around his. "Simon, don't! This is a ball!"

"Damn it, Charity, let go. I'm going to thrash the blackguard."

"No," she pleaded earnestly, casting a despairing glance at the interested throng around them. "It doesn't matter. Nothing happened. I got away from him."

But her words only seemed to infuriate Simon more. His eyes flashed with an unholy fire, and he pulled away from Charity, launching himself at the dazed Reed.

"I'll kill you!" Simon roared, curses spilling from his mouth.

It took three men to haul him off Reed. Another man reached down and helped Reed to his feet. Blood streaked his face, no longer just from Charity's wound, and he swayed as he stood. Several women shrieked at the sight of his blood and began to fan themselves. One lady even managed an elegant swoon into the arms of the gentleman standing next to her. Charity paid them no attention. She was concentrating only on Simon.

"Please, Simon, it was nothing," she begged, curling her fingers into his coat and gazing up into his face. She had never seen this look on his face before; the blind rage was almost chilling.

"If he ever touches you again, I'll kill him," Simon said flatly, but reason was returning to his eyes. He looked down at Charity searchingly. "Are you all right? Did he hurt you?"

"No. No. I'm fine, really. You can see that." Charity tried to smile. "Please, Simon, could you just take me home?"

Simon drew a long breath, bringing himself back under control. "Of course. I'm sorry."

He straightened his coat and offered Charity his arm. "Shall we go, Miss Emerson? I find this is not the sort of party I expected."

A giggle of relief bubbled from Charity's mouth. "Quite right, my lord."

She put her hand in the crook of his arm, and they started across the room. The crowd fell away in front of them, everyone eyeing them with avid curiosity as they walked past. Charity was sure that all the tongues in society would be clacking tomorrow. The Bannerfields had gotten more notoriety from their soiree than they could have imagined.

Simon was stony-faced and silent as they walked out of the house and got into his carriage.

"Are you all right? Truly?" he asked, concerned, as he settled down on the seat across from her. He brushed a hand down her cheek. "I'll call that scoundrel out for this."

"No! Simon, promise me you won't." Charity grabbed his hand anxiously. Dueling had been outlawed for many years, and Charity had not heard of anyone participating in one for a long time. But the mood Simon was in, she was not sure that he would not challenge Reed to a duel.

"What?" He looked down at her with an offended expression. "You think I couldn't outshoot that worm?"

"No. Of course you could. But you could be thrown in jail for it, too."

"I think it would be worth it to get rid of Faraday Reed." His face darkened again, but then he shrugged. "Anyway, it won't come to that. I know Reed. A challenge would send him scurrying to the Continent as quickly as he could pack his bags."

"Oh. Good."

"What happened tonight? What did he do to you?"

"He followed me into the garden," Charity said with a sigh. "I know. Don't say it. I should have had more sense than to go wandering about the garden by myself. But I was bored and hot, and I was tired of trying to avoid Mr. Reed all evening. I thought if I went out, he wouldn't know where I was."

"But instead he saw you and followed you."

"Yes." She cast him a tentative glance. "I'm sorry. I know it was foolish of me."

Simon leaned closer to her, tenderly brushing a stray piece of hair back into place. "Charity, my dear, I'm not blaming you, so you needn't apologize. I just want to know exactly what he did."

"Not much, really. He wanted to know why I wouldn't see him, so I told him that I knew all about him and that I wouldn't have been interested in him, anyway— Honestly, that vainglorious nincompoop thought I would be over-come by passion for him! Then he grabbed me. He caught me off guard. I wasn't expecting him to attack like that, otherwise I would have sidestepped him. But he pulled me up tight, you see, and kissed me."

"How dare he!" Simon's eyes flashed with fury, and his hands clenched into fists. "I should have throttled him when I had the chance."

"It's all right," Charity assured him earnestly. "I took care of him. The shock immobilized me for an instant, you see, but then I came down on his foot, like this." Charity raised her skirt a little to demonstrate the hard jab she had made with her heel. "That distracted him enough that I was able to bring up my knee to, uh, well…strike him in an ex-ceedingly painful place."

Simon stared at Charity, astonishment superseding his fury. "Just when I think nothing I hear about you could astonish me, you manage to prove me wrong." A smile curved his lips as he relished the picture that Charity's words conveyed. "So you set the rogue to singing soprano. By God, I'd have loved to see that."

"Then I popped him."

"What?"

"In the nose," Charity added, and doubled up her fist to show him. "Like this." She frowned slightly. "I think I may have broken it. He bled quite a bit."

"You broke his nose!" Simon gaped at her for a moment, then burst into a roar of laughter. "Heaven help me, I'm marrying a pugilist."

Laughing, he pulled Charity into his lap and wrapped his arms around her. "You never cease to amaze me. *Broke the fellow's nose!* If that gets around, Reed will be the laughingstock of London. My thrashing couldn't begin to equal it."

He squeezed her tightly, resting his head against hers. "Ah, Charity, I think my life will never be boring with you around." He nuzzled her hair.

A little sigh escaped Charity as she snuggled closer to him. It was sweet to sit with his arms around her like this, enveloped in his warmth and scent.

"I'm glad you're home," she murmured.

"So am I." His hand came up to caress the side of her face, then trailed down her neck and onto her shoulder. His fingers moved lightly over her arm and back up, coming once more to caress her neck and face. "I wish I could marry you right now. Tomorrow. I don't like waiting."

"Neither do I," Charity confessed dreamily, entranced by the delicious sensations Simon's fingertips were stirring in her.

She looked up into his face. His eyes were heavy-lidded and his face was faintly flushed as he gazed down at Charity. His chest moved more rapidly against her. Charity reached up and lightly touched his cheek with her hand. His skin flamed beneath hers, and he turned to lay a kiss in the palm of her hand.

"You tempt me," he murmured huskily, and his hand moved down to her chest until it grazed the soft top of her breast above the low neckline of her gown.

Charity drew in a quick breath at the feel of his fingers on her bare skin, and her eyes fluttered closed. Simon gazed down at her raptly, and his hand curved around her breast. He bent and brushed his lips over the quivering flesh above her gown. Charity let out a low sound and sank her fingers into his hair.

Simon caressed her through her gown, his hand sliding down her waist and onto her abdomen, then back up to cup her breasts, and all the while his mouth left a trail of kisses across her chest. Charity could feel the tension rising in him as he stroked and kissed her until he could no longer be content with the partial pleasure of her body. He reached one hand inside her gown, shoving down the neckline and curving his hand around her breast, lifting it until it was free of her dress.

He swallowed hard, gazing at the soft white orb, with its dusky rose center. He bent and touched the nipple with his tongue, so that it hardened and pointed. Simon smiled and took the nipple into his mouth, lashing it with his warm, wet tongue, then gently circling it. Charity moaned, and the sound heightened Simon's arousal. His hand slid down to her skirt and crumpled it, pulling her skirt and petticoat up. He delved beneath it and found her leg.

Charity jumped a little bit, surprised by the touch, but his hand was warm and exciting, and she relaxed. Slowly his fingers slid up her leg, hot through the thin cloth of her pantalets, until he reached her hip. Charity trembled under his touch, excited and uncertain. She had never felt anything like this before, not even when he had kissed her so passionately beneath the stairs at his house. His mouth and hand caressed her intimately, yet so gently and sweetly that she felt giddy and lost, hardly sure whether to laugh and weep or cry out at the wild, shivery sensations he produced in her.

His fingers came around her leg and onto her abdomen, then down to the juncture of her thighs. Charity gasped, but she did not pull away. It seemed impossible that he would touch her there, and she knew that she should feel embarrassed. Yet she felt no shame, only a crazy exhilaration and a strange urge to press herself against his hand.

"Charity." Her name came from him on a deep, shuddering sigh. "Sweet Lord, but I want you." He buried his face in her neck. "I must stop."

"No…please…"

Simon groaned and straightened, pulling his hand away. "I have to. I've done far more than a gentleman should already. You are just so beautiful…. I'm sorry."

Charity smiled at him. "No. Don't apologize. I like what you did."

He simply looked at her for a moment, then squeezed her more tightly against him. "You are a jewel."

Charity giggled at the extravagance of the compliment. The carriage came to a halt at that moment. Simon sighed and reached over to twitch aside one corner of the window curtain.

"Damn. We are at your house."

Charity sighed and slid off his lap onto the seat beside him. Hastily she arranged her clothing and tried to smooth her hair into place so that she looked presentable enough to go into the house.

The coachman's voice came from outside. "It's Lady Bankwell's house, my lord."

"Yes, Botkins," Dure replied, a bit more irritably than he normally would have. "I realize that."

He opened the door and stepped out, then reached up to help Charity down. She took his arm, and they walked to the front door as formally as if moments before they had taken an unexceptional ride home. But Charity was grateful that it was dark, so that no one could see the flush on her face or the heightened sparkle of her eyes.

When the footman opened the door, Simon bowed over

her hand formally, but the extra squeeze he gave her fingertips hinted at deep feeling inside him. "Good night, my dear Miss Emerson. I trust you will sleep well."

"Good night, my lord," Charity replied with equal gravity. "I wish the same for you."

Simon's eyes danced as he looked at her. "That," he said meaningfully, "may take some time, I'm afraid."

Charity chuckled, understanding very well the meaning of his words. "I know. It will be the same for me. It is always thus after so much…excitement."

"Minx," he said under his breath, then turned and walked down the walkway to his carriage. Charity watched him go, then drifted dreamily up the stairs to her room. It would be some time before the rest of her family returned, and it was nice to have an ample amount of time to lie in her bed and dream about Simon.

The next day began well enough. Charity was in a sunny mood from the moment she woke up, still fizzing with happiness from Simon's kisses and caresses in the carriage the night before. She floated through breakfast and the morning, daydreaming about seeing Simon again that night. He had said that he would escort her and her sisters to Lady Symington's soiree.

Her mother insisted that they spend the entire afternoon making calls, as it had been several days since they had made any and there was a backlog of visits that had not been returned, so Charity accompanied her mother on the afternoon's tour of Mayfair.

Late in the afternoon they knocked at the elegant home of Caroline's cousin, Lady Atherton. She was the daughter of the current duke, Caroline's uncle, and a woman who was so aristocratic that even Charity's mother found her boring, though she made regular calls on her out of family duty. The most important thing, in Lady Atherton's estimation, was breeding, a subject on which she was wont to talk for hours. She knew the genealogies not only of her own family and their in-laws, but also of all the noble families who "really counted," which excluded anyone whose family title was not at least five generations old.

Caroline and Charity carried on a halting conversation with Lady Atherton and her companion, a fluttery gray-headed woman whose job in life was to agree with Her Ladyship, and Marian Bellancamp, a shrewd woman, whose husband John was a power in Parliament. A few minutes after they had settled down and started exchanging vague pleasantries, Araminta Bishop came calling on Lady Atherton, too. She bustled in, her cheeks flushed and her eyes sparkling with excitement. When she saw that Charity and her mother were there, her eyes widened appreciatively. She was an inveterate gossip, and it was obvious that she was glad to have a larger audience than she had anticipated.

"Sit down, Araminta," Lady Atherton said in her haughty way. "How are you today?"

"I'm doing excellently, my lady. It's very kind of you to inquire."

Lady Atherton gave a regal nod of agreement. Mrs. Bishop went around the group, greeting everyone, then paused for a moment, letting the drama of the moment build.

"Well, come, Araminta, tell us. It's clear you are bursting to say something."

"Oh, my lady, I've just heard the most dreadful news.

It's hard to believe, but Deidre Cardingham told me, and I know she would never lie….." She paused dramatically, and the others found themselves leaning forward a little, waiting for her news.

"Faraday Reed is dead."

The reaction was everything she could have hoped for. Everyone stared at her, struck dumb.

Mrs. Bishop nodded firmly, as if someone had disputed her words. "It's true. His manservant found him this morning, sprawled on his study floor."

"But I just saw him last night," Mrs. Bellancamp said, as if that would somehow prove that he could not be dead. "He looked fine then."

"It wasn't a *natural* death," Mrs. Bishop continued portentously. "He was murdered."

"Murdered!" Caroline exclaimed, astounded. Lady Atherton and the other women simply stared, mouths open.

Charity's face went as white as flour, and her stomach felt suddenly hot and sick. She thought of the pummeling that Simon had administered to the man. *Had Simon, in his fury, hit Reed so hard that he later died of it?*

"How? What—what happened?" Charity asked.

"He was shot. Right between the eyes."

"Goodness," Lady Atherton said inadequately. "Was it a thief?"

"No one knows, my lady." Mrs. Bishop glanced significantly toward Charity and her mother. "But he did have enemies. Everyone knows that."

"Are you suggesting that *I* shot him?" Charity blurted out.

"Oh, no, Miss Emerson…" Mrs. Bishop began, but Lady Atherton interrupted her.

"Of course not, Charity, don't be silly. Why, you're a Stanhope."

"Yes indeed," the gray-haired companion said. "The Stanhopes would never—"

"I heard," Mrs. Bishop continued slyly, "that Lord Dure and Mr. Reed had a terrible fight last night."

Charity's face hardened, and she leaned forward. "Lord Dure was defending my honor. Mr. Reed had acted in a way not at all befitting a gentleman."

"Oh, my," Caroline said, looking paler and less in command of herself than Charity had ever seen her. "Oh, my."

"Oh, my, indeed," Lady Atherton agreed, her nose wrinkling as if she had smelled something bad. "It would be a scandal of the highest order."

"The highest order," the companion repeated, shaking her head.

"No Stanhope could be aligned with a—"

"Simon did *not* do it!" Charity jumped to her feet, scowling at her mother's cousin.

"Charity! Please, rudeness is not called for. Apologize to Lady Atherton."

"She was implying that Simon—Lord Dure, I mean— killed Mr. Reed! I won't allow that. I don't care who it is!"

"I'm sorry, Cousin Beatrice," Caroline said, her voice strained. "I'm sure Charity doesn't mean to be rude. She is simply overset by this news."

"Indeed, we all are, I'm sure," Marian Bellancamp put in diplomatically.

"Simon would not have killed anyone, even Mr. Reed, who certainly deserved it if anyone did," Charity insisted. "Mother, surely you cannot think that he did!"

"No, of course not," Caroline replied, though her voice was less than firm. "I am sure that Lady Atherton did not mean that he did. After all, the Westports are a very good family. I believe the earldom dates from before the Wars of the Roses."

"Quite true." Lady Atherton seemed taken with that argument.

"Yes, my lady," the companion agreed, nodding vigorously. "A fine family. Not that they can compare to the Stanhopes, of course."

"Oh, Evie, do stop babbling," Lady Atherton snapped, fixing her companion with an icy stare."

"Yes, my lady. I'm so sorry. I do have a tendency…" She trailed off, returning her gaze to the knitting in her lap.

"But I heard that the fight between the earl and Mr. Reed was quite fierce," Mrs. Bishop said pointedly, innocent concern on her face.

Charity narrowed her eyes and started to speak, but her mother trod once on her foot, hard, and Charity closed her mouth. She knew what her mother was trying to get across to her: Araminta Bishop lived on gossip, and she was trying to get a response from Charity so that she would have more gossip to tell. Simon certainly did not need people to have anything else to say about him.

Caroline smiled in a condescending way at Mrs. Bishop. "I'm sure that what happened between the Earl of Dure and Mr. Reed had nothing to do with his death. No doubt it was a thief, as Lady Atherton suggested. Earls are usually not in the practice of going about shooting people." Her tone suggested that Mrs. Bishop would doubtless not realize this, since her own husband lacked a title. As Mrs. Bishop's cheeks began to flush, she went on smoothly, "And I'm sure that Mr. Reed had many enemies."

Mrs. Bishop forgot the previous slight and perked up at the carrot of more gossip. "Indeed?"

"Yes, I've heard many things about him since we came to London. At first I received him, as I didn't know. But then, well, I simply didn't feel right about letting him into the house with proper young unmarried ladies."

Mrs. Bishop goggled and opened her mouth to speak, but Caroline said quickly, "But, then, I'm sure you've heard all the stories about him."

Mrs. Bishop made a strange, gulping noise and closed her mouth. Charity could almost see her thoughts racing across her face. The woman wanted desperately to know what Caroline had heard about Reed, but she would be highly embarrassed to admit that she, who always knew all the latest gossip about everyone of importance, did not know the apparently scandalous tales about Faraday Reed.

Eventually her pride won, and she gave an airy wave of her hand, saying, "Oh, of course, of course. Still, he was always accepted everywhere."

Caroline shrugged, as if to say that she had no understanding of those who did not live by the same exacting moral code as she. "I am, I admit, very careful when it comes to my daughters' reputations."

Despite her shock and anger, Charity almost had to laugh at the neat way her mother had thwarted Mrs. Bishop.

Soon after, Caroline and Charity took their leave of Lady Atherton and the others. They said little as they walked home. Both were too stunned by Mrs. Bishop's news to be able to say much of anything. Charity found it hard to believe that Faraday Reed could actually be dead. She had never before been confronted with the death of someone she knew—or, at least, of someone she knew who was young. Someone with whom she had walked and talked and danced. It seemed impossible. In the few hours since she had seen him last night, he had ceased to exist. No matter how much she had come to dislike him or how angrily they had parted last night, she would not wish death on anyone, even him.

Of course, Charity dismissed out of hand the hints that it might be Dure who had killed him. It was absurd. Laughable. She was certain that no one would be foolish enough to believe that.

Their news set the rest of the household all atwitter. Elspeth collapsed into a faint, and Belinda and Horatia besieged them with questions, most of which Charity and her mother could not answer. Even the usually calm and well-mannered Serena was agog at the news.

When Simon arrived that evening to escort them to the soiree, Charity immediately hurried down the stairs to him, saying, "Oh, Simon, have you heard about the murder? Do you have any more news of it?"

Simon shrugged. "I know only what the fellow from Scotland Yard told me."

"Scotland Yard!" Charity gaped at his mention of the police force that had been formed in London a few years earlier. "You mean, they visited you? But why?"

"Why, to ask me questions, I presume. Several people had been so kind as to point out that Reed and I had quarreled last night."

"Surely they can't suspect you of doing it!"

"They seem to be able to," Simon answered dryly.

"No! He had many enemies—he's bound to have, a scoundrel like that."

"Unfortunately," Simon replied, "I imagine that few of them had a handkerchief embroidered with the Dure crest."

CHAPTER SIXTEEN

CHARITY STARED at her fiancé, momentarily bereft of the power of speech.

Finally she said faintly, "What do you mean?"

"They found one of my handkerchiefs on the floor beside his body."

"You can't be serious. This is a jest, surely."

"I wish it were."

Charity raised a hand to her forehead. The world was spinning around her. "But how? How could one of your handkerchiefs be there?"

"Ah, Charity, you are a jewel." Simon took her hands and raised them to his lips. "Are you so sure of me as that?"

"Sure that you did not kill Faraday Reed?" Charity looked incredulous. "Of course I am. You would not kill anyone, even Faraday Reed. Why, if you weren't driven to kill him years ago over what he did to your sister, I can't imagine why you'd suddenly decide to kill him now."

"I did attack him last night, because he had tried to rape you. According to several who were there, I also threatened him, although I was so angry I'm afraid I don't remember precisely what I said."

"You may have, but it was the sort of threat one often

makes when he is angry. I've threatened Belinda with all sorts of horrid deaths, but I was never serious. Besides, anyone who knows you would realize that if you did kill a man, you would do it openly, in a rage, not cold-blood-edly shoot him hours later in his house. And you would never have been so stupid as to leave your own handker-chief there."

He smiled faintly. "Thank you, my dear. I only wish that the chap from Scotland Yard had your faith in me. He is of the opinion that, in my excitement, I probably paused to wipe the sweat from my brow with it, then accidentally dropped it as I stuffed it back in my pocket."

"He sounds like a ninny," Charity said stoutly. "And I'll be happy to tell him so, if he asks me anything about it." She frowned, then said. "Are they sure that it is your crest?"

"There's no question of it. They showed me the hand-kerchief. It's obviously mine."

"Then someone else put it there. Someone is deliber-ately trying to make it look as if you had done it."

"I'm afraid so."

"But why? Who would hate you so much?"

He cast her a wry look. "The only one I can think of is Faraday Reed." He sighed. "It may be that the killer doesn't hate me. He may be indifferent to me, or only dislike me a little. His main reason could be simply that I was a perfect person on whom to cast suspicion in order to hide his own guilt. Everyone knows that there has been bad blood between Reed and me for years, and after we fought last night…no doubt it seemed a gift from heaven."

"Oh. But how could they have had your handkerchief?"

Simon shook his head and glanced away. He could not keep his mind from straying, as it had done when the detective first told him, to the handkerchief he had lent Venetia a few weeks earlier, when she was crying and telling him about Reed's extorting money from her. He dismissed the thought guiltily. There was no way Venetia could kill anyone, even Reed, and even if she did, she would never cast the blame on Simon.

"That is the question," he said. "No one would have one, unless they stole it out of my drawer."

Charity thought for a moment, then said, "Or else you might have visited them at one time, in the country, say, and accidentally left one of your handkerchiefs in a drawer. Or perhaps one could have fallen out of your pocket at a ball or the opera or, well, almost anywhere."

Simon frowned. "Perhaps. But it doesn't seem likely. Surely I would have noticed it falling out of my pocket, which is not precisely an easy thing. And my valet is quite punctilious about my clothes. I find it hard to believe that he would have forgotten to pack anything on a stay at someone else's house."

"Perhaps not, but it's possible. If a person was desperate enough to kill, he would have been desperate enough to enter your house and steal it—or bribe one of your servants to take it for him."

"I've already questioned the servants about it, and they know nothing."

"Nothing that they'll admit. Considering what was done with the kerchief, I doubt there would be many who would want to admit taking it. They know they would be let go immediately."

"You're right about that...." He paused, and sighed. "The thing is, I don't know how I could go about proving any of those things."

"Is the detective so convinced it is you?"

"I'm not sure. It's rather damning, but he doesn't want to jump off and accuse a peer of the realm of murdering a man, at least not without thoroughly convincing proof."

"I don't see how he could obtain that. He will stop looking in your direction soon, I'm sure. There's bound to be a more likely suspect."

"I hope you're right." Simon rubbed his thumb over the back of her hand, looking down at it steadily. "The thing is, I'm afraid there will be a scandal anyway. People are certain to talk."

Charity shrugged. "For a while, no doubt. But I can't think anyone would seriously believe that you could have killed Reed. It will blow over soon."

But even Charity's cheerfully optimistic spirit was dampened by the party they attended that evening. When Charity walked in on his arm, Serena right behind them, a hush fell over the crowd. It seemed as if every person there turned to stare at them. There was a long silence, then a sudden rush of chatter, as everyone turned back and began to talk to each other.

Charity's fingers tightened on Simon's arm, but her smile never faltered as they advanced into the room. She greeted everyone she knew, and, though no one cut her or her sister, nearly everyone looked obliquely at Simon, curiosity and speculation in their expressions. There was no one brave enough to say anything to her face or to Simon's, but Charity heard the sibilant whispers that spread around her like an eddy of water wherever they walked.

"…shot through the head, by gad."

"…never got along…"

"Suspicious, if you ask me…"

"How can he dare to show his face?"

"Poor Charity Emerson."

"How will the Westports ever hold up their heads again?"

"…his handkerchief, monogrammed…"

"Reed always said he was a blackguard."

Charity realized, in some amazement, that society was already trying and condemning Simon for Reed's murder. Fury flamed up in her at their narrow-minded gossip. However, there was little she could do, as no one directly confronted her with the rumors. Beside her, Simon grew grimmer and tauter as the evening went along, and when he drove her and Serena back to their home, his goodbye was terse.

Over the course of the next few days, the gossip grew worse. Charity had hoped that it would die down, that people would realize that Simon could not have committed murder. But almost every caller, every person at any party, seemed determined to discuss the latest gossip with Charity and her family. Charity, infuriated, defended Simon at every turn, even to the point of one afternoon jumping up in the midst of tea with Emma Scogill, crashing her cup and saucer onto a low table and denouncing the woman's speculation that it would be only a matter of days before Lord Dure was arrested for murder.

"You have no idea what the truth is!" Charity cried, eyes blazing. "You repeat whatever you hear, embellishing it at every turn. One would think Faraday Reed was a saint and the Earl of Dure a monster, the way you people talk. But it was Faraday Reed who was a monster—and Lord Dure did not kill him!"

With that, she slammed out of the room and out of the house, striding home as fast as she could walk, leaving her mother staring after her in dismay.

Her mother upbraided Charity for her discourtesy, so Charity forced herself to sit, lips tightly closed, through the next day's callers. But it was a relief when a servant entered the room and told Charity that her father wished to see her. She moved quickly down the hall to the study, wondering if her father could possibly know how timely his intervention was. She rapped lightly upon the door and swept into the room. A delighted smile spread across her face when she saw that the Earl of Dure was in the room with her father.

"Si— I mean, Lord Dure. What a pleasant surprise."

Both her father and Simon were seated, Simon gazing moodily at the floor and her father seemingly entranced by the picture on the wall across from him. The two men stood at her entrance and turned. It was immediately clear from their stiff expressions that the visit had not been a pleasant one.

Charity faltered as she glanced from her father's grim face to Simon's expressionless one. She closed the door behind her and faced them, her hands clenched tightly together.

"What is it? Is something the matter?"

"Charity, my dear, please sit down," Lytton began, in a serious voice that was most uncharacteristic of him.

Charity edged over to the nearest chair and sat down in it, still looking uneasily from one man to the other. Her father took his seat behind his desk again, but Simon remained standing.

"Lord Dure has come to me on a matter of some importance—concerning you, of course, which is why I sent for you," her father went on. He looked away from Charity's clear, questioning gaze. "Dure, tell her."

Simon's face was blank, though an odd light burned in his eyes and his body was taut. He held his hands clasped tightly behind his back. "I have told your father that I release you from your obligation to me."

Charity stared at him, unable to take in his meaning. "What? My obligation?"

"I am releasing you from your pledge to me."

"To marry you?" Charity's eyes widened, and her face suddenly paled. "You mean…you are breaking our engagement?"

"Don't be a fool," Simon said roughly, then clamped his lips shut and turned away. "I am giving you the opportunity to do so. I will not hold you to your obligation."

"But I have no wish to break the engagement." Charity looked, puzzled, to her father. "Papa? What is happening? What does this mean?"

"Lord Dure is acting as a gentleman should," her father told her sadly. "There is now a scandal attached to his name. The only proper thing is to allow you to detach your name from his."

"Because of the murder?" Charity asked, understanding dawning on her. "You mean to say that he is calling off our engagement because people are whispering that he murdered Faraday Reed?"

Lytton nodded.

"What nonsense!" Charity bounced off her chair, her chest swelling with indignation. "I know he did not kill that… that…pig! Surely you cannot believe that he did, either, Papa!"

"No," her father answered quickly. "But His Lordship

is right—he is tainted now by the rumors. If you married him, you would be subject to the same whispers and innuendos, the same scandal. He does not want that. Neither do I."

"You can't mean that you accepted his offer!" Charity gasped, staring at her father. "That you allowed him to—"

Lytton nodded. "I have to think of you, my dear. It would not be good for you to start out a marriage this way, the prey of gossip, the cynosure of every eye, your good name dragged through the mud."

"But they will find the one who really did it, won't they? Everyone will see that they were wrong, that Simon didn't do it."

Simon shook his head. "They are likely never to know. They have evidence against me, so I doubt they'll look anywhere else. I told you that the Scotland Yard chap thought I did it."

"But that isn't evidence. How could they prove that it was you? They can't arrest you!"

"Perhaps not. But even if they don't arrest me, it won't stop the gossip. The whispers. Do you always want to have to face what happened the other night at the soiree? Every time you enter a room, hearing the voices stop, seeing the eyes all turn to you? And then, of course, the words of whatever 'kind' soul decides to inform you of the things everyone is saying about you. It isn't pleasant."

"I'm aware of that. But I pay no attention to it. That dreadful Emma Scogill was saying all sorts of things yesterday, but I gave her a sharp set-down. I can do the same with anyone else."

Simon shook his head, a faint smile touching his lips. "I have heard of it. You are like a terrier, Charity. You'd never weigh the size of an opponent before you waded in. I am sure that you would be my champion. You are much too loyal and fine not to be. But I will not ask it of you. What if I'm brought to trial? Think about it—going to court to see me standing in the dock, reading my name plastered all over the papers, hearing the criers calling out that your husband is a murderer? I won't allow you to endure that."

"*You* won't allow!" Charity glared at him, then at her father, planting her fists pugnaciously on her hips. "And *you* withdraw your approval for our marriage. Pardon me, but don't *I* have anything to say about the matter?"

"It is a matter between gentlemen," Dure said stiffly.

"Then perhaps you should have been engaged to marry my father, if it is a concern only for gentlemen!" Charity shot back.

"Charity, please! Lord Dure asked me for permission to marry you, and I gave it," Lytton said with unaccustomed firmness. "Now I am withdrawing it. We will send the announcement to the newspapers this week."

Charity stared at her father, stunned into silence. She could not remember when she had not been able to talk her easygoing father into anything. But now, when it was so important, he had turned intransigent.

She drew a breath and began to argue. "What about the dishonor to our name when I break my vow to marry someone? Isn't that a scandal? I thought Emersons never broke their word?"

"Everyone will understand. These are unusual circumstances."

"It's all right to break a vow when the circumstances are unusual? Pray tell me, what else excuses acting dishonorably?"

"Charity, you aren't thinking straight."

"I am! Don't you realize, doesn't either of you see, that it will look even worse for Simon if I break our engagement? Everyone will say, 'He must be guilty. The Emersons refuse to be associated with him. Even his fiancée thinks that he is guilty.' And I don't! I believe in him, and I want everyone to know it. I refuse to break my engagement! I want to marry him!"

A low, choked noise came from Simon. Charity looked at him. His face was twisted with pain. Seizing her advantage, she took a step closer to him.

"Is it that you don't want to marry me?" she asked softly. "Is this an easy way to excuse yourself from a marriage you've realized you no longer desire?"

"This is hardly easy…." Simon ground out the words.

"Then you still wish to marry me?"

"God, yes. More than ever."

"Then do so." Charity spread her arms out to the sides. "I am yours."

There was a moment of silence. Simon's chest rose and fell in deep breaths, and for a second Charity thought that his resolve would break and he would take her in his arms. But then he whirled around and walked rapidly away from her, to the window.

Charity gazed after him, tears filling her eyes. She wanted to burst into tears and run from the room, but she was not the sort to give up. She dashed the tears from her eyes with one hand and stiffened her spine.

She thought for a brief moment, then curled her lips into

a sneer and said, "So, like a coward, you're going to slink off into the night?"

Dure swung around. "I am not slinking off," he retorted through thinned lips.

"No, no, of course not," Lytton interjected anxiously. "Charity really! You mustn't say such things."

"Not even when they are the truth? What else should I call him but a coward? I am willing to stand up and fight for him, for our marriage. But Simon is not. He won't face his accusers with me. He will not even allow me to face them. I never thought I would see the day when Lord Dure broke his word."

"I am *not*—" Simon started toward her, his face blazing, but then he visibly pulled himself under control and continued more calmly. "I am not breaking my word to you. I would not. You should know me better than that."

"I thought I did," Charity responded in a clear, cool voice, her eyes meeting his steadily. "I did not think you were the sort to toy with a girl. To break her heart."

"Charity!" her father protested weakly. "Really, Lord Dure, I'm sorry. She's a trifle overset by all this."

"Lord Dure knows I do not overset easily." Charity lifted her chin in a challenging way, her eyes fixed on Simon's face. "He also knows that I see through this subterfuge. He has tired of me, and has seized the chance to be rid of me."

"Damn it, Charity, stop talking such drivel! You know that isn't true."

"How am I supposed to know that? I see only that you wish to be rid of me. That you are not man enough to marry me in the very teeth of scandal. I have more courage than you."

Dure's face was livid. Charity thought for a moment that he would explode into anger, and her heart lifted in anticipation. She had seen Simon's anger, and it did not frighten her. She hoped that if his fury came flooding out, his feelings and desire for her would come with it, overcoming his reasonable arguments.

But Dure clamped his jaw tight and took a step backward, looking away from her. "Emerson," he said tightly to her father, "pray leave us alone for a moment. I would like to speak to Charity in private."

Lytton cast an uncertain glance at the earl, then at Charity. Charity nodded at him reassuringly. "Go ahead, Papa. It's all right."

"I promise that I shall not harm her," Dure said wryly. "Much as I would like to wring her lovely neck."

"I don't know what Caroline would say…."

"Don't worry, Papa. After all, Lord Dure and I are engaged—at least for a few more moments, anyway. I don't think Mother would object."

Her father looked from one to the other of them once more, seeing similar expressions of stubbornness on both faces, and sighed. "Very well. I will be outside in the hall if you need me."

They watched as he left the room. As soon as the door closed behind him, Charity swung around to face Simon pugnaciously, hands on hips.

For a long moment Simon looked at her. Finally he said in a low voice, "Don't fight me on this, Charity. This is how it must be."

"Why?" Charity went swiftly to him, her hands reaching out for his. "It doesn't *have* to be."

"I will not have you dragged through the mud with me,"

he replied gruffly, clasping his hands behind his back as if to keep himself from reaching out for her. "I will not have you become the wife of an accused murderer."

"*You* will not have. *You* will not allow. What about me, and what I want?"

"I am thinking of you. Do you think this is what *I* want? If I thought only of myself, I would marry you, and damn all the rumors to hell."

"And that is what I would do. I fail to see the problem."

"Because you are so blindly willful! You do not realize what this would mean, what it would do to you. To our children. I cannot ask it of you."

"You are not asking. I am demanding," Charity pointed out.

"You have no idea what you're talking about. You have no idea of the consequences. You're still a child, and your father and I must consider what is best for you."

"You did not seem to think me so much a child a few weeks ago in the garden! When you kissed me and caressed me, you seemed willing enough to think of me as a woman."

"God," Simon groaned, running a hand back through his hair. "Must you remind of me every wrong I do? I should not have been so free with you."

"Yes, but you were, weren't you?" Charity saw a new opening, and was quick to take it. "You touched me in ways no gentleman would."

She moved around so that she was facing him, and looked him straight in the eye, compelling him to gaze back at her. "You kissed me."

His eyes dropped involuntarily to her mouth.

"You loosened my dress and slipped your hand inside."

Simon's eyes dropped lower, to her breasts, fire smoldering in their dark depths.

"You caressed me."

"Stop," Simon said roughly, and moved away. "I should not have acted as I did. I— You know that is why I went to the country."

"It was all right, I thought, because we were to be wed." She heaved a sigh. "But now…how can I ever marry, when another man has had such knowledge of me?"

Simon's eyes narrowed suspiciously. "Stop the playacting, Charity. I know that you are trying to wind me around your finger. God knows, you are usually able enough to do that. But not this time. The matter is too important. You will marry another man. It won't matter that I kissed you or touched you. It isn't as if it were something he will know. I did not bed you. Your chastity is intact."

There was a long moment of silence. Charity could think of no other argument to make, no way to twist or turn it so that Simon would change his mind. She felt suddenly hopeless, helpless, and her heart began to ache inside her chest.

"Then you are determined. You will not marry me."

"I cannot. Damn it, Charity, don't look at me like that! It is for your own good."

"That is always what people say when they do something to hurt you." Charity could feel the tears pressing, threatening to flood her eyes. She blinked them away. She would not let Simon see her cry. She raised her head, facing him with a fierce, unblinking gaze.

"I do not want to hurt you," Simon told her, his voice low and hoarse with emotion. "I am the one who will live in hell the rest of his life."

He turned on his heel and started away, but stopped halfway to the door. Swinging around abruptly, he strode back to her. He took her by the arms and pulled her to him, and his mouth came down to cover hers in a hard, hungry kiss.

Charity went up on tiptoe, kissing him back fiercely, holding on to him as if she could keep him that way. But, all too soon, he stepped back. When she started to move toward him, he gripped her arms and held her away from him.

"No. Goodbye, Charity."

"Please, Simon…"

"I have to. 'Tis the only way."

He swung away and walked out the door. Charity stood staring after him, scarcely able to believe what had just happened. She turned and dropped into the nearest chair, where, curling her knees up and wrapping her arms tightly around them, she bent her head and gave way to sobs.

CHAPTER SEVENTEEN

LYTTON EMERSON sidled into the room a few minutes later. Charity's sobs had subsided, and she looked up at her father, wiping her tears away. "How could you let him do that?" she asked accusingly.

Her father looked abashed as he came across the floor to her and patted her shoulder awkwardly. "There, there, Charity. It was the only way. You will realize that later."

"No, I won't," Charity cried out. "I love him!"

She and her father stared at each other; she was almost as startled as he. But as soon as the words were out of her mouth, she realized how true they were. She did love Simon. She had not set out to, had intended to have the kind of marriage he proposed—without love, both going their own ways. But somehow it had turned into something entirely different. In the past few weeks, she had fallen desperately, completely, in love with Simon. And now he had called off their wedding!

Charity stood up, determination flooding her soul. She loved Simon, and she was not going to let him push her away! He might not love her as she did him, but she knew that he wanted her, that only a few days ago he had been trying to convince her mother to move up the wedding date. She was certain that he had not decided to put her aside because he no longer wished to marry her. He was doing it out of a sense of honor; just as he had said, he was only trying to spare her humiliation and pain. But Charity was not about to let him do that.

The things she had tried this afternoon—reason, guilt, questioning his courage—had failed. She would simply have to find some other method that would work. She had schemed and fought for Serena's happiness; she wasn't about to do any less for her own.

Charity cast a glance at her father, who was still standing with his mouth agape, staring at her in dismay. She knew that Lytton would be no help. He agreed with Simon, and even though he would not want her to be unhappy, he would go along with what had been decided. Though her mother had not been included, Charity felt sure that she would agree with the decision, also. Otherwise, Lytton would never have made it all by himself. There was no one to whom she could turn for advice. Serena would be sympathetic, but she was never any good at schemes; she was too proper. No, Charity knew that it was up to her alone to change the situation.

"Charity," her father began, a trifle cautiously, "what are you thinking about?"

"Nothing," she replied distractedly. "I—I believe I shall go to my room now, if you will excuse me."

"Of course." She swept past him, already deep in thought. Lytton put out a hand, as if to stop her. "Charity…"

"Yes?" She stopped and looked at him.

His hand dropped, and he sighed. "Nothing. I'm sorry. I just want you to remember that I was thinking of you."

"I know, Papa. But *I* have to think of myself, too."

Charity hurried up the stairs to the room she shared with Serena and threw herself onto her bed to think. Her brain whirred uselessly, trying to come up with some way to win Simon over to her point of view. Reasoned argument would not work; he had made up his mind, and he was too stubborn to change it. Besides, she had learned that once a person was bent on doing "what was right" for someone else, there was no talking him out of it. Nor could she think of any way to trick him into it, although she did toy with one or two schemes that were far too complicated and fantastical ever to work. She didn't know what else she could try, besides trickery and reason; she couldn't very well *force* him to do it.

Charity sat bolt upright, her eyes widening, as the perfect plan popped into her head. She got up and began to pace the room, her mind furiously figuring out the scheme. Hope swelled in her breast. *It just might work!*

Others would say it was an insane plan. It made her earlier indiscretion in sneaking over to Dure's house and offering herself as a substitute for her sister seem almost normal and proper. Everyone in her family would be shocked to the core if she did it—and she could not imagine them not finding out. She would be risking everything on this one plan; if it did not work, she might well be ruined forever. But Charity had to do it; any risk was worth it, if it meant she might be able to marry Simon.

Determinedly she set about preparing herself for the evening. She rang for a bath and searched through her wardrobe for the perfect gown to wear tonight. Finally she decided on a rich pearly-white satin ballgown. The short puffed sleeves and low scooped neckline showed off her smooth, snowy white chest and shoulders to perfection, and the corset beneath it would ensure that her breasts were pushed up to swell alluringly above the neckline. The wide skirt, pulled back a little in front and draped in back, would reduce her waist to nothingness. She smiled as she thought of the expression in Simon's eyes when he saw her in it.

She bathed and washed her hair with delicately perfumed soap, then spent a long time before the fire, brushing it dry and curling it around her hand. Afterward, Serena came in, her blue eyes full of sympathy, and helped Charity put her hair up so that it fell in thick, long curls over one shoulder, as bright as burnished gold. She pinned a small clump of tiny white flowers behind her ear, right above the cluster of curls. Then Charity pulled on her prettiest undergarments and was helped into her dress by Serena, who helped Charity do up the myriad of small pearl buttons up the front.

Charity pinched her cheeks and pressed her lips together to put color back into her face, then twisted this way and that in front of the mirror, looking at herself from every possible angle.

"You look beautiful," Serena assured her. She leaned forward to hug her, careful not to muss Charity's hair or dress. "You are so brave to go to the ball tonight. I don't think I could do it."

"I have to," Charity replied, feeling guilty for deceiving her sister. She cast her eyes down and went on softly, "But I'm not sure that I *can* do it."

"I'm sorry." Serena stepped back and took Charity's hands comfortingly in hers. "I'll stay with you the whole time. I won't even dance."

Tears gathered in Charity's eyes, though more from

guilt at her sister's kindness, in contrast to her own lies, than from any sadness. She was too keyed up over what lay ahead to feel sorrow right now. "You are too good to me," she told Serena sincerely.

After that, time crept by. With each passing moment she grew more and more tense, so that by the time she and Serena went downstairs to join her mother and father, it was little more than the truth for her to claim that she had become too sick to go with them. Her family looked at her pale, taut face and believed her.

Caroline sighed and said, "Perhaps it would be better if you stayed here. Although you look so lovely in that gown, it seems a shame for no one to see you. You know, we have to start thinking of your future again."

"You're not—you're not going to tell anyone tonight, are you?" Charity asked in a suffocated voice.

"Of course not. There will be an announcement in a few days, of course, but we certainly don't plan to *talk* about it. I have had more than my share of vulgar questions about your life the last few days. Sometimes I cannot fathom what has happened to good breeding these days. One would think that it was all right to interrogate someone on the most personal details." She heaved a sigh, then said, "Well, run along upstairs, Charity, and lie down. I am sure you will feel better."

"Thank you, Mother."

"I shall stay with you," Serena offered impulsively. "Would you like company? We can have a nice cup of cocoa and talk."

Alarm flared in Charity, and she stammered out, "No! I mean…really, Serena, that's very kind of you. But I just want to go to bed and sleep. And I wouldn't want you to miss the ball. I've heard that the Countess of Ackland always puts on a splendid ball."

"Yes, she does. It's nonsensical for you to stay home, too, Serena," Caroline decreed. "Elspeth is already ensconced amid her remedies upstairs, and now Charity will not be going. You have to go. Besides, things are changed now that Charity is no longer engaged. You may not be able to throw your life away on a poverty-stricken cleric."

Serena paled at her mother's words. "Oh."

"Come along, Serena."

"Yes, Mama."

Serena cast a concerned glance back at Charity, then followed her parents out the door. Charity turned and went upstairs to her bedroom, where she hastily scribbled a note at the small secretary. Folding the note, she wrote Serena's name on the front and left it on the bed. Then she crept softly back down the stairs.

There was no sign of anyone about. The servants were no doubt in the housekeeper's parlor or the kitchen, since they assumed the whole family was out.

Charity threw on her evening cloak, pulling the hood forward to hide her face, and quietly walked out the front door. She started down the street, and in less than a block she spotted a hack and waved it down. The driver looked at her suspiciously, but Charity ignored his expression and climbed in, saying in a firm voice, "Dure House, please."

Simon poured another generous amount of brandy into the wide glass snifter. He raised it to his lips, breathing in its heady fumes. He hoped that this glass would do something to ease the empty ache inside him; the first one hadn't even touched it. It would be nice, he thought, to get so drunk that he could not remember anything about this day.

He took a gulp, letting the brandy roll like fire through his mouth and down his throat, thinking as he did so that it was a waste of good brandy. The cheapest gin would have done as well tonight. He slumped down in the seat behind his desk and raised the glass again.

There was the sound of sharp voices in the hall. Simon frowned and thought about going out to see what was going on, but apathy overwhelmed him. *Let Chaney deal with it.*

The door to his study swung open, and Simon looked up, scowling, ready to let loose some of his ill feeling on whatever hapless servant had disobeyed his orders not to be disturbed. The words froze on his lips.

Charity stood in the doorway. She wore a cloak over her dress, and its hood was up over her head, casting her face into shadows and giving it a haunting, mysterious look. Simon gaped, unable to believe his eyes.

"I'm sorry, my lord." Chaney appeared in the doorway behind her, wringing his hands in distress. "I told Miss Emerson that you were not to be disturbed…."

"He did," Charity agreed, stepping farther into the room and shoving back the concealing hood. "I take full responsibility."

She was so beautiful that it made Simon's heart squeeze in his chest. Her blue eyes were huge, and her skin glowed in the soft evening light. Her golden hair fell in a cluster of long, soft curls over one shoulder, adorned only by a small spray of flowers.

Simon rose to his feet, feeling strangely shaky. "It's all right, Chaney. I shall take care of the matter."

"Very well, my lord." Chaney bowed out of the room, closing the door after him.

For a long moment, Charity and Simon stood facing each other. Charity, whose anger and determination had propelled her through the afternoon and over to Simon's, now was suddenly awkward. Simon had removed his jacket and cravat, and the top two buttons of his shirt were undone, revealing his golden-brown skin and a patch of black, curling hair. She had never seen him so casually dressed; there was an intimacy to the scene, lit by only a single lamp, that made the breath catch in her throat.

"What are you doing here?" Simon asked curtly, bracing his fingers on the desktop. "You should not be here."

Charity raised her chin in a pugnacious gesture so familiar now to Simon that it made him tremble to reach out and take her in his arms.

"I will be where I choose," Charity told him haughtily. "You and my father seem to think that you have my life mapped out, but I have a surprise for you. *I* am the one who will decide what I do."

She began to pull off her supple kid gloves, and Simon said, his voice a mere rasp, "Don't. You aren't staying long enough. I am sending you back to your house immediately." He started around the desk toward her.

"Are you?" Charity quirked an eyebrow at him as she continued to strip off her gloves. He came toward her, one hand extended, his face set. Charity slapped her gloves into his palm as if he were a servant, then turned unconcernedly and walked away, untying her cloak as she went. "You might as well sit down, Simon. I am not going anywhere until I've finished what I came here to say."

"There is nothing to say." Simon clenched the gloves in his hand; they felt incredibly smooth and soft to his skin, and Charity's scent lingered on them. Heat flickered to life in his abdomen. *Hellfire and damnation! Why did the girl have to come here?*

Charity slid her cloak from her shoulders and turned to face Simon, revealing her shimmering white satin ball gown. Standing there before him, her snowy-white shoulders and the tops of her breasts exposed by the low neckline of the dress, she looked pure and beautiful, yet damnably tempting, as well. Even the fire of anger in her eyes as she faced him was arousing.

"I think there is," Charity replied, fixing him with her level gaze. "You see, you and my father may have agreed upon breaking our engagement, but I did not. I still intend to be your wife."

She started toward him, skirts swaying seductively. Simon's eyes were drawn involuntarily to the expanse of her bosom above the neckline of the dress; the soft flesh of her breasts jiggled with every step she took.

"Don't talk nonsense," he said, a trifle weakly. "Put your cloak and gloves back on, and I will drive you home."

"No," she said reasonably. "I am not going home."

"Stop it." He could barely force the words through his constricted throat. His mouth was dry, his skin searing. "Your reputation will be ruined if anyone discovers you visited my house at night."

"Yes, I know." Charity's smile was soft and beckoning. "That's why I'm not leaving."

She stopped only inches away from Simon. Her hands went to his chest and slid slowly up to his shoulders and around his neck. He could feel their warmth through his lawn shirt, traveling over his flesh and igniting a flame wherever they touched.

"Doubtless you made a mistake when you agreed to marry me instead of Serena," Charity said softly. "I believe I told you that I always get what I want. Now, I'm afraid, you are stuck with me."

She went up on tiptoe and brushed her mouth against his. Simon drew in a harsh breath. "Charity, stop it. You are playing with fire."

"I know," Charity replied huskily, and pressed her lips into the hollow of his throat.

A shudder ran through Simon, and he put his hands on either side of her face and tilted it up. He gazed down into her eyes for a moment, his eyes dark and heated, and then he bent his head and kissed her.

His mouth was like fire; his tongue probed deeply. He kissed her with hunger and need, as if time itself had stopped. He told himself that he would kiss her just once, so that he would have this memory to savor through the empty months ahead. But her mouth was so sweet to taste, her response so deliciously eager, that he could not pull away after only one kiss. His mouth took hers again and again, his tongue plundering the treasure there. His breath seared her skin.

Finally, with a low groan, Simon jerked away from her. "No! Sweet Lord, Charity, you are killing me. I would be the worst sort of rogue to take you now. I cannot. But neither can I stand much more of this. You must go."

Charity shook her head slowly, a sensual smile lingering on her lips. She had felt his hunger for her. She was sure now that he wanted her, and that fact gave her courage. She reached up and began to unpin her hair. The heavy mass of hair began to slip out of its moorings, curling and tumbling. Charity tossed the cluster of flowers aside and combed her fingers through her heavy curls.

Simon watched her silken hair twine around her fingers, sliding through them to fall caressingly over her shoulders. Desire rippled through him. He wanted to plunge his hands into the loose tresses, to feel their satiny fire against his skin, to bury his face in her hair and breathe in the sensual scent of her. His fingers moved involuntarily at his side, and he had to clench his hands to keep from reaching out to stroke her hair.

Charity shook back her hair, sending the waistlong mass rippling down her back. Then her fingers went to the top button of her dress. Trembling faintly, she pulled the tiny pearlescent button from its hole. Simon's eyes widened, and he drew in a breath sharply. Charity went on to the next button, and the next, carefully undoing each fastening until the dress parted and fell back, exposing still further the creamy mounds of her breasts, now covered only by a thin chemise.

Simon swallowed, unable to move, unable to speak. He could only gaze, enthralled, at her breasts, round and succulent, pressing against the cloth of her undergarment. A tiny lace frill topped the chemise, grazing the smooth white skin; the tops of her breasts swelled above it, inviting his touch. Below the lace, the large, dark circles of her nipples were visible. He could see their centers peaking as he looked at them. A long shudder ran through him as he thought of how they would respond to his touch. His lips. His tongue.

Air rasped through his throat. He felt as if he were on fire. "Charity," he whispered hoarsely. "Please…"

Charity's fingers paused on the buttons, already down to her waist. The bodice sagged, the little puffed sleeves looping around her elbows, the sides gaping open to reveal her entire upper torso, clad only in her chemise.

"What?" she asked softly. "You do not like it?"

He made a low noise of frustration. "Bloody hell, woman, you know that is not the reason. You are driving me mad."

Charity continued her steady assault on the buttons. "Then you should let me finish. Let me relieve your madness."

"No! Charity, this is insane. You have to stop. I will ruin you! And soon I will not be able to stop myself from doing it."

"I do not want you to stop." The dress fell from her with a swoosh, settling onto the floor at her feet, leaving her in only her petticoats.

CHAPTER EIGHTEEN

CHARITY REACHED for the ties at her waist. One by one she unfastened them, letting each petticoat fall onto the growing heap around her. She stood at last in her pantalets and chemise, blushing, but not covering herself before Simon's avid gaze.

Simon's eyes traveled slowly down her torso, then to her legs. It was the first time he had seen her legs, even covered as they were by cotton, and the blood pounded in his head. He knew that he was on the verge of losing control. He should leave, get out of the room; it was the only way he could keep himself from taking her. But he could not tear his eyes away from her. He could not make himself turn away.

Her hands went to the ties of her chemise. She tugged, and the little blue satin bow came undone. The cloth fell apart, almost to her nipples. Charity's fingers slipped beneath the ribbon and pulled the laces out, one at a time. With each tug the cloth gaped a little more, until finally the two sides were completely apart, showing a swath of white skin all the way down her torso. She reached up and took each side between her fingers. Simon's breath caught in anticipation.

Then she stopped and said huskily, "No, wait. You do it."

Simon shook his head, but even as he did so, he stepped toward her, as if pulled by a force greater than himself. Only inches away from her, he managed somehow to keep himself from reaching up and tearing off the flimsy chemise. Charity took his hands and brought them up to her stomach. The touch of her skin was electric. Simon felt the jolt all through him. She looked up into his face; he could see the dark, hazy passion in her eyes, in the fullness of her lips, the softness of her face. Her lips were parted slightly, and she breathed in fast, shallow spurts. Her cheeks were tinged with pink. He read all the signs of desire on her, and it made his loins tighten and ache.

Her hands were on his wrists now, and she guided his hands up under the chemise. The thin cotton slid across his forearms as she moved his hands slowly upward. He began to tremble. His fingers touched the undersides of her breasts, and every constraint that had held him broke. He groaned and shoved the chemise back. For a moment he stood, gazing at the firm globes of her breasts, crested by the tempting dark pink nipples. He cupped her breasts, squeezing the soft flesh, delighting in the look and feel of her.

"Beautiful," he murmured thickly, then bent and swept her up in his arms.

He carried her to the sofa and laid her down gently upon it. He knelt beside the couch and bent over her to take one nipple in his mouth. He circled the nipple with his tongue, feeling the delightful hardening. His hand covered her other breast, exploring its softness and the contrasting hard thrust of the nipple. He suckled harder, and Charity moaned and moved her hips, raising them up off the couch. The passionate noise shook him. He could no longer think, could only feel the desperate need surging through him.

Moisture flooded between Charity's legs, and she was embarrassed to know that Simon must be able to feel it, but he did not seem to mind, but only stroked and caressed her all the more. Everywhere he touched her, fire played across her body. Charity had come here for the sake of their marriage, but now she found desire taking over her body and shoving out all thought of anything else. She wanted him, needed him, in a way she did not quite understand. Her body moved involuntarily, her hips circling against the sofa. When he jerked down her pantalets in frustration, she did not even feel embarrassment; she only lifted her hips to help him and kicked the garment off over her feet, tumbling her slippers off with it.

Simon's fingers slid softly down the inside of her thigh and back up, then traced the crease between her thighs and hips, moving ever closer to the hot throbbing ache that lay at the center. Then, when Charity was moaning and writhing, he touched the slick satin folds, opening them to his questing fingers. She groaned deeply as he explored her, touching her in a way that she had never dreamed of. She gasped with surprise when his finger entered her. He began to stroke rhythmically, in time with the suckling of her breast, and the fire within her began to pulse harder and faster, filling her with longing. He found a little hard nub of flesh between the folds and stroked it, sending a shocking pleasure through Charity. She moaned and moved against him, urging him on.

Finally he straightened up and looked down at her, his eyes going from her moistened, reddened nipples down her slender torso and on to the curve of her hips. He watched his hand on her, between her legs, hearing the soft sighs and moans coming from Charity as she moved against his hand, lost in pleasure, and he had to bite hard on his lip to keep from disgracing himself right there. His heavy-lidded gaze moved farther down, to the stockings that still clung to her legs, held up by lacy white garters. The sight was almost unbearably exciting. He rolled the garter and stockings down each leg, pausing to plant kisses along the soft flesh of her inner thighs.

"Please, please…" Charity sighed, reaching back to grasp the arm of the sofa and arching her body up toward him.

She did not have to ask again. Simon tore out of his clothes, throwing them haphazardly on the floor. He had never before felt such driving need, such pulsing hunger. It was only with the greatest effort that he kept hold of some remnant of control, knowing that Charity was without experience and he must treat her gently, not take her in a hard, wild rush as he wanted to.

Charity's eyes widened as he stood and pulled off the last of his clothes, revealing the swollen shaft of his manhood. "Simon…"

"No, don't fret," he reassured her huskily, settling onto the couch above her.

And, indeed, the desire in her was too urgent for her to hold back, even for the pang of trepidation she had felt on seeing him. She wanted him; she ached for some unknown joy that her body told her he would bring to her. There was a strange emptiness inside her, a yearning for completion that made her open her legs to him when Simon moved between them. He slid his hand beneath her, lifting her hips a little, and then she felt his flesh probing at the very gates of her femininity.

Charity gasped, her eyes flying wide open. He bent and

kissed her, his mouth consuming her as, slowly, he entered her body. It was a strange and wonderful sensation, somehow exciting and scary and exactly what she was yearning for, all at the same time. There was pain, too, and she stiffened, but Simon soothed her with kisses and soft murmurs.

"Shh... Shh, my love..." he whispered. "I will go slowly. I'll take care of you. It will not be so very bad."

She relaxed, trusting Simon, and gave herself up to the strange sensations. There was a flash of pain, a tearing, and Charity gave a little cry. But then he was deep within her, filling her in a way she would never have imagined possible, and she knew that this was what she had been aching for. He began to move within her, and Charity realized that there was more to it, and that what he did now was even more pleasurable than the satisfaction merely of feeling him inside her. She gasped as he pulled back, then thrust in again, and this time there was almost no pain, only a sweet pleasure, a shock of fulfillment. He thrust again and again, enveloping Charity in the pleasure of the rhythm, the heightening desire that ran through her. She was panting, almost sobbing, wanting something so desperately that it clawed at her.

He reached down between their meshed bodies and found once more that magical little button of flesh, and suddenly Charity exploded into pleasure. It washed over her in waves, and her body shook, unconscious of everything except the joy flooding through her. Simon cried out above her and plunged deep into her, clutching Charity tightly to him. Charity clung to him as they rode out the storm of their passion.

For a long time afterward, they simply lay there, spent. At last Simon shifted and turned, pulling Charity on top of him so that she did not feel the pressure of his weight. He kissed her shoulder, damp and cool from the heat of their lovemaking.

"You've sealed your fate, my darling," he murmured. "You are mine now, and I will not let you go."

Charity, who was exactly where she wanted to be, just smiled.

The banns were read the following Sunday in the little church at Siddley-on-the-Marsh, and Simon and Charity were married there two weeks later. Simon had taken Charity home after their lovemaking and waited with her for her parents to return from the ball. Lytton Emerson had been struck dumb by Simon's terse confession that he had taken Charity's virtue.

But Caroline, his wife, had turned a shrewd look in Charity's direction and said dryly, "Somehow I doubt that you were entirely to blame, Lord Dure." She had shrugged and sighed. "Ah, well, it hardly matters. 'Tis all the same— you two have to be married now."

Caroline had mourned the elaborate plans she had had in mind for the wedding, but Charity hadn't minded a bit. She liked being married in the little church that she had attended all her life, and it was enough for her to have her family there, and Venetia and her husband. It didn't even bother her that the dress she wore as she walked down the aisle was not a new one, encrusted with seed pearls and drowned in layers of lace. She had all she wanted as she looked down the aisle at Simon, standing at the altar, his eyes dark and smiling as she came toward him.

They went to Deerfield Park, the country seat of the Earls of Dure for generations, after the wedding. Closed in their carriage and away from the throng of relatives that had surrounded them for the past two weeks, Simon pulled Charity into his lap and kissed her thoroughly.

"Ah, thank God! I had begun to think I was marrying your mother, not you." He buried his lips in her neck. "I haven't even had a chance to touch you."

Charity giggled. "That's exactly why Mother's been so constantly around. She wants to make sure that there's not a repeat of my scandalous behavior until she gets me safely installed as Lady Dure."

"It's driven me mad." Simon cupped her breast, caressing it through the material of her dress. "I think it's been even worse since the night you came to my house. Before, at least I didn't know precisely how pleasurable it was to make love to you." He kissed his way up her neck to her ear and began to nibble on its lobe.

Charity shivered, the familiar hot ache blossoming between her legs. "It has been the same for me," she murmured, making a little choking noise as his tongue delved into her ear. "Oh, Simon…"

"Mmm-hmm?" he answered distractedly, his attention elsewhere, as he bunched up her skirts in his hand until he found her leg. He slid his hand up her leg, shoving yards of material out of the way. Still, it wasn't entirely satisfying, as her pantalets lay between him and her skin.

Blood pounded through him. All he had to do was touch her, kiss her, even look at her, and he was immediately, achingly hard. Though he might jest about it now, he had spent the past two weeks on tenterhooks, remembering their lovemaking and wishing that he hadn't been so guilt-ridden that he took her home immediately afterward to face her parents.

"Take off your underthings," he whispered hoarsely.

"What? Here?" Charity sat up straight, looking startled. One glance, however, into Simon's hot, passionate eyes made her melt inside, and she quickly moved off his lap and onto the other seat, where she reached up under her skirt and wriggled out of her pantalets. "My petticoats, too?" she asked.

Heat stabbed his loins like a red-hot poker. "I care not. Come here." He reached out and took her by the waist, guiding her onto his lap again, but this time so that she sat astride him.

Charity's eyes opened wide, but she settled herself on him, moving a little, as if to find exactly the right place, eliciting a groan from him.

"Minx," he murmured, in a voice that sounded not at all displeased, and kissed her.

Their tongues intertwined in a long dance of love, while his hands slid eagerly over her clothed torso. His thumbs traced the buttons of her nipples until they were hard and engorged, pressing against her dress. He moved his hands to her legs, sliding up them from the ankles, underneath the petticoats and dress, caressing her smooth, bare flesh, until at last he reached the heated center of her.

When he felt the moisture flooding between her legs, he let out a long, shuddering breath. "Oh, my sweet, sweet girl. You are ready for me so soon."

"I'm sorry," Charity whispered, embarrassed, hiding her flaming face against his shoulder.

"Oh, no, do not be sorry. 'Tis wonderful. You are…delightful." His voice was hoarse, his breath rasping in his throat, and Charity found the sound of it stirring.

She moved restlessly against his hand, and he obliged

her by gently caressing the soft, slick folds of flesh until she was moaning and trembling with pleasure. Finally he took his hand away for a moment to unbutton his trousers and let his manhood spring out, free and pulsing. Charity felt it pushing against her, and her eyes widened a little at this new, different excitement. She raised herself a little and moved against it, caressing the turgid flesh with her own hot femininity. Simon sucked in a sharp breath at the sensation and closed his eyes.

When he could stand the tantalizing play no longer, he guided her onto his shaft, pushing her hips down until she was flush against him. He watched the play of sensual expressions—the flicker of surprise and satisfaction and hunger—across her face as she moved slowly down until at last he was fully embedded in her. Charity's head lolled back, exposing her long white throat, and her face was slack with sexuality. Seeing her passionate enjoyment, feeling himself deep within her, Simon felt as if he might explode. Yet he could not let himself; he was too eager to savor the moment, the joy of taking what she offered so willingly, the supreme pleasure of coming to climax within her and feeling her convulse with pleasure, as well.

He reached up and unbuttoned her dress from behind, letting it slide down to expose her breasts, covered only by the chemise. He trailed kisses across the white expanse of her chest and onto the trembling tops of her breasts. His hands delved inside her chemise, lifting the soft white globes free of the material. Holding them as if they were succulent fruit, he buried his face between her breasts, inhaling her scent, rubbing his cheeks and lips over the soft skin. Then he began to taste her, kissing and nibbling, tracing her nipples with his tongue. Covering his teeth with his lips, he worried her nipples into rosy-red engorgement, then softly, slowly, lashed them with his tongue.

With each new sensation Charity moved unconsciously upon him, arousing new delights in him. Groaning, she dug her fingers into Simon's hair and began to circle her hips. Panting, he struggled to retain control, to savor each moment of ever-heightening pleasure. His hands went to her hips, guiding her, slowing and increasing the pressure and speed of her movements, tantalizing them both almost beyond bearing. Then, at last, Charity cried out and convulsed around him, trembling and jerking, and he could hold out no longer. He buried his face against her breasts, his hands digging into her hips, as he thrust, spilling his seed into her, his hoarse shout of joy muffled against her skin.

They went limp, spent from the rush of joy. Charity rested her head on his shoulder, dazed and weak with happiness. His arms were around her, and his cheek rested against her hair. They were still melded together, touching everywhere, and now and then he brushed a fluttering kiss upon her hair and face, or caressed her lightly.

"Are you comfortable?" he whispered. "Do you want to move?"

"No." Charity shook her head. "Not unless you want me to."

He chuckled and squeezed her. "No. I could stay like this forever."

"Me too." Charity rubbed her head against his shoulder like a cat. "I love feeling you inside me."

Simon made a choked noise, and his arms tightened around her convulsively.

"I'm sorry. Was I wrong to say that?" She lifted her head

and looked up at him. His eyes were bright, and his face was still sensually lax with satisfaction.

"God, no," he murmured, smiling, and lazily traced her lips with his forefinger. "I love to hear you say it."

Charity smiled back at him and daringly flicked her tongue out to taste his finger. The fire that lit his eyes told her that her instinct had been right.

"You're making me hard again already."

"Really?" She straightened up, surprised, leaning back from him a little. It seemed amazing to her, but she knew that it must be true; she could feel him swelling inside her.

"Really," he replied dryly, looking back at the bare chest she had revealed by sitting up.

Her bodice was still pulled down to her waist, her chemise beneath her breasts. Simon studied the smooth white orbs like an artist studying a painting. He ran a finger over her breasts and down each nipple. Her nipples were still rosy and engorged, damp from his mouth, with the softened, faintly swollen look of having been suckled. He thought that he had never seen anything as beautiful, or arousing, as the sight of her right now, half-naked and her hair falling down from its pins. She looked somehow both brazen and innocent…and thoroughly alluring.

"You enjoyed it, didn't you?" he asked softly, wonderingly.

"Why, yes!" Charity was startled. "Didn't you?"

Simon laughed. "Yes. I think you could say I enjoyed it. I knew I would, from the moment I saw you. But I was not as sure that you would feel the same."

He smoothed his hands over her breasts, gazing at the contrast of his hard, tanned skin against her soft whiteness.

"You do not mind when I look at you like this, either, do you?"

Charity blushed. "It is a trifle embarrassing, but I like it, too. It's…exciting. To have you look at me, and to see the way your face changes."

Gently Simon took one nipple between his forefinger and thumb and rolled it. Charity sucked in a soft gasp of pleasure.

"Oh, Charity," he said, pulling her close and squeezing her to him. "You are a woman in a million."

"You mean… Do most women not like it? Am I not normal?"

"I don't know. But please don't change." He buried his face in her hair. "Don't ever change."

"I won't," Charity assured him, adding honestly, "I doubt I could. I like it very much, you see…what we just did."

He chuckled. "So did I. I think we shall deal quite well with each other."

Simon leaned his head back against the seat of the carriage. He had to blink away the moisture that was in his eyes. He felt freer and happier than he had in years. Compared with the peace within him, the fact that he was suspected of murder seemed only a minor annoyance.

"Sybilla hated it, you see," he said, surprising himself. He had never talked to anyone about the lack of joy in his marriage bed.

"Your wife?" Charity asked, sitting up again, a puzzled expression on her face. "Your first wife?"

"Yes. She shrank from my touch."

Charity's mouth dropped open in a gratifyingly shocked way. "You're making jest of me. Aren't you?"

He shook his head. "I wish I were. Sybilla despised

lovemaking—or, at least, my lovemaking. I often wondered if perhaps some other man could have made her happy. I loved her—she loved me. But after we were married, everything changed between us. She avoided me. In bed, she lay stiff and silent beneath me. I came to feel as if—as if I were raping her." He sighed, the old bleak look returning to his face. "I suppose I was. I had the right. She allowed me to bed her. But still, I knew I was forcing her. Conventions, her marriage vows, society, that was what forced her. She *endured* me, she did not give herself to me. I went to her less and less often, only when I was driven by need and could delude myself into thinking that it would be different this time. Every time I left her feeling guilty and crude, an animal. After a time, I stopped. I could not bear it anymore. But it had gone on long enough that she had got pregnant. She died in childbirth."

"And you felt as if you had killed her," Charity said perceptively.

He glanced at her, startled. "How did you know?"

"I saw it on your face. You never tried to squash the rumors that you had killed her—because inside you felt that you really had."

Simon nodded. "It was my passion that was the cause of it. If I had left her alone, as I knew she wanted…"

"You did *not* kill her. Women die in childbirth all the time. It is a common danger. God decides such things, not you. You desired her. That is not unnatural, for a man to desire his wife. Is it?"

"No."

"I would lay you odds that other men have bedded wives who cared no more for lovemaking than your Sybilla, yet the wives have not died in childbirth because of it. *And* there have probably been women who enjoyed the marriage bed and still died bearing a child. It was fate, my love, not your passion."

Simon swallowed hard and brought her hand up to his lips, placing a gentle kiss in her palm. "You are a joy, Charity. I cannot think how I deserved to have you." He gazed deeply into her eyes, reaching out to brush a strand of hair back from her face in a tender gesture. "Until you came to my bed that night, I did not know if Sybilla had been an aberration, or if all women care so little for loving. Or if it was just that I was an animal, too crude and rough to make love to a woman so that she enjoyed it, so low in nature that I enjoyed things that others would find disgusting."

"No!" Charity cried fiercely, taking his hand and pressing it to her cheek. "You are not an animal. You are kind and gentle." Tears glistened in her eyes. "Don't ever believe anything else." She curled his fingers over her hand and began to press kisses along his knuckles, as if to punctuate her words. "You are not low, and the things you do are not disgusting."

She looked up at him flirtatiously, her lips curving into a smile. "In fact, I enjoy the things you do very much."

"Do you?" He smiled back in the same sensual way, his eyes darkening. "Then perhaps you would like to do them again?"

Her eyes widened a little. "So soon?"

"Would you mind?"

Charity giggled. "No, my lord, I would not mind at all."

"Good." He sealed her mouth with a kiss.

CHAPTER NINETEEN

THE TIME THEY SPENT at Deerfield Park was the happiest that either Simon or Charity could remember. They paid their dutiful visits to the small ivy-covered church on Sundays and held a party to introduce the locals to the new Lady Dure. But apart from those things, they spent their days exactly as they pleased: taking long walks through the woods or riding along the river, visiting the village of Deerfield nearby, romping with Lucky. Charity, freed from the constraints of her parents, indulged herself by doing precisely what she wanted when she wanted, and it seemed to her the most fortunate thing in the world that she was able to do it with the man she loved. As for Simon, he found himself engaging in activities he hadn't done for years, and laughing like a boy.

Their nights were filled with lovemaking—and, often, so were their days. Reveling in a willing, joyous partner, Simon was ever thinking of new things and new places to try, and Charity was eager to comply. They learned each other's bodies, each other's wants and needs, their most sensual spots. They spent long, lazy afternoons in bed, talking and exploring, teasing and experimenting. Charity wondered how she could have lived so long without knowing such joy. Simon wondered how he could once have thought that a bland marriage of convenience was all he wanted.

With her sympathetic heart and her habit of bringing home strays, with her mischievous sense of fun and her spirit of adventure, marriage to Charity would never be anything like convenient, he knew. He also knew that anything but marriage to Charity would be deadly dull. She was everything he wanted, even though he had not known before what that was. Simon had sworn that he would never love again, that he would not lay himself open to that sort of pain and heartbreak. But he knew, whatever he might say, that he was rushing headlong toward that precipice and that, moreover, he could not even summon a desire to stop. He remembered Charity's cheerful agreement to a marriage without love, her sunny statement that she doubted that she was capable of falling in love, and he wondered if her words had been true. He was finding, more and more, that he hoped they were not.

They had planned to return to London in three weeks, but they found themselves putting the trip off for one week and then another, until by the time they returned, it had been almost six weeks since their wedding. For that time, they had lived as in a world apart. At Deerfield Park, there had been no gossip, no murder, no one watching their every move and discussing it. They soon found out how unreal that time had been.

The first day in London, Inspector Herbert Gorham came to call on them. He found Charity at home by herself, and when Chaney announced to her that the inspector was there, she quickly agreed to see him. She wanted to see for herself exactly what sort of man he was.

She soon found out. He was small, with a weasel-sharp

face and thinning hair, for which he compensated with an enormous walrus mustache. The result was like that of a child trying on a false mustache: it made him look both small and silly. His eyes, however, disabused one of the impression of silliness. They were light green, and very sharp, as if he saw everything that went on around him.

Charity nodded at him when he entered, trying to address him as her mother would. "Mr. Gorham."

"Lady Dure." He took off his hat and bowed to her. "It is so kind of you to give me this time."

"I am quite eager for you to find the *true* killer of Mr. Reed, of course. As we all are."

"All except the killer, my lady." He allowed himself a thin, supercilious smile.

"Well, yes, one would presume so." She gestured toward a chair. "I am afraid, however, that I have little information to give you. I know nothing about the man's death."

"Sometimes a person may know more than they realize. It can be a dangerous thing." He cast a meaningful look in her direction. Charity simply stared back at him blankly. After a moment, he went on. "I was frankly surprised when I read that you had married His Lordship."

Charity raised her eyebrows coolly. "Indeed? I cannot imagine why."

"So soon after Mr. Reed's death, I mean."

"Why? I wasn't in mourning for him. I scarcely knew him."

"It was not really him I was thinking about, my lady." He paused, then added, "A person who has killed once finds it much easier the second time."

"Are you implying that the murderer is likely to come

after me?" Charity asked, looking perplexed. She knew perfectly well that the obnoxious little man was referring to Simon, but she wasn't about to give him the satisfaction of even seeming to realize it.

"While you may not have known Mr. Reed very well, it might be different with the murderer."

"You mean that the murderer knew Mr. Reed well? I can see that that would be likely."

"No." He frowned, and Charity was pleased to see that she had succeeded in nettling him.

"I meant that *you* might know the murderer very well."

"I?" She looked at him with faint, polite contempt, as if he had committed a social gaffe. "I'm sorry, Mr. Gorham, but I'm afraid Emersons don't associate with murderers."

"Has Lord Dure told you, my lady, that one of his own handkerchiefs, marked with the Dure crest, was found beside the body?"

"Yes. It's most puzzling, isn't it? I wonder, why would Mr. Reed have one of my husband's handkerchiefs? Did he steal it, do you suppose? He was not quite a gentleman, you know, but I hardly would have thought he would be a thief of haberdashery."

"The obvious conclusion is," the man went on, clearly straining to keep hold of his temper, "that the murderer accidentally dropped it."

"So you think the murderer stole Lord Dure's handkerchief. I suppose that is more likely, that a thief would be a killer, as well, but—"

"Lady Dure." He spoke slowly and clearly, as if she were a child, or not quite all there. "The most obvious conclusion is that it was Lord Dure who visited Reed that night. That it was he who pulled the trigger."

Charity looked at him in amazement for a moment, then said, "What nonsense! No wonder you people haven't found the killer, if you go around chasing nonsensical clues. I should think you could spend your time better."

"The night Mr. Reed was killed, my lady, you and Lord Dure attended a party where Mr. Reed was also in attendance. I understand that Lord Dure attacked Mr. Reed that night, that Mr. Reed left the party quite bloodied."

"Well, it was only partly Lord Dure who did that," Charity told him judiciously. "I was the one who bloodied his nose."

Inspector Gorham stared at her. "You, my lady?"

"Yes. He was most impertinent and impolite. A simple set-down did not do the trick. I had to be more forceful with the man."

The inspector continued to gape and blink, looking completely at sea.

"I suppose," Charity went on imperturbably, "you could say, if fighting with him that night was the basis for killing him, that I would be just as likely a candidate for murdering him as my husband. That is what I'm saying to you—there are many people who hated Mr. Reed."

"Lord Dure threatened to kill him that night, did he not?" Gorham recovered enough to ask.

Charity tilted her head to one side, considering. "I'm not sure what Dure said in the heat of anger. It is usually errant nonsense, you know. He may have said something like that."

"I think you know very well that he did," Gorham retorted, heat building up in him as he decided that this strange, lovely young woman before him had been gaming him. *No well-bred lady would bloody a man's nose!* "Lady

Dure, you are playing with fire. A murderer in one's house is not a comfortable thing to live with."

"There is no murderer in this house," Charity replied stonily.

The inspector tried to smile in a friendly way, though it came across looking more like a death rictus. "Lady Dure, you live with the man. It's possible you might see something, hear something…and if you do, it would be to your benefit to come to us. You had best consider your own safety. You are in a very unprotected situation here."

"My husband protects me, sir. I see no further need for protection. As I stated before, I see no reason why Mr. Reed's murderer would come after me. I'm sure he was someone involved in some nefarious business of Mr. Reed's, and 'tis there you should be looking, not at Dure House, which I'm sure Mr. Reed never entered." She rose, dismissing him. "Thank you for coming by, Mr. Gorham. Perhaps you'll come back when you have some *useful* information."

Simon leaned back his head and laughed when Charity described her visit from the inspector in detail. She made a face at him.

"It isn't funny, Simon. Why, he was asking me to spy on you, to try to get information against you. That man thinks that you killed Faraday Reed."

"I know. I could tell that from the first." Simon shrugged. "But he hasn't any evidence apart from that stupid handkerchief. It isn't enough to arrest me."

"But what if he manages to dig up something else that looks suspicious?"

"Such as?"

"I don't know! I don't know how the handkerchief managed to be there, either. But I don't like it. He makes me nervous."

"Refuse to let him in next time. I'll tell Chaney to say that you're out."

"That isn't the answer. We need to find the man who really did kill Reed. 'Tis the only way to completely clear your name."

"Indeed? And how do you propose to do that? Scotland Yard hasn't been able to."

"Well, of course not, if they have ninnies like Mr. Gorham working on it. Besides, we have an advantage over Scotland Yard and Mr. Gorham."

"And what is that?"

"We know that *you* did not do it. He is wasting his time trying to prove it was you. We can start looking elsewhere."

"What do you propose to do?" he asked, smiling down at her determined face. "Question Reed's servants?"

"Not a bad idea." Charity's face brightened. "We could send Chaney or your valet over there to talk to them. I'm certain they'd be more willing to talk to a fellow servant than to the police—or to you and me," she added honestly. "You can even give them some money to open their mouths, if they don't want to talk."

"You're a cunning little thing, aren't you? Why did I never notice this before?"

"I don't know," Charity responded pertly. "It's always been there. As I've pointed out to you, I have a habit of getting what I want."

"So you've told me." His eyes warmed as he remembered the night she had told him that.

"You and I, on the other hand, can talk to people who

knew Reed. Maybe we can find out more about him. He was a perfect cad. I'm sure there were several other people who would have loved to have shot him. His wife would be my first guess. Or maybe someone who he was black-mailing."

Simon's eyes flew to Charity's, alarmed. "Venetia could never have shot him."

Charity cast him a surprised look. "I didn't mean Venetia. But I suspect that if he was extorting money from her, he was extorting it from other people, as well. He would have enjoyed the money, as well as the power over people."

"But to find his other victims, we would have to find out the secrets he might have known about any number of people. A rather large task, I should think, starting from nothing."

"It does seem a little daunting," Charity admitted, but she brightened a moment later. "If we talk about Reed at parties and on calls and such, and we watch everyone else's reaction, we can see if the subject makes someone nervous. Then we will know who to question further."

"I should imagine many of them would be nervous about talking about Reed to his alleged killer," Simon pointed out dryly.

Charity rolled her eyes and went on as if he hadn't spoken. "Then there's the matter of the handkerchief. Who could have had one of your handkerchiefs? We ought to pursue that."

Simon turned and walked away, sighing. "I don't know. I've thought about it a thousand times. I wouldn't have left a handkerchief lying around somewhere. I think it must have been stolen from my house, in which case almost anyone could have done it."

"It seems more likely to me that it would have been

someone who visited your house. That would have been the easiest way to get it. Someone whom no one would have said anything about if they were seen in your house."

"I can't imagine who…"

"I know." Charity sat down on the sofa, curling her legs up under her in a most undignified way. "It's hard to think that someone you know could have taken your handkerchief, especially in order to make it look as if you had committed murder. But I've been thinking about that. What if it was someone who really didn't care about Reed one way or the other?"

"What on earth do you mean?"

"What if Faraday just happened to be handy? What if the person knew that you had fought with him, that it would be you on whom suspicion first fell? So they stole the handkerchief to make it look even more suspicious and went to Reed's house and shot him, then left your handkerchief. Just to get you in trouble."

"A very nice theory, my love, but I don't know anyone who hated me that much, except Reed himself. And who would go to such elaborate lengths, even kill a man, unless they hated me very much?"

"Perhaps it was a bit of both, then. Say they wanted to get rid of Reed and they hated you, too, so this seemed like the perfect solution to get rid of all their problems." She paused, her brow knitting. "Or maybe they wouldn't have to hate you, really, so much as that they would benefit if you were found guilty of murder."

"If I were found guilty, I would hang, so that would mean someone who would benefit by my dying. Aside from you, my dear—"

"Simon!" Charity paled, her eyes wide. "How can you say that!"

"It was only a jest." He went to her quickly and took her in his arms. "I did not mean to hurt you. But you see how silly it is, don't you? No one would benefit from my death except people in my family. You would get the bulk of my unentailed property, and my uncle would get the earldom and the entailed property."

"Well, *I* did not do it," Charity said with heavy sarcasm, pulling away from him. "I wasn't even married to you at the time."

"Do you suspect my uncle?" he asked incredulously.

"I don't know. I hardly even know the man. But someone had to put that handkerchief there for some reason." She paused. "Your cousin Evelyn would have gained, too. He would have been next in line for succession if your uncle received the earldom. But if you married, as you were planning to, and had heirs, his chances of ever receiving it would diminish greatly."

Simon looked at her for a long moment, then said, "No. I cannot believe it. Really, Charity, I cannot see either of them as a murderer. Uncle Ambrose is far too proper, and I can't picture Evelyn making such an effort."

Charity sighed. "No doubt you are right. Which means that 'tis probably someone much more difficult for us to find. Still...don't you think we should have a party, now that we're back in London? A dinner party, say, my first as Lady Dure? Just for your family?"

"Charity!" Simon couldn't keep from chuckling. "Are you planning to line them up and question them?"

"Nothing so obvious, I hope," she replied. "But it

wouldn't hurt, would it, to do a little prying about where they were that night, and so forth?"

He looked at her, shaking his head. "You are going to get me cast out by my family." But there was no anger on his face, only amusement and fondness, and he kissed her on the forehead. "By all means, go ahead and have your dinner party."

Charity started her investigation the very next day. First she had a long and serious talk with Chaney, who promised solemnly to take care of acquiring information from the Reed servants. For her part, she boldly brought up the subject of Faraday Reed when she paid calls or received visitors or attended a social gathering of any kind. She received some strange and uneasy looks from people, but, beyond learning that many women thought he was a perfectly blameless sort and a few looked carved in ice whenever he was mentioned, she found out very little.

She also spent a good deal of time on her upcoming party, consulting with her mother and Venetia, as well as the cook, the housekeeper and Chaney. She set a menu for it and sent out the invitations, then put the housekeeper and maids into a flurry of cleaning, wanting to have the whole house in spotless condition. It was, she thought, a curious task before her: to host the perfect dinner party for Simon's family, as it would be her first for them and she wanted to impress them, yet at the same time to question them all about a murder. It made even Charity uneasy to think of walking such a fine line. Talking to Venetia about planning the party was not as comfortable as usual, as she could not reveal to her that she had an ulterior motive in giving it.

A few days before the party, Charity took a break from her round of calls and planning and decided to go shopping, simply for the pleasure of it. Her first stop was a milliner's, where she tried on several bonnets. The last one was quite tempting, a dashing little thing that more sat on top of her head than covered it, tilting down toward her forehead at a rakish angle. Of course, she did not really need a new hat. But it *was* darling…. She wondered what Simon would say when he saw her in it.

"How lovely that looks on you, Lady Dure!" a low voice cried right behind her.

Charity jumped and whirled, astonished to have her thoughts echoed aloud. A lovely woman with black hair stood behind Charity, smiling. Charity remembered her instantly, although it took her a moment to recall the woman's name. She had met her only that one time in the park.

"I hope I'm not presuming," the woman said humbly. "We have been introduced, but…"

"Of course not." Charity smiled, and felt relieved when the name at last came to her. "You're Mrs. Graves. We met once when you were riding in the park."

"Yes. How kind of you to remember."

"Mr. Reed introduced us." Charity wondered if this woman had been a friend of his.

"Yes." The other woman looked grave. "It was a terrible thing about him, wasn't it?" She gave a little shudder, then added, "Of course, he was not quite the paragon I thought him. I suppose it was no wonder that he was murdered."

"He fooled you, too?"

Mrs. Graves nodded. "I fear he fooled many people. Once he found out I could not help him socially or financially, he no longer bothered with me. That was how I discovered what he was like."

"I see."

A sad look flitted across the other woman's face. "Alas, I am afraid 'tis all too common a trait among men, or, at least, among so-called gentlemen." Then she forced a smile, shaking off her moment of gloom. "But, here, you don't want to listen to my troubles. Not when you're still aglow with happiness. I understand you and Lord Dure are married now. He is a lucky man."

"Why, thank you." Charity beamed. "He's a wonderful man, actually. I am the lucky one. Frankly—" she leaned forward confidentially "—I never realized that marriage would be so much fun."

Mrs. Graves's expression froze.

"I'm sorry," Charity said immediately. "Did I say something amiss?"

"No, of course not. Every young bride should feel that way."

"But you looked so…I don't know…unhappy for a moment."

"You are a most perceptive young woman. It was not your fault. I was only thinking—" She stopped abruptly and shook her head, trying to force another smile onto her face. "No, I shouldn't burden you—indeed, I probably ought not to be seen talking to you. It would not be good for your reputation." She glanced around, a little anxiously, looking to see who might have seen them together.

"Why not? What are you talking about?" Charity stepped closer to the older woman and took her arm, concern wrinkling her forehead. "Why should I not talk to you? What's the matter?"

"You are very kind." Tears glinted in Mrs. Graves's

eyes. "But there is nothing you can do. I am now a…a…" Tears began to flow from her eyes, and she drew a sobbing breath. "I can't… How awful." She pulled a lace-edged handkerchief from her pocket and held it up to her eyes, dabbing away the tears and looking furtively around.

"Here, come with me," Charity decided. She couldn't let the poor woman embarrass herself by bursting into sobs in a milliner's. "My carriage is outside. We shall go for a drive. How does that sound?"

Mrs. Graves looked gratefully at her over her handkerchief, murmuring, "You are too kind."

"Nonsense." Charity set aside the bonnet she had been contemplating and led her companion through the small shop and out to her carriage. "There, now," she said, settling into the seat across from Mrs. Graves, having told the driver to drive anywhere he liked.

"Thank you. I feel such a fool, bursting into tears in a store."

"It probably happens all the time—daughters begging their mothers to purchase a new hat, or moaning that the one they want won't go with their cape or some such thing."

"You are too kind. But you really mustn't let anyone know that you befriended me."

"Why? That's nonsense."

Theodora shook her head and smiled sadly, sweetly. "No, I'm afraid it's not. I pray that you will never have to find out, as I have. My reputation is in shreds. No decent matron would invite me to a soiree any longer."

"But why not?"

"I—" She raised the handkerchief to her eyes again and said in a choked voice, "I have been betrayed by a…a man. I cannot call him a gentleman, no matter what his birth."

Charity sucked in her breath, horrified. "You mean…"

"Yes." She put her hands to her cheeks. "I am so ashamed. It is no excuse, but my dear husband had just died. I—I was so alone, so unhappy."

"Of course you were," Charity murmured sympathetically.

"You will think me faithless to the memory of my husband that I could fall into another man's arms before my mourning was even over. But it was not that I didn't love Douglas. It was, rather, that I missed him so much. It felt so good to be held, almost as if he were there again. I was confused and hurt, and when he told me that he loved me, that I was lovely, it was so easy to believe him. So pleasant. I… He seduced me, playing on my feelings with sweet words and tender caresses. I was a fool, of course, but even though I had been married, I was still very naive. I came from a small town, and I had never loved anyone but Douglas. I believed him when he said he loved me. I loved him, too—so very much. I knew it was a sin, but— it was so nice to be comforted, not to be unhappy."

"That's only natural."

"Perhaps, but women are expected to be better than that, not to risk their reputations no matter how lonely they are or how much they love a man," Theodora said bitterly.

"That is hardly fair."

"What does fairness matter? It is the woman who gets caught, who cannot escape the consequences."

Charity's eyes widened. "Oh, no! You mean…"

Theodora nodded her head, looking down at her lap as

though she could not bring herself to meet Charity's eyes. "Yes. I fear so. I am not sure, but it—I'm very afraid it is true. I went to…him. I thought he would help me, that he would do the right thing. I thought he loved me and would be happy to marry me. But he told me—" Her voice caught on a sob, and she struggled with her emotions for a moment before she was able to go on. "He said he was engaged to marry another, a woman of higher birth and more money. When I told him that I thought we were to be married, he laughed at me! He said I wasn't of his class. My parents were only country gentry, you see, good enough for the third son of a baronet like Douglas, I suppose, but not for him. It would be a disgrace for him to marry someone like me."

"Why, that monster!" Charity's easy sympathy swelled up in her. "How can men be such cads?"

Theodora shook her head. "I would never have thought it of him. But I realized that I had been very, very wrong about him. He gave me a packet of bills and told me to get out of his life."

Charity gasped, shocked.

"Yes, I know." Theodora's lush mouth turned down bitterly. "I thought he loved me. But to him I was only a mistress. He reminded me how he had paid for my rent after Douglas died, when I was in such despair, how he had bought elegant clothes for me. It was true—he had. I hadn't thought about it. Douglas had often bought me loving gifts. I had thought it simply love and kindness on his part. Instead, he had been buying me—as if I were a common whore!"

She burst into sobs, hiding her face in her hands as she wailed. Charity watched helplessly, anger burning in her for the man who had treated this poor woman in such a way. A few months ago she would not have thought it possible that a gentleman could treat a woman thusly, or that Mrs. Graves could have been so fooled by a man. She had thought that evil showed on one's face and in one's manner. But after learning about Faraday Reed, she had realized that she had been hopelessly naive. "Gentlemen" could be as wicked as the commonest of men, and they could hide a snake's soul under a pleasant exterior.

Charity moved across the carriage and sat down beside Mrs. Graves, putting her arm around her shoulders and murmuring soothing words to her. "I am so sorry. I wish I could help you. It's so terribly unfair that you should be treated as a 'fallen woman' while that scoundrel is free to move about, still welcome everywhere, as if he had not sinned at all."

"I know." Theodora had calmed down, and now she wiped away her tears with her sodden handkerchief, looking defeated and sad.

"Well, I won't turn my back on you," Charity promised stoutly. "It was not your fault. I shall invite you to our first ball. After the family dinner, of course, but that's in only two days."

"You must not do that," Theodora murmured. "It wouldn't be right. It would cause you scandal."

Charity considered the thought. "Perhaps I had best tell Dure about it first. But I'm sure that he will not object."

"No!" Theodora gasped. Her lovely face was panicked, and her eyes were wide with horror. "No, pray don't tell Lord Dure!"

"But why not? He's a very intelligent, fair man. He will not condemn you."

"No, please, promise me that you won't tell your

husband, or anyone else, about this. It must be our secret. If it got out, I don't know how I would live it down. You are the only one I've told."

"Well, all right," Charity agreed, a little reluctantly. She was sure that Dure would have a good idea about what the poor woman should do, and she knew that he was not the type to condemn someone out of hand. But she could see how upset and embarrassed Mrs. Graves was at the idea of anyone else knowing, especially a man, and Charity could understand that. She would not bring further grief on the poor woman by airing her troubles, even to her husband. "I won't tell Dure."

Theodora relaxed a little, but insisted, "Do you promise?"

"I promise. I won't tell Dure, or anyone else. And I shall continue to be your friend. I want you to know that you can rely on me."

"Thank you. It means so much to me. If it wouldn't be too much of an imposition, I should love to talk to you again."

"Of course it would not be an imposition! I should love to." Charity squeezed Theodora's hand reassuringly. "You can count on me."

"Thank you, my lady." Theodora looked down, a satisfied grin curving her generous mouth. "I so appreciate your kindness."

CHAPTER TWENTY

IT WAS THE EVENING of their dinner party, and Simon could not imagine where Charity could be. He looked at the clock on the mantel in the drawing room for the fourth time, but it was no more help than it had been the other three times. The dinner party was in only an hour. Charity had gone out almost two hours ago, telling the footman at the door, Patrick, that she was going to buy ribbons for a dress and that she would be home in a few minutes.

Simon experienced a fear, an uneasiness, that once would have been foreign to him. There was little possibility that anything had happened to Charity; she had gone in the carriage, with Botkins driving. Yet, somehow, where Charity was concerned, reason played little part in Simon's thoughts. His horror of losing Charity was so great that even the smallest possibility of it was enough to make him worry. Ever since she had decided to discover Reed's killer and clear Simon's name, he could not help but worry that she might somehow tumble herself into a world of trouble in her usual headlong fashion.

At that moment he heard the front door open, and he went quickly to the open doorway and looked down the hall. Charity swept into the entry, flushed and beautiful, casting her dazzling smile at the footman.

"Good evening, Patrick. I'm afraid I'm desperately late. Where is His Lordship?"

"Right here, my lady." Simon strode down the hallway to her, determined to impress upon her the folly of dilly-dallying when there were a party and an anxious husband waiting for her. He was brought up short by the sight of the creature that suddenly leaped onto Charity's shoulder, having been hidden until now in the flung-back hood of her cloak. "What the devil is that?"

Charity laughed merrily. "It is a monkey, my lord. Surely you must have seen one before."

"Of course I have seen one. But never in this house."

The monkey began to chatter and tip the foolish little red hat, approximately the size and shape of a large thimble, that adorned his head. He grabbed hold of Charity's hair with his other tiny hand and swung around her neck, then onto her other shoulder.

"Churchill, behave," Charity said severely, wincing as the animal's fingers pulled at her hair.

"Churchill?"

"Yes, he's named after the Duke of Marlborough. Absurd, isn't it?"

"In more ways than one." Simon cast a jaundiced eye upon the creature as it scrambled down Charity's front and onto the marble floor.

They watched as Churchill scampered across the floor and up the heavy mahogany hat tree that stood against the wall.

"I imagine you want to know how I happened to come home with a monkey," Charity said.

"I am waiting in breathless suspense."

"I don't precisely know what we'll do with him, but I couldn't leave him there."

"And where was that?"

"With the man who owned him. Or, at least, he said he owned him, but I don't think anyone should own a pet unless he acts more decently toward it."

"I presume this owner did not?" Simon said fatalistically. "And you, of course, decided to uh…free Churchill from him."

Charity smiled sunnily and stepped forward to kiss Simon's cheek. "I knew you would understand."

Simon smiled wryly. "I know you, my dear. However, that's not precisely the same thing as agreeing to having this creature…" He cast a look toward the monkey, who had leaped from the top of the hall tree and caught the bottom of the crystal chandelier and was now swinging from it. Simon groaned and continued, "…having this creature living with us."

"Churchill, come down," Charity ordered firmly, but the monkey paid no attention, chattering merrily as the glass prisms shook around him. "He isn't very well behaved," Charity admitted. "However, I am sure it was because that organ-grinder was cruel to him. Once he comes to know and trust us, no doubt he will learn better to obey."

"Or perhaps Lucky will have him for dinner," Simon offered dryly.

Charity gasped and turned toward her husband, eyes widening. "Oh, Simon, no! Do you think so?"

Simon looked up at the monkey swinging from the light fixture. "Somehow I doubt Lucky will be able to catch him long enough to do him harm. But doubtless that will not stop the dog from trying. Lucky has somehow confused himself with a hunting dog. Patrick!" Simon turned toward the hapless footman standing beside the door. "Get that monkey down and lock him up somewhere—away from the dog."

"Yes, my lord." The footman's expression remained stoically unchanged, but his eyes were eloquent as he gazed up at the monkey.

"I suspect you'll need another person to help you—and a ladder, as well."

"Yes, my lord."

"Thank you, Simon." Charity beamed at her husband. "I knew you'd be willing to take him in. Now I really must change for dinner."

She flew up the stairs and into her room. It was really most annoying, Charity thought, that she should be late on this night, of all nights. She was counting on this dinner party to help her find Reed's killer. All the talking she had done to everyone she could think of over the past few weeks had yielded little important information. To glean something useful from their guests while remaining charming to her new in-laws—as well as keeping a competent eye on the progress of the party—would require her to have all her wits about her. She did not want to be rushing downstairs at the last minute, rattled and harried, to greet the guests.

Fortunately, her maid, Lily, was there, and she had already laid out one of Charity's prettiest dresses on the bed, ready to be put on, with matching shoes on the floor beside the bed. On the vanity table, perfume, hairbrush and an array of hair ornaments stood ready.

"Oh, Lily, you're a jewel…." Charity sighed with relief as Lily sprang up from the low chair in front of the vanity and came around to take off Charity's cloak and begin unfastening the multitude of buttons down Charity's back.

With Lily's considerable help, Charity flew through the task of undressing and washing up, then submitted to the torture of putting on a corset so that she would look her loveliest in the ice-blue satin dress that lay spread across the coverlet. Attired in her dressing gown over her myriad petticoats, Charity sat in front of the mirror and closed her eyes while Lily brushed out her hair, letting the soothing strokes of the hairbrush calm her down. By the time Lily was through coiling and curling her hair, decorating it with the ribbon that Charity had gone to such pains to get, Charity was quite calm, and prepared to subtly interrogate her guests.

She swept downstairs to join Simon in the drawing room, and the way his eyes lit up when she entered the room assured her that she looked as good as nature and Lily's artistry could make her.

"Charity." Simon rose and moved quickly across the room to her. He stopped, gazing down at her with warmth. "You look… delicious." He bent and laid a kiss upon the white expanse of shoulder revealed by the wide scoop neckline of her dress. "Perhaps," he murmured, "we should retire early and let our guests fend for themselves."

The touch of his breath against her skin sent shivers through Charity. She wondered if any woman had ever loved her husband as much as she did Simon. She could not imagine it.

"Now, Simon…" she began as he raised his head and gazed down at her, but the reprimand in her voice was spoiled by the breathy giggle that escaped her, and she looked at him roguishly. "You know we can't do that. 'Twould be exceedingly rude."

"Rude be damned. I find I would very much like to be

alone with my wife." Simon leaned closer to her, his lips hovering over her mouth. Charity waited breathlessly, lifting her lips to his.

"Mr. and Mrs. Nathan Westport," Chaney intoned from the doorway.

Simon and Charity sprang apart guiltily and turned. The butler stood in the doorway, his eyes fixed on nothing, his expression imperturbable. Slightly behind him stood Simon's youngest cousin and his wife, trying to peer around the obstacle of Chaney's frame into the drawing room. Charity blushed and glanced up at Simon.

"Damn," he said under his breath. "Cousin Nathan's timing was always unfortunate."

Charity smothered a giggle as she put her hand on his arm and they started forward to greet their first guests. She knew what would happen after the dinner was over and all their guests had gone, knew how the promise in her husband's eyes would be kept, and she hugged the knowledge to her throughout the evening. Going through the motions of greeting and chatting with her guests, she had in the back of her mind the small, constant titillation of what would take place between them in the bedroom once they got rid of everyone. Still, she could not let the thought distract her from her duty, the hidden layer of the evening's conversations—her determined pursuit of Faraday Reed's real killer.

So she pushed her decidedly licentious thoughts aside and turned her agile mind to questioning her guests without raising their curiosity. It was not easy. No one at this party was likely to bring up a subject so distressful to their host as Reed's murder.

As she chatted politely with her guests, she grew more

and more frustrated at the lack of opportunity to bring up the subject. She had tried in several oblique ways to work this conversation or that around to Reed, but the conversation had always somehow veered away from him. She suspected that it had been done on purpose, one person or another seeing where things might lead and steering the talk away, in order not to inadvertently cause her or Simon any distress. It was exceedingly annoying, and Charity found herself wishing for a less polite group, who would engage in a good gossip.

Finally she approached a small cluster composed of Venetia's husband, Lord Ashford, Simon's Uncle Ambrose, and Ambrose's son, Evelyn. It was Ambrose and his son who had the most reason to implicate Simon in Reed's death, though Charity had trouble envisioning either the pompous Ambrose or his cynical, quick-witted son doing away with Reed.

"Uncle Ambrose," she said, smiling warmly at the older man. "I am so glad you could come tonight."

"Of course, my dear. Always happy to see you and Simon." The older man nodded his head to her in a dignified manner. "Family, you know."

"Of course."

"Hallo, Cuz." Evelyn took her hand and raised it to his lips politely, giving her his usual wry smile. "You are in blooming health, as always."

"Why, thank you." Charity took a breath and plunged in, desperate to pursue her interest. "Frankly, I am quite amazed that I don't look positively ashy. The past few weeks have not been easy."

"What? Have you been ill?" Lord Ashford asked in friendly concern. "Venetia hasn't said a word about it to me."

Ambrose cleared his throat significantly and cast a frowning look at Ashford's genial face. "Might not be the thing to be discussing with you," he pointed out.

"Oh!" Charity realized that he was hinting at a possible pregnancy as the reason for her ill health, and she went on, blushing, "No, it's nothing like that. I was simply saying that it has been difficult…with all this hanging over Simon's head."

"What is that?" Ambrose looked confused.

His son shot him a glance that appeared as exasperated as Charity felt. "I think she's referring to Mr. Reed's unfortunate demise."

"Who? Reed? Oh, that blackguard." Ambrose gave a snort of contempt. "The world's better off without him, I'll tell you. Came from no family, really. A lot of upstarts in Berkshire."

"Still, that's no reason to kill him," Evelyn pointed out languidly.

"What? Of course not. Still, can't see what the fuss is about, personally."

Evelyn's eyebrows rose lazily and he drawled, "Well, the man *was* murdered. It can hardly be overlooked simply because he was a scoundrel."

"Whoever did it did the world a favor, if you ask me," Venetia's husband put in bluntly.

Charity glanced at him, surprised. Lord Ashford had always seemed the mildest and most pleasant of men to her, but the look on his face now was hard, and his eyes glittered unpleasantly.

Evelyn turned toward him, looking as surprised as Charity felt. Ashford glanced around at the others, realizing their amazement at his attitude. "Sorry," he said, his tone a trifle embarrassed, and he moved back slightly, as if to distance himself from his statement. "Shouldn't be talking about such a subject in front of you, my lady."

"Nonsense," Evelyn said, still smiling faintly. "I suspect that's precisely the subject Lady Dure was hoping to hear about." He turned to Charity, his eyes dancing. "Doing a bit of detecting, my lady?"

Charity raised her chin. Evelyn was a pleasant young man, but at that moment she would have liked to kick him in the shins. He was too clever by half. "Don't be absurd, Cousin."

Ambrose frowned at his son. "That's right. You are being damned impudent, my boy. Her Ladyship would have no interest in that rascal, alive or dead. You're the one who brought the subject up, and I must say, it's hardly appropriate for the company of ladies."

"Of course. I beg your pardon, Cousin Charity. However, perhaps you would like to know where I was that particular evening, anyway. Unfortunately, I was with a rather disreputable group of friends at Cecil Harvey's house. All night. What about you, Father? Can you account for what you were doing the night the late, unlamented Faraday Reed was killed?"

Lord Ashford stared at Evelyn in astonishment. "I say, Westport, surely you're not suggesting that Lady Dure thinks one of *us* did the scoundrel in."

"Of course not," Ambrose answered, before Evelyn could open his mouth again. "He's playing his usual foolish games." Ambrose smiled benignly at Charity. "Lady Dure is far too sweet a lass to think such a thing."

"Why, thank you, Uncle." Charity smiled sweetly at him and cast Dure's cousin a quelling look.

Ashford, however, continued to gaze at Charity speculatively, and when Ambrose excused himself a moment later and moved away, Venetia's husband said, "You do suspect one of us, don't you?"

"No, of course not. I mean, not really. It's just that—"

"If it's not Dure," Evelyn continued for her, "then it stands to reason it must be someone else."

"Of course. Stands to reason, surely," Ashford agreed in his bluff way. "But why Westport, or Evelyn here?"

"Or you," Evelyn pointed out reasonably, his brown eyes still alight with humor.

"Me?" Ashford stiffened. "You can't be serious!"

"Everyone is suspect." Evelyn lowered his voice mysteriously. "And did you notice, my dear cousin, that my father did not actually give you an alibi for that night?" He waggled his eyebrows suggestively.

Charity had to laugh. "Stop. You make me feel like a fool."

"Never," he returned gallantly. "Don't worry. Someone murdered the man. It's bound to come out sooner or later. The problem is that there are too many suspects. I am sure there are hundreds of people who would have liked to get rid of him." He turned toward Lord Ashford. "Come along, George. Cousin Charity's probably learned all she can from us. Let us allow her to find new prey."

He sketched a bow to Charity and walked off, taking Ashford along with him. Charity watched them go, a smile lingering on her lips. But she couldn't help thinking how odd Venetia's husband had looked when Evelyn teasingly turned his suspicions on him. Ashford had looked, strangely enough, almost nervous.

But surely he could not have…

Charity could not envision Lord Ashford killing anyone; he was far too placid. But she also knew that he was very much in love with Venetia. *What if he had found out about Reed's threatening her? What if he had even discovered that Venetia had once been in love with the man?* Charity wondered if love and jealousy could prod even a pleasant soul like Ashford to murder. On the other hand, she couldn't see why he would attempt to throw suspicion on Dure, who was his friend, as well as a relation.

Charity roamed around the room, looking for Venetia. She could not find her in the drawing room, so she went into the hallway, where a few of their guests had drifted. Smiling at Dure, who was stuck in earnest conversation with one of his cousins on his mother's side, a man whom Charity had already been unlucky enough to encounter, she hurried on down the hall. Her intent was simply to get away before her husband could try to palm the boring man off on her, but as she swept past the darkened library, she noticed a figure on the couch inside, and she stopped and peered into the unlit room.

She could see that it was a woman by the spread of skirts around her, but the woman's head was turned away, and it was too dim to discern who it was. Charity heard the unmistakable sound of a snuffle.

"Who's there? Can I help?" She went farther into the room.

The figure whirled, letting out a little gasp of dismay. "Oh! Charity!"

"Venetia!" The light from the hall was enough to allow her to make out Venetia's features, now that she was closer to her. "Is something the matter? What are you doing in here?"

Charity went to the sofa and sat down beside her friend, taking one of Venetia's hands. In the other hand Venetia held an embroidered handkerchief, and as she moved slightly, Charity caught the gleam of tears on her cheek.

"Yes, it is I." Venetia gave a watery little chuckle. "I must look a fright. 'Tis as well it's dark in here."

"But what is wrong? Why are you in here crying?"

"I wasn't— Well, only a little bit. You know how it is sometimes, when the slightest thing will upset you."

"Yes," Charity agreed. "But that is not like you. You're usually so levelheaded and calm, like Dure."

Venetia shook her head a little and sighed. "Oh, Charity, I don't know what to do. I thought that everything would be better after Reed died."

A chill ran down Charity's spine at her sister-in-law's words. *What did she mean by that? Surely Venetia could not be responsible for Reed's death!* She couldn't believe it. And she was certain that Venetia would never do it in such a way that it looked as if Dure had done it. Venetia loved her brother too much for that. But Charity could not escape the fact of what Reed had done to Venetia, or how much she had hated him for it.

Venetia looked at her more closely. "Why are you staring at me so? Oh! Are you thinking that I might have killed him?"

"Of course not," Charity responded automatically.

"Well, I had reason enough," Venetia responded darkly. "But I didn't. I haven't the courage. Besides, Dure had told me he would stop him, and I knew he would. I have to confess, I wasn't at all sorry when he was killed. It's awful and uncharitable of me, I know, but I couldn't help thinking that he had reaped what he had sown."

"Yes…if only everyone didn't think Simon killed him!"

"I know." Venetia looked miserable, and fresh tears started

in her eyes. "That is one of the things that's been so awful since then. I hate it that people blame Simon. He would never have shot Reed like that. He might very well have thrashed him, but he would never have done anything sneaky."

Charity nodded. She knew she was right not to believe that Venetia had killed Faraday Reed. She would have relied on Simon to stop him, just as she said. And there was no possibility that she would have implicated her brother in the death by leaving his handkerchief at the scene of the crime; she obviously loved him.

"Did, ah, Ashford know about Mr. Reed's threat?"

Venetia stared at her, eyes open wide. "No! Are you mad? He doesn't even know about what happened between Reed and me. I mean, that was the whole reason for that worm extorting money from me—to keep him from telling Ashford the truth!"

Charity said nothing to her sister-in-law, but she was less sure that Lord Ashford knew nothing about Venetia and Reed's past. After all, people gossiped, and Charity didn't doubt that someone might have suspected what had happened all those years ago between Venetia and Reed— or that some servant or other might have revealed that Venetia had run away and Reed had gone to fetch her back. Everyone knew of the enmity between Reed and Simon. Stories, embroidered through the passage of time and speculation, might have reached Venetia's husband. Or perhaps Reed himself had told Ashford!

Charity's mind raced, thinking of possibilities. Simon might have scared Reed into leaving Venetia alone, but Reed could have decided to get back at Venetia and Simon. He could have gone to Ashford and revealed the secret, as he had threatened to do. It would not have been wise, considering how angry Simon would be, but he might have been too furious to care. Or he might even have hoped to get money from Ashford himself—no gentleman would care to have that sort of story told about his wife to society at large. It would be a blot on the family honor, and Reed might have assumed that Ashford would be willing to pay to avoid it. But, instead, it might have infuriated Lord Ashford to the point of killing Reed.

Maybe Ashford would even have been so angry about Venetia and Simon deceiving him all these years that he would try to make it look as if Simon had killed Reed. *But how would Ashford have gotten one of Dure's handkerchiefs to plant beside the body?* It seemed unlikely that he would have had one ready for such an eventuality.

It was equally unlikely, of course, that the jovial, placid Lord Ashford would be roused to a murderous fury, even by news of his wife's infidelity. Charity sighed and stood up, reaching down a hand to Venetia.

"Come. We'd best get back to the party."

Venetia smiled weakly at Charity, dabbing at her tear-streaked face. "You're right. It wouldn't do for the hostess to go missing halfway through."

"Very true. Besides—" Charity grinned "—it is almost time for dinner to be served. We certainly don't want to miss that."

"You're right." Venetia took Charity's hand and stood up. She smoothed at her hair and skirt, and stuck her sodden handkerchief in her pocket. "There. Do I look presentable? Will everyone know I've been in here crying my eyes out?"

"Of course not," Charity replied staunchly. "You look beautiful, as always. That's what everyone will see."

"Thank you." Venetia's smile wobbled a trifle, and impulsively she stepped forward and hugged Charity. "Thank you. You're so sweet. I am terribly glad Simon married you."

"So am I," Charity confessed.

Venetia chuckled and linked arms with Charity, and together they walked back into the hall.

CHAPTER TWENTY-ONE

CHARITY PROBED AND PRIED as delicately as she could for the rest of the party, but her efforts were largely unsuccessful. She found out little that would indicate anyone's guilt or innocence, and she worried that one or the other of Simon's relatives might take offense at her questions.

She spent the majority of the supper in boredom, caught between a prosaic vicar who was a friend of the elder Westports, and Uncle Ambrose's wife, Hortense, who considered herself a Person of Great Importance and spoke in an affected, clenched-teethed way, all the while tilting her chin so that she looked down her nose at whomever she addressed. Charity realized that the dinner was going to last an eternity.

Midway through the soup course, there was the sound of frantic barking, followed almost immediately by a crash. Charity cringed inside, knowing that Lucky had somehow managed to get into trouble again. She cast a look down the table at Simon, who met her eyes quizzically. There was a shriek from not far away, followed by a—fortunately—unintelligible male shout.

Charity glanced at Chaney, who was overseeing the servers from a position by the door into the butler's pantry. His usually imperturbable face resembled a thundercloud, and he turned purposefully and started into the butler's pantry, through which the servants came and went with the courses. The instant he pushed open the swinging door, however, a small furry bundle shot through it.

Charity stifled a groan. The monkey had gotten free! And judging from the sound of barking and claws clicking on the wooden floor in the room beyond, Lucky was in hot pursuit.

Several ladies shrieked as the monkey scampered across the floor and climbed onto the mahogany sideboard. An instant later, Lucky burst into the room, clawing for purchase on the slick marble floor. His back legs went out from under him, and he slid sideways on his rear end. Right behind him came a footman, face flushed and hair straggling, reaching out for the dog.

"What the devil?" Uncle Ambrose blustered.

The footman glanced toward the tableful of people with an anguished look. "I beg pardon, Your Lordship. My lady. He— I—I don't know how he got out."

"Dennis." Chaney's voice was low, but so icy that Charity felt sorry for the hapless footman. He started toward man and dog.

The monkey cast a single contemptuous glance at Lucky, sprawling across the floor, and turned his back on the dog to admire himself in the narrow mirror across the back of the sideboard. He tilted his head and chattered to himself, using his paws to comb at his face and head. Cousin Evelyn began to chuckle.

By this time, Lucky had recovered his balance, and had spotted his quarry, and he leaped at the sideboard, barking, just as the footman lunged forward to grab him. The footman sprawled on the floor. Chaney stepped forward, reaching for the dog, but Lucky danced out of his way, barking furiously at the monkey, who had now turned and was spitting similar invectives down at the dog. The butler, belatedly realizing that wherever the monkey went, the dog would follow, changed course and grabbed for the monkey. But Churchill jumped easily off the sideboard and ran across the room to the table.

Grabbing the tablecloth in his tiny paws, he quickly climbed up the cloth and onto the table. Lucky followed at full tilt, shoving his way in between two of the guests and planting his front paws on the table.

"Churchill!" Charity exclaimed. "Honestly! Have you no manners? Down, Lucky!"

The footman and butler closed in on Lucky, grabbing him by the collar and dragging him out of the room. They were less fortunate with Churchill. He scampered down the length of the table toward Charity, chattering and pausing to pluck a dark grape from the epergne in the center of the table. Charity pressed her napkin to her mouth to stifle the giggles that threatened to erupt, and stole a glance down the table at her husband, dreading that he was embarrassed or angry or both at this riotous display in front of their guests. But Simon was watching the little creature with great interest, his dark eyes dancing with amusement.

Some of their guests had pushed their chairs back from the table, eyeing the monkey with alarm. Others, like Evelyn, were laughing, and some simply stared, open-mouthed. Churchill seemed to sense the attention focused on him. He was, after all, used to performing. Turning, he doffed his thimble-size red hat to the people seated on one side of the table, then turned and doffed it toward the other side. A roar of laughter went up around the table. Pleased with the response, the animal promptly held out the cap as if asking for coins to be dropped in it, which brought another burst of laughter.

The monkey scurried toward Charity, but before he reached her, he was distracted by a glittering ornament in Aunt Hortenses's hair. Lightning-quick, he leaped onto her shoulder and pulled out her jeweled comb. Hortense shrieked hysterically and swatted at Churchill, but he had already jumped from her shoulder to Charity's. He balanced on Charity's shoulder, clenching one hand in her carefully coiffed hair to steady himself, while he examined his prize in the other hand.

"Churchill, you little imp!" Charity wrenched the comb away from him. Spitting out what sounded very much like a curse, the animal hopped off onto the table and stretched his paws toward Charity's soup.

"Oh, no, you don't," Charity admonished him, whisking her bowl off the table and holding it beyond his reach.

Churchill gave her a long, steady look, then turned and grasped her wineglass and drank from it.

"My word!" Aunt Hortense gasped.

"Eek!" Charity dropped the jeweled comb on the table and reached for her wineglass.

Churchill was loath to give it up, and he held on to the glass stubbornly, even though Charity tugged at it.

"My lady!" The butler, having dispatched the dog and the footman, was now hurrying toward Charity, a horrified look on his face. He turned and shot a significant glare at the serving maid and footman, who were standing flat against the wall at one end of the room, gaping helplessly at the scene before them.

Seeing the danger approaching, Churchill dropped the

wineglass. Charity, still pulling on it, jerked her arm back, and the contents of the glass went flying backward, all over Aunt Hortense's dress. The older woman gasped, and Charity stared in horror at the deep red stain spreading across Aunt Hortense's skirt. Down the length of the table there were several quickly smothered giggles and one outright guffaw. Charity began to babble apologies.

At the other end of the table, Simon stood up and deftly caught the escaping monkey. "Here you go, Chaney," he said calmly, holding Churchill out to the butler. "I believe Lady Dure's wineglass needs to be replaced."

"Yes, my lord."

"I say, my lady," Cousin Evelyn began as Chaney solemnly strode out of the room, carrying the monkey at arm's length before him, "you certainly provide rare entertainment at your dinner parties."

Charity groaned and covered her eyes.

Though everyone returned to the meal, trying to act as if nothing untoward had happened, the rest of the evening was an anticlimax. After the meal, the ladies retired to the drawing room, of course, while the gentlemen paused for brandy and cigars in Simon's study. Shortly after the men rejoined the women, however, the guests began to leave. Charity had the suspicion that they were eager to slip away and discuss the new Lady Dure's bizarre dinner. She was rather downhearted as she and Simon made their way upstairs to their bedroom.

"Come, my love," he said, accurately assessing her mood and the reason for it. "There's nothing to be upset about."

"But all your relatives were there," Charity moaned.

"Your uncle is so stuffy, and it was *his* wife who got my wine spilled all over her—not to mention Churchill's stealing her hair comb."

"You gave the comb back," Simon said evenly. "And her dress needed to be retired. It was quite hideous."

Charity's lips twitched, but she said sternly, "Don't make fun. I offended your relatives."

"Some of them, perhaps, but I caught several of them laughing. Evelyn thought it was grand."

"I know. But what about the others?"

"I never much cared for them, anyway," Simon said as he opened her bedroom door and stepped aside to let her in. "Believe me, my love, in case you haven't noticed it before now, I don't live or die by what others think, including my relatives."

Simon followed her inside, closing the door behind them, and pulled Charity around to face him. He dropped a light kiss on her nose. "Besides, there was nothing you could do to stop it. Churchill and Lucky were supposed to be put up, you know."

"Yes, but if I hadn't brought him home in the first place, none of it would have happened."

"That's true. But then I wouldn't have had anything to lighten a boring evening with my relatives, and, more importantly, you would not be you." He shrugged off his coat and dropped it across a chair.

"But don't you think it would be better if I learned some decorum?"

"Ah, I hear your mother speaking." Simon shook his head at her, undoing his cravat as he spoke. "It wasn't she whom I wanted to marry. It was your very beautiful, very indecorous self."

He bent and kissed her on the lips, lingering at the sweet taste of her mouth. When they parted, Charity smiled blindingly up at him. "Truly?"

"Truly." He took her hand and raised it to his mouth, planting slow, searing kisses across her palm and up her wrist to the tender skin on the inside of her arm.

Charity melted against him, her head on his shoulder, as his lips worked their way up her arm to the short, puffed sleeves of her evening dress.

"Did I tell you how lovely you looked in that dress tonight?" he murmured, raising his head to nuzzle her hair.

"I'm not sure." Charity let out a languid sigh as she snuggled into his shoulder. "You can tell me again, though."

"You were beautiful." He kissed her with each word, moving over her hair and down to her cheek and neck. "Stunning. Glorious."

Simon paused at the top of her low-cut gown, then gently kissed the quivering slope of her breast. Charity smiled with deep satisfaction and breathed, "I love to hear you say so."

Simon's mouth moved to her other breast, brushing over its tantalizing softness. "I would rather show you." His voice was low, and a trifle uneven.

"Mmm…" Charity tangled her fingers through his thick hair. "I think I'd rather that, too."

He raised his head, a sensual smile curving his lips. His eyes were heavy with desire, and his face was slackening. "You are the most desirable, most responsive—"

Simon kissed her, his mouth hot and seeking, and Charity opened her mouth to him. Their tongues twined around each other softly, silkily, exploring with a lazy heat that would soon build to an all-consuming fire.

Finally they pulled apart, and Simon began to undo the buttons of his shirt. Charity reached up and took the pins from her hair, releasing the heavy mass to tumble down around her shoulders.

"I am afraid I need some assistance," she told him, turning her back to him and sweeping aside her hair to show the long row of buttons that fastened her dress.

"You know that I am always pleased to help you." His fingers went to the first of her buttons and began to work their way downward. It was a task he often performed for her. Indeed, Charity's maid had learned not to wait up for her mistress to retire, as her presence was usually in the way, rather than necessary. Simon was becoming rather adept at handling the little buttons and hooks and eyes that fastened his wife's clothing.

When he undid the last button, Charity released the bodice of her dress and it tumbled to the floor, pooling around her feet. Simon grumbled when he saw her corset beneath the dress, for he did not like its hard encumbrance. He unlaced it quickly and tossed it aside, gently lifting the soft cloth of the chemise from Charity's skin, where the tight corset had stuck.

Across the room stood Charity's long cheval mirror, and Simon could see their reflection in it, Charity facing the mirror in her chemise and petticoats, himself standing behind her. There was something arousing about watching them in the mirror, and he looked into it as he ran his hands up over Charity's shoulders and down onto her chest. He tenderly cupped her breasts, then slid his hands down to her waist. Unfastening the drawstrings of her petticoats, he slipped them off her, then let his hands roam down her abdomen and her cotton-clad legs.

"You are so beautiful," he murmured, burying his face in her hair.

Charity leaned back against him, enjoying the sensations his fingers aroused in her as they moved over her body, touching her through the thin layer of clothing. His hand slid between her legs, caressing her through cloth dampened by the thick moisture of passion. He raised his head to watch his hand stroking her there, his own blood heating as he watched her face relax into passion.

Simon stepped back and ripped his shirt off, then tugged and shoved off the rest of his clothing, releasing the throbbing staff of his desire. While he did so, Charity slipped out of her undergarments, so that when they came together, they were both naked. They stood for a moment, looking at each other, drinking in each other's bodies. It seemed that even as they grew familiar with one another, their bodies remained alluring, for each spot now reminded them of pleasures past, of a kiss or a caress or a breathless moment of loving.

Charity reached out and placed her hands on Simon's chest, slowly sliding them down his torso to his hipbones, enjoying the pleasure that pulsed so visibly in him at her touch. She ran her fingers along the lines of his ribs and played with the hard, masculine nipples, then twined her fingers through the dark, curling hairs that adorned his chest. Simon sucked in his breath at the exquisite torture of her fingers, hunger surging up in him anew. When at last her hand settled on his manhood, he groaned and clenched his hands into fists, struggling to hold back the pounding tide of passion. She caressed him with delicate fingers, exploring the tender softness of the skin that stretched over the hard shaft and tracing her way down to the soft sacs below.

Simon's breath was ragged, and sweat dampened his body. He wanted to sink himself into Charity now, but he knew that the pleasure would be all the sweeter for the waiting. Charity leaned forward and touched her tongue to his nipple. He jerked and reached for her, twining his hands through her hair. Her tongue flickered over the flat bud again and again; then she paused to suckle it, intensely aware of how Simon's passion surged with each new movement. As she sucked, her hands crept down to take him once again. With both hands and mouth she aroused him, until his body was trembling with tension.

He bent then and picked her up, carrying her to her bed and laying her out upon it. Charity lifted up her arms, welcoming him as he slid between her legs. He thrust deep inside her, filling her completely, and she wrapped her legs around him. Together they began to move in a primal rhythm, their bodies taut and sweating, until the tension was too much to bear, and then, at last, with a cry, they exploded in a paroxysm of love.

Charity awakened the next morning nestled against her husband's side. His arm was thrown across her, and the heat of his body warmed her. She smiled to herself. It was wonderful waking up this way.

For a time she lay there, thinking about the party the night before and what she had and hadn't learned. She was beginning to think that the task she had set for herself was nearly impossible. After all the talking she had done with people, she was no closer to figuring out who had killed Faraday Reed, or why. Nor had Chaney been able to come up with anything helpful from Reed's servants, other than that none of them seemed to have liked Reed.

There must be a better way to go about it, she told herself. Perhaps she should hire someone who had experience in such things, someone who could investigate Reed's past and discover other people with a motive to kill him. But she wasn't sure where one could find that sort of person, or even if they existed.

Sighing, she slipped out of bed, careful not to disturb Simon. Wrapping her dressing gown around her for warmth, she walked across to the door to her dressing room. She opened it and stopped, her eyes going to the floor in front of her.

She screamed.

In a flash, Simon was out of bed and beside her. "What? What is it?" He looked around wildly, as if expecting an armed man to come charging into the room.

Charity's hand was clapped to her mouth, and her eyes were wide with horror. She did not answer, simply pointed to the floor of the dressing room. Simon looked down.

"Churchill?"

The little monkey lay still on the floor. Simon stared in amazement for a moment, then looked at Charity. "What happened to him?"

"I don't know," Charity wailed, and her eyes filled with tears. "Simon, he's dead, isn't he?"

He looked back at the unmoving creature. "I fear so."

Simon bent down and picked up the monkey. His body was cold. Simon carried him over to the window and pulled the drape aside to give him better light.

"Did Lucky kill him?" Charity asked. "Oh, I shouldn't have brought him here. I should have realized that Lucky would get him."

"No," Simon said thoughtfully, frowning down at the

monkey. "I don't think this was anything to do with Lucky. There are no marks on him. He isn't cut or torn at all."

"He must have shaken him until he broke his neck. He was probably only playing."

"I don't think so. His neck doesn't seem broken, either. Besides, he was in the dressing room, wasn't he? And the door was closed. How could Lucky have gotten to him?"

"You're right. Do you think one of the servants could have killed him?"

"Then tossed him in your dressing room, where you would be sure to find him? I think not." Simon lowered his head to the little animal and sniffed.

"Simon, what on earth are you doing?"

"There's a faint odor…. I'm not sure—" Simon broke off and strode across the room to the connecting door that led into his own bedroom. He laid the monkey carefully on a chair and hastily began to dress.

"Simon, what are you doing? Why are you dressing? And why haven't you called Thomkins? What about Churchill?"

"I haven't time for the valet. I'm going round to see Dr. Cargill."

"Dr. Cargill?"

"Yes, he's been my family's doctor for years."

"But why do you suddenly want to see him? Are you ill?"

"No. I'm taking Churchill's body to him."

Charity goggled at him. "But he's a doctor for people. Why would you— Do you think Churchill may have had a disease that you could have caught?"

"No. I'm not sure what I think. There's just something about such a sudden death that bothers me. Obviously the servants locked him in that little room so he wouldn't be able to get out again. How did he manage to die in there? With no marks on his body, no broken bones?"

"Perhaps he ate something earlier that disagreed with him," Charity suggested.

"That's what I suspect. That he ate something that disagreed with him very much—poison."

"But why would anyone want to poison a poor little monkey?" Charity asked, wondering if Simon had lost his senses.

"I don't think anyone would," he replied grimly. "But, if you'll remember, he drank from your wineglass last night, before he spilled it all over Aunt Hortense. The reason I'm taking the body to Dr. Cargill to find out if Churchill was poisoned is that I'm afraid someone might have tried to poison *you*."

CHAPTER TWENTY-TWO

CHARITY WAS TOO STUNNED to protest. Simon dressed and left in a hurry, taking the poor dead monkey with him, wrapped up in a cloth. Charity went about her toilette more slowly, thinking. She could not believe that someone had tried to poison her. Why would anyone wish to kill her? It seemed utterly absurd, and she soon decided that Simon was being overprotective. The thought that he was so concerned about her warmed her heart, but she was certain she did not need to worry, and she soon went on about her business. When she sat down at the breakfast table, it gave her a little qualm, but she pushed the doubt aside and ate—though she did avoid drinking anything.

Simon came home some time later, grim-faced, and Charity's heart began to thud as soon as she saw him.

"I was right," he said, settling heavily in a chair in the morning room, where Charity sat, embroidering. "The animal was poisoned. Dr. Cargill confirmed it."

Charity simply sat, looking at him. She had convinced herself so well that nothing was wrong that it was a shock all over again to hear him say it. "But…even so, that doesn't mean it was from my wine. Someone could have given him poison earlier. Someone who disliked his antics. Some cruel person. Perhaps even one of the servants grew so tired of him that they fed it to him. He would have eaten whatever anyone gave him. Probably someone put it in a sweet and—"

"It was in the wine," Simon said heavily. "The doctor cut him open. There was nothing in his stomach except wine and poison. That's where he got it. There's no doubt that it was intended for you."

"But why?" Charity jumped to her feet, her hands clenching nervously. "Why would anyone try to kill me?"

"Perhaps because you have been running all over London asking questions about Faraday Reed's murder. Perhaps you struck too close to home for someone's comfort. Damn it, Charity, you nearly got yourself killed!"

The color drained from Charity's face as an even worse thought occurred to her. "But, Simon, if it was in my wine last night, that must mean that—that someone at the party put it there. One of your—"

"Oh, God." He stood up, shoving his hands into his hair, and began to pace. "It couldn't be. Wait, it wasn't necessarily put there by a guest. One of the servants could have done it."

"The servants!"

"Yes. Perhaps someone bribed one of them into doing it. Or—or didn't Chaney take on some extra men to help serve?"

"Yes." Charity brightened. "Yes, he did. That large man was one of them. And I think there was one other. He needed extra help for the number of guests."

Chaney, when called for, confirmed that he had hired two extra servers for the previous evening. Both of them had been sent by an agency with which he had dealt many times before.

"Go there today and find out about both men. I want to know who they are. I want to question them. In the meantime, Chaney, Lady Dure is to eat nothing that hasn't been prepared and served by you personally. Is that clear?"

"Yes, my lord." Even the usually imperturbable Chaney's face showed amazement.

"Someone has tried to kill her, Chaney."

"My lord!"

"It's true. That foolish monkey is all that saved her." He explained what had happened. "But I don't know that he will try poison again. It could come in some other way. That's why you must watch her, also. Whenever I am not here, you must not let anything happen to her."

"Yes, my lord. Either Patrick or I will stand outside her door the whole time. Patrick is my sister's boy, and I trust him absolutely."

"Very good."

"I will go to the agency right now, my lord." Chaney bowed and left the room.

"Simon, I don't really think that's necessary," Charity began.

He whirled, his eyes stabbing her. "Isn't necessary? Do you actually think I'm going to stand by and not protect you?"

"Of course not, but—"

"No buts about it. In fact, I'm thinking that it would be probably be best if you went back to Deerfield Park."

"No! Not without you. Besides, we'll never be able to find out who did it from Deerfield Park. We have to stay in London. We should send for that obnoxious Gorham person and tell him. Perhaps he will realize then that he is chasing the wrong person."

"More likely he will think we are trying to pull the wool over his eyes." Simon paced back and forth across the room, his forehead drawn together in a scowl. Finally, abruptly, he said, "I have to go to Venetia."

"Venetia?" Charity stared. "But why? Anyway, you can't. She told me they were leaving first thing this morning for Ashford Court."

"In Sussex? Damn!" He made a few more turns around the room, then said, "I shall simply have to go there. I fear I won't be back until tomorrow evening. Chaney and Patrick will guard you. You have to promise me that you will *not* leave the house. For any reason. Is that understood?"

"Simon!"

"I mean it, Charity. I don't know what I would do if anything happened to you."

Charity could not speak. What he had said was almost a declaration of love, and even in the midst of her fear, it lifted her heart. At that moment, she thought, she would have agreed to almost anything he asked.

"Yes, Simon, I promise. I won't go anywhere. And with Chaney and Patrick standing by, I am sure I shall be utterly safe."

"Better let Lucky eat a bit of everything from your plate before you do."

Charity rolled her eyes. "Chaney is going to oversee my meals."

"Just to be safe."

"Why is it so important that you visit Venetia? Surely you don't think that she—that she could have done it, do you?"

"God, I hope not." Simon closed his eyes, in pain. "I— The thing is, you see, I gave her my handkerchief. Before

I left for Deerfield Park, two weeks before Reed was killed, I went to see her, and she was crying, and I gave her my handkerchief. She forgot to give it back to me before I left."

Charity looked at him, stunned by the implication of what he had just said. "Oh, Simon!" she breathed. "Oh, my poor darling!" She hurried across the room and put her arms around him. "All these weeks, have you been thinking about that? Is that why you have seemed reluctant to find the killer? Why you discouraged my talking to people about Reed?"

He nodded. "Partly. I can't believe that Venetia could kill anyone, even Reed. I told her that I would take care of things, so she did not need to fear him anymore. Still…she detested him and feared him. And I knew that she had that damned handkerchief. I couldn't bring myself to ask her. I didn't want to suspect her, didn't want her to know that the thought had even crossed my mind. But as long as there was a possibility that it would turn out to be she, I preferred to let the inspector keep me as his main suspect. I didn't want him turning an eye toward Venetia."

"Or George. He would have had access to the handkerchief, too, if Venetia had it. And I told you how odd he looked yesterday when I mentioned Reed's name."

Simon sighed. "I suppose George might be more likely to kill someone than Venetia. Though that, too, seems a trifle farfetched." He walked over to the sofa and sat upon it with her. "But now I have to know for sure. I don't care if she did kill Reed—God knows, he deserved it many times over. But if she tried to harm you—I have to stop it."

Simon left in the carriage not long afterward. He drove hard all afternoon, and arrived at Ashford Court just as

Venetia and her husband were sitting down to dinner. Dure strode into the dining room on the heels of the servant who announced him. Venetia jumped to her feet, astonishment on her face.

"I say!" Ashford exclaimed, standing up as well. "Dure! What the devil are you doing here?"

"I had to talk to you. Or, rather, to Venetia."

Venetia stared at him. "But, Simon, we saw you last night. Why have you come all the way out here? We've just barely got here ourselves."

"It's important," Simon said flatly. "It's about Charity."

"Charity?" Venetia sucked in a breath, worry spreading across her face. "Why? What's the matter? Has something happened to her?"

Simon looked at his sister coolly. "Why do you say that? Should something have?"

Venetia's face knotted in confusion. "But you said that you had come here to talk about Charity. I assumed... Simon, whatever is the matter?"

"Yes. Out with it, man," Ashford urged him. "I can't understand what you're talking about."

"I think someone tried to poison Charity last night."

"Oh, Simon! No!" Venetia leaped to her feet and hurried across the room to her brother, taking his arm solicitously. "Is she all right?"

"What the devil are you doing chasing out here?" Ashford demanded bluntly. "I would think you'd be at home with her."

Fear and pain flitted across Dure's features as he gazed down at his sister. "She's well. She did not drink the poison. It killed the monkey, instead."

"Thank God," Venetia breathed.

"The monkey!" Ashford exclaimed. "How the devil did that happen? Dure, you're not making sense. Sit down. Have a cup of tea. Venetia…"

"Of course." Venetia steered her brother to the chair across the table from hers, then sat down herself and began to pour him a cup of amber liquid. "I don't understand, Simon. How do you know the monkey was poisoned? Or that it was meant for Charity?"

"We found the creature dead in her room. We thought at first it was the dog, of course, but there wasn't a mark on him."

"Perhaps someone wrung his neck. Doesn't seem unlikely to me," Ashford pointed out.

A half smile touched Simon's lips, and he sighed. "I thought of that, believe me. But I checked. His neck hadn't been broken. And he hadn't shown any sign of being ill earlier. You saw the way he scampered around. The main thing is, he smelled of almonds."

"Almonds? Someone poisoned the almonds?" Ashford goggled.

"No. 'Tis a kind of poison. It smells like bitter almonds. I recognized it."

"But what does that have to do with Charity?" Venetia asked.

"The monkey drank from her wine cup at dinner. Remember? When it was scampering all over the table, disturbing everyone."

"Damn, that's right, I remember." Ashford agreed. "But…why would anyone want to murder Charity? She's a likeable gel. Are you sure it wasn't your Aunt Hortense's glass the rascal took? There's someone I can see wanting to poison."

"George!" Venetia exclaimed.

Dure let out a laugh at his brother-in-law's words, then groaned and shoved his hands into his hair. "Oh, God, I don't know what to do. Or what to think."

"But why did you come to us?" Venetia asked, frowning. "I mean, of course, we are glad you informed us, but…"

"I came because I had to ask you something." Simon raised his head and looked at her bleakly. "Venetia…where is my handkerchief?"

"Your handkerchief!" Ashford stared at Dure as if he had lost his mind. "What a thing to be thinking about at a time like this! You must have dozens of handkerchiefs, man."

But Venetia understood the import of his question. Her face drained of color, and she rose slowly. "You mean… you think that I…"

"I know you had my handkerchief—that day when you and I talked, and you began to cry, I gave you one."

"What the devil is all this talk about handkerchiefs?" Ashford blurted out in frustration. "Venetia, why do you look as if you'd just seen a ghost? What is going on?"

"Perhaps I'd better talk to my sister alone," Simon said stiffly, his face limned with pain.

"I should say not! You are obviously upsetting her. Damn it, Simon, I won't have it. Whatever your problem is, you and I shall sit down and talk about it, man to man. Over a glass of brandy. Venetia, why don't you go upstairs while I try to thrash this out?"

"No," Venetia replied colorlessly. "You can't thrash it out with him. It's me he suspects of murder. Isn't it, Simon?"

"I don't know!" Simon cried out. "That's why I'm here. I couldn't believe it. I didn't want to believe it. But there was the handkerchief…. I could not forget that. And the reasons you have to hate him."

Ashford, who had been standing with his jaw hanging open, staring at them, suddenly came to life. Flushing red, he started forward. "You think…that Venetia…that Reed fellow… Hellfire and damnation, man, you are accusing your own sister of murder?"

Simon's eyes flashed fire. "I am not accusing her of anything. I am simply asking. I have to know. Damn it, Charity's life is at stake here! I cannot go on not knowing."

"Well, it wasn't Venetia," Ashford retorted. "She was with me that night, all night. I'll swear to it."

"But, George, that's not true." Venetia swung around to look at him.

"Blast it, Venetia, if I say we were together, we were."

Venetia smiled tenderly at her husband and reached out to take his hands. "Dear George. You would lie for me?"

"It won't work, Ashford," Simon said flatly. "Everyone saw Venetia at the Willingham party, and you were not with her."

"Yes, dear," Venetia reminded him gently. "You were at your club, and I am sure there are a dozen gentlemen who can testify to that."

"But I left," Ashford maintained stoutly. "I must have been out of the club by three."

"We both know you were not in my bed that night, though, don't we? I heard you come to your room, but you never came to my door."

His eyes slid away. "It was late. I didn't want to disturb you."

"Just as you haven't all these past few months?" Venetia asked softly. Then, as Ashford's face flushed red again, she shook her head, turning away. "No. There's no use in getting into that. The problem now is whether I killed Faraday Reed." She looked at Simon squarely, her chin coming up. "Wait here a moment. I shall be right back."

She swept out of the room. Simon and Ashford looked at each other uncomfortably; then Simon turned away and walked to the window. He looked steadfastly out into the dark. The air was heavy with their silence.

Finally Ashford said, "She couldn't have killed him. You don't know. If anyone had any reason to kill him, it was I, not Venetia."

"You?" Simon turned to him, amazed. "What are you talking about?"

"The jealous husband. He's always the one with the best motive, is he not? I could have taken your handkerchief from Venetia's drawer, you know. I could have killed him and dropped it there to throw suspicion on you. Much more likely a thing for me to do than your own sister, don't you think?"

Simon stared at him. "My God, George, are you saying that *you* killed him?"

Ashford set his jaw. "It is what I shall say if you accuse Venetia."

"George!"

Both men turned to see Venetia standing in the doorway. Her face was white, and her eyes blazed in her pale face. She stared at her husband. "Do you mean that you would confess to a crime you didn't commit in order to save me?"

Ashford cleared his throat, looking uncomfortable. "Well, I couldn't very well let them take you to jail, could I?"

"Oh, George!" Her voice was choked with tears. She

hurried across the room to him, and gazed up at him, heedless of the teardrops beginning to spill from her eyes and trickle down her cheeks. "You love me that much?"

His eyes shifted away from her. "Of course. You are my wife, after all. You…I…you must know I've been mad for you since the day I met you."

"Oh, George!" Venetia threw her arms around his neck and clung to him. "Then why—why have you been so cool to me these last weeks? Why—?" She broke off suddenly and stepped back, her eyes searching his face. "Unless *you* thought I killed him, too?"

"Good gad, no. Why would I think you killed the rat? You loved him. *I'm* the one who lay in bed every night thinking about choking the life from him. Wouldn't have shot him, though—not satisfying enough. I wanted to kill him with my own two hands. But I couldn't, of course. I mean, it would have made you unhappy, and I couldn't do that. You know I can't bear for you to be unhappy. I will admit I was glad to hear he was dead. But then, every time I hear you crying in your bed at night, I hate myself for being glad."

Venetia stared at him, puzzled. "Unhappy? You think I have been unhappy because Faraday Reed is dead? That I cried at night because of him? Good heavens, why?"

He looked back at her in equal puzzlement. "Why? What do you mean? Because you loved him."

"I hated him!" Venetia's face twisted, as if she had tasted something bitter. "How could you think I loved him still after what he'd done?"

There was a long silence as George gazed at his wife in bafflement. "But you were lovers. I— Weaver followed you. He saw you meeting. He saw…" His voice trembled a little, and he paused to swallow before he went on. "He saw Reed kiss you that day in the park. I knew about your affair."

"No!" Venetia cried, stepping back from him, her hands flying to her face. "No… Oh, George, you thought— I didn't love him! I despised him. I hated him. We were not having an affair. He was extorting money from me! That day in the park, he grabbed my arm and pulled me to him and kissed me, but I didn't want him to! I struggled to get out of his embrace, but he was too strong. And he was only having fun at my expense. He knew how much I hated him, but he knew I couldn't cry out, because it might attract attention."

"He wasn't your lover?" Ashford's taut face softened as he absorbed this news. "Venetia…my love… I've wronged you. Good God, can you ever forgive me?" He reached out and pulled her close, wrapping his arms around her and squeezing her to him.

"But wait—" Ashford released Venetia and looked down into her face. "You say the scoundrel was trying to get money from you?" His gaze flew over to Simon. "And you knew about this?"

Simon nodded.

"Why? What hold did he have on you?"

Venetia stepped away from her husband, releasing a sigh. "Obviously I cannot keep it from you any longer. I— Mayhap you will hate me just as much as when you thought I was trysting with him."

"No. I did not hate you. I could never hate you."

"Don't speak so soon." Venetia closed her eyes for a moment, then opened them and gazed unflinchingly at her husband. She told him her story, of the way Reed had wooed and deceived her when she was young, how he had convinced her to elope with him and then had demanded money not to reveal the blot on her reputation when Simon caught up with them.

As she spoke, anger grew on Ashford's face, and as it did, her voice began to falter. She finished in a rush, almost in tears at the end. Ashford looked thunderous.

"That blackguard!" he roared as Venetia stopped. "I should have killed him!" He glared at Simon. "*You* should have killed him, long ago!"

"Believe me, there have been times when I wished I had. I think all our lives would have been much simpler," Simon retorted dryly. "But there was Venetia's reputation to consider."

Ashford grunted. "He was a cur, a scoundrel, a— To do that to an innocent young girl and then have the gall to expect her to pay him to keep his mouth shut! I wish he had told me. I'd have given him 'full payment.' You shouldn't have paid him a cent, Ven. You should have come straight to me."

"But, George. I was so afraid of what you would think, how you would feel. I was afraid that you would hate me. That you would cast me off."

"Venetia! How could you think that? I would never have cast you off. Even when I thought you were having an affair with Reed, I never thought of doing that. I simply prayed that it would not last. That you would come back to me."

"I never left you." Venetia smiled tremulously at him.

"I know that now. Oh, my love." He took her in his arms again. Kissing her hair, he whispered into her ear, "Do you think I didn't know that I was not the first? I didn't care.

All I wanted was you. All I cared about was that it was me you had chosen in the end."

"Oh, George…" Venetia wrapped her arms around him tightly, crying softly against his chest. "You are the best man in the world. I don't deserve you for a husband."

"Nonsense. You deserve much better."

Simon, who had been watching this emotional scene before him with the distinctly uncomfortable feeling of being a Peeping Tom, turned discreetly away. Once again he gazed out the window, trying to ignore the sniffles and sighs, and the soft sound of a kiss. More and more every moment he was sure that he had come on a fool's errand. His concern for Charity's safety had muddled his thinking; Venetia could not have murdered a man—not even a cur like Faraday Reed. She was too gentle, too sweet. She was much more likely to do what she *had* done: turn to him with her problem. And she would have trusted that he would handle it; she had always relied on him as her big brother.

Now, Charity—she was a woman he could very well envision deciding to take matters into her own hands, even if it meant toting a gun over to a man's house. She was also one who would be willing to use the weapon if the man attacked her. He had grown too used to Charity's spirit and independence, and he had started assuming that another woman, like his sister, might act the same.

Simon sighed and turned back to the other couple, who were still locked in each other's arms, Venetia's head upon Ashford's chest and his cheek resting tenderly on the top of her head.

Simon cleared his throat and began stiffly, "I'm sorry, Venetia. I have been an idiot in coming here. I can see that.

I just—I wasn't thinking clearly. I knew it wasn't you, couldn't be you, and yet there was this doubt niggling at me all the time because of the handkerchief. When that bloody monkey dropped dead and I realized Charity was in danger, I jumped to conclusions and came tearing off down here to find you."

"Of course Venetia didn't do it," George agreed bluffly. "Thing is, who did? That's what you need to find out."

"Will you forgive me, sister?" Simon looked at Venetia tentatively.

She smiled back at him warmly. "At this moment, I could forgive anyone anything, I think." She crossed the room to him and took his hands in hers. "Yes, I forgive you. It was a shock to me at first, but I can see that it was only natural to wonder, knowing the enmity between Reed and me, and knowing that I had your handkerchief. I am sure that you are wild with fear for Charity. However, I need to return the item in question, anyway." She reached into her pocket and pulled out a neatly folded white square. "Here is your handkerchief—washed and pressed."

Simon took the handkerchief, smiling shamefacedly, and tucked it into his pocket. "Thank you. You are an angel not to hate me for suspecting you, even for a moment."

"I understand. You love her."

Simon swallowed and looked away. "Yes. I do."

"Well, come now, and eat with us."

"No, I need to get back to Charity." Simon frowned.

"Surely you can't mean to ride back to London tonight! Why, it's pitch-black outside, and you've already ridden all day. Your horses can't stand it, even if you could. You need to eat and rest. Tomorrow you can go back. Charity is safe. You said that Chaney is watching over her."

"Yes. I suppose you're right. It's just that I feel so uneasy…. One never knows what Charity might decide to do. Still, she promised not to go out. Surely she can't get into any trouble before tomorrow evening."

CHAPTER TWENTY-THREE

CHARITY DROPPED her sewing in her lap and sighed. She was restless. Simon had been so adamant about her staying inside and away from danger that she had not left the house even once, today or the day before. And everywhere she turned, there was either Chaney or Patrick, watching her as if she might disappear right before their eyes.

That odious man from Scotland Yard had come by to ask a lot of questions. He had been by turns sly and humble in a way that made Charity long to slap him, and he had alluded vaguely to "new information," looking meaningfully into her eyes. Charity hadn't been able to decide whether he actually did have new information or was simply hoping that he could scare her into saying something damaging about her husband. Charity had told him about the monkey's death, but, just as Simon had predicted, Gorham had been disbelieving.

She had worried about his visit for the rest of the afternoon, wondering if there really was new information, and if, as Gorham had implied, it was damaging to Simon. She wished that Simon would return so that they could talk about it.

Charity could not believe that Venetia had murdered or even helped to murder Faraday Reed. However, she was a good deal less certain that Ashford had not. It seemed possible to her that George, despite his affable temper, could have risen to a rage if Reed told him how he had hurt and misused Venetia. Throwing the blame on Simon hardly seemed like something he would do, but then, she reasoned, one really didn't know to what lengths a person might go if he was afraid of being caught.

Chaney stepped into the room, his face, as always, carefully blank, his figure rigid. He carried a small silver salver, and on it lay an envelope.

"My lady? This just came for you."

Charity brightened and reached for the letter. The writing on the front bore no frank, and for an instant she felt a frisson of fear as she remembered the other notes she had gotten, before she married Dure. But, of course, it was impossible for it to be another like that, she reminded herself. It was Reed who had sent her the notes, and he was dead.

Charity's name on the front was written in elegant copperplate handwriting, dispelling any reminder of the other notes. Charity slit it open and pulled out the sweetly fragranced piece of paper inside.

Dear Lady Dure,
I beg you will not find me overbold in writing you. Please forgive my importunity, but I have nowhere else to turn. I would consider it a great kindness in you to agree to visit me today. You are such a kind woman that I hoped I could impose on you this way. Perhaps you remember the matter of which we spoke last time we met. I have found that my worst fears are confirmed. I dread being seen, and I know that,

in my shame, you should not be seen with me. Therefore, I am waiting for you in the carriage outside in the hopes that you will ride with me and talk. Pray do not tell Lord Dure or anyone else, or he would forbid you to see one who is so fallen as I.

With highest regards,
Theodora Graves

"The poor thing," Charity murmured, her own troubles momentarily forgotten as she thought about the poor woman's plight. Abandoned by some arrogant nobleman—a cad much like Faraday Reed, no doubt. It was she alone who would bear the burden of society's condemnation.

It didn't take Charity a moment to make up her mind. She stood up, saying, "Chaney."

The perfect-mannered butler reappeared almost immediately from the hallway where he had discreetly withdrawn while Charity read her missive.

"Yes, my lady?"

"I am going for a ride with a friend."

Chaney's usually expressionless face showed that he was appalled. "My lady! His Lordship said specifically that you were not to leave the house."

Charity grimaced. "Dure House is not a prison, is it?"

"No, of course not, my lady. But Lord Dure—"

"Is concerned for my safety," Charity ended impatiently. "Yes, I know, but there's no call to worry. I won't be alone. I have a friend, you see, waiting for me in the carriage. She doubtless has a coachman driving her carriage, and he can protect us. We are merely going for a ride."

"But, my lady…" Chaney was almost moaning now.

"There's nothing to worry about. I will not be in any danger."

"My lady," Chaney reminded her doggedly, using the argument he knew would hold the most sway with her, "Lord Dure will have our heads for letting you go out alone."

There was a long pause, during which Charity and Chaney looked at one another. "Oh, all right, then," Charity agreed grumpily. "I will take one of the footmen with me, as well. Will that satisfy you?"

Chaney could not suppress a broad smile. "That would be splendid, my lady."

While Charity put on her bonnet, Chaney went looking for Patrick. Chaney himself opened the door for Charity, saying as she stepped outside, "And who is my lady visiting with this afternoon, if I may ask?"

Charity cast him a quizzical look. "Another thing that will keep Lord Dure from having your heads?"

"Yes, my lady, I am afraid so."

"Well, it's a widow. Mrs. Graves. Mrs. Theodora Graves."

Charity swept down the steps and out to the carriage without a backward glance, leaving Chaney at the door, gaping after her.

The coachman, who had climbed down in order to assist her, looked surprised at Patrick's presence, but he stepped back as Patrick helped Charity up into the coach. He and Patrick climbed up to the high coachman's seat while Charity settled in across from Theodora. The carriage took off, leaving Chaney behind, stupefied.

"I am so glad you came," Theodora said, a little pitifully. "I was afraid you would not."

Charity, looking across at her, thought that Mrs. Graves's problems must indeed be wearing on her. Her color was unusually high, and her eyes were very bright. Her hands clutched a carriage robe, though in Charity's opinion it seemed unseasonably warm for her to require a blanket.

"Are you feeling ill?" Charity inquired gently.

To her surprise, Theodora giggled. "Ill? No. In fact, right now I think I feel better than I have in months."

The look on Theodora's face made Charity uneasy. It was somehow odd and unnatural. Charity shifted in her seat and glanced away, wondering if Mrs. Grave's problems had unbalanced her mind slightly. She found herself wishing that she had not agreed to come. She had no idea what to do if Theodora should have hysterics or some such thing.

"What can I do to help you?" Charity asked finally.

Again Theodora chuckled. "Why, nothing, *my lady.* Absolutely nothing. You already have."

Charity looked back up at her, startled by the woman's strangely sarcastic tone, and saw that Theodora Graves had a small silver gun in her hand, and was pointing it straight at her.

For a long moment Charity could only stare at Mrs. Graves in astonishment. Theodora laughed again; it was almost a cackle this time.

"Even now you don't understand, do you?" she asked. "How could he have married you? A country girl! No sophistication, no charms. A complete ninny, always so bright and smiling and full of good cheer, as if the world were your play yard." Theodora's features grew tighter and more twisted as she talked, until she was snarling. "I'm sure he regrets it now. He couldn't get any joy out your childish charms in bed. No, I'm sure he regrets marrying you now!"

"Simon!" Charity asked in amazement. "You are doing this because of Simon?"

"Yes! You little fool! Don't you realize that he was in love with me? He would have married me, too, if you hadn't come along."

Charity gazed at her, trying to assimilate the other woman's words. Finally she asked, "Are you saying that Simon is your nobleman?"

"Yes!" Theodora hissed, her eyes narrowed almost to slits. "He loved me. He panted after me. Then you came along and ruined it!"

"Don't be absurd," Charity said crisply. Anger flickered up in her, sweeping away her momentary paralysis of fear and astonishment. "Simon would not have treated a woman the way you said your lover had. He told me straight out that he had had mistresses, and I am sure that that is what you were. I would say it is much more likely that you were a very 'available' widow, not an innocent, grief-stricken one, and he was attracted by your quite obvious charms."

Theodora actually preened at Charity's words, raising her chin a little so that it showed the white column of her throat to its best advantage. "He worshiped at my feet."

Charity let out a dry chuckle. "I seriously doubt that. Simon does not worship at one's feet. Knowing him, I am sure he was quite generous and fair with you. No doubt he paid for your clothes, your carriage, your servants...."

"Of course." Pride still covered Theodora's face.

"And no doubt he considered it a business arrangement,

not a love affair. He paid you for what you offered him, and that was all it was. He didn't love you. He told me he loved no one. He certainly would not have ruined his family name by marrying a woman of the streets."

Color flooded Theodora's face. "I was not a whore! I was a respectable widow. And he loved me. He did! He would have married me!"

"You must be mad!"

"Mad!" Theodora's face turned almost purple with rage, and she shook the little gun wildly at Charity. "I'm mad? You think a mad person could have planned this? You think a bedlamite could have thought of all the other things? You little fool! You have no idea what you're talking about."

"The other things?" Complete understanding dawned on Charity at last. "You mean, the monkey?"

"That bloody animal! And Hubbell couldn't return to do it again."

"And—and Mr. Reed?" Charity almost stopped breathing as she asked the question. *Could this madwoman actually have killed someone?*

"Yes, of course Mr. Reed. That worm—trying to back out of our deal. The blasted coward."

"The deal?"

"I was going to stop the marriage, you see, and Faraday agreed to help me. He had always hated Simon. He was eager to despoil Simon's future bride."

"Despoil—" Charity felt a blush spreading across her face. "Do you mean he always intended to rape me?"

Theodora grimaced. "No, the stupid man thought that you would fall into his arms instead of Simon's. But if that didn't work, yes, he intended to force you. It didn't matter, as long as you were soiled, a scandal."

Cold spread through Charity at the thought of this woman's icy indifference to her pain and humiliation. She wanted to turn away from Mrs. Graves, to retreat into silence. However, she realized that the best thing to do now, the only thing she could do, really, was to keep Theodora talking. Otherwise the woman might decide to shoot her. Obviously Theodora had no qualms about killing. But as long as Theodora was talking, at least Charity could try to think of a way to escape.

Charity searched her brain for something else to say. "Was it you, too, who sent the notes to me?"

Theodora smiled, as if Charity had complimented her. "Yes. When they didn't work, Faraday thought he could use them to worm his way into your friendship. But then he was too much of a coward to continue." She sneered. "He told me he was even afraid of you."

"So you shot him?" Charity tried to keep all blame out of her voice.

Theodora shrugged. "We argued. He was being most unreasonable. Finally he began to threaten me. *Me!*" The idea clearly amazed Theodora. "We struggled and...well, I had to shoot him."

"But what about the handkerchief? How did that get there?"

Theodora smiled, pleased at her cleverness. "After he died, I ran away. I was terribly frightened, but then I remembered that I still had one of Simon's handkerchiefs, one he had left at my house on a 'visit.' So I got it and returned to Reed's. Fortunately, no one had come into the room and found him. I could see into the room through the side window. The window was open, so I tossed the handkerchief in. No one saw me leave the house or return."

"But if you wanted to marry Simon, why did you leave his handkerchief there? I thought you loved him."

"Love him? Did I say that? I would not say it is love, no. I wanted to marry him, that's all." She shrugged again. "He is a pleasant lover, much better than so many men, who only want to grab and paw and get their own satisfaction as soon as they can. It would not be so bad to have him in my bed. And he is wealthy. If he married me, I would have whatever I wanted. I would be a respected member of society."

"But it's rather hard to marry someone who is in jail for murder, isn't it?"

"I don't think his handkerchief is enough to hang him. I mean, here he is, many weeks later, and nothing has happened to him. I did not want him arrested. Mostly, I wanted to cast suspicion away from me. I had, after all, been seen with Faraday rather often recently. I hoped merely that it would implicate Simon enough that you would call off the engagement."

Theodora frowned at Charity, adding in irritation, "Why didn't you? I was sure that the scandal would frighten your ever-so-noble family. I thought Simon would be too much of a gentleman to keep you to your word, either. I was counting on it." She looked downcast and puzzled.

Charity shifted; she didn't want to give Theodora any time to think. "So then, the poison—it was to get rid of me, so that Simon would be free to marry you?"

"Of course. It would have worked, too, if it hadn't been for that damned monkey." She glared at Charity. "Why would you have such a silly animal in the house, anyway?"

"I—I'm not sure. It was quite cute." Charity didn't know what to say. She felt as if she were in some mad world where all the normal values and rules were turned upside down. What did one say to keep calm a woman who had killed, who saw human lives only as obstacles in her way?

Charity rubbed her palms down her skirt to dry them. It was hot and stuffy in the carriage. She didn't know how her head could feel so hot and her stomach so cold. She wished she had some idea what to do to stop Theodora. She had never faced a person with a gun before; it frightened her far more than Reed's clumsy attack in the garden. She could not leap at Theodora and try to take the gun away, because Theodora would be able to shoot her before she reached her. Charity contemplated the idea of jumping out of the carriage; she was willing to risk the injury when she hit the ground, but, again, it was all too likely that she would be shot before she reached the door latch. But Charity was not about to wait passively for Theodora to kill her when and where she chose.

She wondered if Theodora had seen Patrick outside when he helped her up into the carriage. If she had not, then Charity had a surprise weapon. Patrick would try to save her when they stepped out of the carriage.

"Would you mind if I raised the curtain?" Charity asked, reaching toward the heavy curtain that obscured the windows. *At least she could find out where she was.*

"No!" Theodora's gun hand had drooped a little, but at Charity's movement, it snapped back up and she pointed the gun squarely at Charity's chest again. "Do you think I'm stupid?"

"I only want to get a little fresh air. It's terribly hot in here."

"I will not let you be seen in my carriage. I will not allow you to call for help."

A thought popped into Charity's head suddenly, and she smiled. "But I told Chaney who you were. I said your name. They will notice that I am missing."

"You're lying!"

"Am I?" Charity smiled and leaned back, crossing her arms. "Can you risk it? Everyone will know that you killed me. You will be hanged. I'm sure you would not like that. It makes you terribly ugly, I've heard. Your face turns purple, and your eyes bulge out."

"Shut up!" Theodora screeched. "Shut up!"

The gun wavered dangerously in her hand, and Charity wisely decided to be quiet. For a few moments there was silence in the vehicle, except for the rumble of the wheels as it rolled over the cobblestones. The carriage jiggled and bounced, and Charity eyed the gun nervously as it bobbed in Theodora's hand. *What if it went off accidentally when they hit a bump?*

Theodora was much too nervous; her fingers trembled on the gun. Charity thought that almost any bump or anything that startled Theodora might cause enough of an extra jerk to make her pull the trigger. Sweat trickled down Charity's sides in the stuffy carriage; she hoped her incipient panic didn't show on her face. Fear, she thought, might incite Theodora to violence.

"Ah…where are we going?" Charity asked, almost as much to take her mind off the shaking gun as to lull her captor with conversation.

"Someplace you wouldn't know," Theodora said with a sneer. "It's among the common folk, the sort of place you've never been in your life."

The carriage had slowed almost to a stop, and their path seemed to twist and turn. The sudden strong stench of an open sewer made Charity almost gag, and she quickly put one hand over her mouth and nose.

Theodora, watching her, chuckled. "You see? You would never have soiled your pretty little feet by walking in here—not that you would have made it out unharmed if you had."

"Why?"

"Because it's the sort of place where a gun can go off and no one will pay the slightest attention. No one will rouse Scotland Yard or admit to seeing anything. It's perfect for disposing of unwanted things."

Charity could think of nothing to say to that, and she lapsed into silence.

The carriage rumbled to a stop. Charity heard the sound of the two men climbing down from the carriage. Theodora moved quickly to Charity's side. Grasping the younger woman's elbow with one hand, Theodora pressed the snout of her stubby gun to Charity temple. A moment later the door to the carriage opened. Theodora's coachman stood outside, at the foot of the steps he'd let down. Behind him stood Patrick, looking puzzled, worried and angry all at once. He glanced around him uneasily.

Theodora pulled on Charity's elbow, propelling her out the door, with Theodora as close to her as a second skin, the snub-nosed pistol still tight against Charity's head. Patrick's mouth dropped open when he saw them, and his face drained of all color. Charity realized that Theodora had been expecting this; that was why she had moved over and put the gun to her head before the door opened. She had known about Patrick all along.

Red rushed back into Patrick's cheeks, and he took a step forward, reaching out toward Charity.

"Stay back!" Theodora barked, grinding her gun against Charity's temple so hard that tears came to Charity's eyes.

"'ere!" the coachman said, pushing Patrick back. "''ave some sense, will ye? Ye try to take that popgun away from 'er, and yer fine lady'll be dead 'fore you can even touch 'er."

"He's right," Theodora said. Charity could hear the sound of Theodora's rapid breathing, and though she could not turn to see because of the gun pressed hard against her head, she suspected that Theodora's face was flushed and her eyes were wild. "The only thing you can do to keep her from dying is to walk along quietly with us. Say nothing to anyone, and do not try to signal for help. Do you understand?"

Patrick swallowed hard and nodded.

"Right, then, let's go," the coachman said.

He reached out and grabbed Patrick's arm, swiveling him about and shoving him forward. Theodora removed the gun from Charity's temple and stuck it in her side. They fell in behind the two men. It was evening, but it was far darker here than normal, even for this time of day. A jumble of ramshackle buildings rose up all around them, blocking out all light, and there were no gas lamps anywhere to add even a small glow. They walked along a path far too narrow for the carriage. The place stank of sweat and sewage and mildew. A skinny, half-naked child stared at them dully, his finger in his mouth, and behind him a woman sat against a wall in a stupor, mumbling to herself.

A man with blackened teeth lurched out of a low doorway and peered after them. An unkempt urchin on crutches hobbled after them, begging for coins. Charity twisted to look at the child.

"The poor thing," she murmured.

Theodora jabbed the gun deeper into Charity's side. "You're in worse danger than that cripple."

"Couldn't I give him just a few coins?"

"Are you daft?" Theodora came to a standstill, gaping at her.

"Please?" Charity looked at her pleadingly and reached down into her pocket.

Theodora narrowed her eyes suspiciously. "What do you have in there?"

"I don't normally carry a weapon about," Charity retorted crisply. "Will you not allow me to do a final good deed?"

She gazed steadily at Theodora, willing all the power of the centuries of privilege and entitlement that lay behind her into her eyes.

"All right," Theodora agreed grudgingly. "But do it slowly. I'll shoot you if you pull out anything but coins."

Charity nodded and slowly took out her small coin purse. She held it out to the boy and smiled. He moved forward as quickly as he could and stretched out his hand. Charity tossed the soft leather purse into his hand, then turned, as regally as a queen going to the block, and followed the path the coachman and Patrick had taken.

Behind her, she heard the boy let out a soft breath of discovery. Her coin purse, she knew, had a guinea in it, as well as several shillings. She was sure it was more money than the lad had ever seen in his life. He would be sure to remember the two women who had passed his way this day—if only Simon could track her this far.

CHAPTER TWENTY-FOUR

AS CHARITY WALKED slowly along, she clasped her hands together and surreptitiously pulled off the large square-cut emerald ring that Simon had given her when they became engaged. Then, just as secretively, she slipped it onto the middle finger of her right hand, next to the much smaller amethyst that had been given her by her grandmother. The emerald ring was too small for the finger, of course, but she shoved it as far down on her knuckle as it would go. The two rings combined would inflict far more pain if she was able to swing at anyone.

Ahead of them, the coachman and Patrick stood waiting in front of a door, the coachman behind Patrick and with a heavy hand encircling his arm. As they neared the small door where the men stood, Charity slowed her steps, trying to show panic developing on her face.

"No," she said softly. "Please, Mrs. Graves… Theodora… I never meant you any harm. Isn't there some other way?"

"Oh, so now you start to beg," Theodora said with a smirk. "Not so full of yourself now, are you?"

Theodora motioned to the coachman, who opened the door and shoved Patrick inside. Theodora steered Charity in after them. They were in a small, dim, squalid room. The smell was so rank that Charity could barely breathe.

"Why—why have you brought us here?" Charity asked, stalling for time, though it was clear to her that Theodora had brought her to kill her.

Theodora chuckled. "Why? I should think it's clear. At first I thought I'd have Hubbell here drop you into the river with a stone tied to your hands, but then I realized that if you simply disappeared, Simon would not be free to marry again. I have to let them discover your body. I was planning on shooting you and leaving you here. Then your footman's presence gave me a better idea."

Theodora smiled archly and leaned close to Charity, saying, "I'll make it look like a lover's quarrel, as if you and he were having an assignation in this squalid place. But you argued, and he shot you, then turned the gun on himself. Yes, that will do very nicely. It will explain your death to everyone's satisfaction. And it will guarantee that Simon won't grieve for his bride. He will know that his *suitable* wife was a whore at heart, that she betrayed him. In his rage, of course, he will come back to me."

"He will not!" Charity cried, too furious to worry about spurring Theodora into shooting her immediately. "Simon wouldn't go to you. He *loves* me. He knows me far too well to believe that I had a lover."

Theodora's brows drew together menacingly. "He does not. He couldn't love you."

In truth, Charity was not at all sure whether Simon loved her or not. He had called her his love a few times, but that was a fairly common endearment. It could mean no more than that he was fond of her. But she wasn't about to admit her uncertainty to Theodora. However, neither could she argue with her; Theodora was too obviously unstable. She might pull the trigger on the little gun just because Charity dared to dispute what she said. So Charity kept her lips clamped shut.

Theodora nodded her head, as if Charity's silence were her vindication. She turned to Patrick and said, "Now, you, take off your clothes."

The young man's eyes bulged, and his face turned a bright crimson. "Wot?" he yelped, forgetting the distinguished accent he had worked so hard to develop the past few years.

"You heard me. Take off your clothes—unless you want your lady shot right in front of you."

"But— But— That's indecent!" Patrick looked far more outraged than he had at any time since he and Charity had been in Mrs. Graves's power. At any other time Charity would have laughed at his expression. Now she could only think of whether his protests would distract Theodora enough for Charity to make her move.

"I'm sure that Lord Dure will appreciate your nicety very much," Theodora snapped, "when his wife is bleeding on the floor because of it."

Patrick gulped, glanced at Charity, then at Theodora again. He shrugged out of his elegant jacket and took off his shoes, taking his time about it. When there was no sign of mercy from Theodora, he turned away from the women and began to unbutton his shirt.

"Must you humiliate him?" Charity hissed.

"It's essential," Theodora answered softly, amusement in her voice. "Otherwise my plan wouldn't work. Lovers don't tryst fully clothed, now, do they?"

Charity sucked in her breath sharply, her eyes widening with shock. She had been sure that Simon would not believe that she had been unfaithful, but if she and Patrick were found in such an incriminating way, then he might. *Would she not only die but leave Simon cursing her memory, as well?* Her name would be a scandal in everyone's mouth. Pure, scalding anger poured through her.

Theodora laughed. "Ah, I can see that knocked some of that famous courage out of you. You're right to be afraid. There's nothing you can do."

Charity turned her face aside, glad that Theodora had mistaken her stunned silence for fear. She must not let Theodora catch sight of the fury that she knew must be blazing in her eyes. She needed to trick Theodora into believing that she was weak and scared; otherwise Theodora would never be fooled by the case of hysterics Charity hoped to throw at the right opportunity.

"Please," Charity said, still looking away, "please, there's no need for this. If you will let us go, I won't tell anyone, and neither will Patrick. I shall guarantee it. I won't tell even Simon."

"What good will that do me?" Theodora sneered. "I wouldn't have Simon—and after all this effort, too. I'm certainly not about to give up now."

Finally poor Patrick was down to his unmentionables, and he stopped, looking back pleadingly at Theodora. Theodora simply said in a steely voice, "The rest of it, too."

Patrick's hands clenched, and he started toward Theodora, but the woman brought her gun up to Charity's temple again, reminding him of what would happen to her if he did not cooperate. The footman stopped and set his jaw, then began to unbutton his underclothes with short, jerky movements, all the time staring at Theodora as if he would gladly murder her.

Charity felt sorry for him and turned her face aside, giving him at least a modicum of privacy. Theodora watched, a faint smile playing on her lips.

"A well-set-up young man," she murmured archly. "It's rather too bad to do away with one like that."

"Have you no shame?" Charity cried out, putting a sob in her voice. She brought her hands up to her face.

"Oh, am I too low for my lady's fine tastes?" Theodora sneered, then called to her henchman, "All right, Hubbell, tie him up now."

Charity peeked through her fingers and saw that Hubbell had picked up a rope and was now tying it around Patrick's wrists, pulling his hands behind his back. When Patrick's hands were tied, Hubbell made the footman lie down, and he looped the rope around his feet as well.

"Will you— You aren't going to make me…do that, as well…?" Charity said, and the tremor in her voice wasn't entirely for effect. "I mean, take off my clothes."

Theodora grinned evilly and said, "Yes, and more. That's one of Hubbell's rewards for doing this. He gets to undress you and make sure that it's obvious you've had a man."

The blood drained from Charity's face, and for a moment she feared that she might actually faint. "No! You wouldn't—you wouldn't allow him to do that."

"Why not? It's something I've had to do for years. Do you think you're too fine to have some sweaty, grunting man on top of you, taking what he wants with never a thought to you?"

Charity could do nothing but stare at her.

"All right, Hubbell, she's yours now," Theodora said, stepping back from Charity.

The coachman strode toward Charity, a gleam in his

eye. Theodora moved away, still keeping the gun trained on her. Charity knew that this was her one chance.

She threw her hands out pleadingly toward Theodora and began to wail, "No, please, please, don't do this! You can't do this to me!"

Theodora stopped to watch her, a little smile of satisfaction playing about her mouth. Charity could see that behind her, Patrick, though lying tied and almost helpless on the floor, was inching his way painfully toward Theodora. Charity didn't know exactly how he could help, but she knew she had to stretch the time out.

Charity shrieked and wailed and flung her arms about, throwing a perfect fit of hysteria. She begged and pleaded with Theodora, punctuating her words with sobs and moans. Hubbell hesitated, looking back at his employer, and Theodora impatiently motioned to him to go on.

Hubbell reached out to take Charity's arm, and she shrank back. "Don't touch me!"

"Bloody hell!" Theodora cursed. "Hubbell, just slap her and stop that caterwauling."

"No!" Charity shrieked, and sank artfully to the floor, curling over as if too overcome with fear even to stand and face him.

"Go ahead, Hubbell, shut her up. We can't stay here all day."

Charity peeped between her fingers, looking through Hubbell's legs across the room. Patrick still had not reached Theodora, but at least Theodora had lowered her gun while she watched Charity's display of hysterics. Charity knew she could wait no longer. She curled her right hand into a fist, the stones of the two rings sticking out.

As Hubbell bent over to pull her up, Charity jumped up,

her arm thrusting directly into Hubbell's face. She meant to hit his eye, but she missed slightly, and the force of her blow struck his cheek, the jewels razoring jaggedly along his cheekbone.

The man howled in pain, staggering back and clutching his cheek. Charity streaked toward the door. Theodora raised the gun and fired.

Simon was in a fine mood when he stepped out of the carriage in front of his house. He no longer had to worry that Venetia might be the one who had killed Faraday Reed and, far worse, tried to kill Charity. Charity was still in danger, but he planned to keep an eye on her every minute of every day until he figured out who had really murdered Reed. Now, at least, he would be able to work on that problem with a clear conscience, no longer half fearing that it was his beloved sister whose name would turn up if he investigated. It would be no small task, of course, to keep Charity from jumping into the middle of the investigation and putting herself in danger, but Simon had discovered that anything he did with Charity, even trying to convince her of something, had its pleasures.

He hurried toward the house, eager to see Charity again. It had been only a little over a day since he had been with her, but even that period of time was enough to make him feel as if a part of him were missing. He wanted to see her smile, to hear her laugh, to celebrate with her that Venetia was no longer a suspect, to plan how he would smoke out the killer…to take her in his arms and kiss her, the way he had been wanting to do all the way back from Ashford Court.

The door flew open so hard that it crashed against the

wall, and Chaney ran out, a look of panic on his face such as Simon had never seen. "My lord! My lord! Thank God!" He turned toward the carriage, which was just pulling away from the curb on the way to the mews, and waved his arms frantically. "Wait! Botkins, stop!"

"Chaney, what the devil is going on?" Simon gripped the butler's arm, icy fear forming in the pit of his stomach. He was sure that there was only one thing that could bring the staid butler to this state: Charity. "Has something happened to her?"

"Yes, my lord. I mean, I'm not sure. I don't know."

"Damn it, man, out with it! Stop dithering about. What happened to her?"

The youngest of the footmen came pelting out the door, too, his neat white powdered wig absurdly askew and his elegant frogged coat abandoned. Sweat stained the front of his shirt, and his chest was heaving, as if he had run a race.

"I followed her, my lord. Or, at least, most of the way."

"Followed her! Where the devil is she?" Simon's brows drew together thunderously, and he swung back to Chaney. "Blast it, man, you said you would take care of her while I was gone. It was only a day."

"Yes, my lord. It is my fault, my lord. I shall never be able to live with myself if anything happens to her. But at least it's a woman. Surely she isn't the one who tried—"

"*It?* What is *it?* Who is it?" Simon barely resisted the urge to grab the older man's shoulders and shake him. It wouldn't help his obviously befuddled thoughts.

"Mrs. Graves!"

"Theodora!" Simon stared at him, stunned. "Lady Dure is with Theodora Graves?"

Chaney nodded.

"How in the name of all that's holy does Charity know Theodora?" He stopped and shook his head. "No, that's a foolish thing to ask. She could know the king of Siam and it would not be astonishing."

"Lady Dure said a friend, a widow, was waiting outside in a carriage for her. I brought her a note. Lady Dure said she had to talk to her, and that there would be a coachman to protect them. She agreed to take Patrick with her."

Simon relaxed a little. "Good. Then she at least had protection." Now all he needed to worry about was whatever Theodora might be filling Charity's head with. He groaned inwardly. Charity was likely to come home hating him. No young wife would like to meet her husband's former mistress.

Chaney nodded. "Yes, but as she was leaving, sir, she told me the widow's name. Of course, I, uh, recognized it."

Simon nodded and said dryly, "Of course."

"I couldn't imagine why she was meeting *her,* or where they were going, but I didn't think you would like it, sir. So I sent Thomas here after them. And…and…" he began to wring his hands "…and that's what is troubling, my lord. They went, well, into St. Giles."

"St. Giles!" Simon straightened, whatever peace of mind he had felt fleeing instantly at the mention of the most notorious slum in London. "What the devil were they doing there?" He fixed the footman with a hard stare. "Are you sure that's where they went?"

"Yes, my lord. I swear to you," Thomas assured him, nodding vigorously. "I caught a hack and followed them. I'm certain it were the same carriage, my lord, on account of this little gold stripe all around the top and along the doors. Right smart little thing, it was."

Simon felt sick. "Yes, that's Mrs. Graves's carriage."

"It went into the East End, my lord, and after it reached St. Giles, the hack wouldn't take me further. He made me get out, and I couldn't get him to change his noggin for nothin'. So I had to leave, ya see, or I woulda lost sight of 'em altogether. So I run after it. Lucky they had to move kinda slow like, or I'd of never kept up at all."

He stopped, and Simon prodded, "Well, man? Where did they go?"

Thomas looked away shamefacedly. "I lost 'em, my lord. In this rookery. A woman carryin' two great pails of water got in my way, and they was way ahead of me. When I got around her and down to the street where they'd turned, there weren't no sight of 'em at all."

"Sweet Jesus." In his mind, Simon saw Theodora's face, contorted with fury when he had said he was about to wed another. Her eyes had looked capable of shooting darts into him. She had shrieked that he had been about to marry her, and he had wondered how she could have thought something so unlikely. Suddenly, sickeningly, he was certain of one thing: Theodora Graves hated Charity. She might just be insane enough to kill her. Poison, he recalled, was reputed to be a woman's weapon.

Simon turned away. The world was crumbling under his feet. "Come with me," he said hoarsely to Thomas. "You can show me where you lost them."

He walked rapidly toward the carriage, Thomas on his heels. Thomas climbed on top of the carriage to give the coachman directions, and Simon swung inside, saying, "Go wherever he says, and drive like the devil himself was on your tail."

Behind them, Lucky came bounding out of the house and across the small yard, jumping over the fence with ease and leaping up into the carriage. Simon did not even reprimand the dog. He simply leaned down and sank his hand into the animal's fur, saying softly, "Pray God you live up to your name."

The carriage rattled through the streets of London, at first dashing along faster than Simon had ever ridden in town. But as they reached the narrower streets of the city, they had to slow down. They twisted and turned, and Simon's nerves were shredded by their slow pace. At last the carriage came to a stop, and as Simon opened the door, Thomas hopped down.

"This is it, my lord. This is where I lost 'em. I ain't sure where they went from 'ere."

"Then we shall have to ask."

They questioned everyone they met along the streets. Some shied away; others eyed them in suspicious silence. But now and then a man or woman would answer, pointing the way they had seen a carriage go. Simon would toss them a coin and follow their directions, hoping that they were not simply lying, or too drunk to be sure what they had seen and where it had gone. The streets grew too narrow to drive the coach, and Thomas and Simon walked the rest of the way, leaving the coachman behind to guard the carriage. Lucky, of course, padded along beside Simon, his tail up and his ears on alert, pleased with this latest adventure.

Simon's stomach was knotted with fear. He knew that Theodora could have brought Charity here with no other purpose than to kill her. He hated Theodora, and he hated himself for ever having been involved with her. Why had he not sensed the madness that must have been lurking beneath her provocative exterior?

If he did not reach Charity in time, she would be killed,

and it would be his fault, he knew. Simon did not know how he could live if that happened. He could no longer imagine life without Charity. She had become the sun around which his world revolved. He tightened his grip on the gun in his pocket and kept on walking.

There was a movement off to his right, and he turned his head sharply. A boy's head pulled back into the shadows.

"Here! Lad! Come out!"

Slowly the boy limped out, moving on crutches, and looked warily at Simon, then at the dog. "Wotcher want?"

"A lady. I'm looking for a lady. Have you seen one with another woman?"

"A lady wot looks like a angel?" the lad asked.

"Yes!" Hope surged in Simon's chest. "Blond hair, beautiful. And the other one has black hair, very curvaceous." He made a movement with his hands, as if drawing a voluptuous figure.

The boy nodded his head sharply. "She were nice, the angel lady. She give me money. Ye aren't goin' to take it back now, are ye?"

"No. The money is yours. If she was kind to you, tell me where she went. She is in grave danger."

The boy shook his head. "Aye, she is. T'other one, the she-devil, 'ad a gun in 'er side, she did." He turned and pointed down the street. "There were two men, too, and they all went down there." He pointed down a narrow lane that branched off from the street they were on. Buildings rose up darkly on either side. "They went up them steps and into that building."

"Thank you." Simon reached in his pocket and pulled out several coins and threw them to the lad. Then he wheeled and started quickly toward the dim doorway the boy had indicated.

At that moment, a shot rang out. Simon began to run, and Lucky lunged forward, barking ferociously.

Theodora's shot went wide, smacking into the wall. But Hubbell, cheek bleeding and one eye closed, staggered to his feet and charged after Charity. He threw himself upon her just as she reached the door, and they crashed to the ground. Hubbell landed on top of Charity, knocking the breath out of her. Behind them, Theodora struggled to reload the small single-shot weapon. Patrick gave up stealth and all thought of personal safety and rolled violently forward. He hit Theodora in the back of her legs, knocking them out from under her, and she fell heavily, the gun flying from her hand.

She shrieked and tried to struggle to her feet, but Patrick, far heavier than she, rolled over on her. She kicked and punched at him, but he lay where he was, and she could not roll him off or squirm out from beneath him.

Charity recovered her breath and began to struggle with Hubbell, hitting and kicking at him. He put his hands around her throat and began to squeeze, and, as his arms were much longer than hers, her blows fell harmlessly on his arms.

She heard her name bellowed outside, but she couldn't get out even a squeak. Something pounded against the door, once, then twice, and suddenly it flew open. Just as black began to creep around the edges of her vision, a large furry thing launched itself straight at them.

It knocked Hubbell's arms aside, and air once again rushed down Charity's painful throat. Lucky, wriggling all over, paid no attention to the man he had dislodged but proceeded to lick Charity's face.

Hubbell roared in rage and tried to kick out at Lucky and scramble to his feet all at the same time. But before he could manage to rise, Simon was upon him, pulling him up by his collar. Simon hit the man flush on his jaw, then delivered another blow to his stomach. Hubbell bent over in pain, and Simon finished him off with another hard fist to his chin. The burly man went down on the floor like a load of bricks, making the ramshackle building shake.

Thomas, in the meantime, had gone to help his fellow footman, who was still draped over Theodora's squirming form.

"Good God, man, wot you doin' all trussed up like that—and naked as the day you were born?"

"Simon!" Charity at last gasped out his name as Simon turned from Hubbell and came toward her.

"Charity! Oh, my God, Charity, are you all right?" Simon went down on his knees beside her, lifting her up into a sitting position and cradling her to his chest.

"Oh, Simon!" Charity whispered hoarsely, and clung to him, unable to say anything more.

"Love, sweet love, tell me you're all right."

Charity nodded, saying nothing, simply holding on to Simon for dear life. He swept her into his arms and rose. He glanced back toward Thomas, who had cut through Patrick's bonds with his knife and was busy wrapping some of the fragments of rope around the struggling Theodora's hands. Theodora's eyes met Simon's. Her gaze was wild, the white showing around her eyes, and she began to scream imprecations at him.

Simon looked back at her with eyes as cold and hard as

death. "You and Patrick take her to Scotland Yard, Thomas. I'm taking my wife home."

Simon turned and strode out of the door, carrying Charity in his arms like a prize.

EPILOGUE

CHARITY LAY PROPPED up in bed, pillows behind her head and back, her hair loose and spread all around her. Dr. Cargill had come and gone, and Lily and the other maids and even the housekeeper had fussed around her, giving her hot tea and helping her into a nightgown, then settling her in bed. Simon had at last ordered everyone else out, leaving him alone with his wife.

He sat down now on the side of her bed and brushed a stray lock of hair back from her face. "Feeling better?"

Charity nodded. "Yes, now that we're alone."

Her voice was still hoarse from Hubbell's hands squeezing her throat, but it was now firm and at full volume, unlike the faint, trembling voice that had first answered Simon back in the slums of St. Giles.

Simon took her hand and raised it to his lips, then turned her hand to lay her palm against his cheek. "Thank God you're still alive. I am sorry, Charity. I did not protect you well at all. I almost let you get killed."

"But you didn't. You found me, and I am alive. That's all that matters."

He nodded and turned his face to kiss her palm. Charity thought she felt a trace of moisture on his face, but she couldn't be sure. *Was he crying?* Her heart swelled within her, and she felt so full of love and happiness that she was not sure she could contain it. Two hours ago she had been struggling for her life, and now here she was, warm and well and loved, safely ensconced in her own bed.

"What happened to Theodora?"

"Patrick and Thomas were happy to take her to Scotland Yard after the carriage let us off here."

"What will happen to her?"

"God knows. She will be hanged, I suppose, or perhaps sent to Bedlam. What mad idea possessed her, anyway? What did she hope to gain by killing you?"

Charity explained Theodora's plan to a dumbfounded Simon. He shook his head disbelievingly. "God, how could she have thought—?" He groaned and turned to Charity, dropping his head to his hands.

"I never loved her. I don't know what she told you, but I never loved her. I desired her once, it is true, but there was never love, only an exchange of her body for my money. It was no more than that, I swear to you."

"I know."

"Do you hate me?" Simon asked in a stifled voice.

"Hate you? No! Why would I hate you?"

"For having had a mistress."

Charity reached out and laid her hand upon his arm. Softly, she said, "'Tis a practice that is not uncommon among gentlemen, I've heard. And it was before I even knew you, was it not?"

"Yes," Simon answered fervently, turning to gaze into her eyes now. "It was. The day that I asked for your hand, I ended it with Theodora. I never dreamed that she would react so—I thought it was clear, that she understood. It was never aught but a business arrangement."

"Much as our marriage was," Charity murmured.

"No!" Simon looked shocked.

"At first it was," Charity reminded him. "That was what you wanted. An heir from a wife of good family and spotless reputation, in exchange for the benefits of your fortune."

Simon cocked an eyebrow at her. "Once I met you, it was never a business arrangement." He leaned forward and kissed her on the forehead, then on each eyelid. "It was only desire...and good sense...and love."

"Oh, Simon!" Charity threw her arms around his neck. "I don't care if you had a hundred mistresses before you married. All I care about is now. All I want to know is that you love me, that you have no one else but me *now.*"

"You know that is true." He kissed her again, lingeringly, on the mouth. "What about you?" he murmured when he raised his head at last.

"What do you mean? What about me?"

"Do you love me?" His face was carefully blank, but Charity could see the flicker of uncertainty in his eyes. "Or is it still an 'arrangement' for you?"

"Once I met you," Charity repeated his words, "it was never a business arrangement. I was terribly, terribly glad that Serena had not wanted to marry you. I love you. I've loved you for ages, since before the wedding. I realized it when you broke off the engagement, and I knew I would do anything to marry you. I love you, I love you, I love you."

She began to kiss him all over his face, punctuating her kisses with more words of love. Simon chuckled and caught her face in his hands, holding her still while his mouth took hers. A long time later, he lay down beside Charity, gathering her into his arms.

"I don't plan ever to let you go again," he told her.

Charity closed her eyes. After a moment she murmured, "Simon, that little boy who helped me, the crippled child…"

She could feel the rumble of Simon's laughter start in his chest. "Yes, my dear. Another stray. I shall send for him immediately."

Charity smiled and snuggled up to him. "I knew you would."

* * * * *

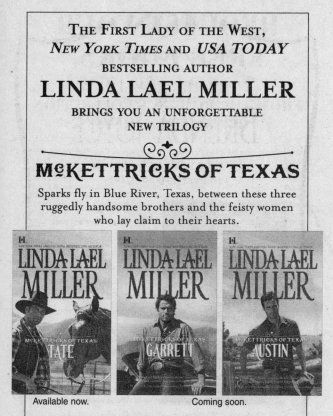

REQUEST YOUR FREE BOOKS!

2 FREE NOVELS
FROM THE ROMANCE COLLECTION
PLUS 2 FREE GIFTS!

YES! Please send me 2 FREE novels from the Romance Collection and my 2 FREE gifts (gifts are worth about $10). After receiving them, if I don't wish to receive any more books, I can return the shipping statement marked "cancel." If I don't cancel, I will receive 4 brand-new novels every month and be billed just $5.74 per book in the U.S. or $6.24 per book in Canada. That's a saving of at least 28% off the cover price. It's quite a bargain! Shipping and handling is just 50¢ per book in the U.S. and 75¢ per book in Canada.* I understand that accepting the 2 free books and gifts places me under no obligation to buy anything. I can always return a shipment and cancel at any time. Even if I never buy another book, the two free books and gifts are mine to keep forever.

194 MDN E4LY   394 MDN E4MC

Name _____ (PLEASE PRINT) _____

Address _____ Apt. # _____

City _____ State/Prov. _____ Zip/Postal Code _____

Signature (if under 18, a parent or guardian must sign) _____

Mail to The Reader Service:
IN U.S.A.: P.O. Box 1867, Buffalo, NY 14240-1867
IN CANADA: P.O. Box 609, Fort Erie, Ontario L2A 5X3

Not valid for current subscribers to the Romance Collection
or the Romance/Suspense Collection.

Want to try two free books from another line?
Call 1-800-873-8635 or visit www.morefreebooks.com.

* Terms and prices subject to change without notice. Prices do not include applicable taxes. N.Y. residents add applicable sales tax. Canadian residents will be charged applicable provincial taxes and GST. Offer not valid in Quebec. This offer is limited to one order per household. All orders subject to approval. Credit or debit balances in a customer's account(s) may be offset by any other outstanding balance owed by or to the customer. Please allow 4 to 6 weeks for delivery. Offer available while quantities last.

Your Privacy: Harlequin Books is committed to protecting your privacy. Our Privacy Policy is available online at www.eHarlequin.com or upon request from the Reader Service. From time to time we make our lists of customers available to reputable third parties who may have a product or service of interest to you. If you would prefer we not share your name and address, please check here. ☐

Help us get it right—We strive for accurate, respectful and relevant communications. To clarify or modify your communication preferences, visit us at www.ReaderService.com/consumerschoice.

CANDACE CAMP

77354 THE COURTSHIP DANCE	___$6.99 U.S.	___$6.99 CAN.
77308 THE WEDDING CHALLENGE	___$6.99 U.S.	___$6.99 CAN.
77257 THE BRIDAL QUEST	___$6.99 U.S.	___$8.50 CAN.
77243 THE MARRIAGE WAGER	___$6.99 U.S.	___$8.50 CAN.
77136 A DANGEROUS MAN	___$6.99 U.S.	___$8.50 CAN.

(limited quantities available)

TOTAL AMOUNT $ _____
POSTAGE & HANDLING $ _____
($1.00 FOR 1 BOOK, 50¢ for each additional)
APPLICABLE TAXES* $ _____
TOTAL PAYABLE $ _____

(check or money order—please do not send cash)

To order, complete this form and send it, along with a check or money order for the total above, payable to HQN Books, to: **In the U.S.:** 3010 Walden Avenue, P.O. Box 9077, Buffalo, NY 14269-9077; **In Canada:** P.O. Box 636, Fort Erie, Ontario, L2A 5X3.

Name: _____
Address: _____ City: _____
State/Prov.: _____ Zip/Postal Code: _____
Account Number (if applicable): _____

075 CSAS

*New York residents remit applicable sales taxes.
*Canadian residents remit applicable GST and provincial taxes.

HQN™

We *are* romance™

www.HQNBooks.com   PHCC0210BL